W9-ADJ-903

Run the Risk

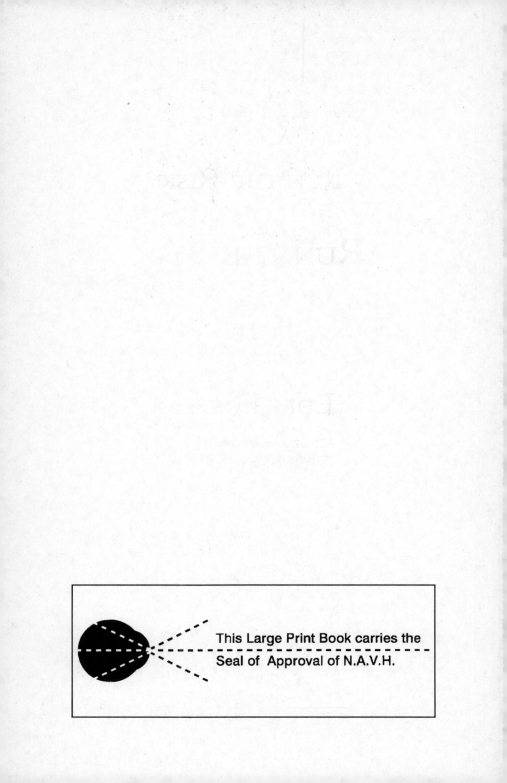

RUN THE RISK

LORI FOSTER

THORNDIKE PRESS
A part of Gale, Cengage Learning

GALE
CENGAGE Learning®

Detroit • New York • San Francisco • New Haven, Conn • Waterville, Maine • London

GALE
CENGAGE Learning®

Copyright © 2012 by Lori Foster.
Thorndike Press, a part of Gale, Cengage Learning.

LIBRARY OF CONGRESS CATALOGING-IN-PUBLICATION DATA

Foster, Lori, 1958–
    Run the risk / by Lori Foster. — Large Print edition.
       pages cm. — (Thorndike Press Large Print Romance)
    ISBN 978-1-4104-5475-1 (hardcover) — ISBN 1-4104-5475-4 (hardcover) 1.
Murder—Investigation—Fiction. 2. Large type books. I. Title.
PS3556.O767R86 2013
813'.54—dc23   2012038893

Published in 2013 by arrangement with Harlequin Books S.A.

Printed in the United States of America
1 2 3 4 5 6 7 17 16 15 14 13

Dear Reader,

As I draw to a close on each series, wonderful readers always ask me for more. You can't know how much that means to me! I'm thrilled that you enjoyed the Men Who Walk the Edge of Honor books, and it's very rewarding to know you'd be happy for more stories with those characters. But I always go where my muse takes me, and now, with my new Love Undercover series, it's taken me to some wonderfully complicated relationships where, out of necessity, the hero or heroine — or both! — are hiding their true identities . . . and falling in love anyway! How fun is that?

Well, I think it's fun! I grin a lot while writing, so I hope you grin while reading.

And I especially hope that by the time this series draws to a close (several books from now!) you'll write to me . . . and ask for more.

That's the best compliment an author can get!

Here's to happy reading!

Lori Foster

To Jenna Scott and Gary Tabke,
I have immense respect for
all law enforcement officers,
but I know little about the inner workings.

Thank you both for all the insight,
the research help, and for
answering my numerous questions.

Any errors or exaggerations are my own
(because really, sometimes we writers
need to make things work!) but hopefully,
thanks to you both, the story is
believable.

Here's to the writing community —
authors and readers alike.

CHAPTER ONE

Pepper Yates felt the intense scrutiny stroking over her as she made her way to her apartment building. She'd been feeling it for over two weeks now, ever since her new neighbor had moved in, but she'd never get used to it.

Dangerous anticipation crawled up her spine.

She didn't acknowledge the man leaning over his balcony, muscular arms folded along the railing, shirtless, smiling — tracking her every move.

She didn't, in any way, encourage him. He was out of her league in a big way. His attention made her tense, more so with every incident.

Uncertainty gave her a faltering step, causing her cheap canvas slip-on sneakers to make an obnoxious shuffling sound. Her long skirt kicked around her shins. Her chest constricted.

Keeping her head down, her paper bags of groceries held securely in her arms, she pretended not to notice him.

She should win an Oscar for her performance, because seriously, who wouldn't notice him? If she had to guess, she'd say women came to him easily. He had that type of raw, cocky presence.

The kind of presence that left her on edge.

It probably ate him up that she ignored him. That was the only explanation for his continued attention. But what else could she do?

The hot August sun beat down on her head. She would dearly love a cool swim right about now. But not with him around.

Actually . . . not ever.

It seemed her carefree days of swimming were well behind her. It made her sad to think of all that had been lost, all that she'd had to forfeit, in the name of survival.

But thanks to her brother, she had survived, she reminded herself. And that's what mattered most.

It was also the number one reason she couldn't be drawn in by the new neighbor's lure.

He should have a big *D* for *danger* on his oft-naked chest.

As she hastened her steps in, Pepper

dropped her head so far that her chin nearly touched her chest.

Of course he called out to her. He always called out to her. It made no sense, but her rebuffs hadn't dissuaded him at all.

The man had a rock-solid ego.

"Evening, Ms. Meeks."

When she'd taken the alias, it hadn't been a big deal, because she wasn't a big deal. Few ever spoke to her. None ever called out to her.

But he did.

She drew a fortifying breath, peeked up at him and gave a subdued nod. "Evening."

He disappeared off the balcony and she just *knew* he was coming inside to corral her in the narrow hallway.

Why wouldn't he leave her alone?

The apartment building was . . . unpleasant. Peeling paint from the walls, mold in the corners, carpet with stains she didn't want to investigate too closely . . .

She knew why she was there.

Why was he?

Dreading every foot that brought her closer to him, she went up the squeaking steps to her second-floor apartment, and . . . there he was.

Knowing he waited for her, she stalled.

He lounged back against his door, which

11

was right next to hers, arms crossed over his bare chest, his brown hair disheveled, five o'clock shadow on his jaw. He wore only wrinkled khaki shorts that hung low on his lean hips — and he took her breath away.

Seeing him again had the same impact it'd had the first time she'd laid eyes on him. He was so sinfully appealing that it staggered her senses.

What did he want?

Not the usual, not with how he looked, and how . . . she looked. So then, why did he so relentlessly pursue her?

The long walk to the grocery and back again — something she usually enjoyed — left her hot, damp with perspiration and in no mood for playing games.

At least, not these games.

She had to avoid his gaze or — humiliating thought — he just might see everything she felt, everything she thought.

About him. About the incredible body that he insisted on displaying.

And how she'd like to rub *her* body all over his . . .

"Hey."

Before she could figure out a way to dodge him, he pushed away from the wall, his smile welcoming, his dark eyes warm. She swallowed her sigh. "Hello."

"Here, let me help you with that."

Like she couldn't handle a few bags of groceries? *Why* was he bothering her like this? Flustered, talking too fast, Pepper said, "That's okay, really. I've got —"

He scooped the bags away from her and gestured for her to precede him to her apartment.

"— it." Left empty-armed and unnerved, she kept her shoulders slumped and did her best to bank her reaction to him. "Really, Mr. Stark, I don't —"

"We're neighbors, so call me Logan."

She didn't want to call him anything and tried to convey that with a show of umbrage. "Really, *Mr. Stark,* I don't need any help."

His grin widened. Teasing. Flirting. "You are so prickly."

How could he make that sound like a compliment? "I am not —"

He snatched her keys from her, too, and short of grabbing for them, which would only make her look foolish, she had no choice but to follow him.

"— prickly," she muttered — probably in a really prickly way. While he unlocked her door, she stared at his broad back. He was tanned, his sleek skin almost as damp as her own.

Her fingers twitched with the need to

touch him, to coast her palms over his heated skin and taut muscles.

He turned toward her, and she got the up close and personal view of his chest. It shocked her, but she noticed his small brown nipples, how soft chest hair half hid them . . .

"If not prickly, then what?"

She glanced up, saw he'd been watching her as she studied him, and wanted to sink into the floor. Her face went hot, her body hotter — but probably not for the reasons he assumed.

"I'm *private.*" Although, the way she'd just looked at him, sort of eye-raping him — *oh, God* — it was no wonder he didn't understand that.

Every single time he got within her view, she visually molested him. His fault in part, because he always had so much skin on display; she wasn't used to anyone like him, anyone who looked as good as he did.

A touch to her chin brought up her face and nearly stopped her heart. "Saying hi to a neighbor somehow intrudes on your privacy?"

No, no, no. He couldn't *touch* her. She couldn't *let* him touch her. Time to escape.

Ducking around him, Pepper swung the door open, stepped in fast ahead of him, then turned to block his way. "I barely know you."

"I'm trying to remedy that, right?" He looked into her apartment with curiosity and surprise. One brow lifted at the mess she knew he saw.

So she wasn't übertidy. So she was actually a slob. Maybe that would repel him.

"I keep to myself." She awkwardly snatched back her groceries and straightened her spine. "Others should do the same."

"Yeah, maybe I could." Giving up his scrutiny of her cluttered living space, he leaned in her door frame — all six-feet-plus of him. His broad shoulders kept her from closing the door.

Patient, silent, he waited for her to meet his gaze.

Girding herself, Pepper looked up — and felt caressed by his suggestive, intimate attention. She cleared her throat and prompted him with, "You could . . . what?"

"Maybe stop chasing your skirt." His voice dropped. "If you weren't so damn cute."

Shock took her back a step.

Cute? He must be deranged, because no way was he desperate. Why would he say such an absurd thing?

His expression softened. "You don't think

you're cute?"

The laugh strangled in her throat, and her automatic "No" sounded like a croak.

Cute? Hardly. She kept her dull blond hair pulled back in a low, unflattering ponytail at the nape of her neck, showcasing a face devoid of even the most subtle makeup. She wore clothes any respectable grandmother would disdain, with shoes so ugly they made her sad when she stepped into them.

She slumped when she walked, mumbled when she talked. Or at least, she remembered to mumble when a certain neighbor didn't push her past the breaking point.

"Well, I think you are," he said, still watching her, his tone almost . . . pitying.

How dare he feel sorry for her?

Pride rose to the forefront, returning her backbone. "Is that a joke, Mr. Stark?"

Shifting his stance, he leaned in and — while she held her breath — said with distinct insistence, "Call me Logan."

Oh, good Lord. He was close enough that she felt his warm, moist breath and could see the thick, dark lashes on his eyes.

Bedroom eyes.

Her temperature spiked. "Oh, umm . . ."

Those sexy lips lifted into a satisfied grin. "And I'll call you . . . ?"

When Pepper only stared at him, a little

dazed, his grin twitched. And man, oh, man, she wanted to kiss that mouth of his.

Kiss it and . . . other things.

Catching herself, Pepper shook her head and tried to ease the door shut. "Goodbye, Mr. Stark."

His big hand flattened on the door near her shoulder. "Come on, throw me a bone here." Without much effort, he held the door open. "How will it hurt if I have your name?"

What to do, what to do?

He was so pushy that her continued refusal looked absurd.

Grudgingly, she said, "Sue."

Now more amused, he admitted, "I know."

"Beg pardon?"

"You manage the building, so I already saw your name on my rental agreement." He tweaked her chin again. "But I wanted to hear you say it anyway."

Her huff of affront did nothing to get him out of her doorway.

"So." He looked up and down the hallway. "You're a woman alone, and this isn't the best apartment building, or the best neighborhood."

Now he was a master of understatement? "You're insulting my management skills?" Did he think that'd win her over?

"You're only responsible for notifying the owner if rent is late or repairs are needed, right?" Without letting her reply to that, he said, "Let me leave you my number. Anything comes up, or if anyone bothers you —"

"*You're* bothering me."

His gaze zeroed in on her mouth. "That's why you're flushed?"

Oh, God. More heat rushed to her skin's surface. "Really, Mr. Stark —"

"Logan," he corrected softly. "Say it for me. Just once. Then I'll go."

He wanted to . . . seduce her?

So it appeared. And worse, he succeeded just by presence alone. "Logan," she agreed through stiff lips. "I need to go." *Before I do something stupid — like invite you in.*

Or kiss you.

Or drag you down to the floor and —

He pulled a card from his pocket. "My number. Seriously. Any problem at all — or if you just want to visit — give me a call, okay?"

"All right." *Not on your life.* "Thank you."

As if he knew her thoughts, he gave a warm laugh and stepped out of the doorway. "See you later, Sue."

Not if I see you first. "Goodbye, Logan." She started to close the door.

And he said, "Now that wasn't so painful, was it?"

She clicked the door shut in his face, then dropped against it.

Painful? Not exactly.

Stirring? She felt like a blender on high speed, all her emotions, all her dormant desires, churning together in a frenzy.

It had been too long — like forever — and she was too deprived to be around a specimen like him without imagining the impossible. She needed to find a way to avoid him, but she'd have to do it without causing suspicion. And there was the rub.

Avoiding him *was* suspicious.

Pepper turned so that it was her shoulders against her door. Head down, eyes closed, she struggled to come up with a plan.

Maybe, she reasoned to herself, she was going about this all wrong. Any woman would be flattered by Mr. Stark's attention.

A woman like her, especially so.

Slowly, she lifted her head. Did she have a good reason to engage him in conversation? To get to know him better?

She pressed her hands to her cheeks and fought off a smile.

Yes, that's what she would do. She would stop deflecting him, and instead — she'd shyly reciprocate. If that didn't scare him off once and for all, she didn't know what would.

Logan Riske sauntered back to his temporary digs with a feeling of encouragement.

So he'd had to be pushy. Again.

So he'd had to practically force a conversation on her. At least this time, he'd been successful.

More than successful.

The lady could deny it till doomsday, but he felt her awareness. If her damned brother didn't have her so cowed, she'd probably be knocking on his door right now.

Thinking of her brother, Rowdy Yates, always soured his mood. No doubt Rowdy had run roughshod over her for years, so Logan had to proceed cautiously.

He ran a hand over his chest, considering all the twists and turns of her ruse. It *was* a ruse — he couldn't be wrong about that. Yes, she looked different from the photos he had, but there was something in the eyes, in the way she looked at him.

Pepper Yates.

After two years of searching, the end drew near.

She was the one woman he needed, the link that'd get him everything he'd worked for.

He thought about the small grainy photos online, the newspaper reports. Her wide-eyed innocence had shown through. She looked a little worse now than she had two years ago, but he supposed running, and hiding, and putting up with her brother could do that to a woman.

His hands curled into fists.

Most everything he'd uncovered had been on Rowdy Yates, but bits and pieces of Pepper had surfaced, as well. He knew she was younger than thirty, and he knew she was shy.

He hadn't known she would be so tall. At around five-ten, she stood only three inches shorter than him. And while no one would accuse her of being pretty, he hadn't known that her light brown eyes would be so expressive. When she looked directly at him, he felt it.

All over.

Her hair was so dark a blond, it was nearly brown. Long, but lank. Dull. Untidy, with frizzy ends, despite her habit of securing it in a ponytail.

And still he wanted to see it loose. He wanted to feel it in his hands.

And speaking of untidy . . . His quick glimpse of her living room had been a shocker. He'd just naturally assumed that a

21

plain Jane like her would be ultraneat, like the stereotypical mousy woman who lived like a maiden aunt.

Ha! Not even close.

Clothes, magazines, empty cola cans and a pizza box had all littered her small living space. Beyond that area he'd seen a towel on the floor of her bathroom, and through an open door, her unmade bed with a quilt more off the bed than on it.

For some reason, knowing she wasn't a neat freak made him smile. It was such a contradiction to his assumptions.

He again pictured her sloppy bed and wondered if she'd had a sleepless night. He knew for certain she'd spent the night — every night — alone.

Maybe that was why, more than once, she'd stolen a glimpse of his body.

And that rosy flush?

Yeah, that hadn't been annoyance he'd seen stirring in her expressive eyes.

Eyes that couldn't hide her secrets.

Not from him. As a cop, he excelled in uncovering mysteries.

As a man, he knew how to seduce a woman.

Sue Meeks — what a joke — would be no different.

What he found odd was his own reaction.

She wasn't outright homely; he knew women well enough to see that with some work, she could be attractive. Women had an amazing knack of highlighting their best features while downplaying their flaws.

Not Pepper Yates. The woman didn't seem to have a clue how to promote her strong features.

And her body . . . well, who could know? She didn't exactly look thick or thin, just . . . shapeless.

He hadn't found any photos of her that really showed off her figure. And beneath the dated, ill-fitting clothes she now wore, she could be concealing anything.

Yet while talking to her, he'd felt alive. Hell, he'd felt alive just watching her stride down the sidewalk, her enormous, sloppy purse throwing her off-kilter more than the overloaded bags of groceries had. She'd kept her head down, but her stride had been long and confident.

Until she'd seen him.

Then she'd dragged her feet like a reluctant sacrifice.

Which, though she couldn't have realized it, was a pretty apt description for what he had planned.

He would not feel guilty about it, Logan told himself. She'd be fine. He'd see to it.

She might be timid, but she had a spark of fire.

Once he got things ignited, he'd find out everything he needed to know about her brother — but he'd do so gently. He'd treat her with respect, and he'd be generous with his attention, both emotionally and physically.

No, Pepper Yates wasn't a beauty, but having her wouldn't be a hardship. Hell, he felt taut with anticipation just thinking about it. *Enough on that.*

Logan secured the locks on his door, then headed back to the balcony. Since the building didn't have air, and the windows were small and difficult to open or close, the balcony offered the only respite from the smothering, humid heat.

But, yeah, the August weather wasn't his only reason for venturing out to the crumbling balcony.

He'd seen the steak in her grocery bag.

Pepper Yates, aka Sue Meeks, prepared a lot of her meals on a small propane grill. Too many evenings he'd lurked inside, observing her through the vertical blinds, watching her as she'd cooked a single potato with a piece of chicken, a pork chop or a steak.

Did she hate cooking for one as much as he did?

Didn't she ever tire of eating alone?

He knew for a fact she didn't date, didn't have any visitors of any kind — not even her damned brother.

She didn't drive, didn't leave the apartment any longer than it took to run errands, and as she said, she kept to herself.

No social life.

He knew, because he'd been watching her for longer than he'd been in the apartment building. Weeks longer.

Would she venture out to her grill with him sitting outside, his balcony right beside hers, close enough that they could chat?

Would she give in to the curiosity he'd seen in her expression?

Or would she avoid him as she'd done so far?

After dropping into a lounge chair, Logan finished off his beer, sprawled onto his back, closed his eyes against the evening sun, and thought about things yet to occur.

Things that had to do with her.

Things that would no doubt prove . . . interesting.

Even exciting.

The thrill of the chase.

This was what he lived for. The reason

he'd become a cop. The core of his basic nature.

And now, finally, he was moving in on his prey.

Why did he have to be out there? For over an hour, Pepper waited to see if Logan Stark would go inside. He didn't budge.

And she didn't stop watching him.

He appeared to be sleeping, his broad chest expanding with deep, slow breaths. Legs sprawled, hands loose, face relaxed.

Body enticing.

She swallowed and thought about the card he'd given her — now on the top of her refrigerator for safekeeping. It didn't mention a job, just his name, address and cell phone number. He didn't have the look of the poor. His demeanor defied the defeat of unemployment, and his body defied a lack of activity.

He wanted conversation. She bit her lip.

Okay, so maybe she'd ask him where he worked. Maybe, given his absurd pursuit, he would expect her to want to learn more about him.

God, he looked good all lounged out like that.

He had one arm up and over his head, showing off his biceps and the tuft of darker hair under his arm. Sinfully sexy. He kept the other bent at his side, his big hand opened over a tautly muscled abdomen. The setting sun glinted off his brown chest hair, turning it almost golden. He wasn't overly hairy, just earthy and masculine.

No shaved chest for this guy, thank God.

His chest hair narrowed to a fine line down his body, skirted around his navel, and then, growing darker, disappeared into his shorts.

And below that, behind the fly of his shorts, a nice, full bulge.

Stepping farther out, she stared hard, enrapt.

Her heartbeat slowed, her breath deepened.

Logan opened one eye and found her visually molesting him again.

For several seconds they stared at each other, and then he said, "Hey," in a deep, lazy, *interested* way.

Oh, no, no, no. Why did he have to be so . . . *potent?*

Busted, but never a coward, Pepper stepped out fully to the balcony. Hands clasped together in front of her, nervous smile in place, she said, "I, ah, didn't mean to wake you."

"Just dozing." A low rumbling growl accompanied a deep stretch. "No biggie."

The stretch did interesting things to all those muscles: flexing, bulging, then letting them relax again, still prominent, but no longer tense.

So unfair. How could he look so good doing nothing?

Sitting up, he swung his long, hairy legs over the side of the chair. Even his big feet were beautiful!

After running a hand over his head, then his chest, he focused on her. "Getting ready to grill?"

How did he know that? "Um . . ."

"I could join you." His gaze drilled into her. "I have my own steak I'd planned to throw on anyway. No reason we can't share the grill, right?" And as an enticement, he added, "I'll even bring the beer."

That much proximity, given her sizzling awareness, could be treacherous. A little time with him, maybe. But the entirety of dinner? She'd be a fool to agree to such a . . . "Okay." *What?*

Oh, my God, had that really come out of her mouth? Well of course it had. Look at him, sitting there like physical temptation, legs apart, expression lazy and skin sunwarmed.

She covered her mouth with a hand.

But she was only human after all, and if her downtrodden appearance didn't keep him at bay, well then, what would it hurt?

As surprised as she, he said, "Seriously?" He straightened, his manner suspicious, his gaze going all over her.

What, did he think she had a concealed weapon? Did he expect her to wield a steak knife?

Did he expect ulterior motives?

Yes, of course, she had them — but they weren't motives he'd ever guess.

Pepper dropped her hand and filled her lungs with the thick evening air. "As you said, there's no reason for us to fire up both grills."

"Well, hot damn." Smiling, Logan pushed to his feet. "I got time to take a shower?"

Oh, she wished he wouldn't. Her nose twitched with the need to smell him, to drink in his hot scent. "If you must."

"Give me five minutes." Without another word, he ducked back inside.

Hugging herself, Pepper sat down on her single patio chair. She felt deflated, concerned and absolutely filled with anticipation.

CHAPTER TWO

After breaking speed records for a shower and shave, Logan punched in the number, then dried off one-handed while using his shoulder to hold his cell phone to his ear.

The second he got an answer, he said, "She took the bait."

His partner, Reese, bit back a curse. "What does that mean, exactly? What did you do to her?"

Around a rough laugh, Logan said, "I didn't *do* anything to her." Ignoring the fact that he hoped to do a lot of things to her, he tossed aside the towel. "She agreed to share dinner with me, that's all." For now. But if things went right . . .

"I wish you'd rethink this, Logan."

Why did Reese have to act as if he planned to molest her? "Fuck that. If I don't get to the bottom of this, then who will?" No one else was willing to track down the truth. No one else dared go up against that scum,

Morton Andrews.

No one else cared what had happened two years ago.

"Logan —"

Skin still damp, Logan skipped his boxers and pulled on another pair of soft, well-worn jean shorts. Long ago he'd decided to eschew the trappings of inherited wealth and go for comfort instead. As a detective, he had to wear suits, a tie, the whole she-bang. He'd gotten used to it, and didn't even think about it anymore.

But in his leisure time, he wore whatever felt best.

This new gig masquerading as a middle class construction worker fit him just fine. More often than not, a pair of shorts was all he needed. "I'm too close to pull back now, so save the lecture." He dragged up the zipper with care.

Resigned, Reese got down to business. "Have you seen her brother?"

"No." Not even a glimpse. "But he's around, I'm sure of it."

"If it turns out you're right, the walls could start crumbling down. But if you're wrong . . ."

He wasn't wrong. No way. He trusted his instincts and his gut; both told him he was on to something here. He and Jack Carmin had gone through school together, college together, but while Logan had set his sights on becoming a detective, Jack had veered off into a different type of public work: politics. He'd died at the hands of a madman. Senseless murder — all for greed and corruption.

"He was my best friend, Reese."

Morton Andrews would pay, even if it took him a lifetime.

"I know." Tiredly, Reese said, "Keep me posted, okay? Don't push too hard, and don't do anything stupid or dangerous."

That made Logan laugh, but not with any real humor. "Don't act like you? Is that what you're saying?" Known for championing the underdog, Reese resembled Jack in many ways. In the face of injustice, he often reacted before thinking, but usually, at least in Logan's opinion, he was dead-on. Logan trusted him with his life, and that was saying something. He trusted only a select few.

Now with a smile in his tone, Reese said, "Exactly."

"I'll check in tomorrow."

"Not tonight?"

With any luck, he'd be busy till late. "Let's keep the calls to a minimum, just in case."

Reese hesitated. "Forget the task force and your assignment — if you need backup, don't trust anyone else, understand? Get hold of me, and only me."

"That's a given." Jack's murder had been all the incentive Logan needed to accept the position as head of a special task force. To clean up a lot of the rampant corruption in Warfield, Ohio, his lieutenant had given him carte blanche.

But because some of that corruption had infiltrated the force, Logan had immediately brought Reese on board.

"I've lined up a few unies if we need them. Kids I know we can count on."

By "kids," Reese meant young uniformed cops, still bright-eyed with the need to see justice served. "You didn't tell them anything yet?"

"Nope. Just checked out their backgrounds, family histories and their records. If you find Rowdy, they can make the actual arrest to keep it clean."

"Thanks." To really make a difference, Logan needed people he could count on, and that meant Reese had to do a lot of setup.

But he also needed an eyewitness to a two-year-old murder.

And that meant he needed Pepper's brother, Rowdy Yates.

Through tons of research and a little luck,

he'd found Pepper. At first he hadn't been certain it was her; Rowdy had done an amazing job of covering their tracks. But now that he'd seen her up close, talked with her, he was sure he had the right woman.

Through her, he'd eventually get Rowdy.

And with Rowdy, he'd get that scumbag club owner, Morton Andrews, the man he *knew* was responsible for many deaths, including Jack's.

Hell, he wasn't the only one who knew it. Plenty of people made the link. But Morton owned enough people, bought enough alibis that, for all intents and purposes, he remained untouchable.

With Rowdy's eyewitness account, he'd finally be able to put Morton away.

With that end goal in mind, Logan said, "I gotta go. The lady is waiting."

Dropping his cell phone into his pocket, along with his keys and a wallet holding false ID, a rubber and a few bills, Logan detoured into the kitchen.

Using his real first name made the undercover work easier. It was enough to remember that Pepper Yates was Sue Meeks without trying to carry his own alias. It was all too easy to fuck up when you tried to change too much. That's why construction work was part of his undercover persona.

Sure, he and his brother Dash had inherited a shit ton of money from their family. But neither of them flaunted the money, and neither of them felt content being idle or, God forbid, sitting in boardrooms. They invested wisely, donated generously and got on with their lives.

As owner of a construction company, Dash could employ Logan when necessary, giving him the background he needed in case Rowdy got on to him and did any checking.

It was a stroke of luck that he'd found Pepper in a different county. Anyone who knew him might unwittingly blow his cover, but the different locale made a chance encounter with cops in the field less likely.

Logan grabbed his packaged steak, a potato and a six-pack of beer, minus one.

He locked the door behind him and stepped over to tap on Pepper's door. As if she'd been waiting for him, it opened almost before he'd dropped his hand.

Standing before him, shifting her feet nervously, she said, "Hi."

She looked adorably unsure of herself, her gaze avoiding his, her teeth nibbling on her bottom lip.

Again flushed.

"Hi yourself." Logan took his time looking her over, not that she'd changed a thing. She still wore the ugly canvas sneakers, long skirt and baggy pullover top. Her hair remained dragged back in that hideous ponytail.

But he saw the movement of her chest as she drank in deep, nervous breaths, and the way her hands trembled a little.

Emotion, awareness and his dick all swelled. He felt ruthless, and he felt territorial. "You want to let me in, Sue?"

She continued to look at him, all over him.

Logan lowered his voice more and said with certainty, "I'm coming in."

"Oh." Closing her eyes in embarrassment, she stepped aside. "Yes, of course."

He hadn't planned to rush things. He'd intended to be smooth, patient. But the moment just felt right, so as he moved past her, he bent and put a firm kiss to her soft mouth. "Thanks."

The brief contact proved addictive — sparking awareness, firing his blood.

Over a simple kiss.

He made it all the way to her kitchen before he realized she still stood at her open door, staring after him, frozen in shock. She watched him set down the beer, the steak and potato.

She looked ready to flee the apartment.

Pretending he didn't understand the reason, Logan asked low, "Everything okay?"

She treated him to another intent stare, consuming him with her innocent gaze. "Yes." Letting out a long breath, she closed the door, faltered a second, then stepped forward. "Yes, everything is fine." Head down, mouth pinched, she bustled past him. "I already started the grill. Another minute or two and we can put on the steaks."

Logan caught her arm, his fingers wrapping around her. She was slim, her bones delicate.

Why hadn't he noticed that before?

"You picked up the place." She'd closed the door on her bedroom and bathroom, so he didn't know about those spaces, but the cardboard pizza box, empty cans and papers were gone. "I hope you didn't tidy up on my account."

"Oh, no, not at all." Sidling out of his reach, she plumped a throw pillow at the end of a love seat, putting the entire piece of furniture between them as a barrier. "That stuff was leftover from last night."

Her efforts to distance him only made him feel more predatory. Alarm filled her gaze as he approached. She jerked around, turning her back on him, but then just . . . stood there, waffling, uncertain.

A defense mechanism? How badly had her damned brother mistreated her?

Savage, protective instincts sharpened. She was so damn sweet, so shy.

Having her would be sweet, too. Not that it mattered; his reasons for being here with her now, for using her, had little enough to do with her growing appeal.

An appeal he hadn't noticed before getting close to her.

Using the back of one finger, Logan stroked the side of her neck and was rewarded with her shiver. Her incredible softness stirred him more and roughened his voice. "You ate pizza all alone last night?" The image pained him.

"I . . . Of course." She swayed back into him. "I *am* alone."

Amazed by how quickly she melted, he settled both hands on her shoulders. Again he noted her slimness. Not skinny, but most definitely slight in the way of females.

Would it really be this easy? Did she not possess a single iota of self-preservation? She wore her heart on her sleeve, her need for affection painstakingly obvious.

He wanted to pull her closer, wrap his arms around her, but he didn't want to scare her off.

Using his thumbs to rub the backs of her upper arms, he said, "You could have invited me over."

"I . . ." She shook her head. "No. I couldn't."

Because her brother wouldn't allow it? Bastard.

Logan leaned closer, his breath on her nape, his whisper near her ear. "Anytime, Sue. You have my number." His lips just touched her lobe. "Or just knock at my door."

Breathing hard, she shifted — then lurched out of his reach. "No, I'm sorry," she said in a rush, "but I won't ever do that." She all but raced out to the patio. With her out of the room, Logan looked around.

Her furniture, ragtag and mismatched, had probably come with the apartment, same as his. As an acting manager for the four-unit building, did she get to live here rent-free? Where did she get money for food? For clothes? Lack of funds likely accounted for her secondhand clothing. She didn't have a car — because she couldn't afford one?

It disturbed Logan, how isolated and alone she was. He always empathized with those less fortunate; never in his life had he wanted for a single thing — except justice. But with this woman, it went beyond a sense of social responsibility to the needy.

It went beyond anything familiar.

Where the hell was her brother? Why did Rowdy leave her so unguarded?

From what he'd uncovered, he hadn't considered Rowdy Yates a "bad" man, just a man of poor choices and, in the case of his employment with Morton Andrews, worse acquaintances. Now, knowing Pepper? Rowdy had to be the lowest type of villain. How else could you explain her circumstances?

Other than a work history that included everything from dishwasher to deliveryman, carpenter to bouncer, there'd been little on Rowdy, and even less on Pepper.

Logan knew her brother worked, he drifted, he teetered on the edge of trouble — and he dragged Pepper along for the ride.

Logan hadn't been able to find anything on their educations, parents or other relatives.

But Rowdy had worked at Checkers — which was the wrong club at the wrong time. While employed there he'd gotten embroiled in corruption. His testimony was needed to bring down Andrews, but for two years now, he'd dodged involvement. The last anyone had heard from Rowdy was right before a reporter had his throat cut.

After that, nada.

Until now.

Now, Logan had Rowdy's kid sister, and much as it went against the grain, he *would* use her to get what he wanted.

Justice.

Revenge.

Peace of mind.

Unwavering, Logan picked up his food, snagged two beers, and went out to the patio to join her.

Pepper lay in her bed, wide-awake, miserably hot, and dissatisfied.

The fan in her window stirred the humid air, pushing it around the room and over her mostly bare body.

A cold shower hadn't helped, not after four long hours of Logan Stark's personal brand of seduction.

God, she felt singed. The intimate way he'd looked at her, the suggestive way he talked.

Even the way he ate his steak somehow affected her to the point that she'd barely touched her own, when she'd been anticipating the dinner.

She had planned to ask Logan some

personal questions, but he'd kept her on the defensive with small touches and warm smiles. It had taken all her wits to keep from falling under his spell.

But she wanted to. Badly.

Actually, she wanted to be under him.

Impossible.

Rolling to her back, she stared at the shadowed ceiling and wondered if he was asleep. After that spontaneous kiss he'd given her before walking into her apartment, she'd been on guard. When she'd finally gotten him to the door, ready to say goodbye, she'd stuck out her hand.

A handshake she could handle. It was civilized. Socially acceptable.

But he'd done her in even then, lifting her hand, pressing his firm mouth to her palm. Inundated with the sensations all over again, she curled her fingers and groaned.

When her phone beeped, she jumped, then quickly sat up. No one had her number — except Rowdy.

She turned on a light, pressed a button on the phone and put it to her ear. "Hey."

"Did I wake you?"

"No." They both kept strange hours, but even if they didn't, Rowdy would always call when others least expected it. Because it was always a looming threat, she asked, "Is anything wrong?"

"You had company."

She gulped. How did he find that out so quickly? "A neighbor."

"A man."

Since Rowdy actually owned the apartment building, buying it outright under yet another alias, she could understand his consternation. "I don't know too much about him —"

"But you had him over anyway?"

She understood his incredulity. "It's not like that. His name is Logan Stark and for some reason . . ." Well, she couldn't just tell her brother that Logan hit on her. That'd not only infuriate him, it'd also make him as suspicious as she was. "He wanted to share dinner, that's all."

Cold silence.

"C'mon, Rowdy," she cajoled. "I'm careful, you know that."

"You're playing with fire."

Maybe. "It's not a big deal. Dinner, that's all."

"Then tell me why."

She shrugged to herself. "I wondered the same thing. It's not like I'd be appealing to him."

He cursed low. "I didn't mean that."

"You did," she corrected. "But it's okay. A

low profile is what's most important, right?"

"I don't like it."

"There's not much you do like these days." She sighed, feeling for her brother, worried about him, and so tired of all the subterfuge. "Please, believe me, Rowdy. I won't take any risks."

"Maybe not on purpose, but that was a risk you took last night, so I'm going to check into him."

Hmm . . . "Maybe you could find out where he works."

"Ask him," Rowdy said. "We'll see if what he says to you meshes with what I find."

"All right." If the opportunity presented itself, she could try a little prying.

"Give me a week or two to find out what I can about him. Until then, watch your ass."

Of course she would. Not like anyone else was watching it. Well, except her brother — and she could do with a little less vigilance from him, especially now that Logan was in the picture. "Love you, Rowdy."

His voice softened. "Love you, too, kid." And then, right before he hung up, he admonished, "Behave."

Pepper put the phone back on her night-stand. It would be so nice to visit with Rowdy, to spend an entire day with him.

But he wouldn't allow it.

She understood why, but that didn't stop her from missing him, more and more each day.

It saddened her, but as she tried to get to sleep, it was Logan she thought of, not her brother.

And that disturbed her most of all.

On the third floor of his exclusive, all-service club, Morton Andrews held court. Idiots surrounded him, but they were his idiots, loyal to him, afraid of his influence, so he tolerated them.

He eyed the cop who'd just entered. No, he wouldn't offer a seat. He'd show no courtesy at all.

Cops had to remember their place — as hired help. "Is it true that Rowdy Yates has turned up?"

Surprise showed, but then was quickly covered. "Where did you hear that?"

Interesting. So maybe there was some truth to it. "You forget my many tentacles? I have ears everywhere. You know that."

A nod of acknowledgment. "Yes, I know that."

Morton accepted he had few virtues, and patience definitely wasn't one of them. "Well?"

"There's nothing concrete on Rowdy."

It irked him sometimes, that cool confidence, the near disdain. Others cowered around him. Others understood the threat. But not this one. "You'll let me know when there is?"

"Of course."

Truth, or false assurances? Didn't matter. In his own way, and in his own time, Morton knew he'd get to the bottom of it. For now, it amused him to let the illusion of trust exist. "All right, then." And just to be a prick, he said, "You can go now."

Taking the dismissal with no show of insult, the cop turned and left.

Morton shook his head. To his way of thinking, the only good cop was dirty — or dead. He'd yet to decide the fate of this one. But soon . . .

For three days, Logan kept his distance. It wasn't easy, but he wanted Pepper to think about him, to anticipate seeing him. Anticipation could break down her barriers, and that's what he needed.

After spending the day working for his brother Dash, he'd expended a lot of tension. Physical labor always did that for him. Sunshine, sweat, using his hands, working his shoulders and thighs . . . he enjoyed it.

46

Likely Dash did as well, which would explain why he'd not only bought the company, but worked alongside the laborers on a regular basis.

There'd been a lot of concrete work throughout the afternoon. Sweat flattened his hair to his head and kept his T-shirt glued to his back. Everywhere he stepped, his dusty boots left footprints. Too much sun made his face feel tight.

And still he loved it.

Dash had the right idea. Make his own way doing good, honest labor, and build a great reputation at the same time.

It didn't hurt that the construction company gave Logan great cover. No one knew he and Dash were related, so no one paid him any attention. On the construction site, he was just one more grunt, there to help with the physical workload.

Just as he reached his door, Pepper's opened.

Satisfaction burned in his gut.

He glanced up, saw her standing there uncertainly, and smiled. "Hey, Sue." He continued to unlock his door, pushed it open. "What's up?"

"I, ah . . ."

He glanced at her again, a brow raised.

"I haven't seen you for a few days."

"Been working." He leaned in the door to drop a thermos and hard hat. "That's how construction is. You don't work for a month, then you're nonstop busy for a while."

"Construction?" She eased farther into the hallway.

Seeing this as a prime opportunity, Logan rubbed the back of his neck tiredly. "Yeah." He gestured. "You want to come in? I need to shower and grab some dinner, but then we can visit."

"Oh." Shaking her head, she retreated a step. "No, I —"

Keeping his gaze locked on hers, he reached for her, caught her hand, and pulled her forward into the hall and then into his apartment. "I only need a few minutes. What'd you have planned for dinner? I'm starving."

Not the most subtle hint, but maybe she'd be female enough to pick up on it and take pity on him.

"I was going to order a pizza." She looked around his apartment with interest but jumped when he closed the door. Apprehension welled up. "I should go."

"I'd rather you stay." He dropped down to his couch but didn't lean back into the cushions, not with his shirt damp through and through. He began unlacing his work boots. "I'd put off the shower, but I'm a sweaty mess. It's bad enough that it's in the nineties, but add in the humidity, and it was miserable today."

"Yes."

At that faint agreement, he looked at her, found her staring at his shoulders, and smiled. "I probably smell like a locker room."

Her face again warmed, and she breathed, "No."

Logan reveled in her response. Had he reduced her to one word replies? Just to keep her tongue-tied, he stood and pulled off his shirt.

Her jaw loosened, and she drew in a shuddering breath.

Damn, could a woman be more enticing? More in need of a long hard ride? She damn near fainted when he reached past her to set his boots on the floor inside the door.

Close to her, crowding her a little, he emptied his pockets on the table, setting out his wallet, cell phone and some change. "Stay put, okay? I'll be right back."

She stared at his throat.

Remember what you're doing. Giving her a verbal nudge, Logan whispered, "Sue?"

Her gaze jumped up to his.

"Tell me you'll be here when I get out of

the shower."

"Yes." She nodded slowly. "I'll be here."

He couldn't resist touching her, but because he was a mess, he used only his baby finger to stroke her warm, downy cheek. Then, before he lost it, he said, "Make yourself at home," and turned to head into the bathroom.

He hoped she would use the time alone to snoop a little; it was why he'd left his wallet and second cell phone sitting right there. Anything she found would only reinforce his cover.

Scrubbing head to toe, he removed the grime even as the cool water helped to temper his explosive lust.

Not that he should have been exploding with lust. It made no sense. This was a job, just like any other. His association with her was a means to an end, and Pepper Yates, aka Sue Meeks, was as far from a femme fatale as a woman could get.

But knowing she waited in the other room left him half hard, his guts knotted and his balls tight.

Shit.

In a hurry to get back to her, he turned off the shower and dried. Now that he'd gotten her into his place, he didn't want her to turn tail and run before he could take advantage of the situation and advance his goal.

But as he walked back in, snapping his jeans along the way, he found her still at the door, his belongings untouched, her expression a little lost. It appeared she hadn't moved an inch. Hell, it almost looked as if she held her breath.

New sensations tensed his muscles. He didn't know for sure what he felt, but he felt it in spades, unsettling and blistering hot.

Without saying a word, their gazes locked, he approached her. For several seconds they stood there, staring at each other while the charge between them arced and crackled, growing stronger with each beat of his heart.

Softly, he said, "You look ready to bolt."

She rolled in her lips and shook her head.

Because he couldn't not touch her, Logan put a hand to the top of her head. Her hair was silky soft, warm. He stroked back to her nape, and then down the length of that long ponytail, stopping with his hand open on the small of her back. "Everything okay?"

"Yes." Then, as he nudged her closer, she blurted, "I hadn't heard from you . . ."

His strategy had obviously worked — so then why did he feel like such a prick? "After working on the construction site, I

51

came home each day pretty beat."

"I didn't mean . . . You don't owe me anything."

Her vulnerability chewed on his conscience. "No?"

Without his urging, she drew closer, her attention on his mouth. "I just . . . You had said . . . so I thought . . ." She clamped her mouth closed and squeezed her eyes shut. "Never mind."

"I gave you my number," he reminded her.

Her tone now more strident, she shot right back, "I told you I wouldn't call."

So she had.

He probably should've kissed her already to avoid this little conflict.

Better late than never.

But he didn't take her mouth. Instead, he lowered his head and brushed a kiss over her heated cheek, down to her firm jaw, and then to the side of her silken neck.

She locked her hands behind her, confounding him.

"You smell good, Sue." He nuzzled her ear, filling his lungs with her scent. "Like sunshine."

"I was outside." Breathless, she added, "The building has termites."

"Yeah?" He didn't give a damn. His hand on her back contracted; she felt supple, trim, but so soft.

"I had to meet with the exterminator." She tipped her head to make it easier for him to get to her throat. "We were outside for over an hour."

This dump had an exterminator? Okay, so he'd never seen any bugs, it still surprised him. "Thanks for taking care of that."

"I probably need a shower, too."

"No." He opened his mouth on her throat, moved his tongue over her, tasting her skin, licking her, then whispering in her ear, "But you could have showered with me if you'd —"

She left his arms so quickly, it took him a second to figure out what had happened.

She had that deer caught in the headlights look about her.

Time to regroup.

Pretending he hadn't panicked her, Logan said, "You mentioned ordering pizza." He took a step back, giving her some space so she could breathe easier. "How about I pay, and we can eat here?"

Indecision kept her on the edge of retreat. "I didn't mean to intrude."

"You'd be doing me a favor." When she hesitated, he handed her his phone. "Go ahead and order it. I'll get us something to drink in the meantime."

He walked away, hoping she'd settle down and stay with him — but prepared to go after her if she didn't.

Then he heard her soft voice ordering the pizza, loaded, just as he liked it.

He got out glasses. "You want a beer or a Coke?"

She looked at his beer with longing, but said, "A Coke, please."

Another mystery. If she wanted a beer, why not say so? Did she think it unladylike — or did she worry that alcohol, even a simple beer, would lower her resistance, maybe allow her to divulge secrets better kept concealed?

Logan disliked her brother more by the minute. "Over ice?"

She nodded.

"How long for the pizza? I'm starved."

"Fifteen minutes or so." She inched closer. "They're just around the corner."

"Good to know."

"You can also get Thai and Chinese pretty quickly. And hoagies or chili only takes half an hour."

"You do a lot of fast food, too, huh?"

"During the summer I usually grill dinner. You know that. But at night, after it gets quiet, sometimes I . . ." She shrugged.

"You can't sleep?"

"I enjoy the peace," she corrected. "I don't have a set schedule, so when I want to watch an old movie, or catch up on the news, I do. I think I'm a natural night owl."

"So you curl up on the couch with some fast food?" It was a cute picture. What type of pajamas did she wear? A granny gown? T-shirt and panties? Somehow he couldn't picture her in lingerie. "Maybe you can share the numbers of the local restaurants with me."

"All right." Though she hung back in the kitchen doorway, she asked, "Can I do anything?"

Oh, hell yeah. She could do all sorts of things. He gave her a smile but said, "Don't worry about it. We'll just grab some plates and napkins when it gets here." He handed her drink to her. "Want to watch TV now, or sit on the balcony?"

She looked toward his balcony but again hesitated, so he took the decision away from her.

"Let's see what's on TV." Taking her hand, he led her to the sofa. He sat down and pulled her down beside him, probably closer than she liked, but not as close as he wanted.

She sat stiff, silent and wary. After setting her drink on the coffee table, she clasped her hands together in her lap, pressed her knees and ankles together, kept her back military straight.

All because he sat beside her? "Relax."

"I am relaxed," she said too fast.

After a long look, he grinned at her and shook his head. "I think I'll have to teach you how to loosen up."

Her eyes flared, especially when he put aside his beer and reached for her shoulders.

But he only pressed her back against the couch, and began kneading her tensed muscles. "C'mon, Sue. Take out the starch. Inhale a big breath . . . that's it. Now let it out nice and slow."

She tried, but she was still far too rigid.

"Don't worry. We'll get there eventually." He settled back beside her. "That's a promise, by the way." Using the remote, he turned on the set and flipped through the channels until he found a movie in the middle of a love scene.

"There you go." He took a swig of his beer. "Better than suffering more of that broiling sun."

For a minute or two she watched the movie, her breathing deep and even, until the sex scene faded to dark. When the commercial came on, he flipped channels again, finding a sports update.

She half turned toward him, and, tension

mounting, Logan waited to see what she'd do.

Using one hand, she touched his jaw. It was so unexpected, that spontaneous contact from her, that it rendered him mute, immobile and combustible.

"Men do seem to enjoy controlling the remote, don't they?"

What did she know of men and their preferences on control? He found his voice to say, "You want me to go back to the movie?"

"I don't care what we watch, but I'm glad you chose to stay inside." She brushed her fingertips down to the side of his neck. "You've already gotten a little too much sun."

Jesus, how could one simple touch do that to him? "On my shoulders, too," he said huskily. "Hazard of the job, I guess. Half the time we work shirtless."

Her gaze drifted to his shoulders, followed by her hand. "Construction is why you're so tanned?"

"That, and I like the outdoors." Blindly, he set aside his beer. "Swimming, boating, just being outside. I enjoy nature." His brother had a very secret retreat on a lake. They'd each used it when they wanted to get away, when even female companionship didn't appeal.

The log cabin was so rustic that anything more than a five-minute shower used all the hot water. Dishes had to be washed by hand — and so did clothing. The all-wood panel interior boasted three sparsely furnished bedrooms, a tiny kitchen with the barest essentials and a bathroom barely big enough to turn around in. The massive front deck, flanked by towering trees, overlooked the small secluded lake that was big enough for fishing, swimming and a rowboat or small trolling motor.

"Does it hurt?" she asked softly, teasing the skin of his shoulders.

"What?" He ached with lust, but he didn't think she meant that.

"The sunburn." She drifted her hand up to his nape, around to his collarbone.

It was such a bold move for her, so unexpected, that he forgot his plan. He caught her wrist, kissed her palm and then flattened her hand against his chest. "Sue?"

She stared at his mouth with yearning. "Your skin is so hot."

Fuck it. She begged for a kiss, and God knew he wasn't a saint. In the end, what did it matter if he made his move now or later? One way or the other, she'd be his.

His to enjoy.

And then his to use.

He put his hand around her nape and pulled her in as he leaned forward. At the first touch of his mouth on hers, she made a sound of pleasure, and Logan knew he was a goner.

CHAPTER THREE

Could any man taste better, smell better, or be more tempting?

Heat poured off him, and Pepper wanted to feel it all over her body. She pictured him working outside, all macho in jeans and heavy boots, the sun on his bare shoulders and chest, and her pulse raced. As his mouth moved over hers, his chest hair drew her fingers again and again. Using care not to exacerbate his sun-kissed skin, she stroked him, carefully, over his shoulders, his chest — and down to his taut abdomen.

Oh, God, she wanted to feel every inch of him.

He made a sound of approval and somehow, at the same time, lowered her to her back on the couch. The plush cushions gave way to their combined weight, and she sank into them.

Having a man's solid body over her, pressing into her — she'd missed it. So damn much.

Each kiss grew deeper, hungrier, until they were both breathing hard. He had his tongue in her mouth, exploring, and she just naturally twined her own with his.

He ran a hand down her side to her hip, his spread fingers covering a wide path, touching so much of her. He squeezed at her hip with appreciation, and even through her long skirt and underwear, it electrified her senses.

He moved his hand down her thigh until she stiffened, ready to stop him if he took things too far.

Instead, he brought that seeking hand back up her body, up, up, to her left breast.

Before she could think better of it, she arched her back, pressing into his palm, alive with sensation.

He cuddled her, but his movements slowed, became more of a search than a caress.

Lifting his head but staying very close, he said with a touch of confusion, "What kind of bra is that?"

No, she didn't want reality to intrude. Not yet. Not now. "Sports bra," she breathed, and took his mouth again.

A very tight, very restrictive sports bra.

Hoping he might not think too much of it, she caught his wrist and tugged his hand away. *Please let me have a little more.*

"I want to touch you," he murmured, and his hand went back to her waist, this time slipping up under her loose shirt.

Sexual frustration mounted, warring against desperation, against common sense. She knew she had to be strong, but then she felt his rough palm at her waist, at her ribs, and her resistance began crumbling — until a knock sounded on his door.

She jumped, at first alarmed, and then, reluctantly . . . relieved for the jolt back to sanity.

The pizza delivery boy had saved her, because she hadn't been strong enough to save herself. She'd take the interruption as a warning — to show more care.

Logan pressed his forehead to hers. His heartbeat rapped against her breasts, and the tension in his shoulders amplified.

"Rotten timing." Using both hands, he held her face, his thumbs stroking her jaw, his breath hot. "I don't suppose you'd want to put off dinner?"

She couldn't look at him. If she did, she'd cave. Staring at his left shoulder, she shook her head.

His sigh teased her lips. "All right then.

Pizza it is." As he sat up, he pulled her up, too.

She closed her eyes with stark regret, and when she opened them again, she encountered his intense scrutiny.

His smile went crooked as he tweaked a long hank of her hair. "You are so sweet." And with that, he left the couch.

Sweet? What was that about? Pepper checked her hair and felt the way her ponytail had come undone. Worse, her top was all displaced, her skirt hiked up on one side all the way to her knee, and she'd lost one slip-on canvas shoe.

While Logan answered the door, she decided to make a hasty exit to right herself. "Excuse me." She snatched up her shoe and rushed down the short hall into his bathroom. She closed and locked the door.

Get a grip, she ordered herself. But it was oh-so-difficult after those scorching kisses and exciting touches.

A few deep breaths helped a little. She stepped into her shoe, tugged her shirt into place, and moved away from the door. One glance in the mirror over the sink and she winced. Her hair was more out of the ponytail than in it. Hastily, she pulled the band free and finger-combed her long hair back, then resecured it.

She straightened her clothes again, but could do nothing about her aroused flush. Blast her fair skin.

A tap sounded at the door. "Everything okay, Sue?"

"Yes." Other than unfulfilled lust, she was just peachy. Head down, Pepper opened the door and walked around him, up the hallway and into the kitchen.

He'd already put slices of pizza on plates, set out napkins, and moved their drinks to the table. Surprising her, he pulled out her chair.

Why, oh, why couldn't he be wearing a shirt instead of flaunting that awesome body? As to that, why couldn't he be out of shape instead of so ripped? Or unattractive instead of so appealing? Or —

"It's just pizza, Sue." He tipped his head. "I won't pounce on you while you're eating, I promise."

She didn't want to get that close to him again, but she didn't want to look overly foolish, either. "Thank you." She brushed past him and sat.

After trailing the backs of his fingers over her cheek, he took his own seat. "Dig in."

"Thank you," she said again.

He thoughtfully watched her as he ate. "You know, I just had my tongue in your mouth, so you don't have to be so formal."

Pepper gasped — and choked on her pizza. What was he thinking, saying something like that over dinner? Did he have no sense of propriety at all?

After a bout of wheezing, she caught her breath, looked at him, saw he was still eating while studying her reaction, and decided that no, he did not have any sense of decorum.

"It bothers you?" he asked. "Kissing me, I mean? Is that why you're over there strangling yourself?"

"No —"

"Sure looked bothered to me."

"I didn't expect to discuss it over dinner!"

He ignored that. "I'm wondering," he said, "if I mentioned how bad I want to get you naked, would you keel right over?"

Throwing the slice of pizza at him seemed like a good idea. Instead she put it back on her plate. Should she leave? Show disdain? Embarrassment?

She decided on a dose of honesty instead. "You'll never see me naked."

"No?" As if only mildly curious, he asked, "Why not?"

"Because I won't allow it."

His eyes narrowed — and his gaze went to her chest. "Too shy, huh?"

She sat back in her seat. "You don't talk like a man who ever hopes to be successful. You're so mocking, it's almost an insult."

"Don't mean to be." He put another gigantic slice of pizza onto his plate. "Truth is, Sue, you confound me."

"Confound you?"

She had to wait while he devoured half the pizza. After he wiped his mouth with a napkin, he crossed his arms over the table. "You're as interested as I am. I wasn't the only one on the couch who wanted more."

Since he waited, she said, "No." She'd probably been far needier than he was. For certain, she'd been celibate longer.

"So why are you so skittish? Why the mixed messages?"

Shoot. She had been pretty inconsistent. But how could she possibly explain the past that held her back, the fears that dictated she show discretion in all things?

He saved her by reaching for her hand. "You can tell me, you know."

No, she most definitely could not. She eyed him warily. "Tell you what?"

"If someone hurt you. If you're just inexperienced. If you're modest or afraid or . . . whatever the problem might be."

All that? What exactly did he think? That she'd lived in a convent? That she'd been a

66

victim of abuse? For certain she couldn't tell him any part of the truth. Even with the passing of time, even with Morton Andrews's club, Checkers, being in another county — distant enough that they wouldn't run into him, close enough that Rowdy could keep tabs on him — the truth would be risky.

But she had to say *something,* so she looked at his big hand holding hers. "I am shy. And I am modest." A really good liar, too.

"But you want me."

Did she ever. Whether she should or not, whether it was wise or not.

"Sue? Whatever you tell me, it's okay. I'm not going to start rushing you."

Baloney. That's all he'd done so far. She met his gaze. "Yes."

It took several heartbeats before he repeated, "Yes . . . what?"

"I want you." Let him deal with that. "Your interest has been flattering," she added, trying to sound a little more uncertain. "But I'm not comfortable with anyone seeing me."

His sharpened attention moved over her. "Naked, you mean?"

"Yes, that's what I mean."

A heated stillness fell over him. "You don't

have anything I haven't already seen, right?"

She almost choked again. He had no idea the surprises she kept hidden. "I'm not disfigured, if that's what you're asking."

"No, I wasn't. Just making a point, that's all. And if modesty is the only problem —"

"It's not." No, there were a million reasons why she shouldn't get too involved with him, physically or otherwise.

And yet, here she sat. Having pizza. Talking.

After allowing him to kiss her into oblivion and grope her on the sofa. She put her head in her hands and fought off a groan.

Pushing his chair back from the table, his dinner forgotten, he concentrated on her. "What else?"

Because it felt as if he might pounce on her at any moment despite his promise not to rush her, Pepper left her chair and stood behind it. Judging by the look on his face, he saw it as a defensive move. She knew it was more a matter of control: around him, she had none.

Slowly, he stood.

Before he took a step toward her — and before she pounced on him — she said, "I barely know you."

"Okay." He held out his arms. "I'm an open book. What do you want to know?"

Why do you want me so badly? No, she couldn't ask him anything that blunt. "Everything, I guess."

"Will you sit down and finish eating while I give you a verbal resume?"

Why not? She was still hungry, the pizza still hot. "Okay." Not looking at him, she took her seat and again bit into her pizza.

"Long or short version?"

Everything, in minute detail. She shook her head. "I don't mean to pry exactly —"

"Long it is." He smiled, waited until she got a mouthful, then said, "Never been married, but was engaged once. Have a degree in business, but haven't used it because I enjoy the freedom of construction more. I've been all over the country, but prefer the Midwest. I'm thirty-two, love watching all sports and enjoy playing softball or football. I detest shopping of any kind, even for groceries, but I'm a fair cook when forced to it. I really like animals, but don't have any because, well, living in a place like this, it wouldn't be fair to the animal, right? Dogs especially deserve a big backyard. In fact, now that I'm thinking about it, I don't really trust anyone who doesn't like animals, so do you?"

It took Pepper a moment to realize he'd slipped a question in there. She swallowed down her bite and nodded. "Yes, but for the same reasons you just gave —" *and many more* "— I don't have any pets, either." Someday, in her fantasy future, she'd love to have pets, lots of them. Kids, too . . . no, she wouldn't, couldn't think that way.

It'd only depress her.

"So we have that in common," Logan said. "My folks have an ancient German shepherd that loves to swim. I think it's easier for him than running, less stress on his hips."

Slipping in her own question, she asked, "Why didn't you marry?"

"Haven't met the right woman, I guess. I want to someday." He gestured. "You know, home, hearth, holidays with two kids, a cat and a dog. All that."

"You were engaged?" she prompted.

"Yeah, for over a year." He ran a hand through his hair. "It was all good until she decided I had to take a job with her daddy, and her daddy was a grade-A prick, so . . ." He shrugged. "Couldn't work it out."

That sounded like the absolute truth, but could that really be the whole story? "You don't sound particularly heartbroken over it."

His expression warmed. Belatedly, she decided that prim and proper Sue Meeks

70

should have reacted some to his language. But, oh, well. Too late now.

"Funny thing, that. I never was." Done eating, he slouched back in his chair and cradled his beer on his midsection. "I mean, I was pissed. Maybe even a little . . ." He searched for a word and settled on, "Disappointed. But I guess I never really loved her, not the way you should love someone if you're going to spend a lifetime together."

"How long ago was that?"

"Few years." He gave her a searching look. "What about you? Ever been serious about anyone?"

"No."

Because she'd answered so quickly, he laughed. "Okay." He nodded at her empty plate. "All done?"

Thrown by the change in topic, she looked at her plate and was surprised that she'd eaten so much. "Yes, thank you."

"So." He stood and carried the dishes to the sink. "What now?"

Bemused, she watched as he rinsed each plate, loaded them in the dishwasher and did a general cleaning of their dinner mess.

By the time he finished, no sign of dinner remained. "You're a lot tidier than I am."

"No offense, but I'm thinking a lot of people are probably tidier than you."

"It's true." She didn't really get into the whole domestic routine. She let out a sigh. "My place isn't really dirty or anything, but it is cluttered." She wrinkled her nose. "I don't like to fuss."

"Good. Fussy women are annoying."

Distant thunder rumbled, and they both looked toward the balcony. The bright evening sunshine had faded beneath thick gray clouds that darkened the sky. A troubled breeze carried in cooler air.

"Don't get me wrong," Logan said, "but this is the weirdest date I've ever had."

That brought her back around to face him. "It wasn't a date!"

"Sure it was." Mood teasing, he came closer. "A little necking, dinner and conversation, getting to know each other."

Oh, God. Maybe it was a date.

"Usually doesn't happen in that order, and I can't recall ever talking marriage on a first date."

"You brought it up!"

"To appease your curiosity." A light patter of rain danced over the patio doors. "But it wasn't bad for our first. Was it?"

Not bad at all. In fact, it was the first time in ages that she'd forgotten, for just a little while, how much her life had changed. "No, I suppose it —"

Bright lightning splintered the sky, chased by a deafening crack of thunder that reverberated in the floor beneath their feet.

She said, "Wow." And the electricity died.

It needed only this.

The combination of no lights and black sky left the apartment cast in deep mysterious shadows.

Logan walked to the patio doors just as the storm hit in earnest, pounding the earth with a deluge of rain. It blew in against his bare chest, dampening his skin, his hair and the front of those well-worn jeans.

He shut his doors and, after swiping off his face, crossed the floor to get the kitchen window, too.

Because she stood there in a lustful daze, he prompted her. "What about your windows? They open?"

How had she forgotten that? "Damn it," she said, and bolted back to her own apartment. She didn't want Logan to follow her, but she didn't take the time to tell him not to. The way the rain blew in, everything she owned would be soaked in under a minute.

She got the balcony doors closed while he shut the kitchen window for her. She darted into the bathroom to get that small window, and Logan . . . went into her bedroom.

No, no, *no*.

Face soaked, shirt and shoes wet, she waited, but he didn't come back out. Knowing proximity could get the best of her, she nonetheless stepped into the bedroom behind him. He had his back to her, eyeing her treadmill.

"Logan?"

When he turned, she saw his jeans clinging to his body, his chest hair darker with the rain, his nipples tight from the chill.

Her mouth went dry.

"Sorry." He ran a hand over his face and pushed back his hair. "It was coming in pretty good. Your floor's wet, and so is the bottom of your bed."

She stayed by the door, her thoughts rioting with explicit images of him naked, the things he'd do, the things she wanted to do to him.

A sudden shift in the air, in his mood, sent a thread of excited alarm up her spine.

He took a step toward her. "What about you, Sue?"

Not knowing what he asked, she shook her head in confusion.

"It's too damn dark for me to tell," he whispered, coming closer. In a husky, suggestive tone, he said, "I'm betting you're wet, too."

So many ways she wanted to reply — all

of them dangerous.

She couldn't think when she looked at him, so she turned her back and tried to order herself to caution.

"Thank you for the help." It was an obvious hint for him to go, but at the same time, she had that image of him standing there, at the foot of her unmade bed. Tall, bare-chested, sexy as sin . . .

His hands settled on her shoulders; his scent settled around her.

And before he said a single word, she knew she was a goner.

Logan ignored the not-so-subtle suggestion for him to hit the road, especially since her voice had gone all thin and high. She was nervous, he got that.

Why, he didn't yet know.

But he had her in a bedroom, in the near-dark, and with every fiber of his being, he was aware of her as a woman.

Not of his plan to get hold of her brother. Not of how she could assist him in his goal to obtain justice.

Just . . . *her.*

The way she trembled, the scent of her damp skin, her arousal.

They stood in the shadows while lightning flashed outside and occasional thunder rattled the windows.

Holding her shoulders, he drew her back into his chest and bent to inhale the heady fragrance of her damp skin. "I don't want to leave you alone in this storm."

The silence grew taut, and he knew she warred with herself, with what she wanted — and probably her damned brother's rules.

Finally she whispered, "I'll be fine."

"You want me to stay." And knowing that, he went about convincing her, putting soft love bites on her throat, teasing her ear with his breath and his tongue, wrapping his arms around her and holding her close enough that she felt his erection against her soft ass.

"Logan . . ."

"Your shirt is wet," he told her and boldly smoothed a hand up and over her breast. The restrictive bra confounded him. It couldn't be comfortable.

"Don't." She caught his wrist and drew his hand down to her waist, but she didn't step away from him.

"Okay." He pressed his hand lower, to her belly, and asked, "Is this better?"

She shocked him by nodding.

Need held him in a powerful grip; he pressed his hand lower, between her thighs, cupping her through the long skirt and insubstantial underwear.

They both breathed harder.

She parted her thighs.

Amazing. So this was okay, but her breasts were off-limits? Prodded by concern, by the idea that she could be scarred, or worse, he asked, "Why, honey?"

Pressing back against him, she put her hand over his, encouraging him to continue while muttering low, "No questions."

Not being a fool, Logan agreed. When he got her in bed, he'd get her naked, and then he'd figure it out on his own. He'd reassure her and let her know whatever it was, it didn't matter, not between them.

She flattened her hands on his thighs, and her nails dug into him. He heard the catch in her breathing, savored the heat of her, how she moved against his exploring fingers.

For the longest time they stood there like that, in the dark with the storm all around them, damp, hot, necking and petting. He grinned against her shoulder. "I haven't done this since high school."

It took a little while before she asked, "This?"

"Making out. Fooling around with my clothes on." He pressed his hard-on against her. "Getting so frustrated, I almost can't take it."

She groaned — and started to step away.

Logan turned them both instead and brought her down to the bed. He sprawled out over her, kissing her hard, deep, hoping to obliterate any objections.

She had none.

Of her own accord she parted her legs so that he fit between them. Her hands tangled in his hair, and she held him close while he kissed her.

When he again reached for her breast — dying to see her, to touch her — she stalled. "Wait."

Of course he did. Balanced over her, edgy with need, their breaths mingling, he . . . waited.

Her body beneath his was an indistinct form, but he felt her urgency, the way she stared at him, and her indecision.

Her hands kneaded his chest. "If we're going to do this —"

"I hope we are."

"— then I need the curtains closed."

Even though it was black as pitch outside? He looked toward the window. Was she afraid a flash of lightning would show him something? *Like what?* Thinking to encourage her, he said, "You don't need to —"

"And you have to keep your hands to yourself."

Thoughts, ugly suspicions, bounded this way and that. He gave her a gentle kiss. "I don't understand." Any of it, including the driving need to discover her hang-ups. "I've got my hands on you now." He emphasized that by tucking her hair back, smoothing her cheek with his thumb.

"I don't want you . . . feeling around on me."

Moving his body over hers, he growled, "I can feel you. All of you." He closed his eyes at the giving softness of her curves, the open cradle of her thighs. "You're soft and hot and —"

A little panicked — or else very close to the edge of release — she said in a high voice, "Promise me right now, or we're done."

Unease warred with conviction. He couldn't keep from brushing gentle kisses on the bridge of her nose, her brow, and he wanted to go on kissing her. Everywhere. "Whatever it is, honey, I swear to you, it's okay."

"It's me." Stroking her hands around to his back, fraught with uncertainty, she clutched at him. "I need my clothes on. I need the lights out. I need you to keep your hands mostly to yourself."

Jesus. "When I mentioned high school, I

wasn't looking for a reenactment."

She sucked in a breath. "Fine." Shaking, she pushed against him while trying to turn away from him. "Then let's forget about —"

"No way." He brought her face back around to his and again kissed her, softer, deeper. "You can trust me, Sue." *Like hell.* "I won't hurt you." *Damn it.*

In the near darkness, they watched each other. Her eyes glimmered, but he couldn't see her well enough to decipher her thoughts.

She touched his jaw. "Let me up."

Damn, damn, damn. Flopping over to his back with a groan, Logan stared toward the ceiling, hot, frustrated, but mostly troubled. From the knees down, his legs hung over the end of the bed.

The part the rain had soaked.

The wind howled eerily, suiting his mood. Thunder crashed, and he felt it in his chest.

He didn't want things to end like this.

He rose up on one arm. "Sue?" It amazed him that he kept the forethought to continue using her alias. There remained just enough light filtering in for him to see her shadowy form as she lifted her skirt.

Lust tied him in knots. He drew in necessary oxygen. "What are you doing?"

"Taking off my panties." She dropped them on the floor and crossed to the window to close the heavy curtains. "*Only* my panties."

His heart thundered. "Yeah, all right." Lust cut into him. When he felt her approach, he dropped back to the bed in an agony of suspense, breath held, erection straining.

Her hands went to the fastening of his jeans. With a small tug, she opened the snap. "I shouldn't do this," she said.

He heartily disagreed.

She pushed his jeans down to his knees. "I'll probably regret it."

He wouldn't let her feel regret. Somehow he'd make it okay —

Her hand curled around him, and his thoughts shattered on a rough groan.

Keeping his cock held tight in her small, hot hand, she climbed onto the bed to straddle his hips. She'd lifted her skirt; her panties were indeed gone. "Please don't ruin this for me, Logan."

"No." Hell, no. "I won't."

Sitting back a little, she stroked him once, then released him. "Can you put on this condom?"

Where the hell had she gotten it?

Screw it, he didn't care. He found her

hand in the darkness and took the rubber from her. "Yeah, no problem." Amazing that he felt so close; it hadn't been that long for him. He shouldn't be so wired, so fucking desperate to get inside her.

She was plain, timid, with a nondescript build and more secrets than he could count.

She was a pawn in his scheme to corral the murderous Morton Andrews.

But he couldn't remember the last time he'd felt like this.

CHAPTER FOUR

Logan loved sex, always had, always would. No two ways about that. Somehow, with Pepper Yates and all her coy rules and seductive timidity, it felt different. Scorching. Salacious.

Like a kinky fantasy come to life.

Her soft bare thighs opened over his hips. Not touching her was one of the hardest things he'd ever done. He fisted his hands in the damp sheets of her bed.

Again she wrapped her small hand around him. "I can feel you pulsing," she whispered.

God. "Tell me what you need, honey."

"You," she said. "Inside me." And with that, she moved over him, positioning him, moving the head of his cock against her hot, slick flesh.

He couldn't remember ever being so turned on, so primed. "You're wet," he said with savage satisfaction. She gave him so little . . . but he had this.

"I know." She sank down the tiniest bit, caught her breath and hesitated.

Shaking all over, Logan held himself as still as he could. Jaw tight, he waited. He could barely see her, but her scent was stronger now, her body clamping around him, alternately squeezing him, then softening again with devastating effect.

It was a snug fit, and with her only working the sensitive head, he thought he'd lose it. Through his teeth, he said, "More, Sue." He drew a harsh breath. "Now, or it'll be over before it begins."

"I'm sorry." She braced a hand flat on his chest and pressed down, rocking a little, working herself down over him. "It's been a while for me."

"You need me to touch you, to help ready you —"

"No." Now with both hands on his chest, she gasped, and sank more.

Heels to the floor, Logan lifted up and pressed himself as deep as he could go until he'd buried himself inside her.

He heard her vibrating groan and felt the way her inner muscles worked him.

"Yeah?" Anchoring himself so he wouldn't forget and reach for her, he waited.

"Yes," she breathed.

Thank God. He drove up into her again

and again. He wanted to hold her hips, he wanted to free her breasts and suck on her nipples.

But all he had was this, and it was so damned erotic, he had to concentrate hard to keep from coming.

They found the perfect rhythm together. Her nails curled into his pectoral muscles, then kneaded him in pleasure. He growled, and she purred.

"Let me kiss you," he said. He needed at least that. "Give me your mouth."

Lowering to her forearms, she bit his bottom lip, kissed him hard, licked her tongue against his. This new position drove him even deeper, brought her clitoris into contact with his shaft with each solid thrust — and he felt the start of her climax.

Against his mouth she cried out, still kissing him with hunger, grinding herself against him, harder and faster.

Suddenly she arched back with a harsh moan, riding out her orgasm, and more than anything Logan wished he could see her.

Letting himself go, he groaned with her, stunned by the power of what she made him feel, by her physical and emotional appeal. The release continued until he was drained, until the aftershocks faded and she sprawled down over him, a limp, sweet weight over his heart.

They were half off the bed, half on it, as lax as the sheets.

Carefully, Logan settled his hands on her narrow back. "Okay?"

"Mmm." She kissed his sweaty chest, nuzzled her nose against him and said with clear regret, "It's such a shame that you have to go."

He Went Still beneath her, then rigid. "Is that a joke?"

On a long, melancholy sigh, Pepper levered herself up over him. "No." She patted his rock-hard shoulder, disengaged their bodies, and left the bed. "I wish you could stay." She really, really did. "But I'm sorry. You can't."

"You're kicking me out?" He sat up in disbelief. *"Now?"*

"Yes." If only the lights would come back on first so she could get a good look at him. But darkness prevailed. She moved away and opened the curtains again. "It's getting late."

"It's only half an hour later than it was before we got in bed!"

True. Unfortunately, prolonged foreplay wasn't in the works for them. Trying to ignore his irritation, she started out of the room. "I need a shower."

He was off the bed in a heartbeat, stepping into her path, blocking her retreat.

Offended.

Given her current frame of mind — sort of soft and distracted and . . . susceptible — it was a good thing he'd pulled up his jeans. They were still open, and now that she'd parted the drapes again, she could see his abdomen . . . and lower. But at least she didn't see all of him, everything that she'd touched, stroked.

The thick flesh that had filled her up.

Her heart beat in a slow, steady rhythm. Resisting the urge to touch him, Pepper put her hands behind her and backed up.

Incredulous, he glared. "No fucking way are you afraid of me."

After everything they'd just done? "No." She was afraid of herself, of her reactions to him. She couldn't do this — but she had. And it had been so wonderful . . .

He tried a different tack. Taking her shoulders, caressing her, he cajoled, "Let me stay the night."

"I can't." She took another quick step back — out of his reach.

His hands dropped. "I don't fucking believe this."

His coarse language grated on her. They'd

had sex — weird, restrained sex, but still, that didn't give him the right to treat her without respect.

"I don't believe you're cursing me."

"Not *you.*" Working off what was clearly a very short fuse, he pinched the bridge of his nose. "It's this situation. I thought we were getting closer. I thought . . ."

That it meant something? He sounded like a scorned woman, and she felt like a jerk.

It seemed a wise thing to get out of the bedroom. Pepper went as far as the small sofa and paused. *Don't do it, Pepper. Don't do it* — "We could share dinner again. Tomorrow I mean." *She squeezed her eyes shut.* "If you're not busy."

The sudden silence nearly choked her. Had the storm finally quieted, too? She wasn't in the habit of propositioning men. Even before her life had changed so drastically, she hadn't thrown out dinner invitations.

She hadn't needed to.

Wondering what Logan thought, if he'd accept her offer, she turned to him. He'd crossed his arms, but his nonchalant stance couldn't hide his antagonism.

"Well?" She wished he'd say something.

"I'm trying to figure out if you're really inviting me for dinner, or for sex."

Both. Feeling a little foolish, she shook her head. "Never mind. It was a bad idea."

"Oh, no, you don't." In three long strides he reached her. "Whatever we just did, I liked it."

Her knees went weak. "Me, too."

"Yeah?" He caressed her again. "It was unusual —"

He meant odd. Weird. Bizarre.

"— but I don't think I've ever been that turned on."

"Really?" Sure, *she'd* loved it, but then even a crumb was delicious to a starving woman. And that had been no more than a crumb.

Guys were always easy, but still, she couldn't believe he'd be that accepting of her restrictions.

"Absolutely." With two fingers, Logan touched her chin. "If you're asking me over for more of the same, I'm in."

Could she make the apartment dark enough? Would she have an opportunity to buy blackout blinds? Did she dare have an encore of that unique and somewhat torturous intimacy?

"But," he said, interrupting her thoughts, "if it's only dinner you want, I'm in for that, too."

No way. If he accepted a "dinner only"

invite, it'd be because he figured he'd eventually get back in her bed. "Okay."

Proving her right, he slid both hands around her neck. "You know I'm rooting for the first option, right?"

"Yes." She was sort of rooting for it, too. "I understand that. I just don't know . . ."

He kissed her. "We'll play it by ear, see where things take us."

"Okay." And if she could find a way around Rowdy's temper over it all, then for sure, the bed would win. But she had no illusions about keeping this from her brother. He knew everything she did, and who she did it with.

Well, not the sexual details, of course. But he always watched her so closely, no way would he miss the fact that Logan had been in her apartment, during a power outage, without a lot to do to keep them busy.

Rowdy wouldn't be happy. She sometimes thought if he could have his way, he'd keep her locked up, out of sight.

Out of the way.

Thinking about that bothered her, so she again said to Logan, "You need to go."

Something dark and dangerous — probably ego — glittered in his eyes. "You have my number handy?"

"On top of the fridge."

Despite his menacing expression, his touch remained gentle, persuasive. "Keep it by your bedside, all right? Better, program it into your cell phone. Just in case you need me."

Need him? Did he mean for sexual satisfaction or physical protection? Either way . . . "I'll be fine."

Answering her question, he said, "If this blackout lasts, you don't know what kind of trouble might come knocking at your door."

True enough, but she wasn't worried. "It's just a storm." God knew she had survived worse things than weather. "And actually . . . I'm good with numbers."

"Meaning you've memorized it already?"

She shrugged.

"Good." Still he hesitated. "I'm leaving under duress."

Never had she known anyone like him. Sure, most men would take sex in just about any circumstances that they could get it. But what they had just done had to top the list of peculiar sexual encounters.

Still, she knew he'd reached satisfaction. His harsh groans had been wonderful to hear, and the way his body had tensed, the heat pouring off him during his release — she'd loved every second of it.

He'd gotten what he wanted. But now,

instead of being glad to escape further involvement, he wanted to hang around.

That sort of made her smile. "Thank you."

Taking her by surprise, he wrapped one arm around her waist, the other under her backside, and he lifted her off her feet. Given her height, that was no easy feat, but he didn't look strained.

Actually, he looked turned on. Again.

With her pelvis flattened to his hard abdomen, her legs aligned with his, she braced her hands on his bare shoulders. *Hot.*

"Logan!" She gasped. "What are you doing?"

Her well-covered breasts were even with his chin, but he stared into her eyes. "I need another taste to tide me over until tomorrow."

"Oh." She found no fault with that plan. "Okay."

Treating her to the full effect of his potent appeal, he kissed her — and this kiss was different from the others. Not entirely sexual, but not exactly sweet and innocent, either.

It was maybe a kiss of . . . understanding. And interest.

As he lowered her back to her feet, he said, "Think about me tonight, Sue. And think about what we'll do tomorrow." He gave her one more kiss before leaving.

Pepper watched him go. Think about him? She doubted she'd be able to think of anything else.

Hat pulled low, collar up, Rowdy Yates hung back in the shadows, shielded from the downpour by the slight overhang of the building across from the apartment complex. He chewed the end of a toothpick until there was nothing left of it.

What the hell was she thinking, fooling around with the new neighbor? She knew better, damn it.

Because he'd taught her better.

Having random, well-hidden cameras in the building hadn't proved useful until now. Usually, she took no chances. He'd felt safe with the occasional contact, knowing Pepper could reach him in case of an emergency.

But ever since Logan Stark had moved in, he'd been more vigilant — mostly because Pepper had been different. It seemed that, despite all his precautions, she'd come to the end of her rope. He'd have to deal with that, with her — but first he'd deal with Logan Stark.

Down the street, somewhere in the darkness, a car alarm blared. Glass broke. Sirens split the night.

A streetlamp flickered back on, disturbing the concealing cocoon of the blackout, sending a river of light to shimmer across the washed-out roadway.

The woman on his arm shivered from the rain and pressed her heavy breasts into his side. "It's cold."

"Not really." He'd already forgotten her name but didn't care. He wouldn't see her again after tonight. Wrapping an arm around her, Rowdy asked, "Better?"

"Are we going in or not?"

"Yeah." He could smell her perfume, felt the heat of her small body. He threw the toothpick away. "Remember, I've got an hour or less. That's all."

Running a hand down his chest and smiling, she said, "Sugar, that's all the time I need."

Still curled in her bed, relaxed from a good night's sleep, Pepper watched the sun begin filtering through the curtains. She had that type of lethargy that only came from sex.

She stretched, smiling, wondering what the coming day — and the night — might bring. More time with Logan? More sex? She hoped so.

Her cell phone rang.

She frowned toward it, but she knew it

would be Rowdy, and she knew he'd be angry. Much as she wanted to keep reality at bay, she had to answer.

Rolling to the side of the bed, she snatched up the phone and pressed the button to accept the call. "You're up early."

"But you're not?"

Smiling again, she fell to her back. "I slept in." To daydream. To remember.

"We have to talk, Pepper."

Uh-oh. Hearing Rowdy's exasperation, she shook off her dreamy preoccupation. "What's the matter?"

"You already know, so don't play dumb." And then, sharper, "What do you know about him?"

"He's . . . harmless." A neighbor, an oversexed guy willing to abide by her stipulations for a little fun in the sack. In other words . . . *perfect.*

"He's working construction."

Shrugging to herself, she said, "He told me."

"But you didn't *know* it, not until I checked."

She looked at the clock. It was after ten. "Is that where he's at now?"

"Yeah."

"And you figure it's legitimate?"

"Since he just shot a nail through his

hand, I'd say so."

She bolted upright in the bed. "Is he okay?"

Rowdy fell silent.

"Is he?"

"You care about him," Rowdy accused.

"I barely know him." Not a lie; but she knew him better than she knew most people.

Because she'd gotten intimate with him. A strange sort of intimacy, but still . . .

"He got sloppy with the nail gun, but I'm sure it's not a big deal."

Only another guy would think that. "Did he go to the hospital?"

"No. A few of the other guys patched him up."

Her anxiety lifted. It must not have been too awful. "So you're convinced he's on the level?"

"Hell, no. You shouldn't see him again."

But she would. "Why not?"

"You know why." Disgust mixed with anger in his tone. "Think about it, Pepper. What does he really want from you?"

Sex. "I don't know." *And dinner. And . . . conversation?* She shook her head. "Maybe he just wants to know a friendly face here."

With silky menace, Rowdy asked, "And have you been friendly?"

Oops. Bad wording on her part. "Not

exactly." She propped her back against the headboard. Anxious to get off the topic, she said, "So you only called to caution me?"

"To *warn* you. You're playing a dangerous game."

She didn't ask her brother if he'd been celibate; she knew the answer already. Double standards always annoyed her. "Duly noted. Now I need to go. I have to see how much damage the storm did to *your* building."

"Wait."

Pepper could almost picture him grinding his teeth, and she smiled. "Yes, Rowdy?"

A beat of silence, and then: "Until I get a chance to do a more thorough check on him, keep him out of your apartment."

Her lips compressed. Rowdy had gotten awfully good at giving her orders — and expecting them to be obeyed. "Fine." She wondered if Logan had been sent home from work but didn't dare ask Rowdy. He was surly enough already. It never paid for her to tweak his temper. "Let me know if you find out anything more."

"Might take a few days, but I'll be in touch."

The connection died, and so did her good mood. She tossed aside the phone and bounded out of bed. She had a lot to get done, so she might as well get to it.

Going to her closet, she chose another drab, ugly outfit and carried it into her small bathroom. Looking at herself in the mirror, she touched her dull hair and even duller complexion.

She hated to face the truth, but Rowdy had a valid point. Though he hadn't come right out and said it, they both had to wonder what Logan saw in her.

Easy sex? Accomplished.

So now what? More sex? For most of the men she'd known, it was all about the conquest. Once they got what they wanted, they moved on to more challenging territory.

For now, Logan was an enigma.

She'd shower, dress and get through her errands which, despite what Rowdy said, included buying heavier drapes and blackout blinds for her bedroom — just in case. It was bad enough that Logan had seen her treadmill.

She didn't need him seeing anything else.

Being a woman of her word, she'd insist that dinner be at his place tonight. And after dinner, maybe she'd be able to talk him into round two.

Letting out a long sigh, she cooled the temp on her shower and stepped in.

She knew better than to hope for too much; nothing in her life had really changed. She still lived a lie, and she needed to remain in isolation.

But she couldn't seem to stop herself from reaching for this one pleasure.

Her very restrictive existence suddenly looked brighter. For the first time in a long time she had reason to anticipate the day.

Given half a chance, she'd thank Logan for that — in the limited ways left to her.

With his cell phone on speaker, Logan paced his small living room and stewed. His hand ached, but he deserved it. Luckily, it was his left he'd injured, not his gun hand. He could shoot adequately with his left, but he had improved aim with his right.

Even luckier — depending on your point of view — it wasn't an uncommon accident to have happen on the job site. While he'd cursed a blue streak, the other workers had laughed at him, proof positive that they'd seen it happen before.

Dash had remembered not to single him out with concern and had, in fact, chewed his ass for being careless, as he would do with any worker.

But now he'd have a few days off work, and that'd fuck with his cover and his control. He needed to stay busy, to keep his thoughts occupied.

What the hell was Pepper Yates hiding under those hand-me-down clothes?

What didn't she want him to see? To touch?

Men were simple creatures, women not so much. They always wanted physical attention during sex. Hell, they *needed* it to get off.

Not Pepper.

He could still feel her sliding down his shaft, at first so slowly that she'd made him nuts, then taking him deep. And he could still feel the way her body had tightened around him during her climax.

A climax she'd reached with little help from him.

All while dressed. Without a single seductive stroke of his fingers.

Or his tongue.

He hadn't seduced her, hadn't incited her.

He hadn't done anything except supply a dick and then react to her lead. It burned his ass big-time that he felt used.

It burned him even more that he wanted her to want more.

Reese finally picked up on the fourth ring and said with irritation, "Anything wrong?"

His mood gave Logan pause. "Not really, no."

Reese cursed. "Then this better be good."

"Am I interrupting something?"

"Actually, yeah, you are."

Logan grinned. "New woman?"

"New puppy. It's destroying my place."

That was so far from what Logan had expected to hear, it threw him. "You got a dog?"

"It sort of got me. Long story."

So he'd taken in a stray? Logan grinned. "You're such a big softie."

Reese snorted. "You want me to come there and kick your ass? Is that it? You're all lonely and, instead of admitting it, you're finding a reason to piss me off so I'll hunt you up?"

Logan laughed outright.

Reese said, "Dog, no. No! Damn it." Then with a growl to Logan, "What's up?"

It took some effort to fight off another laugh, but Logan took pity on Reese and got to the point. "I need you to do some specific searching through our collection of photos."

"Rowdy?"

"No." He knew Reese wouldn't be happy, but what the hell? Logan had his reasons. "Pepper."

Reese paused. "We don't have much on her. Some small black-and-whites, that's all."

"I know." And if there was any way Logan could do this himself, he would. The last thing he wanted was another man scrutinizing Pepper's body. But it'd be too dangerous for him to have the photos around, so he'd have to rely on Reese. "Look at what we have, see if we have any body shots."

"Body shots?"

Forging on, Logan said, "Try to get a read on her . . . body."

"Come again?"

At least now Reese sounded more interested. "She's hiding something, something physical I mean."

"And you know this . . . how?"

No way in hell would he give Reese the nitty-gritty. Pepper Yates was a pawn in the big scheme of things, but for whatever reason, Logan didn't want to betray her.

So fucking stupid.

"Look to see if there are any shots showing her in a blouse, or hell, even a T-shirt. Anything that'll show . . ." The words dropped off. What could he say?

"The size of her rack?" Reese finished for him.

Logan rubbed his face with his uninjured

hand. "Yeah. But more than that, too. Body type. Like is she shapely all over, or athletic, or maybe extra slim —"

"Damn it, Logan, what the hell are you doing now?"

"Nothing." Nothing that he'd share anyway. "I just need to know what I'm dealing with."

"Because you're dealing with her boobs?" Reese grunted. "Never mind. Forget I asked. At least I know you haven't had sex with her, or you'd know the answer to that one yourself."

No, he wouldn't. But again, not Reese's business. "Can you try to find some pics or not?"

"Yeah. Give me till tomorrow morning."

Logan looked at the bruising on his hand, flexed his fingers and winced. Being done with the topic of Pepper's body — for now — he asked, "So did you name the dog?"

"Cash."

"Nice name."

"It was either that or Debt." Reese made a sound of frustration. "He's been expensive. And speaking of that, I need to go. He's eating one of my shoes."

Logan heard Reese call out to the dog, then drop the phone, and with a laugh, he ended the call. Next time he and Reese got

together, he'd find out more about the
animal. But for right now, he had other,
more important issues on his mind.

Like how he'd get Pepper Yates naked.

No time like the present to start working
on that.

CHAPTER FIVE

Wearing jeans and a T-shirt, Logan stepped out of the apartment, locked the door, turned — and found Pepper standing there.

By the looks of it, she'd just left her apartment, as well.

"Sue. Hey. I was just coming over to see you."

How she could look so shy after last night, he didn't know. The woman had used him up, and they'd both loved every second of it.

She licked her lips — which now, to his curious libido, appeared soft and lush — and nodded at him. "Hi." Clutching a big purse to her chest, she turned toward the stairway to the apartment building entrance. "I was just on my way out."

"Hold up." Logan fell into step beside her. Bright sunshine poured through the glass entry doors, gilding her long, dark eyelashes, highlighting her lack of makeup. He hadn't noticed it before, but she had amazing skin.

And when the hell had he ever noticed a woman's skin, unless it was on an interesting place on her body? "Where are you off to?"

"Shopping."

"I could give you a lift."

"No. Thank you." She trotted down the steps. "That's okay."

"What's the rush?" He tried a laugh that, even to him, sounded fake as hell. But damn it, she was running from him. Still.

First the hurried sex in the dark with her clothes on. Then the abrupt goodbye. And now she didn't want to take a single second to talk with him.

"Sorry," she said again. "I have a lot to get done today."

"I could help," he offered, but she was already shaking her head. "Why?" he demanded. "What's different today?"

But he knew. Intimacy, mixed with sunshine. She wanted to keep her damned secrets.

He wouldn't let her.

Eyes wide, she stared at him. "Nothing has changed. Why would you think it has?"

Now, that pissed him off. He leaned toward her. "I was inside you last night."

As her face went hot, she dropped her

gaze to his shoulders, then lower to his crotch. "Yes," she breathed, and she touched his chest. "You were deep inside me."

God, the way she looked at him made him feel it all over again. His cock twitched, his heart started popping against his ribs. He covered her hand with his own. "You liked it."

"I did." She looked into his eyes and pulled her hand away. "But that doesn't change anything. I still can't . . ." She gestured from him to herself and back again. "Can't. But if you want, we can still do dinner tonight."

Only dinner? Like hell. He'd squelch that idea at the first opportunity. "My place or yours?" he said as a challenge, then wanted to smack himself when she jumped on the offer.

"Yours."

Figuring her out could take a lifetime. But he'd already spent considerable time getting to this point. He wouldn't waste a minute more. "Okay, sure."

Maybe after he had her brother, he'd be able to nail Andrews and ultimately get justice for his best friend's murder.

And then he could work on unraveling the mystery of Pepper Yates.

He looked her over in the faded jumper

107

that she wore over a blouse with elbow-length sleeves. "What do you feel like?" God Almighty, she had horrid taste in clothes. "Besides me, I mean."

Her eyes narrowed the tiniest bit, making them look darker and somehow more mysterious. "Besides you — I don't care."

Damn. So sex was still on the table with no effort on his part at all?

He'd never known a woman to be all timid one minute, then so verbally ballsy the next.

The contradictions left him singed.

"I'll be over at seven." Tentatively, she reached out and touched his chest again in a vague, barely-there goodbye gesture. "See you then."

Logan rubbed the spot where she'd just stroked him.

What was it about her? She may as well have stroked his junk for the way it affected him.

She hadn't asked about his hand, or why he wasn't at work, but then, he'd already told her he didn't work every day. And really, with her attention on his body, who cared if she noticed a stupid injury or not?

He didn't.

Before she got too far down the walkway, Logan stuck his head out the doors. "I'm cooking barbecue."

Her head down, her shoulders forward, she gave a negligent wave of her hand and kept going in a brisk walk.

Almost like the hounds of hell dogged her heels.

Logan watched her until she was out of sight. Damn it. He hadn't even realized he was staring after her until he couldn't see her anymore.

He had to get it together.

Preferably by getting her under him. Without clothes. Lights on. And with enough time for him to explore every inch of her.

Once he had her, *all of her,* then he'd be better able to focus.

But for now . . . what to do?

He looked up the steps, considered breaking into her apartment to snoop around, but if Rowdy had any booby traps set, he could end up blowing his cover.

Best not to push it.

Tromping back up to his own apartment, he got his shoes and a shirt, and headed out to the grocery. His culinary skills were limited. He knew only how to cook what he liked best, which meant meat and potatoes. He'd pick up the barbecue, and maybe grab a cake or something from the bakery.

He made a point of driving around the

block so that Pepper wouldn't think he followed her. They could still run into each other, but it wouldn't be on purpose — not on his part, anyway. Along the way he thought about Morton Andrews. So far, Andrews had gotten away with a lot, including murder. So many times, in so many ways, the trail led to him.

Unfortunately, Andrews had connections everywhere, which meant he always had an alias.

Logan needed Rowdy Yates's eyewitness account to nail the bastard for good. The facts bolstered his belief that he'd eventually be successful.

Yates had worked at Andrews's club, Checkers, a few years ago. For all Logan knew, Yates had been legitimate muscle for the club, but either way, he'd been in the right place at the right time to have the inside scoop.

A reporter had claimed to have a breaking story about Jack's murder — thanks to confidential info from Yates.

That story had died with the reporter, but Yates was still around, and soon, Logan would be able to question him.

He could hardly wait.

Thoughts of Morton Andrews continued to plague him even as he parked and did his shopping. He could still see the smug prick: fifty years old, tall, trim, and as dirty as they came. Women seemed to find him handsome with his dyed white-blond hair, near-black eyes and slick wardrobe.

As one of the wealthier club owners in the state, he always had a babe on his arm. The women either didn't know, or didn't care, that Andrews dealt drugs and was suspected of forced labor trade and everything from theft to murder.

What would Pepper think if she knew of her brother's association with Morton Andrews? Did she even know her brother had worked at Checkers?

As Logan grabbed the few things he needed off the shelves, he could have sworn he felt someone watching him. Not casual curiosity but intense observation. He paid for his groceries and walked out to the parking lot.

The sense of being watched sharpened. After slipping on mirrored sunglasses, he looked around, nonchalantly checking parked cars, customers and shadows.

Though he saw no one in particular, he'd been on the job long enough to know he hadn't imagined it. Only Reese and the lieutenant knew he was currently undercover, but Andrews was always a threat. For that reason, Logan remained cautious. But he was damn good at his job, and he doubted Andrews could have had him followed, not without Logan knowing it before now.

So who then? Possibly Rowdy Yates?

He stowed the groceries in the rear of his pickup and opened the driver's door. The fine hairs on the nape of his neck prickled; would he end up with a bullet in his back? Anyone with a rifle could pick him off with ease. Was Rowdy corrupt enough for cold-blooded murder?

"What are you doing here?"

Logan jerked around and found Pepper standing there, a hand shading her eyes from the sun, a soft breeze playing with a few loose tendrils of her dark blond hair.

When he pulled off his sunglasses to greet her, he noted her look of unease.

Logan knew her damn brother was the most likely threat to him . . . but was he also a threat to her? "I had to get stuff for dinner." To make it more difficult for anyone with a rifle scope, he maneuvered her between his body and the grocery store entrance. He had his own truck at his back. "What are you doing here?"

"I needed some groceries myself." Looking beyond him, expression wary and anxious, she scrunched her face against the glare off the blacktop parking lot. "I could have gotten your stuff for you, but since you're here anyway —" she took his arm and began hauling him back toward the store "— you may as well give me a ride home when I'm finished."

That attitude was so different from what she'd expressed back at the apartment that his suspicions darkened. Was she hoping to protect him from Rowdy?

He said only, "Glad to." And he freed his wrist from her grip so that he could put a hand to the small of her back.

The rain from the night before had ramped up the humidity, but it also left behind that stirring breeze that plastered her skirt to her legs. The skirt kicked up with each hurried step she took.

"Stop staring," she said. "You're embarrassing me."

He'd been about to ask her why she was rushing him, but she effectively sidetracked him. "I find it hard not to watch you."

"Why?" she asked.

Before, he'd studied her to make her aware of him, not out of any real intimate interest of his own.

Now . . . her every move enthralled him. He needed to see her body, to touch her all over. At every moment, some part of his brain churned over the body hidden from him. In a very short time, he'd become obsessed.

"You have long legs," he mused aloud.

She missed a step, then moved ahead of him, out of his reach.

Knowing he had her on the run, Logan smiled. "Slim hips, too."

She charged forward, grabbed a cart and shoved her way down an aisle. Hanging back a little, aware of the concentrated way she resisted any sway to her walk, Logan watched her.

Suddenly she stopped and turned to glare at him.

And it was a glare of pure fire, taking him by surprise.

"Stop it," she ordered him, "or leave."

Mesmerizing, that small sign of her temper. "You asked me to give you a ride home."

"Yes, but if you can't behave in a civilized way, I'd rather walk. In fact, I like walking. It's good exercise and —"

"Forget it, honey." Logan put his arm around her and started her forward again. "I'll pretend you're not hiding a sweet body, okay?"

Her mouth opened, but nothing came out.

She clung to the cart, almost using it for support as he urged her down the bread aisle.

As she shopped, Logan stayed attuned to their surroundings, but he no longer felt the scrutiny of prying eyes.

Come out, you bastard, Logan thought to himself. *Come out so I can get to you.*

But he didn't see Rowdy Yates anywhere around, and he didn't feel that burning gaze, either. His disappointment would have been more pronounced if he weren't so fascinated with Pepper. The no-nonsense way she shopped, how she moved, even her junk food choices were a source of interest.

Add to all that her awareness of him, which he felt in spades.

Even in the middle of a grocery store, that damned sexual chemistry arced between them, live, hot and alarmingly real. Possibly the most real thing he'd felt in two long years.

"Turn in here."

Logan glanced at her. "What?"

"I need to go to the department store, too. Turn in here." He'd been silent too long, and she didn't know if it was because he'd sensed her brother's nosiness, or his curiosity about her body that kept him brooding.

Neither possibility boded well for her peace of mind.

As he pulled into a parking spot, she opened her seat belt. Already preoccupied with thoughts of her brother and his domineering presence, she said, "You don't need to wait. Thank you for the lift, but I'll walk the rest of the way after I've finished."

Before she moved an inch, he caught her arm in a gentle but unbreakable hold. Far too seriously, he said, "I don't mind waiting."

He had such big, strong hands, but she couldn't imagine him ever hurting her. "What happened there?" She nodded at his left hand, braced on the steering wheel. The nail gun had left behind some grisly bruising.

As if he'd forgotten the injury, he looked at it. "I screwed up at work, that's all."

Pepper couldn't resist reaching for his wrist, drawing his hand toward her. At the base of his thumb and halfway up his index finger, purple, blue and green colored his skin. At the fleshiest part of his thumb, where it webbed, she saw a puncture.

"What did you do?" she asked softly, pretending she didn't already know.

"Drove a nail through it." He curled his fingers around hers. "It's fine."

"Ouch," she said in sympathy. The urge to kiss his hand nearly overwhelmed her. But she didn't know for sure if Rowdy had followed them, and she didn't want to do anything to set off her brother's temper. When it came to her, he had enough anger for ten men. "Did you go to the hospital?"

"No need. I already had a tetanus shot and I didn't hit anything vital — just my pride."

She smiled with him.

Almost as a suggestion, he said, "I'll be off work for a few days."

She waited . . . for what, she wasn't sure.

"I was hoping we could spend more time together."

And there it was, the reason for Rowdy's suspicions. She tried to think of what to say, tried to muster up the conviction to turn him away.

He didn't give her a chance.

"I have so many things to ask you."

Alarm took her breath. "Like what?"

Teasing, he kissed the end of her nose, then her cheek and finally her mouth. He lingered, a soft press of lips, breath mingling, heartbeats accelerating. Finally he sat back. "How is it a woman as shy as you are has a rubber handy?"

Oh. Not a horrible question. "I, um . . ."

"Why don't you run in the park instead of on a treadmill?"

She winced. She knew sooner or later he'd ask about that. "The thing is . . ."

He put a finger to her lips. "And why don't you realize how pretty you could be."

Could be. Out of all the people who'd looked past her, even through her, did Logan actually see her, not a disguise, not the bland facade, but a real woman? The tension left her shoulders. "Logan."

"Not that you aren't cute now." He ran the backs of his fingers over her cheek. "It's there, even though you don't want it to be."

"It?"

"Your physical appeal. I know you'd rather I didn't notice, but I can't seem to help it."

No, she didn't want him to see much of anything at all. "I'm not cute." She really wasn't. Not like this. "I have mirrors."

Leaning in for another kiss, he murmured, "If you give me a chance, I can convince you."

He was soooo tempting. "A chance . . . how?"

His mouth brushed the corner of hers. "Spend some time with me. We can do dinner out and a movie, or nothing at all. Your choice."

"But you want to have sex again?" She

could care less about the other stuff, but the physical intimacy — she craved a repeat performance.

His mouth quirked. Then he laughed. "Yeah, I wouldn't object to it." He traced a fingertip over her jaw, her chin and down her throat. "It doesn't have to be all or nothing, you know. We can mix it up a little."

The way he looked at her, almost as if he meant it, as if he really did think her cute, had her drowning in need. She drew in necessary oxygen — and her cell phone buzzed in her purse.

Rowdy.

Oh, God, she had to get away from Logan, and fast. She didn't know if Rowdy was watching them right now, and she didn't know if Logan realized her phone was on vibrate. But she'd taken enough chances for one day.

She opened the door and slid off the seat. "Sorry, but I do need to go, and no, I don't want you to wait for me. Please don't argue with me, Logan. I want to walk. I need the fresh air." And then, because that all felt so abrupt and maybe even unkind, she added, "I'll see you tonight, okay?"

Confusion narrowed his eyes. "That was an awful lot, said awfully quick."

"Logan, *please.*"

He searched her face, scowled darkly, and nodded. "All right. If you're sure."

"I am. Thank you." She reached for her groceries, but he stopped her.

"I'll take them home. You can get them from me later."

Rather than debate with him, she agreed. "Okay, fine."

"And, Sue?"

She detested that stupid name more each day. "Yes?"

"You'll answer my questions for me? Tonight at dinner, I mean."

Right. Rubbers, treadmill and cuteness. She could handle that. "Okay."

He smiled. "Tonight then."

She hurried off — forgetting, *again* — to shuffle her feet.

Rowdy would have her head before this was over.

But if Logan got her body, well then, she'd consider it a fair trade-off.

CHAPTER SIX

Now that Pepper had walked away, Rowdy relaxed. What the hell did Logan Stark want with his sister? Through the binoculars, Rowdy watched her cross the parking lot and enter the relative safety of the department store.

Was he missing something?

No, he didn't miss anything, especially when it came to women, and most definitely not when it concerned his troublesome sister.

Maybe Logan was after something other than the usual.

He brought his gaze back to the neighbor. Sitting there in his truck, Logan Stark peered around as if he felt Rowdy's attention. Huh. Perceptive bastard.

Finally the neighbor put his truck in gear and drove away.

Stowing the binoculars in the glove box, Rowdy got out of his car, locked it up and pocketed the keys. The bar he'd chosen to use for surveillance had an ideal location. With his binoculars he could see all the way up the road to the apartment building, as well as the grocery and small strip mall — basically any place his sister was likely to go.

While debating his next move, he strode toward the bar. He noticed a "For Sale" sign crudely attached to the brick wall above a collapsing cardboard box of trash. Old papers, a few cans and a broken bottle had already spilled out. Hazardous.

He thought of Checkers, the upscale club Morton owned. Pricey liquor, chic decor, classy-looking women and high-stakes activities. Checkers had been kept visually pristine, but he'd bet his life that more filth had happened inside its walls than could ever occur in the back alleys of the town where he now kept his sister under wraps.

Checkers boasted three floors. It was the main floor where Rowdy had usually worked, overseeing lap dances, ensuring none of the ordinary men got too grabby or overstepped the services they'd paid for. More adventurous activity was reserved for the second floor and for men with deeper pockets. On the second floor, patrons could buy hand jobs, blow jobs and a variety of sex ranging from one partner to three.

Morton's sprawling office was on the third floor, along with a private boardroom and other, smaller offices.

Rowdy had been paid well to know the difference in the clientele, to keep his mouth shut about illegal sex acts, and to alert the guards stationed at the upper levels whenever the law came calling.

It all ran smoothly, even in moments of chaos. And when it didn't . . . Rowdy closed his eyes, not wanting to think about the city commissioner who'd been murdered. Jack Carmin had died at a young thirty-two — and Rowdy hadn't done a damn thing about it.

Acid burned in his gut. Rumor had it that Morton would be expanding his enterprise into human trafficking. Rowdy knew he'd have to do something about that, and soon. But now, with Pepper's admirer putting him on edge, he couldn't act. He had to guarantee her safety first.

His sister would always be his top priority.

If it turned out Logan Stark was on the up-and-up, well then, maybe she'd be safe without Rowdy keeping tabs on her. At least for a short time.

Long enough for him to take care of

Morton as he should have two long years ago.

A drunk loitered outside the bar entrance. Off to the side, two youths smoked and talked too loud.

Distractions like that would never have happened at Checkers, but for here and now, an uninterested owner worked to Rowdy's advantage; the less accountability at the bar, the safer it was for him.

While wondering if the bar would end up abandoned, he almost missed the woman smiling at him. She stepped out of the shadows, tall, slender, sexy — and probably for sale. Too bad he avoided hookers. Not because of moral scruples, but because he never spent money so unwisely.

"What do you say, sugar?" She traced a finger up and down her exposed cleavage. "Got some free time?"

Nothing but. "Sorry, but you look out of my price range."

"For you, I'd offer a . . . special."

Yeah, he could just imagine. "Appreciate it, but not this time." After a farewell nod, he entered the dim establishment. Sluggish music played. Regulars filled the booths and the bar. Up on a ramshackle stage, exposed bodies gyrated.

More women looked his way, so he tried

not to make prolonged eye contact. In his current mood, he didn't want to encourage anyone. He had a few things to work out before he sought company for the night.

A nod here, a half hearted smile there. He always appreciated the female attention. But he didn't always take advantage of it. Sometimes, though, when the dark past intruded and his turbulent thoughts made sleep impossible, he needed a woman's softness to get him through the night.

And at those times, he always despised his own weakness.

Grabbing a seat at a small table, slouching back comfortably, Rowdy glanced toward one attentive woman who looked too young, another who looked too mature. He settled on watching a pole dancer who had a great ass.

Other women worked the floor in skimpy dresses, some nearly topless, all in mile-high heels. Matching small aprons distinguished them as employees of the bar.

He rubbed his mouth, wondering if a fast tumble would help clear his thoughts. Not that anyone had really grabbed his interest yet. Hell, he felt no spark, not even for the mostly naked blonde; he definitely didn't appreciate her substantial curves as he should have.

"What can I get for you?"

At the intrusion of that brisk female voice, Rowdy glanced up — and got lost in pale blue eyes.

But not for long.

While the gyrating blonde left him cold, this woman set off a spark. He trailed his gaze over her, from thick, dark red hair held back by a headband, to a narrow nose and wide mouth, to her petite little bod.

No sexy uniform for her.

She wore straight jeans with slip-on shoes and a regular crew-necked T-shirt. That same apron, a little messier than the others, loosely circled her waist.

Rowdy looked back at her face. "You're a trim little package, aren't you?"

Her chin tucked in. "You have two options, okay? You can give me your drink order, or you can get a different table."

Well, well, well. A challenge? A chase?

The spark caught flame.

Rowdy smiled at her — and saw her blink. A little predatory, a lot cynical, he kept quiet and watched her.

"Okay," she said. "I have to admit, that look is effective. Dangerously so. But as it is, I live on tips, so if you don't want anything —"

"I want."

She filled her lungs on a deep breath. Shifted her stance. Looked up at the ceiling, then off to her right. "The thing is, honestly, I need to take a drink order. But that's it. That's my job, nothing more."

"No pole dancing, huh?" He relaxed a little more, sliding back in his chair, one hand on the table, one resting on his thigh. "Well, damn."

Her brows pinched over his mild show of disappointment. "The place would go broke, believe me."

"I assume it's already going broke." When that confused her, he said, "The 'for sale' sign?"

"Oh, yeah." She scrunched up her nose. "Are you thinking of buying?"

"Could I reassign you to the pole if I do?"

"Not if you wanted to continue employing me."

Had the current owner already tried that? Interesting. "Got other prospects, huh?"

She gave a hesitant pause, then without invitation, she pulled out a chair and sat opposite him. Prim and proper. Spine straight, shoulders back. "So what's your name?"

"You can call me anything you like." As long as it wasn't his actual name. For those who might care, Rowdy Yates had fallen off the face of the earth, and he planned to keep it that way.

"All right. Here's the thing, Walter."

"Walter?"

"That's the name I'm choosing. You did say anything would do."

He chided her with a small frown. "But not Walter."

She let out an exaggerated sigh. "I'm working, *sir.*"

"That's not much better." Hell, no one had ever called him sir. The people he associated with either had no manners at all, or were the ones he deferred to, not the other way around.

She forged on. "I have responsibilities, sir. I know that the bar encourages outrageousness. I understand that. It's a guys' hangout." She glanced around with clear contempt, murmuring low, "There's a lot of sexism, and a lot of inappropriate activity going on."

"Yet you're still here," Rowdy pointed out softly.

"Yes, sir. For the pay, which I need. But I'm not part of any of . . ." She waved toward the floor. "That."

He ignored the "sir" business. "By choice?"

She dropped her head to the table with a

thunk. Rowdy winced for her. She looked tired and a little fed up.

Unable to resist, he ran his fingers through the dark ropes of red hair spilling over the table. Warm, thick, silky.

Was she a true redhead?

Something primal in his nature gave him a real weakness for petite women. For a redhead . . . yeah, he was a goner.

Without raising her head, she snagged his wrist, lifted it away from her hair, and sat up.

She maintained her hold on his thick wrist. Her slender fingers didn't quite circle all the way around him.

Rowdy didn't object, and she didn't let go. The physical connection felt more intimate than it should have.

Anticipating what she'd say or do next, he watched her.

She met his gaze squarely. "On the off chance that you might be a buyer for the . . . establishment, I want you to understand that I'm too short, too lacking in curves and far too modest to ever do justice to any stage performance."

"You think?" Because he didn't. "You could audition and let me make that decision —"

Cutting him off, she held up her free

hand. "And if you're not a buyer, then know that I have no interest in flirting, the nuances of sexy banter elude me, and no way, ever, would I date anyone from this bar — regardless of how attractive he might be."

Date? He didn't *date.* No time and no interest. He said only, as a taunt, "Bet I could change your mind."

She made a funny sound. "Take a look around, sir. Plenty of other women are hoping you'll notice them. I'm sure they'll provide an easier route for your intentions."

She didn't know his intentions, and he didn't look, because he didn't care. "I think you're attractive, too."

That gave her pause. She glanced down at her person and made a face. "I was going for something altogether different."

"Like?"

"Perhaps plain, uninteresting. Maybe even invisible."

So the clothes she wore were supposed to . . . hide her? He again took in her shoes which, despite being unadorned, were still feminine, almost like dainty little ballet slippers. The straight-legged jeans, likely new, showed the length of her legs. And that crew-necked T-shirt, even being a little big, displayed the narrowness of her bone structure and the soft swell of her breasts.

Whatever her intent, she made an enticing, overall package. Small, female, understated.

But with that dark red hair . . .

Intriguing.

That made him frown. Did Logan look at his sister like that? Did he see beyond Pepper's outward image?

It wasn't at all the same thing, given this woman only downplayed her looks instead of attempting to conceal them. But his sister . . .

"I'm glad we were able to clear all that up." Mistaking his silence for lack of interest, she stood. "So would you like a drink or not? And believe me, if you give the wrong answer this time, I'll leave and let another waitress deal with you."

Not for a second did he believe that, but he played along. "I'll take a beer."

"Of course. I'll bring that to you right away."

On impulse, he sat forward. "Let me ask you something first."

She cocked her hip in a stance ripe with attitude. "I have other tables to wait on."

"I'll double your tip if give me the truth."

"Truly?" Her eyes gleamed. "I promise not to sugarcoat a single word."

She hadn't pulled her punches, so he

131

believed her. "Is this getup meant to turn off guys, to maybe cover your assets?" *As his sister tried to do.* "Or is this how you usually dress?"

For several seconds she studied him, probably trying to figure out his angle.

Not in a million years would she even come close.

She gave in without any fuss. "I started here a few weeks ago. Other than the apron, there isn't a dress code, so I wore my regular wardrobe, which, believe me, isn't designed to beguile."

Interesting. "No low-cut tops or miniskirts or anything like that, huh?"

"I'm casual clothes all the way."

If the clothes came from her everyday attire, did that mean she didn't own any low-cut tops or miniskirts? If so, it'd be a pity. Even being petite, she had long legs. He'd love to see them. Hell, he'd love to be between them. "So, the other women?"

"I believe they dress to get tips." She showed not a single sign of judgment.

So her derision was aimed only at the male customers, not the female workers? By the second, his interest grew. "Dressing sexier works for them?"

"Yes, it does, but it also comes with a lot of extra hassle."

Spoken like a woman who knew. "In your regular clothes, you got hit on?"

She didn't confirm or deny that. "I decided it'd be better to discourage interest as much as I could."

Rowdy didn't bother telling her that all she'd done — at least for him — was stimulate his curiosity. "So this —" he nodded at her body "— is your attempt to dial down the sex appeal?"

"Yes, and I'm sure I'm successful."

Raising a brow, Rowdy sat back in his seat. "Sorry, love, but I'm seeing it all, every sexy inch."

"Annnnd . . ." she said, "there goes your last chance."

Amused by her drama, Rowdy watched her march off. He appreciated the back view of her as much as he did the front.

She probably stood no more than five-two, and he doubted she'd weigh over a buck-ten. But with each step, that thick auburn hair caught the bar lights, coiling down her back to the bottom of her shoulder blades, sort of pointing the way to that pert little ass. Even the baggy seat of her boy jeans couldn't detract from that nice asset.

Yeah, he saw it all. And one way or another, he'd get her under him.

Unfortunately, he hadn't even thought to

ask her name. If she wore a name badge, he hadn't seen it. Another deliberate move on her part?

For now, wondering if Logan also saw his sister in spite of her camouflage kept Rowdy from turning on the charm.

First things first. He would put a GPS tracker on Logan's truck to see where he went. That'd give him a starting place for unraveling the neighbor's mysterious interest in his sister. He'd take care of that tonight.

If Logan Stark had anything to hide, Rowdy would find out, and then he'd deal with it.

A woman sidled up to his table. "Hi."

Rowdy glanced at her. Light brown hair tumbled over her shoulders, framing a lot of cleavage. A cloud of perfume wafted in her wake.

Unlike the waitress, this woman had all her curves on display, and they were many. She suited his normal preferences, but tonight didn't feel ordinary in any way.

Already bored, he said, "Hey, yourself."

"You're not drinking alone, are you?"

Normally, at that point, he'd start the process that'd ensure he had a bed partner for the night. This time, he flat-out didn't feel like it. Never mind that minutes ago he'd been thinking a tumble was just what he needed. "Yeah, I am."

"How about I join you?"

"A persuasive offer, if all you want is conversation."

She paused, coy, suggestive. "And if I wanted more?"

"Tonight's a no-go for me, honey. Sorry."

His rejection surprised her and set her to pouting. "Should I ask why?"

"I have something I need to do."

She slipped into the chair opposite him. Touching his shoulder with one manicured fingertip, her eyes heavy, her mouth smiling, she whispered, "Do me."

"Ah, now that's tempting." He took her warm hand and relocated it to the tabletop. "But I still have to decline."

"I could be a nice distraction."

"I don't doubt it." Admiration at her confidence gentled his tone. "But it doesn't change anything."

"Tomorrow, then?"

He half smiled. "So you don't just want to share a drink, huh? All right then. If I'm here tomorrow, feel free to hit me up."

She flattened both hands on the table in front of him, bent forward, and said close to his mouth, "Be here." And with that, she straightened and sashayed off.

Damn, but he enjoyed women. The more brazen and confident and upfront, the better.

"The other waitress was busy," said that familiar husky voice.

Usually he liked brazen and up-front. This time, something altogether different appealed to him. Rowdy switched his attention to the redhead.

She plunked his beer down on the table hard enough to slosh some out of the glass.

"Thanks." That she hadn't abandoned him as she'd threatened didn't really surprise him. Women could be adorably predictable. Teasing her, he asked, "Something wrong?"

"Not at all. Is there anything else I can get you — and, no, no innuendo, please."

Her prim voice amused him. "Would I be that clichéd?"

"My apologies for assuming that you would." She started to leave.

"There is one thing."

Even over the loud music and drone of conversation, he heard her groan of exasperation.

Keeping her back to him, she stopped, inhaled and finally looked over her shoulder. "Yes?"

Folding his arms on the table, Rowdy

leaned forward. "I need your name."

"Noooo," she said on a laugh. "You most definitely do not."

Three women approached, stepping around her and crowding his table. Rowdy wanted to curse the interruption.

"Just a sec, girls." Impatient, he stood to see around them. The waitress, checking in at other tables, was already a few feet away. To the ladies, he said, "Be right back."

Not caring what they thought of that, he took several long strides and snagged the waitress by the apron tie at the small of her back, drawing her up short.

In silky tones, he said, "Now, don't run off."

"I was not running. I have work to do."

"If you say so." Still holding on to that tie, he drew her closer. "You may as well give me a name. Otherwise I'll have to ask around."

Losing some of her good humor, she stiffened. "Why ever would you do that?"

Near her ear, Rowdy whispered, "Pure, hot, male . . . curiosity?" The warm scent of her made his gut clench as he breathed her in.

That pushed her over the edge.

She jerked around to blast him with temper but went still as she took in his size.

Staring down at her, anticipation heightened, Rowdy waited to see what she'd do or say. He had a feeling she wouldn't bore him.

"Good grief." She tipped her head way back and stared into his eyes. "You're big!"

Pleasure warmed him. *She* warmed him. "I think you mean tall."

Still looking him over, she asked absently, "What?"

"You're commenting on my height, yes?"

"Of course. You're what? Six and a half feet?"

"Six-four. But as to me being big . . ." He touched her chin. "Wanna find out?"

She finally caught on, but rather than be insulted by his come-on, she laughed.

Laughed.

"That wasn't a joke." For some reason, the sound of her laughter turned him on more.

Still amused, she said, "Sir, you are too outrageous."

Her mouth looked even sexier when she smiled like that. Such a soft, full mouth. No lipstick. Nothing to get in the way of a nice, deep kiss . . .

She waved a hand in front of his face. "Are you still with me?"

He was with her just a little too much. "Yeah."

"Then perhaps you'd like to focus — no, not on me." She nodded back at his table. "You have a bevy of women waiting on you, so we really should wrap this up."

A bevy? He glanced back. Sure enough, his small table now overflowed with women — and it did look like they were waiting. Impatiently so. Not a big deal. He'd had females after him most of his life.

Let them wait.

But when he turned back to the waitress, she was already gone, disappeared into the milling crowd. Well, damn. He wouldn't chase her again. When she came to bring him another beer, he'd get a name and take it from there.

Until then . . . he surveyed the women at his table with narrowed eyes. Even the brunette from earlier had rejoined them.

They acted warm and friendly — flirtatious women looking for a good time and a little fun, and he had no problem with that.

They didn't really engage his awareness. Not like the waitress had. But for right now, for an hour or so, he'd take what he could get.

No, he didn't forget about Logan or Pepper, but with time to kill, why not make use of the company?

Unfortunately, almost an hour later, it was

a different waitress who came to offer him another beer. When Rowdy asked after the petite gal, he was told she'd gotten off half an hour ago.

She'd left without saying goodbye.

Playing hard to get?

He could play. He enjoyed a good game every now and then. He'd be back at the bar over the next few days, and eventually he'd find her again.

Putting her from his mind, he paid his tab, and amidst complaints and more pouting, he bid farewell to the lovelies.

As he went back out to the parking lot, he surveyed every dark corner, shifting shadow and person passing by. The caution was now an ingrained trait; he never took safety for granted.

He saw nothing and no one of interest.

Time to thwart Pepper's annoying neighbor. Everything else, including cute waitresses, would just have to wait.

CHAPTER SEVEN

"Oh, Rowdy, *no.*" Distrust for her brother's plan added a quaver to Pepper's voice. "I can't believe you'd ask me to —"

"Just keep him busy, that's all you have to do. I'll be in and out in a flash."

Somehow this might backfire. It was dangerous. Too dangerous. *"I don't want to."*

Resolute, Rowdy said, "Do it anyway."

With her heart hammering, she dropped to sit on the edge of the couch. "Please, Rowdy. Stop and think about this. There's no reason —"

"I know what I saw, Pepper. You started this, so now I have no choice."

Unfair! He made her feel guilty for making one small move toward companionship. "You're a bully."

"You have twenty minutes, so don't leave me hanging." He disconnected the call.

Folding her arms around her middle and leaning forward, Pepper struggled with a vortex of emotions — the guilt her brother had just heaped on her. Sadness, exhaustion at continued deception, a yearning for something different, something real.

She also felt sharp anticipation.

Rowdy wanted her to keep Logan preoccupied so he could put the GPS tracker on his truck. She knew only one way to truly ensure Logan stayed busy. Definitely not what her brother had in mind, but still —

Suddenly, as if she'd summoned him, Logan called to her from his balcony. "Sue?"

At the sound of his voice, her heart stuttered and her eyes flared. Logan! Had he heard her conversation?

For only a moment, she knotted her hands in her hair. And then, because she'd just mussed her ponytail, she pulled out the band and refastened the mass.

How much had he heard?

"Sue, are you all right?"

Enough to make him worry. What to do now?

Pushing away from the couch in a rush, she slid the screen aside and stuck her head out to the balcony. Standing there with the blue sky as a backdrop, his dark gaze vigilant, he nearly took her breath away, he looked so good. Rugged. Sexy.

The same as always.

A little wistful, Pepper waggled her fingers at him. "Hi."

Concern narrowed his gaze. He looked her over as if seeking an injury. "Everything okay?"

"Yes." *Think, Pepper. He's going to ask, so come up with a story and fast.*

"I heard you talking." Logan rested his forearms on the railing, leaning toward her.

The positioning did interesting things to his shoulders, his biceps.

And her imagination.

"You sounded . . . upset."

"Oh." *Focus, Pepper.* She should have thought about their sliding doors being open. But until Logan, she'd never had to. Not for a very long time had any man showed interest. "No, I'm fine."

He tipped his head, scrutinizing her. "You look upset, too."

More like agitated. Where creeps and criminals were concerned, Rowdy was far more recognizable than she'd ever been. Anytime he showed himself, he ran the risk of one of Morton Andrews's flunkies noticing him. Granted, Morton and his following had no reason to be around here. They were well away from his domain, but still . . .

"Sue?"

Think, think. "Are you ready for me?" That

blurted question held very distracting overtones. Pepper prayed that it worked.

And it did.

Logan slowly straightened. "Ready?"

She nodded. "I've been thinking about . . . you know." *Sex.* "I can come over . . . now?" *So pushy.* But thanks to Rowdy, she had to be. "That is, if there's time before dinner."

A new, hotter emotion replaced the concern in his dark eyes. "Yeah, you can come over. Anytime. I told you that, remember? Dinner isn't ready yet, but I —"

She walked off in the middle of him talking. Now that she'd decided what to do, a pulse beat of anticipation expanded throughout her system, throbbing, curling in her lower belly.

Snatching up her keys and purse, she went out her door, closed it, and as she turned toward Logan's door, it opened.

Sexual tension held them both still, gazes locked. They stared at each other as expectation built with every breath. She felt a little uncertain. He just looked turned on.

What to say, how to explain? "I, um . . ."

"C'mere." Logan reached for her, dragged her into his apartment, and pinned her back against his door the second he got it closed. "I need —"

His mouth on hers cut off her attempt to

steer them into the bedroom.

Knees going weak, she let him have his way, relishing the damp heat of his mouth, the slide of his tongue past hers, the urgency.

He held her upper arms as he ate at her mouth — and she liked it. A lot.

God, truthfully, she liked him. How he seemed to care. His interest and patience and his keen sensuality.

"You're a tease," he whispered against her mouth, then kissed his way to her cheek, her throat.

"Mmm." That felt *so* good. But she had to get it together. Rowdy would only be safe if they were off in another room, door closed, fully involved.

If he ever found out, her brother would detest her tactics, but too bad for him.

Putting her hands flat to Logan's chest, she levered him back. "Bedroom."

He pressed her shoulders to the door, his breath coming fast, aroused color slashing his cheekbones. "I like the idea of taking you right here." He wedged in closer to her. "Like this."

Oh, such a wonderful idea — but like so many things in her life, not possible.

Sad, she whispered, "I can't."

Butterfly kisses teased her temple, her jaw.

"Tell me why."

"I'm sorry, Logan." Closing her eyes, Pepper swallowed hard and shook her head. "It's either in the bedroom, right now." A deep breath didn't help. "Or not at all."

She expected an argument. She waited for irritation, maybe even anger.

Given how wonderful he'd been so far, she should have known better.

His small smile personified sex appeal. "Then let's go, honey. Right now."

God love the man, could he be more considerate?

Logan caught her hand as he stepped away to lead her down the hall. Once inside the room, he went about closing the drapes without her having to ask. "Okay?"

That was so . . . sweet. When was the last time a man had been sweet to her?

Touched, her throat tight with emotion, Pepper covered her mouth and nodded. "Yes. Thank you." And then, before he could steal the lead, she went to the foot of the bed. "Do you think we could try something a little different?"

The heavy shadows didn't hide everything. Soon their eyes would adjust. She had to rush things — and honestly, that worked for her.

"Whatever you want, honey." He moved

nearer but didn't touch her. "Tell me what you have in mind."

Boy, it wasn't easy to spell it out. She started with the first priority. "I need my clothes on."

"All right."

She heard the click of his snap, then the slow hiss of his zipper coming down. "You don't mind if I get naked, do you?"

Her mouth went dry. Her heart started pumping hard. "No."

"Thanks." He pushed his shorts down and off, then kicked them away.

A hot, naked, buff temptation stood before her, waiting, expectant, obliterating her priorities. Pepper could hear him breathing, feel his heat.

Smell his unique scent.

Blindly she reached out. In deference to the dark quiet of the room, she kept her voice low. "Do you mind if I touch you a little?"

Replying in the same way, he said, "I'd prefer that you touch me a lot."

Oh, yeah, she'd prefer that, too. "Okay." Laying her palms over his shoulders, she absorbed the warmth of his flesh, the tautness of his muscles. Coasting down over his collarbone, she spread her fingers wide, dragging them through his chest hair to his nipples.

His breath hitched, and he shifted the smallest bit. "I picked up a box of condoms."

His abdomen was nice and tight — the muscles getting tighter and more defined as she touched him. "Thank you."

"They're on —" he paused, shifted again, breathed a little faster "— my nightstand."

"Okay." With both hands, she held his erection. Her eyes closed at the feel of him flexing, swelling more. It amazed her that something so firm and solid could be encased in such velvety softness. Using her thumb, she brushed over the head and found a bead of fluid.

Logan whispered, "Damn."

"Shh." Enthralled, excited, Pepper loved the freedom he gave her. She explored his testicles with one hand while clasping his erection with the other. There was just so much of him to enjoy, so much —

"You're killing me," he growled. "You know that, right?"

"It's just . . ." She wrapped her fingers around the base of him. "I love how you feel."

Moving his hand over hers, he helped her to squeeze tighter, encouraged her toward a slow, back and forth stroke. After three audible breaths, he asked, "How do I feel?"

Incredibly sexy. Still holding him, Pepper sank to her knees. "Probably not as good as you taste."

"Jesus." He gave a ragged groan and widened his stance.

Sliding her mouth down along the length of him, Pepper savored his taste, the richness of his scent, how he flinched with escalating need.

Lightly, his hands touched the top of her head.

She could have gone on tasting him until he lost control — but suddenly he caught her arms and pulled her back to her feet.

"Logan?"

"How are we doing this, honey? Tell me quick, because I'm on a hair trigger here."

Lost to subtleties and subterfuge, Pepper reached beneath her skirt to pull off her panties. "Get a condom."

As if her words threw him, he hesitated, but not for long. They fumbled against each other in the small, dim room, Pepper attempting to get her underwear off without showing anything, Logan getting to the box of rubbers. She heard him opening the little packet, saw his dark form shifting, and knew what he was doing.

When he made his way back to her, she turned and positioned herself.

Bent over the foot of the bed.

She yanked up her skirt so that it bunched around her waist, then knotted her hands in the soft cotton sheets that carried his stirring scent. Firmly braced, she waited.

Other than the sound of his breathing, silence filled the room.

"Logan?"

No answer. But she knew he was there, behind her. She could feel him standing close, knew he tried to see her, tried to adjust to the immediacy.

If he mistook her intent, it would end, and she couldn't bear that. Emotion closed her throat, thickened her words. "Please don't ruin this."

His hair-rough thighs brushed the backs of hers. "Tell me what you need."

"You inside me. Just that."

His fingertips trailed over the top of her behind.

"Logan!" If he got too familiar, if he explored her body, she'd have to —

Without warning, two fingers pressed into her.

The hot, slick intrusion wrenched a ragged groan from her.

He turned his hand, pressed deep again.

150

Voice gravelly with lust, he whispered, "I want to make sure you're ready."

She was so ready that she just might leave him behind. Every breath grew deeper, harsher. He put one hand at her waist — not caressing or exploring, just . . . holding. Keeping her steady.

And with the other, he played her. Made her insane. Pushed her to her limit.

"You're getting close," he crooned, "aren't you, honey?"

She should tell him to get on with it. She should direct every aspect, keeping him from too much familiarity.

Sex. That's all it could be. Rushed. Impersonal. Anything more would be too dangerous —

He stopped stroking her but left his hand there, his fingers firm inside her. "Tell me," he said, his voice low and rough. "Tell me you like it."

Oh, God. "Don't stop."

Triumphant, he promised, "Not until you come." With his free hand, he moved her ponytail over her shoulder, while with his other he continued to work her, his fingers sliding deep, twisting, finding hidden spots of pleasure.

Her body writhed with the start of an orgasm, a wave that expanded, receded, pulsed brighter and hotter.

"Logan . . ."

He said nothing, didn't lose his rhythm —
and suddenly the climax grabbed her.

She tried to muffle her groans in the covers, tried not to move with his fingers. But
he didn't stop, and she couldn't hold back.

As the bliss finally receded, her legs gave
out and she ended up sprawled facedown
on the bed. Immediately Logan came down
over her, body to body, masculine weight
crushing her feminine form into the bedding. He touched her, opened her and filled
her in one powerful thrust.

Oh, God. If his fingers had felt good —
and they definitely had — it was nothing
compared to this.

Balancing on his forearms, his mouth
touching her temple, he drove into her in
an unbreakable, heavy rhythm. The bed
rocked under her; his chest brushed her
shoulder blades. Her skirt bunched between
them, but he didn't let that get in his way.

Her excitement must've spurred his own,
because in no time at all, he nuzzled against
her, his face tucked close to her neck. A low,
feral growl vibrated against her skin, and he
opened his mouth on her shoulder before
stiffening.

Knowing it would have to be brief, Pepper

152

cherished the contact. Holding her tight, he closed in around her as he gave in to his release and, finally, went utterly calm and replete over her.

It felt . . . oddly protective. Entirely too familiar. Way too comfortable.

She could have stayed like that for an hour or a day.

Maybe even a lifetime.

It distressed her that she couldn't spare even a moment more. She cleared her throat. Twice. And still, when she whispered, "Logan?" she could hear the tears in her voice.

Without a word, he struggled up to his forearms again. He took a moment before gently kissing her cheek, and then he rolled to his back beside her.

It was so incredibly tempting to stay put, to turn and snuggle into him, to kiss him.

And have him kiss her.

To start all over again.

If she stayed even a second more, the tears would get the best of her. So instead she scuttled from the bed, slapped down her skirt, and rushed back to his living room where she collected her purse. Seeing through a blurry haze of regret, she opened and closed his door quietly, grateful that he hadn't followed, that he hadn't questioned her, or . . . even seemed to care all that much.

Choking on her own vulnerability, eyes damp with sadness, she let herself into her darkened apartment.

Now, after Logan, the small, worn-down space felt more lonely than ever.

CHAPTER EIGHT

After Pepper literally fled his bedroom, Logan continued to lie there, sprawled out, a spent condom still in place.

Fuck.

He fisted his hands, squeezed his eyes shut. At thirty-two, he'd had sex with plenty of partners. Younger women, some more mature. Women looking for a good match and women just out to have a good time at a honky-tonk bar. Wealthy women and women down on their luck. Hell, he was more than experienced.

But sex with Pepper Yates was beyond confounding and more satisfying than anything he'd ever known.

Clothes on — again.

No touching — again.

Mind-blowing release — again.

How did she do it? What was it about her? She'd bent over the foot of the bed, her rump in the air, and he'd been a goner. He couldn't see her clearly, didn't dare feel the soft flesh of her thighs or hips for fear she'd bolt. And still he'd been wild for her.

Her scent made him savage with lust. Her voice stroked him as surely as an erotic touch.

What was she hiding, damn it?

Disgust — at himself, at what he did with her, what she had him do — got Logan off the bed. The urge to go to her clamored in his head, matching the rhythm of his still galloping heartbeat. But he resisted and instead went into the bathroom to take a long shower. He hoped it would help to clear his head.

It didn't.

If anything, the cool water against his still-sensitized body only left him more agitated. Not just because he'd let her use him, and not just because he enjoyed it so much.

Logan had to face the awful truth.

When he was with her, he forgot why he'd started all this in the first place. He forgot she was a link to an unsolved murder. He forgot that her brother could tie up loose ends and give him the means to prosecute the ones responsible for the death of his friend.

Pepper equaled Rowdy, and Rowdy equaled Morton Andrews.

But when he was with her, he thought only about pleasure. His, and hers.

Naked, chased by personal demons, Logan went into his bedroom to get clothes. The second he flipped on the light, he saw her panties on the floor.

Time seemed to stand still. For far too long he stood there staring at them.

Black. Lacy.

A skimpy little bit of nothing with a single tiny pink bow in the front.

Un-fucking-believable.

Like a sleepwalker, he picked them up, rubbing his thumb over the material, thinking of them on her, how she'd look, and what other surprises she kept from him.

From everyone.

To the world, Pepper Yates might be a plain-Jane wallflower bullied by her brother, but deep down — *with him* — she was as sensual as a woman could be.

Damn it all to hell, he was starting to like her.

Sitting on the side of the mattress, Logan tried to decide how to proceed. He was in too deep to give up the progress he'd made undercover. If he blew it now, he might never get another opportunity. Lieutenant Peterson had given him a grace period to get things done. She had big ambitions for the department, so her patience on resolving this had a very definite time limit. His best bet would be to accelerate things — by utilizing his relationship with Pepper.

He couldn't be the only one leveled by their sexual chemistry. Pepper felt it, too. His hand crushed her panties as he thought of how she'd tightened around him, the rush of wetness, her broken, unrestrained groans while coming.

Yeah, they were in this together.

He'd play off that, use it against her instead of letting it trip him up. Then, when he finally closed the case, he'd find a way to make it up to her.

Should he go to her tonight?

He heard the rattling of pipes as her shower started.

No. Let her stew a little. Let her think about what they'd shared, because he knew damn good and well he'd be thinking about it.

Tomorrow he'd talk her into another "date." She'd learn to trust him, and then she'd confide information about Rowdy.

Logan finished dressing, stuffed the panties into his pocket, and headed out for his truck. He needed to burn off some energy. He needed Pepper.

But for tonight, he'd settle for a stiff drink.

■ ■ ■ ■

Annoyed, Morton tapped a pen against the desk and considered his options now that he knew of Logan Riske, a detective bent on revenge. For what, Morton didn't know. Could be any number of things.

That made him laugh as he eyed his quarry. "So you knew there was a cop investigating me?" Morton waited for explanations, excuses and a rush of assurances to avoid punishment.

All he got was a shrug and palpable indifference.

"There are always cops investigating you." Direct eye contact never wavered. "You own enough of the department that it's never a problem for you."

He wouldn't let it become a problem this time either, but that wasn't the point. "Why does Riske want me?"

"It's assumed you had a friend of his murdered."

Since that didn't narrow it down at all, Morton demanded, "Who?"

"A city commissioner."

"Ah. The murder that Rowdy Yates supposedly witnessed." Sitting down, Morton tried to remember, but came up blank.

"What was his name again?"

"Jack Carmin."

He snapped his fingers. "That's right. Old Jack Carmin," he murmured. "He was a righteous prick."

"Honest, yes. There's no solid proof against you, but it's believed that you tried to corrupt him, and he refused."

There wasn't any proof because Rowdy Yates, the bastard, had fallen off the face of the earth. Not before talking to a reporter — who Morton had later dispatched to hell — but since then, nothing. "I remember thinking Yates had promise. He was a quick learner, strong as a bull and unimposing."

Nothing, not even a sound of acknowledgment.

"So," Morton said, watching the cop carefully. "Now Rowdy has turned up again?"

"Possibly. But it's not an issue."

"And if it becomes an issue?"

"I'll take care of him."

Truth rang in the words, so Morton nodded. "Perfect. I have a new venture in the works, and I don't need any distractions." When the cop still stood there, Morton flattened his expression. "Was there anything else?"

"No."

"Then I'll see you for the next report."

He watched the cop leave, and damn if admiration didn't bloom — but then, he'd always had respect for cold, calculated ruthlessness.

The next morning, Pepper pushed herself on the treadmill, running hard and fast until her thighs and shoulders burned and sweat covered her body. She could barely breathe — and still she felt needy.

For Logan.

So much had happened to her over the past two years. Awful things. Life-changing things. She should have been immune to hurt. She should have learned to live without dreams.

Until Logan, she'd been doing okay.

Now . . . now everything felt raw and new and as fresh as that first day when she'd been forced to accept that dreams made no difference, not to her.

She turned down the treadmill to an idle jog, letting her heartbeat slow, giving her body a chance to cool, to adjust.

Her efforts to exhaust herself with exercise, to leave her thoughts and her emotions empty, had failed.

They were anything but.

Memories of Logan, how he smiled, how he looked at her, how he tasted, filled every void of her mind. For her own sake, she had to make a clean break from him.

Rowdy was right — she took far too many risks.

No more playing with fire. No more playing with her sexy neighbor.

No more stealing bits of a normal life.

She'd just finished a quick, cool shower when a firm knock sounded on her door.

Logan.

Despite everything she'd just told herself, joy filled her. She wanted to put off the inevitable, but that'd be cowardly, and it'd leave her with lingering hope.

Dangerous.

She'd had the night and most of the morning to get herself together. It wasn't enough time.

"Be right there," she called out. The walls were so thin that she knew he heard her. After wrapping a towel around her head and hurriedly dressing in a depressing outfit fit for the homeless, she went to the door.

Logan stood there, patiently waiting on her, again wearing no more than shorts. Why did he have to keep doing that to her?

As his gaze moved over her, his smile slipped. "I took you from the shower?"

"What? Oh." She touched the towel on her head. She'd been so focused on his

162

thighs, remembering the press of them against her backside, that she'd forgotten herself. "I was finished before you knocked."

His gaze probing, he reached out and stroked two fingertips over her cheekbone.

Yes, she remembered those fingers, as well. Liquid heat coursed through her, weakening her spine, her resolve.

He dropped his hand. "You look different without the ponytail."

No, no, she did not. *She couldn't.* Alarmed, she took a step back, away from his disturbing proximity. "I need to go." She gestured at the bathroom. "I have to blowdry it . . ."

He stepped in.

Oh, crap. "Logan . . ."

"We didn't get a chance to eat the barbecue last night."

Because she'd rushed him to bed as a distraction so that her brother could put a tracking device on his car.

Because she and Rowdy lived like criminals on the run.

Because they trusted no one, even neighbors with no apparent agenda other than a sexual relationship.

Sometimes, she almost hated herself.

"I know." She swallowed. "I'm sorry."

"Don't be." He shut the door behind him. "I'm not."

Heart slamming, Pepper tried to figure out what to do.

"Having you," he whispered, "beats the hell out of dinner any day."

She'd die if Rowdy found out just how involved she'd gotten, or the methods she'd used to keep Logan occupied. That meant she had to steer clear of him. "I . . . Things got out of hand last night."

He appeared to think about that. "So have dinner with me tonight."

Dinner, instead of sex? "No."

Pretending he hadn't heard her, he said, "We'll eat the barbecue and then afterward . . ." The way he watched her did crazy things to her insides. "Things can get out of hand again."

So tempting. She shook her head.

Attention almost predatory, Logan shifted closer. "Then have breakfast with me now."

She started to refuse yet again — and he held out her panties.

Her jaw loosened, her heart dropped into her stomach, and heat flooded her face. *So stupid, Pepper!*

Unnecessarily, he said, "You left these on my bedroom floor."

She already knew that! Oh, God, what had she been thinking? Bolstering herself with a thickly indrawn breath, she muttered,

"Thank you."

But when she reached for them, he put them behind his back. Not smiling, looking dead serious now, he said, "I think I'd like to hang on to these."

"No." Palm up, arm extended, she waited.

"Have dinner with me." Still no smile.

He was taking this all so seriously. "I don't think that's a good idea."

"Why?"

Temples throbbing, she turned away but came right back. "You know why."

His intent gaze steady on her face, he tucked the panties into his back pocket. "Because there's red-hot chemistry between us? So what? You enjoyed it as much as I did."

Surely she'd enjoyed it even more. "Give me my underwear."

"I will. Tonight. After dinner."

To keep him from reading all the emotions on her face, Pepper spun away again. How could she resist him if he found so many ways to challenge her? *Think, think, think.*

She didn't hear him move, but suddenly his arms closed around her. It felt *so* good.

"You don't have to be shy with me, Sue."

It wasn't about being shy; it was about self-preservation. *Please don't do this to me.*

165

Her resistance was at an all-time low.

"It's just dinner," he murmured, not giving an inch.

"We both know it's not."

"That's your decision, Sue. Always."

And every time she got alone with him, she decided on sex. "You know what will happen."

At her whispered admission, he went still, and then his arms tightened around her. "If you don't want sex, if you're saying you didn't enjoy it —"

"I did." She couldn't lie to him about that. "Too much."

"Not possible," he declared. "But if you prefer we cool things a little, then how about if we go dancing after dinner? That'll keep us occupied, right?"

She almost choked. What man made such a suggestion? What man gave up on the idea of sex to *dance?*

"No."

Keeping her back snugged up close to his chest, he said, "We could hit up a club."

"No!" Oh, God, she wanted nothing to do with that idea, but she shouldn't have reacted so strongly. No way did Logan mean Checkers. It'd take an hour to get there, so he'd probably thought to visit someplace closer.

She didn't know of any clubs, though.

"What's wrong, Sue?"

She lied. "I . . . don't dance." *She loved dancing.* As to cooling things — was it possible?

Could he honestly be content just spending time with her? Doubtful. She wasn't an idiot.

"Then jog with me." He rocked her side to side. "I know you like to run, or you wouldn't have the treadmill, right?"

Diabolical. The offer of jogging was even more tempting than dance. But she couldn't do that, either.

And why did he keep asking, trying to find a way to sway her?

Turning in his arms, Pepper gave up with a disgruntled, "Dinner, and only dinner."

Satisfaction showed in his dark eyes, and she finally got that smile she'd been watching for. "Come early. Say, five?"

Incredible. "Logan, are you sure you want to do this?"

Mocking her a little, he said, "Yes, Sue, I'm very sure." He released her and backed up to the door. "Stop being so skeptical. We'll have fun. I promise."

It wasn't possible to have more fun with him out of bed than in it, but she only nodded. "Five o'clock, then."

His gaze dropped to her mouth. "I'd kiss you, but I'm not sure —"

"Better not to test things." He might be able to resist, but she'd crumble for sure.

As if he knew that, he looked down at the floor a moment, then met her gaze resolutely. "I like you, Sue Meeks. Remember that, okay?"

She couldn't help but shake her head — and she even laughed. The sound so surprised her, she covered her mouth.

Logan's expression warmed. "Tonight," he said softly.

When the door closed behind him, Pepper sank down to her couch.

She was in too deep, and worse, she liked it.

Three days later, Pepper watched the sunset with Logan while sharing an ice-cream sundae. The mood was relaxed and mellow — until her phone rang.

Their gazes met.

He said, "Go ahead. I don't mind."

No, he wouldn't, but she knew it had to be Rowdy. No one else ever called her. "I'll be right back." She pushed up from the lounge chair on his balcony and stepped inside. On the fourth ring, she had her phone out of her purse. "Hello."

"What took you so long?"

"I was . . . busy."

"With your neighbor." Rowdy made a sound of displeasure. "It's looking awfully cozy."

Her heart hung heavy in her chest. "Yes." Very cozy. She relished her every minute with him.

And she missed the sex a lot.

"Should I check the GPS tracker?" Impatient, he asked, "Has he had any unaccountable time away? Any reason for suspicion?"

"No." And with every day, she became more convinced that Rowdy was chasing down a dead end. Other than quick trips to the grocery, where Logan often invited her along, he went very few places. Occasionally he jogged, and she so badly wanted to join him . . .

"His hand's still injured?"

"Yes. But it's better." He'd even grumbled about being bored.

"Do you know when he'll get back to work?"

Logan remained on the balcony, his back to her, seemingly uninterested in her conversation. But just in case he could hear her, she lowered her voice more. "Tomorrow." And she'd grown so accustomed to having him around she would miss him while he was gone.

"I'll give him a little time, then, before I check it. If he's making any stops he shouldn't, we'll know."

"Yes." But she just couldn't imagine it. From what she could tell, Logan was exactly what he claimed to be: a bachelor who liked her company.

They watched rented movies, shared newspaper articles, cooked meals together. They talked and laughed. She liked him and admired him.

She loved the casual company.

Not quite as much as she'd loved the physical release, but close enough to cherish their time together.

"While you're making yourself at home there," Rowdy said with an edge in his tone, "at least scope out the place. Keep your eyes open to anything that seems out of place, any clue that'll tell us more about him. Don't let your infatuation —"

"Okay." Oh, shoot. She hadn't meant to snap. Logan looked back at her, smiled and then stood to lean over the railing, watching the street traffic beyond. Pepper dropped her head forward, took a breath. "Of course I will."

Rowdy was quiet for several seconds. "I'll call again in a few days. Just don't do anything crazy, okay?"

Like have sex with an almost-stranger whom her brother suspected of nefarious dealings? She let out a sigh. "All right."

"Love ya, kiddo."

"You, too." She disconnected the call but hesitated to rejoin Logan.

He fixed that by coming in behind her, and though he didn't quite look at her on his way to the kitchen, she felt the tension surrounding him.

She cleared her throat. "Sorry about that."

"Don't be." He set the empty ice-cream dish in the sink. "Not a big deal."

He waited, but what could she tell him?

She shook her head and said again, "Sorry."

Clearly disgusted, he smirked. "You can keep your secrets, Sue. If you have another guy calling you, hey, we don't have any agreements, right? We're not even having sex anymore. Is that why? You've found someone else?"

What? That's what he thought? She laughed at the absurdity of it.

Eyes narrowing with menace, he crossed his arms. "That's funny?"

"Well . . . yes. A little."

"Glad I could amuse you."

Wow, he really did sound angry. "I'm sorry."

He muttered, "Fuck." Then with just as much annoyance, he said, "Stop apologizing already."

She approached him. "That wasn't another man."

"Then who was it?"

Blast. She'd really gotten herself into a corner. "I mean, it was a man, but not in the way you're thinking."

"What other way is there?"

She made a split decision. A good way to test him would be to give him just a tiny taste of information — and watch how he reacted to it. "My brother."

Chagrined, he took that in, then smiled. "Oh." After an awkward moment, the smile turned into a laugh. "Shit."

She tipped her head, gauging the sincerity of the sound. "Now you think it's funny?"

"Considering I was jealous, yeah."

"Jealous?"

"What did you think?" Taking her by surprise, he kissed her, quick and light. "I didn't know you had a brother."

Jealousy was outrageous and sort of endearing. "We don't see each other often."

"How come?" As if it didn't really matter, he took her hand and led her to the couch.

"You're not close?"

"It's not that. We're actually very close. We only have each other. But he doesn't live around here."

"You lost your parents?"

She nodded. "A very long time ago."

Solemn, he cupped her face. "You never told me."

"Because it's not an uplifting story."

His thumb brushed her cheek while he studied her face. "I'd still be a good listener."

He seemed so sincere, so sympathetic, that she wondered how a few truths would hurt. She'd never had anyone whom she could confide in. Only Rowdy.

But no one knew the details of their background, so it wasn't information Logan could use against her — even if he was a threat, which she didn't believe. Out of necessity, she'd learned to be a good judge of character.

Logan didn't feel like a bad guy to her, not in any way.

"My brother and I grew up in a trailer on the riverbank." Memories crowded in: days spent swimming, playing in the mud; Rowdy teaching her how to fish, and how to fight; sunburns and late nights camping out and watching the stars. As kids, they'd had some good times — just not enough. "My parents weren't . . . great. Neither of them kept a job, and they drank too much. My brother and I were pretty much left to raise ourselves."

"Damn." Appearing genuinely hurt for her, he took her hand. "What's the age difference between you and your brother?"

"Just three years." She couldn't help but smile. "But he's so alpha, way more outgoing than I am, you'd think there was a bigger age span."

"Alpha?"

Mega alpha. She smiled at Logan. "He's pretty fearless, and too daring for his own good."

Logan stilled, then lifted her hand to his mouth to kiss her knuckles. "How did your folks die?"

"Just a dumb car wreck. Dad was driving, but they were both drunk. There were a total of about six cars involved, but luckily no one else died."

Though she'd tried to keep a physical distance between them, she found herself leaning on Logan's shoulder, accepting the arm he put around her and the kiss he pressed to her temple.

"How old were you?"

"Fifteen. Young and dumb and . . ." Vivid

memories settled over her, making her heart heavy, her chest tight. "Unprepared for social services to take me away."

"Shit." He turned her face up to his. "That's what happened?"

She nodded. In a mere whisper, she confided what only Rowdy knew. "It scared me so badly, I spent two days crying. I didn't want to go to a foster home. I didn't want to lose my brother."

Logan's strong arms closed around her, holding her tenderly, protectively. "Of course not. No young girl should be put in that position."

"My brother took care of it." *He took care of me.*

"How's that?"

Much as she enjoyed Logan's embrace, his warm attention and especially his caring, she put a little space between them. The more she depended on him, the more she wanted to, and that was a dangerous path to go down.

Rowdy wasn't wrong about that.

"He knew they wouldn't let him be my guardian, so he packed us up and we ran off together."

Disbelief, and maybe a little pity, showed in Logan's expression. "An eighteen-year-old and a fifteen-year-old?"

She nodded. Rowdy had promised her that they'd never be separated, and he'd done his best. But despite all his efforts, too many promises had been impossible to keep.

Introspective, too quiet, Logan stroked his hand over her head, down the length of her ponytail. Finally he asked, "He got a job?"

"We both found work wherever we could." They'd learned to be pretty tough, too. Out of necessity, they'd stayed in cheap, sleazy places. Danger abounded, so Rowdy taught her how to defend herself.

But more often than not, he followed up whenever he found out anyone had hassled her. Guys learned to leave her alone unless she showed an interest. And even then, Rowdy never missed a thing. He'd started hovering, and to this day, he kept a quiet vigilance over her. There wasn't much she did, there wasn't much she thought, without Rowdy knowing.

"Must have been really rough."

Logan sounded far too maudlin, causing her to smile. "We survived off a very limited budget. But it wasn't all bad. I looked at it like an adventure. My brother sort of made it seem that way. He'd tell me that we were free, independent, that we could do anything, be anything." Remembering so many different times that Rowdy had been there for her, she grew somber. "We didn't have a lot, but we had each other."

After a long stretch of silence, Logan spoke. "I'd love to meet him sometime."

That'd never happen. Not in this lifetime. "Maybe someday," she hedged. She sat back to look at him again. "But now you know I'm not talking to another guy. I don't even know any other guys that I'd want to talk to, or who'd be all that anxious to talk to me." She bit her lip but had to admit the truth. "You're the only one I'm interested in visiting. I promise."

Logan's gaze went to her mouth and then back to her eyes. "I'm glad that I'm here, with you."

But for how long? A man like Logan would quickly grow discontented with celibacy. Maybe after her brother checked the GPS and found out Logan was safe, she could resume a real relationship with him. If she told him everything, how would he react?

Would he understand? Would he help to keep her cover?

Would he want her enough to live with the convoluted lie of her life?

Pepper realized they were sitting there watching each other in a taut silence. She'd gotten way ahead of herself, so she faked a yawn. "I need to get going."

Instead of trying to dissuade her, Logan nodded. They stood together, and he walked her to the door.

"Sue?"

"Hmm?"

His hand slid around her skull, holding her still. "I could really use a good-night kiss right about now. I promise it'll be that and nothing more."

Dangerous, dangerous, dangerous, but . . . "Me, too."

It felt different, the slow, gentle way his mouth moved over hers, just as hot, but now somehow more personal. As he lifted away, he said, "I'll work tomorrow, but I'd love to share dinner again."

"My turn to cook," she said. And because she couldn't stop herself, she kissed him again, quickly, then not so quickly. It'd be easy enough to segue into the bedroom, to get carried away one more time . . .

Again, Logan ended the kiss. "Soon as you're ready, honey, let me know." He touched the corner of her mouth, put his forehead to hers. "The second you give me the word, I'm as willing as any man can be. Until then, I'm doing my best not to push you. But much more of that, and I'm going to forget myself."

So noble. So incredibly considerate. "Thank you." Smiling from the inside out, Pepper stepped out to the hall. "Good night, Logan."

"Good night, Sue. Sweet dreams."

Like a true gentleman, he stood in the hallway watching over her until she got into her apartment.

Closing the door, choking on a resurgence of hope, Pepper hugged herself. If she couldn't have a normal life, she at least had this, now, with Logan.

It was more than she'd learned to expect.

And maybe it was far more than she deserved.

CHAPTER NINE

A little more than a week later, Rowdy sat in the parking lot of the bar, his laptop in his lap, disbelieving the results of his GPS tracker. Every day he'd wanted to check it, yet day after day, he'd put it off.

Pepper seemed so damned hopeful that he hadn't wanted to burst her bubble by grabbing solid evidence off the tracker any faster than necessary. Neither did he want to check the damn thing too soon, thereby missing something important.

He'd kept a close watch on things, waiting to attack if Logan Stark made the wrong move, while hoping he wouldn't. He knew he couldn't put it off any longer, so while his sister sat all cozy with the bastard, watching a movie and eating pizza, he'd retrieved it.

With dread, Rowdy had anticipated how he'd break the news to her, how he'd explained that she'd been used . . .

Now, with the results right there in front of him, it looked as if he might not have to. Logan Stark had gone shopping, to various establishments in the area to eat or get a quick drink, back to his construction site only recently and to the apartment building.

The apartment where he spent an inordinate amount of time with Pepper.

Sitting back, restless on many levels, Rowdy thought about things. He and Pepper had survived by being cautious and by trusting instincts.

For some reason, despite the data before him, everything about Logan screamed a warning. But maybe that was Rowdy's own prejudice.

How could any red-blooded guy be so attracted to Pepper for so long? Most times when Rowdy saw her, she looked like a drudge, like a plain-Jane with no redeeming features to draw in a man.

Being a guy, too, he understood how the male mind worked. At first he'd written off the attraction as a challenge for Logan. After all, Rowdy himself had recently suffered the same type of challenge with the little waitress. He'd gone back to the bar a few times, but he hadn't seen her again, which accounted for part of his restlessness.

But Logan saw Pepper damn near every day, so that reasoning didn't make sense.

If he'd hoped to score with her . . . no, Rowdy hated thinking along those lines. Besides, that'd be impossible without Pepper blowing her cover, and she'd never do that. In so many ways, she was more protective than he could ever be.

So what the hell was happening between them? It made no sense. Logan had to be working an angle.

As a safeguard against all threats, Rowdy had furtively kept up with his past, with Checkers and with any info he could find on Morton Andrews.

For all intents and purposes, it was business as usual. Crimes committed without proof of personal transgression. Accusations that didn't pan out. Cutthroat business that expanded by the day.

Ripe frustration among a select few in the police force.

But no mention, ever, of Rowdy or Pepper Yates. It seemed they'd been forgotten. Perhaps even the most corrupt villains gave up on loose ends after enough time had passed.

Could it maybe all be over?

Could Logan Stark really be no more than an honest guy looking for companionship?

Rowdy snorted. Before he made that leap, he wanted some assurances. And that meant breaking into Logan's apartment, going through his things and seeing what he could turn up.

He'd uncover the man's entire background, one way or another.

And he'd get started tonight . . . as soon as he got Pepper to cooperate.

Feeling like a hunted man, Logan paced his small living room. Pepper would expect him in another hour. She didn't realize that her personal style of platonic socializing had left him tightly strung.

With lust. Sympathy. Concern.

But mostly lust.

Jesus, each small smile from her was so precious that it left him in a vortex of conflicting emotion. And when she laughed — a very rare occurrence — it reduced him to a basic male animal, an animal who wanted to make a permanent impression on her in the time-honored way of men.

But she'd ruled that out. Though he knew she wanted him, too, she continued to draw back anytime things got too heated. That put him back at square one, having to cajole his way into her narrow social calendar all over again.

Now that he knew part of her background, it only amplified his growing feelings for her. God, but she'd had it rough, and her brother hadn't helped. As a kid, she hadn't wanted foster care. But she hadn't been mature enough to decide what would be best for her.

And really . . . neither had Rowdy. Eighteen. Damn. That was so young to have so much responsibility. Logan could understand how easy it'd be to get off the straight and narrow. At eighteen, he'd had the world by the ass. Parents who spoiled both him and Dash. Independence given to him by indulgent parents. He'd wanted for nothing, certainly not security, comfort, support.

Or love.

Rowdy and Pepper had had none of that. Ever. As children, they'd been neglected by disinterested parents. As very young adults, they'd been threatened by an unknown system. He hated to admit it, but Logan could sympathize with Rowdy. He'd made tough decisions.

But he shouldn't have dragged Pepper into that atmosphere. Though Reese had tried, he hadn't found any clearer photos of Pepper. Nothing in color. Nothing of her body.

Not that it mattered. He couldn't be more

obsessed.

Thanks to the paper-thin walls, Logan needed no more than a handheld audio listening device to keep track of her routine. Whenever he wasn't with her, he could still hear her moving around, occasionally listening to the radio or television, showering or doing dishes.

Or talking with her brother.

Many times, after he left her, she ran on her treadmill.

Endlessly.

She probably tried working off the same sexual tension that plagued him. He could have told her not to bother. Nothing but the real deal would do.

They could be so good together if she'd trust him a little, if she'd . . . but then again, she had good reason not to trust him.

Logan rubbed his face. Everything was far more complicated than he'd expected — because he couldn't stay detached. He couldn't stay cold and indifferent to Pepper, because she wasn't cold or indifferent. Warm, funny, fickle and so damn sexy . . . yeah, he hadn't expected that. Not from the grainy little black-and-white photos of her. Not when she hid all that fire behind concealing clothes and a reserved persona.

Her physical appeal wasn't out there and

in your face.

It was subtle, something that came from her as a woman, her gentle nature and wounded soul. It was far more potent than a stacked body could ever be.

When the rattle of her water pipes quieted, Logan paced closer to the adjoining wall.

She'd finished her shower.

Closing his eyes, he tried to picture her naked . . . but came up with an incomplete image. She hid so much from him, every inch of skin from her collarbone to her elbows, her waist to her ankles.

And still, somehow, she turned him on until he almost couldn't take it. Her outfits were so well suited to disguising her figure that most times he strained his eyes trying to figure out the curves of her body.

Frustration mixed with imagination kept him from sleeping at night, leaving him mostly antsy.

She seemed so starved for company, his company, that it broke his cynical heart and nearly corrupted his convictions.

If he only wanted sex, he could have it.

But he wanted *her.*

Naked, lights on, hair loose and that special little smile in place . . .

"Shit." On edge, he scrubbed a hand over the back of his neck, laughing at himself.

Any more of that and he'd be prowling his apartment with a hard-on. He had to work it out with her, and soon.

He'd tried things her way. Too many days of sensual torture hadn't gotten him the desired outcome. Tonight he'd press her, emotionally and physically. Because of his end goal, he'd feel like a bastard, but he'd do it anyway. If it blew his cover, then he'd suffer the consequences, but he had to —

The ringing of her cell phone stilled his turbulent thoughts.

He knew it was her damned brother keeping tabs on her. Calls from Rowdy Yates were the main reason Logan had the hand-held audio device; bugging her apartment would have been too risky.

Listening through the thin walls was safer.

Retrieving the audio device from beneath a desk drawer, he put in the earbuds and pressed the receiver to the wall. He missed the first few words of Pepper's greeting, but he caught her distress right away.

Every call from her brother seemed to cause her grief.

"What if he catches you?" she asked with worry, and then, "It's entirely possible. Even if I try to keep him here . . . well, no."

Logan frowned. What if who caught him? He adjusted the volume and waited.

"Rowdy, listen to me, *please*." She lowered her voice but not enough. "It's too dangerous. Of course I trust you, but if Logan catches you in his apartment, he'll probably call the police. Then what will we do?"

Rage coalesced, crowding out guilt, pity — annihilating every other emotion. Rowdy Yates planned to break into his apartment.

Bingo, you bastard. I have you now.

Even if he didn't hear a specific time for this break-in, he'd let Reese know. He'd get things set up in advance so that —

"There's no reason. He's just a nice guy." A pause, and then, "I just know, that's all."

Jesus. She thought he was nice? Logan closed his eyes, but that did nothing to alleviate the remorse. Before it was all said and done, Pepper Yates would be badly hurt. By her brother and by him.

In the end, she'd consider him far from *nice*.

"When you find nothing, then will you let it go?"

Logan held his breath — until Pepper said, "Thank you."

So she agreed to whatever scheme her brother cooked up? That's probably how it had gone throughout their lifetimes —

Rowdy leading her down the wrong side of the law.

Never mind that she didn't know he was the law.

"I was supposed to go to his place tonight, but I can ask him over here instead. Yes, I'm sure. I just want it done."

Logan curled a hand into a fist. *Tonight would be the night.* After so many dead ends, he should have been relieved, even exuberant.

Instead, he felt the great weight of his conscience and sadness for what he would lose, and for what he never had.

With Pepper Yates.

As Reese started up the steps to his second-floor apartment, one of his female neighbors came out her door. He paused to give her a smile, a greeting, but she didn't acknowledge him. She locked her door, checked it twice and went past him as if he didn't exist.

No eye contact. Not even a quick glance. She avoided him like the plague.

Because for sure, she saw him.

Not like anyone could miss a man of his size. Women teased him about being a hulk. Men walked a wide path around him. He'd been blessed with good genes from the males in his family lineage, giving him height and strength. As a bachelor he had time to hit the gym a few times a week, so he stayed in shape.

Women noticed him, damn it.

But she acted as if she didn't.

Snooty gal. Alice-something-or-other. Sort of classic looks; baby-fine brown hair cut in a blunt, shoulder-length style, soft brown eyes, very fair skin, average build on the slim side.

He glanced back at her, but she appeared lost in thought as she went out the entry door with single-minded purpose. He'd noticed that about her a few times already. Wherever she went, it was as if she was on a mission. Even when she took out her trash, she did it with extreme focus, as if it took a lot of concentration to get anything done.

It was part of Reese's nature to size up everyone in the building. Hell, everyone in his area. This particular neighbor didn't necessarily interest him any more than the others, but male ego deigned that he disliked being ignored. By anyone. He was a friendly guy. Jovial even, damn it.

But he couldn't be real jovial with a woman who shut him out so completely.

Reese shook his head and continued on to his apartment. It had been a hellishly long day at the station, and he looked forward to a beer, televised sports and a thick ham sandwich. Alice-something-or-other wasn't worth additional thought.

Arms loaded down with purchases, he got the key in the lock — and heard the maniacal barking.

With a heavy sigh, he opened the door to the destruction of his belongings. The dog, all black with long ears and soft curly fur and a hyper disposition, yowled and barked and whined while running a frantic circle around him.

He left a wet trail everywhere he went.

Great. At least he had hardwood floors. Carpet would have been . . . no, Reese didn't want to think about that.

Resigned, he set down the bag and dug out the leash and collar. "Thought I wouldn't come back, huh?"

Dropping to his back in a submissive posture, the dog wiggled his way toward Reese.

Reese couldn't help but smile. "I think you've already drained your pipes, but we may as well start a routine, right?" He fastened the collar around the dog and attached the leash. After pocketing a few of the plastic bags used for cleanup — a really distasteful idea — he stroked the silky fur along the dog's back. "Let's go, Cash."

With the dog alternately refusing to budge, then bounding this way and that, Reese re-locked the door and went back out front. Sweat glued his dress shirt to his skin, heat wilted the tie around his neck, and an old injury set his left thigh to throbbing.

Being more social than Alice-something-or-other, the other neighbors in the building greeted him. One hot blonde flirted, as she always did, but Reese wasn't dumb enough to bring trouble to where he lived.

Well, except for Cash.

The dog jumped up on an elderly neighbor who didn't much appreciate it. Before Reese could duly chastise him, Cash charged another dog, only to run out of leash and nearly choke himself. He sniffed every blade of grass, refusing to go, until Alice-something-or-other suddenly re-turned. Then Cash chose to stare her in the eyes while doing his business.

Great.

Reese figured what the hell, and he stared at her, too.

Even with Cash involved in something so . . . un-smile-worthy, she smiled at him.

Reese, she ignored, or at least, she tried to.

Screw that. "New dog," Reese said to her.

"He cried all day while you were gone."
Direct and to the point.

Great. Why waste time with pleasantries?
"Sorry about that. He'll settle down." I
hope.

She nodded and continued on. Reese saw
that she carried a bag of jelly beans. Was
that why she'd gone out? Just to get jelly
beans? Huh.

Cash finished up and bounded after her,
and wonder of wonders, she stopped and
knelt down to pet him.

Good dog, Reese thought. "He disturbed
you?"

"I felt bad for him. He needs attention.
He's still a puppy."

"Yeah, see, the thing is, I sort of found
him. Or rather, he found me. I wasn't really
planning on having a dog, but —"

"It was kind of you to take him in." She
seated her narrow rump on a concrete step
and good old Cash practically crawled into
her lap.

And, her smile soft and amused, she let
him.

Who knew a dog had so many uses? Alice
looked very peaceful while loving on his
dog. Her average brown hair fell forward,
half hiding her average face. She didn't
seem concerned with getting her beige

slacks dirty or getting dog hair on her green tank.

She set aside her purse and the candy and put all that extreme focus on his dog.

So how did a stray accomplish what Reese couldn't, in such a short time?

Determined to find out, Reese started to sit beside her, but his cell phone rang. He pulled it from his pocket, saw it was Logan and groaned.

Alice glanced at him.

He handed her the leash. "You mind? Just for a sec." Without waiting for her reply, he turned his back on her, took a few steps away, and answered the call.

"Make it fast," Reese said. He didn't want to be too rude to the neighbor lady, now that Cash had finally managed to break the ice.

"He plans to break in to my place tonight."

For the sake of privacy, Reese took a few more steps away, dismissing the dog and Alice-something-or-other. Undercover operations were kept tightly compartmentalized to avoid security leaks. No way in hell did he want a civilian listening in. "Rowdy Yates?"

"None other."

Unexpected. "You know this, how?"

A pause, and then Logan said, "Overheard her talking on the phone with him."

"She talked with him in front of you?"

"Not exactly."

"Then how —"

"I listened through the wall. With an audio device."

Damn it. Reese looked up at the blazing sun, now in shades of red, pink and purple. Lately, the nights hadn't been much cooler than the days. "I'm betting you didn't have a search warrant for that?"

"No."

So he couldn't mention it. It couldn't come up, ever. Again . . . great. "You tell the lieutenant?"

"Not yet. Only you."

At least there was that. "Let's keep it that way."

"She expects me to keep her apprised."

Yeah, Lieutenant Peterson liked to stay in the loop on everything. She remained inflexible in her efforts toward a clean sweep of the force, and grumbling from the ranks hadn't swayed her off that course.

Reese was just as determined to keep her in the dark on this. "I'll take care of it then." In his own way, in his own time, with everyone's best interests at heart. Logan wouldn't like that, but that's how it had to be.

There was more at play than his need for justice and revenge.

"I'm short on time anyway, so that works." Reese glanced back at his neighbor. She stood now, walking Cash over to a shady spot in the grass. "If I'm on surveillance, then I can just happen to catch Rowdy breaking in." For Alice, Cash followed along politely.

Stupid dog. He shook his head and smiled.

He hoped Alice watched her step, because he hadn't yet had a chance to clean up any messes.

"That's how I figured it," Logan said. "No one needs to know I overheard the details."

Reese checked his watch. He felt the neighbor watching him with curiosity. *Not the best time to finally show interest, honey.*

"Might take me an hour or more to get there." He had his own team on hold, ready to go at the drop of a dime. They were loyal to him, not to the lieutenant, and not to Logan.

He wouldn't have it any other way.

"I don't have an exact time," Logan said, "but I have to be at her place soon, so it won't be until then."

"Put it on hold for as long as you can.

Maybe be out on the balcony or something. Even after I get there, I'll need time to set up. You can do that?"

"No problem."

Could it be true? Could Logan have really caught up with the elusive Yates? Wondering at what cost, Reese asked, "What about the sister?"

Logan's silence worried him more than anything.

Just to piss him off, Reese said, "Want me to have her cuffed, too?"

"Don't touch her."

Well, well, well. That sentiment was clear enough. "She's going to be hurt, Logan. No way around it."

"You think I don't already know that?"

If only Logan had let it go. But he hadn't — maybe because he didn't realize just how persuasive Morton Andrews could be. "I take it she doesn't yet know what motivates you?"

Logan laughed without humor. "No."

It seemed believable to Reese that Logan no longer knew his motives, either. "Well, don't worry about it. She won't be your problem after tonight." Or would she? By the day, it seemed problems were adding up. Reese would have to deal with them before it all got insurmountable.

After an exaggerated silence, Reese prompted him. "Logan?"

"This is totally fucked, but . . . I like her."

Oh, hell. "Come again?"

"I like her, damn it. She's . . . not what I expected."

No, she wouldn't be. Alice gave Reese a look of impatience. He shrugged at her. "How's that?"

"She's nice, Reese. An innocent stuck in the middle of this mess."

"Yeah, her situation is pretty tough. Can't be helped, though, right? Not with her brother still around."

"It's more than her being nice."

Reese looked up at the sky but found no inspiration, so he just waited.

Logan said, "I'm interested in her."

That bald statement gave him pause. "As in helping her through this, you mean? Making amends after you get Rowdy? Because you feel bad for disrupting her life —"

"As a woman, damn it."

"Bullshit." His raised voice drew Alice's sharpened attention. Again Reese turned his back on her.

"I don't believe it." Guilt, okay, he got that. Logan was one of the most honorable men he knew. It's why he was so resolved to bring his friend's murderers to justice. But . . . "I've seen the pictures of her, remember. She's not your type." He'd scoured the photos at Logan's request and saw that she was plain at best, damn near dumpy at worst.

Sounding defensive, Logan said, "She's smart. And sweet."

"So is my new dog, but that doesn't mean —"

Logan all but snarled, "Fuck off, Reese." And then more quietly, "You don't know her."

He squeezed the phone and kept his tone low. "And you think you do? Jesus man, you're *undercover.* Any relationship you think you have with her is a fucking sham."

Ice filled Logan's voice. "Get here as soon as you can. I'll stall her for an hour or so. Later."

After Logan disconnected the call, Reese dropped his phone into his pocket and turned back to Alice and Cash.

They sat beneath the only tree in the lot, trying to hog the sliver of shade. Ready to get on his way, Reese strode across the grass to stand over her.

As usual, she paid him no mind.

"You like my dog."

"He's beautiful."

"Busy tonight?"

She blanched. Literally. Looking up at him with big dark eyes and something that felt remarkably like fear, Alice-something-or-other tried to speak, but nothing came out.

"Jesus." Reese knelt down in front of her. "I wasn't going to proposition you. I just need someone to look after Cash."

After a pregnant silence, color rushed back into her face. "Oh. You mean your dog?"

"Yeah. I have a . . . an emergency. Gotta go back out and it might take a while, so I was thinking —"

"Yes," she blurted. Pushing back and away from him, she scrambled up to her feet. "Yes, I'll watch him for you."

Odd. To the point of being weird. "Great." Slowly, Reese regained his own feet. "He's not entirely housebroken yet, so . . . You want to watch him at my place instead of yours?"

"Mine."

What a relief — and yet, still annoying. "Then I'll go get the stuff I just bought for him." He walked away from her, and he didn't care if it was rude or not. The dog, damn him, didn't give a shit now that he had Alice-something-or-other fawning all over him.

Reese used his cell to organize the stake-out while bounding up the steps to his apartment. He took time to clean up Cash's mess and change into jeans and a black T-shirt before heading back out front in under ten minutes. He handed a bag of Cash's new belongings, including food, a chew toy and a blanket, to Alice — who still stood out in the yard.

He thanked her, gave the dog a pat and the admonishment to be good — yeah, right — and got on his way. No matter how tonight rolled out, it was going to end up an apocalyptic mess. He felt it deep in his bones. Things were about to implode — for good or bad, he didn't yet know. Logan was getting in a little too deep. Maybe he was discovering things better left undiscovered.

Reese would have to keep an eye on him.

And while he was on it, he'd keep an eye on Pepper Yates, too.

CHAPTER TEN

It wasn't easy, putting on a front and keeping Pepper in the dark when every instinct Logan had urged him to protect her from what would happen tonight.

What *he* would instigate.

Despite her brother's orders, she seemed genuinely happy to see him. Maybe a little more reserved than usual, but hard to tell when she was always so introverted.

Except during sex.

He had planned to have her again, to seduce her in whatever way necessary. But with it all going down tonight, Logan knew he couldn't do that. Not to her.

Not again.

To help keep things in check, he'd worn jeans and a T-shirt. Not much in the way of barriers, but at least he wasn't deliberately trying to draw her in.

"Let's go inside," she suggested for the fifth time. "It's hot out here."

Normally, Logan would follow her lead. Tonight, he continued to lean against the railing, staring out at the colorful sky. He needed another twenty minutes or so to ensure Reese was in position. Damned if he'd miss this opportunity now that he finally had Rowdy taking the bait.

He hated putting Pepper in this position, caught between following her brother's orders and having to lie to him, but it couldn't be helped.

"Look at that sunset." Only a shimmer of sun remained over the horizon, but it left behind a colorful display that made even warehouses and factories look good. "Amazing, isn't it?"

She closed her eyes, uncaring about the beauty of nature when duty to her brother weighed so heavily on her delicate shoulders. "Yes, very pretty."

Logan badly wanted to soothe her, to hold her close and promise her it would be all right. But he'd lied to her enough already. "You feeling all right?"

Her eyes snapped open, and she stared at him, flushed — maybe with guilt.

But . . . maybe not.

Speculative, Logan surveyed her expression. He'd seen it before, that heat in her beautiful eyes, in her cheeks. "Sue?"

"I'm . . . I'm fine."

Turning, he leaned back on the railing, now watching her instead of the sunset. "You know how you look?"

She shook her head.

"A little turned on." And maybe that'd work to his advantage. Would her physical desire help ease her past her hurt feelings once he took her brother into custody?

She let out a breath, didn't deny it and smoothed her hand over the soft cotton of his T-shirt.

Logan felt the touch everywhere. Emotions clashed.

She had set the boundaries of no sex, but now she wanted to lure him.

For her goddamned brother.

Covering her hand with his, Logan pulled her around beside him. Much more of that, and he'd forget himself. At least her touch hadn't been against his bare skin.

But with Pepper, no amount of clothes would be enough deterrent.

He'd thought on it long and hard, and while he still didn't know what it was about her specifically that pushed his buttons, it was a reality all the same.

He wanted her. All the fucking time. More so every damned day. Hoping he hid it, Logan smiled at her. "Relax, honey."

She didn't. If anything, she tensed up more. "Are you . . . punishing me, Logan?" She kept her head down, her gaze avoiding his.

What was this about? Punishment? "I don't know what you mean."

"Yes, you do. I put you off, and now you're paying me back in kind."

His determination softened. "That's what you think?" Yes, it burned his ass that she'd bow to her brother's instructions, but he couldn't bear seeing that particular look on her face.

To hell with it. He didn't give a shit if Reese, Rowdy, or both were watching.

"No." Logan lifted her chin. "Even if I wanted to, I couldn't." He kissed her with pent-up frustration, tilting his head, sinking his tongue in to play with hers, consuming her — and pushing himself dangerously close to the point of no return.

She pulled back, but not far. In a broken whisper, she said, "*Now* can we go inside? Please?"

He had to remember that this was a game, her brother's game. She was only a player.

Keeping her close, Logan looped his arms around her. She was tall, but so slender. Soft and warm. "Tell me what you want first."

"You."

Damn, but that fired his blood. He stared at her mouth, then down over her body. "That's a mighty quick turnaround."

"Quick?" She stared at him. "It's been days."

True enough. Knowing she still had to hide from him, Logan whispered, "All right. Tell me how you want me."

Beneath the cotton material of her blouse, her chest expanded with a deep breath. A pulse raced in her pale throat. Her eyelashes fluttered.

So turned on and so damned appealing.

She glanced around the area, at his empty balcony, the sparse traffic, the few disinterested pedestrians across the street. Sounding scandalized, she whispered, "Out here?"

"No one's listening to us." At least, he didn't think anyone could hear them. But it was feasible her brother had set up an audio device, same as Logan had done. There were gadgets that amplified sound across space; Rowdy could be in a building across the street and still hear them.

That possibility disturbed him. "There's only you and me, Sue." Logan watched her. "Right?"

"Yes, but . . ." Stepping away from him, she smoothed a nervous hand over the material of her skirt. "You know I like . . . the dark."

"So that I can't see you, I know." And sooner or later, he'd find out why. He leaned on the railing, pretending an ease he didn't feel. "But you can still talk to me. You can still give me that."

The way she lifted her chin surprised him. "Okay." She licked her bottom lip. "I want to pull your jeans down to your knees, then sit on your lap."

The visual nearly leveled Logan. He could so easily picture how it'd be. Straightening from the railing, he said, "Facing me?"

"Yes."

He fingered a fold in her skirt. "With this bunched up around your hips?"

Her breathing deepened. "Yes."

"Your thighs wide open around me. No panties." He'd finally be able to see her legs, maybe stroke her thighs, her hips. He felt the start of wood and didn't care. Stepping closer, he whispered, "And me deep inside you?"

A soft sound of excitement parted her lips, and she nodded. "Yes."

He kissed her again. Gentler this time, with apology — although she wouldn't know that.

Hugging her close, her head to his shoulder, he wrapped his arms around her. "I would never want to punish you for doing what you thought best, Sue."

"Okay, well then, we could —"

He cut her off. "It's for that reason, your insistence that we cool things, that I'd rather we hold off for a while." *At least until after your brother is arrested so I can get answers out of him.* "I want you to be sure —"

"I am," she rushed to say.

"Shh. I don't want you to have regrets." *More* regrets . . . because he knew she'd be racked with shame after tonight.

Stillness settled over her. Did she fear he'd caught on to her? He didn't want her distressed. He didn't want her hurt ever again.

"I care about you." *Believe it, please, even after I crush you.* Surely enough time had passed for Reese to get everything in place. "Let's go in. We'll watch a movie, talk, and afterward, if you feel the same, then believe me, I'm game."

He saw that she wanted to argue, but mostly she wanted him off the balcony.

Conflicting emotions passed over her features — worry, shame, need . . . and finally an expression of iron will. "Okay."

So often she took him by surprise. That particular look was a new one for her. He imagined it took a lot of strength to have survived the harsh life she'd led with Rowdy Yates, to do the things her brother coerced her into doing.

Like deceiving him.

Logan's reasons for going after Rowdy added up by the second.

"I won't change my mind," Pepper assured him.

Forcing a smile, Logan said, "I'm glad." He hoped she felt the same in the morning, but he didn't kid himself. It was going to take a lot of finesse on his part to appease her after all his deceptions.

No matter how long it took, he wouldn't give up on her.

Watching Logan lead his sister into the apartment left Rowdy incandescent with fury. That was no friendly peck he'd just witnessed. For a heart-stopping moment, he feared Logan would take Pepper right there on the goddamned balcony.

Son-of-a-bitch.

Rowdy almost threw the binoculars, but instead, he tossed them through the driver's side window and into the front seat of his car.

On the one hand, he wanted to take Logan apart for daring to get so familiar.

On the other . . . he had grudging optimism that maybe his sister had found something real. He hoped he wouldn't discover anything incriminating in Logan's apartment. He hoped his sister wasn't being used.

But he didn't trust hope and never had. Long ago he'd learned that was a fool's game.

He hadn't survived by being a fool.

Leaving his locked car in the designated spot down the street from the apartment building, he put on his hat and started walking. Tension crawled into every muscle until he couldn't ignore it.

Something felt off. Wrong, in a big way.

If it wasn't for Pepper, he'd go with his gut and put off this little search for another night. But even as he scanned the area, studying every shadow and leaving his senses open to all threats, Rowdy had to face the fact that Pepper was in her apartment — with Logan Stark — because that's what he'd asked her to do.

He owed her closure on this. Asking her to go through it all again at a later date would be grossly unfair.

Pausing in the building across from the apartment, he watched the facade, the light coming from Pepper's sliding doors, the dark beyond Logan's. The fine hairs on the nape of his neck stood on end. Two young ladies came down the walkway, talking quietly, laughing. They paused when they saw him. One smiled, the other gave him a blatant once-over.

In no mood for feminine attention, Rowdy nodded. "Ladies." They strode on but not without a few glances back at him.

Several cars drove past, then a bus. He continued to wait, every few seconds checking the lights and shadows, looking for anything that didn't belong. The sun sank completely and streetlamps flickered on.

It was almost too still.

But if he delayed any longer, he ran the risk of Logan returning to his apartment.

Mind made up, Rowdy crossed the street. Not in a rush, but not with any real caution, either. He needed to blend in. Just a passerby. Nothing more, and nothing less.

Both Pepper and Logan had apartments on the second floor, side by side. He'd placed Pepper in that particular apartment because a large tree that grew too close to the building made it possible to sneak out the small bathroom window if it became necessary.

It also made it possible for Rowdy to sneak in undetected.

Sure, he had a key . . . but going in the front door would leave him too exposed. If anyone saw him, he could be recognized — as Pepper's brother. Never would he risk that.

Reaching Logan's window could get dicey, but he'd figure it out.

By design, the security lights didn't reach the side yard, and the tree helped to conceal his movements as he climbed. Years ago, when he and Pepper had been river rats, they'd climb trees all the time. Sometimes, in summer weather, he'd tie a rope up high and they'd swing out to drop into the cold river water.

Other times, they'd sit up in a tree for hours, and he'd talk with her, keeping her out of the trailer when their mom or dad had drunk too much. Usually his folks just got stupid with drink.

But occasionally they had gotten mean.

Shaking off those disturbing memories, Rowdy ventured out onto a sturdy branch. Like riding a bike, it was a learned trait, once ingrained, never forgotten. It took some maneuvering, but he jimmied open the window. Even more difficult was fitting his frame through the opening. Pepper with her narrower shoulders and hips wouldn't have the same difficulty.

After dropping into the dark room, he paused to listen. He heard nothing, so he left his hat on the bathroom counter and pulled out the penlight to start his inspection. He checked the medicine cabinet. Any prescribed meds would have a name on the label — but he found none, just the usual OTC stuff, enough to look as though Logan truly lived there. A razor, a toothbrush . . . okay, so the guy had settled in long-term. That proved nothing.

Rowdy crept through the apartment. Because he'd lived on the edge, he knew how to cover his tracks. Without a trace of his presence, he went through the bedroom and back out again. No drawers were left askew, not even a shift in the blankets on the unmade bed.

He didn't find anything.

Both relieved and frustrated, he saved the living room for last. Standing in the middle of the floor, he looked around, orienting himself to the shadows, the placement of furniture and lamps. He could hear noise from Pepper's apartment next door — the sound of the television, occasional conversation.

The closet held nothing out of the ordinary. That in itself was a little strange. Most people stored stuff in the closets. There was no box of photos, no unused sports equipment. Nothing much at all, other than a lightweight jacket and a spare pair of sneakers.

Disturbed by that, Rowdy opened up the desk. Typical bills, checkbook, mail. All the props necessary to pull off a cover — or to actually occupy a place.

Still unconvinced, he searched beneath the drawers — and found wires.

His focus narrowed, his thoughts centered.

Pulling them free, he held the penlight in his teeth and examined the device . . . and it hit him.

Fuck.

He no sooner realized that Logan had been listening in on Pepper than he heard running footsteps in the hallway outside.

More than one person.

Hell, it sounded like a fucking battalion charging forth.

He shut off the light and hurried back to the bathroom where he'd come in, but at the open window he heard men outside. Damn it.

They'd cornered him.

On silent feet, intent on trying Logan's bedroom window, he got as far as the hall just as men entered the apartment. He detected the hush of their movements and the clinking of their weapons.

Thoughts of his sister pounded on his brain. Was she in danger? Had this whole thing been a setup?

Rage coalesced. If anyone touched her, hurt her in any way, he'd pay. Breathing steadily, Rowdy slid his knife free —

The overhead light in the narrow hall came on, momentarily blinding him. Three men faced him, all armed, their aim steady. His hand tightened on the knife hilt.

From behind him, a voice said, "I wouldn't."

Fuck, fuck, *fuck.*

With few choices left to him, Rowdy dropped the knife. His hands in the air and his heart in his throat, he slowly turned to face the voice. Rowdy was tall, but this dude stood inches over him, with wide shoulders.

Despite the jeans and T-shirt, Rowdy sensed that the blond behemoth standing there was a cop. To verify the truth, he said, "Officer . . . ?"

"Detective Bareden." To the other men, Bareden said, "Shoot him if he moves." He holstered the gun and produced handcuffs.

Laughing, Rowdy lowered his arms and only half listened as Bareden read him his rights.

So someone had seen him go in the window and had called the law? He'd be busted for breaking and entering? Big deal. Piece of cake.

Far fucking better than having a real threat on his ass.

But as Bareden led him back out the front door of the apartment, he paused to knock on Pepper's door.

Going on the alert, Rowdy tensed all over again. "What's this? What are you doing?"

"Be quiet," Bareden said.

"You don't need her." Rowdy would not overreact. He'd schooled Pepper on just such a situation. Surely, she'd follow protocol. "She has nothing to do with anything."

It was Logan who answered the knock. His gaze landed on Rowdy, and the smug prick had satisfaction written all over him.

Behind him, face white and expression haunted, Pepper stared at him. Her lips trembled. She put a hand to her mouth.

"Say nothing," Rowdy told her. "Get inside and don't say a goddamned word!"

Vision narrowing, blackness closing in, Pepper took in the sight of her brother in handcuffs. Logan was tall, her brother taller. But the brawny blond looming over Rowdy topped them all.

She reached out to steady herself — and

grabbed hold of Logan.

Through his teeth, Logan told the iron-man, "Get him out of here."

Confusion left her knees like noodles. "Logan —" She didn't understand. A strange sickness expanded, making her stomach pitch, her heart thump heavily.

Logan drew her close to his side.

"Get your fucking hands off her." Her brother resisted, lunging for Logan.

"Wait . . ." She made to move toward him.

Logan pulled her back.

Rowdy's handsome face twisted as he stared at her with dogged insistence. "This has nothing to do with you. Stay the hell out of it, do you understand me?"

He couldn't be serious. She tried to reach out to him.

Putting an arm around her, Logan locked her to his side. "Drag him if you have to, but I want him out of here. *Now.*"

"Yes, sir," one of the uniformed officers said.

Sir? The awful, undeniable truth of the situation sank in and Pepper eased away from Logan. An invisible fist clamped around her throat. Her eyes burned, with anger and with hurt. "Who are you?"

Implacable will sharpened his gaze. "Detective Logan Riske."

Detective? Fear kept her thoughts in a jumble. "You're a . . . a cop?"

Rowdy caused a ruckus, struggling on the stairs, making one cop stumble, another fall. "Stop talking to him!"

The big blond crossed his arms and stared at Logan. "You want to give some orders here, or am I taking over?"

Logan clamped a hand around her arm, drawing her away from the door and into the apartment. "Stay here. I'll be back up to talk to you as soon as I can."

When she didn't answer, he caught her chin.

"Do you hear me?"

She searched his face and hated what she saw. "You're arresting him?"

He remained cold, distant. "I'll explain everything later."

Like an explanation existed beyond the obvious? Her past had caught up to her. Logan either was or wasn't in league with Morton Andrews, but either way, it didn't much matter. Not when he exposed Rowdy, and by association, left her exposed, as well.

After all their years of caution, all they'd gone through to stay invisible and safe — she'd destroyed it all.

Thinking of how badly she'd been duped, she laughed, then quickly covered her mouth to muffle the near-hysterical sound. Tears tried to blur her vision, but she blinked them away.

Logan hesitated. "Pepper —"

"You know my name," she realized aloud. Oh, God, oh, God. "You know everything."

The other cop uncrossed his arms with a sigh. "Yeah, why don't I just go handle things? Looks like you have your hands full here."

After a last searching look, Pepper shoved past them both.

"Pepper!"

Holding her long skirt high above her knees, she went down the steps two at a time and hit the front door hard, flinging it open. She got into the yard in time to see one cop holding open the back door of an unmarked sedan. Another told Rowdy to get inside.

This couldn't be happening.

Horribly afraid that if they took him, she'd never see him again, she raced toward them. Were they legit cops? Were they *good* cops?

She had so many reasons for doubt.

Logan called out to her again, but she ignored him. Later, she would have to deal with that, with how incredibly gullible she'd been, how easy she'd made it for him to get to her brother, to use her — in more ways

219

than one.

For now, she needed to talk to her brother.

"Wait!" She got close, but one of the officers — how damn many were there, anyway? — stopped her when she was still several yards away.

Rowdy gave her his darkest, most imposing scowl. "Back inside. Now."

"I'm so sorry," she said, choking on the words, on her escalating fear and the awful, grinding shame. "I should have known. I should have listened to you."

"Say *nothing*," he ordered again.

Oh, God. "I'm sorry . . ." She took a step toward him.

"Stay away from me, damn it."

No. No, he couldn't face this alone. He couldn't do this to her.

He couldn't leave her.

"Please . . ."

"You know what to do, now do it."

"Get him in the car!" Logan grabbed her arm, and this time she couldn't shake him off.

Seeing that, Rowdy narrowed his eyes more — and continued to resist the efforts of the cops. Infusing his tone with iron, he ordered, *"Tell me you understand."*

"Shut him up," Logan barked.

The officer tried to stuff Rowdy into the

car, but he shouldered the younger guy hard and sent him reeling. *"Damn you, answer me!"*

Two cops swarmed in on him, and still he fought.

Her heart broke into shattered pieces. "I understand," she whispered. And then again, louder so that he could actually hear her, she shouted, "I understand!"

Rowdy wanted her to follow the fallback instructions. Did he honestly think she'd forgotten?

Of course he did, and with good reason. Because she had. For a little while there, with Logan, she'd forgotten . . . everything.

With her agreement out there, Rowdy stopped struggling. Rough hands pulled him around, someone knotted a fist in his hair. He got shoved into the car even though he'd stopped resisting.

Her brother was tough, one of the toughest men she knew. *He will be okay.* Pepper had to keep telling herself that or she'd fall apart.

Now wasn't the time for excesses of emotion. She had to be strong, if not for herself, then for her brother.

All along her back, she felt the heat of Logan standing close behind her. He had used her. He had set her up. And she'd made it absurdly easy.

Yes, she remembered everything Rowdy had ever taught her. But this time, to atone for her guilt, she'd do what was best for him, instead of what was best for her.

The officers waited for instructions.

From Logan.

Burying deep the hurt, the fractured hope, the absurd injured feelings, Pepper turned to face him. She needed information. She needed Logan to go on thinking he had the upper hand.

Beyond him, the big blond said, "I grabbed you a shirt."

Staring at her, Logan nodded. "Thanks, Reese." He took the dress shirt and pulled it on. As he buttoned it up, he said to Pepper, "I want you to wait in your apartment until I —"

"Go to hell."

He paused at her cold, flat tone, then nodded as if he simply accepted her reaction.

Almost as if he didn't care. But . . . of course he didn't. All of it was for show. His friendly smiles, his caring, his sexual interest . . .

Her stomach cramped at the appalling reality: everything he'd said and done had only been meant to win her over.

God, she hated herself in that moment.

To two of the officers, Logan said coolly, without emotion, "Stay here with her. See that she's safe."

So he'd leave her with guard dogs? Pepper smiled at Logan. *Perfect.*

It perplexed him and made him wary, just as she intended.

He studied her face, his gaze direct but guarded. "Your brother will be fine."

"He will be," she agreed. "No thanks to you." She'd see to Rowdy's safety. She'd do what she should have done long ago. She'd been thinking about it for a while now. Logan's deception had only spurred her to act more quickly. Thanks to him, the decision was no longer hers alone to make.

She looked past Logan to the other detective. "Reese?"

Logan frowned, but his buddy only arched an eyebrow. "Detective Bareden, Reese to my friends."

"Am I under arrest, Detective Bareden?"

"I can't imagine why you would be." He deferred to Logan. "Care to chime in?"

Disgusted, Logan tucked in his shirt. He looked a little mismatched in the button-up shirt and jeans, but then, he'd been a walking contradiction all along.

If only she'd grasped that sooner.

"I have no reason to arrest you. The men

will stay to see to your safety until I can get back."

She ignored Logan and again spoke to Reese. "You're arresting my brother?"

Morbidly amused, Reese grinned at her. "Taking him in for questioning. For now."

"Questioning about what?"

Logan stepped in front of Reese. Teeth locked, he gritted out, "I will explain to you later."

She leaned around him to see Reese. The blond sighed and shook his head as if exasperated with her.

She didn't care what they thought. She couldn't care. "Where are you taking him?"

Reese gave her the name of the police station — in the same area where Morton Andrews ran his damned club. Was that even legal? She didn't know. And what did it matter when she couldn't involve lawyers?

"When can I see him?"

Logan again blocked her view. "You want to talk to him, Pepper, you'll go through me. Now if you'll just —"

"You're wasting that arrogance on me, Detective. I'm not impressed, I'm not intimidated, and I'm no longer trusting."

His gaze sympathetic, Logan held silent.

She could take just about anything — except his pity. "You think you played me for a fool, don't you?" She wrought a credible laugh. "You're the fool. I only wish I could be around when you realize it."

"You aren't going anywhere."

After everything that had just happened, did he honestly think he could stop her? "I'm going away from you." She stepped around him and headed for her apartment. "For now, that's more than enough."

Logan said nothing, but she felt his gaze burning into her back as she retreated to her apartment.

She had a lot to do, a lot to accomplish tonight. She wouldn't waste another single second on lost causes.

And whatever his real name might be, Detective Logan was most definitely a lost cause.

CHAPTER ELEVEN

"Guess you're in the doghouse," Reese said to Logan. They rode in a car behind the sedan carrying Rowdy. Logan wasn't ready yet to deal with him. He needed to tamp down his rage — and his conscience.

The look on Pepper's face . . . God, it ate at him. "She'll come around." Somehow, he'd make it so.

"You think so, do you?" Reese followed the sedan closely. "She looked more pissed than hurt."

Reese only thought that because he didn't know her well. "She's sweet and tender-hearted. She doesn't belong in this mess."

"She's in it all the same."

Thanks to him. "Quit needling me with the obvious, damn it."

"Just saying." Reese glanced at him. "You know, I can handle this shit with Yates, if you want to be with her."

"No." Difficult as it might be, he'd remember his priorities.

"The more time you give her, the less she's going to want to hear you. Women have a way of working themselves into a lather over stuff, especially when embarrassed. I'd say using her to get her brother would qualify as an embarrassing situation."

"Until I talk to Rowdy, until I get what I need, she's not going to want to listen to anything I have to say." She'd only want to follow Rowdy's order — to be quiet, to shut him out.

Logan thought again of how the brother had shouted at her, his lack of gentleness with her. It infuriated him. "Once I have the info, I can reason with her, make her understand how important it is."

Reese let that go to ask, "How long do you think you can hold him?"

"After catching him in my place? Long enough." He hoped. "What did the lieutenant say?"

Reese squeezed the steering wheel. "I didn't tell her yet."

After giving Reese a long look, Logan put his head back. Shit. It needed only this. "She's going to be pissed."

"We'll hit the station in another ten minutes. Even if you don't call her, she'll find out soon enough."

It actually worked to his advantage that Reese hadn't gotten around to calling her. "I'll talk to her after I question Rowdy. In the meantime, I want him in holding, and I want him watched 24/7."

"I'll do it." Reese glanced at Logan again. "Better not to trust anyone else at this point."

Because Logan felt the same, he nodded. He wouldn't take a single chance that Rowdy Yates would walk before he had the opportunity to get the details needed.

Once he had the right info, he'd find a way to protect Rowdy — and he'd start building the case to get Morton Andrews, once and for all.

And after that, after all the details were in place, he'd go back to Pepper. He'd reassure her, he'd apologize to her, and he'd explain.

But he kept seeing that look on her face, and deep down, he just didn't know if any of that would matter to her.

The two officers that Logan left behind crowded into her doorway. Pepper gave them direct stares. "You can leave now. I'm not going anywhere."

"Ma'am." The lankier of the two gave her a look of apology. "We're just here to see to your safety. It'll be easier if we're inside."

"I need to shower." Yeah, not her most immediate concern, but it was as good an excuse as any. "I need to change clothes and go to my brother —"

"Detective Riske was clear, ma'am. He'd prefer that you wait here."

"I don't care about his preferences."

They looked at each other. The shorter guy stepped in farther. "You won't be able to see your brother until he's processed anyway. If you try going there, it might just slow things down."

Processed. She wanted to groan. Thanks to Morton, she knew far more about how the criminal element worked than the procedure for law enforcement. "How long will that take?"

"Depends. They'll take him to the station to be interviewed —"

"You mean interrogated."

He said nothing to that. "It takes time to do the booking paperwork, photo, finger-prints and all that. I don't know if he'll be transported to the county detention center for holding until bail or trial."

The lanky one said, "He could go straight to county. We won't know until Detective Riske returns."

So they weren't informed of the whole procedure that'd be taken? Was that a security thing, or were they just grunts who didn't deserve the details?

It really had nothing to do with anything, but Pepper heard herself ask, "Is his name really Logan?"

"Ma'am?"

She waved a hand in impatience. "Detective Riske. Is his first name Logan?"

"Yes, ma'am. Logan Riske."

Probably he'd used his first name to keep from tripping himself up while . . . seducing her.

Humiliation rolled over her in suffocating waves.

He thought her shy and introverted. He'd smiled at her while she'd shared her wretched background. He'd been gently accepting when she insisted on sex in the dark.

He'd been inside her.

It felt as if an elephant sat on her chest, crushing her heart, all but crippling her. Wrapping her arms around herself, she struggled to hold it all together.

Numb, sick, Pepper whispered, "Thank you." To keep their suspicions at bay, she gestured to her couch. "Make yourselves at home. I'm going to get ready just in case Logan calls or returns more quickly than expected."

They gave her pitying looks, thinking her

naive, thinking she didn't grasp the nuances involved.

That could be, but she understood the most important fact: people outside the law and in it wanted her brother. He could die if she didn't react quickly.

"I won't be long." And with that, Pepper turned away. Time to get things under way.

She went to her bedroom first. Buried inside the bedsprings, she found her stash of cash, her knife and .38 revolver, and the keys she'd need. She put it all inside her purse, then wrapped it up in a change of clothes, bundling everything together. As she left the bedroom for the bathroom, she glanced shyly at the officers.

Neither had sat down. They both stood at the ready, watchful, wary. Maybe they were good cops. After all, they hadn't yet tried to murder her. They hadn't called in the goons. They hadn't even threatened her.

But they did stand by her front door, trying to block her escape.

Knowing the flimsy lock offered little real protection, she locked the bathroom door behind her, turned on the shower, and wasted no time changing into jeans and a T-shirt. Putting the strap of the purse over her shoulder and across her body, she opened the window and climbed out. It had been a while, but she scurried down the tree limbs with ease, then dropped the last several feet to the ground, landing in a crouch. Anxiety making her breathless, she waited, but no one seemed to notice her. No alarms sounded.

No one gave chase.

To help disguise her, she pulled the band from her ponytail and let her long hair hang free. She didn't head for the road but instead darted to the back of the building and went down alleyways until she'd crossed a mile or more. The bright moon and security lights for other buildings made it tough to stay in the shadows.

She found Rowdy's car in the agreed-upon location. Holding back, she watched it, worried that it might be a trap, that others could have it under surveillance. But with little time to spare, she swallowed her misgivings and fear and ran to the car to quickly unlock it.

Once she had the engine started, she breathed a sigh of relief.

For too many years she hadn't been behind the wheel. She'd missed it. Even as she drove out of the lot, she watched for anyone shadowing her. She stayed alert as she stopped at a convenience store for a quick shopping spree of necessary items.

She constantly scanned the surroundings as she went next to the motel room where Rowdy had last been staying.

It took her a few precious seconds to pick the lock, and when she got the door open, she found a woman there in his bed. Un-freaking-believable.

Rowdy was such a hypocrite.

Furious, Pepper swept into the room, stormed over to the bed and jerked away the covers. The drowsy — naked — brunette stirred, looked at her, and sat up to object. "Who are you?"

"Out," Pepper said, cutting off the complaints and questions. "Now."

Confusion kept the woman huddled on the bed. "I'm not going anywhere! I'm waiting for —"

Pepper didn't want to know what alias Rowdy had used. She withdrew her knife. "Take your clothes," she enunciated clearly, "and *leave.*"

"Ohmigod!" With great haste, the woman scampered out of the bed, stepped into a slinky dress and grabbed up her sandals and purse. "You're insane!"

"I noticed." Pepper held the door for her until she'd cleared it. Insane? Maybe. Driven with her purpose? Most definitely.

Boy, would she give Rowdy hell. Later.

At least, she hoped she'd be able to.

Please, God, let him be okay.

In less than five minutes she'd cleared out all signs of Rowdy's presence. Luckily, her brother kept the majority of his meager possessions in the trunk of his car. He had only a change of clothes and toiletries in the motel room, never anything incriminating. But they couldn't take chances, and so Pepper did as she'd been taught and removed all traces of his stay. She didn't leave behind a fingerprint or even a hair.

Since the run-down place was a pay-as-you-go establishment, and no way would Rowdy have given his best-known alias, she didn't have to bother checking him out. She loaded his stuff into the car, got back behind the wheel, and headed to the safe location they'd established long ago.

Rowdy had kept tabs on it, making sure it remained abandoned, secured and well-stocked with supplies.

He expected her to go there, so she knew her brother would die before giving up the address.

In the dark of the night, without security lights and with little moonlight, the big deserted warehouse gave her the creeps. Rodents had surely inhabited it by now, and after so many years, it looked capable of crumbling down around her.

But she unlocked the rolling metal door, drove the car inside and parked in the back behind heavy, broken machinery.

The car would make her transformation easier.

And the transformation would aid in everything else.

Not knowing what to expect, Rowdy sat still, silent, in the interrogation room. A bruise under his left eye swelled, but he barely noticed. His shoulders burned from the scuffle in handcuffs before the cops had gotten him into the backseat of that car, but the small aches and pains were the least of his concerns.

He didn't know what it all meant, but he knew he had reason to worry. For himself, but especially for Pepper.

Out of necessity, the times he saw her were few and far between. To see her tonight, in the middle of a nightmare situation . . . *damn it.*

At any moment, he half expected someone to come in and gig him. It'd be easy enough for cops to do — he knew that much first-hand.

Had Pepper gotten away? Please God, don't let her —

Logan Stark — no, Riske, Rowdy had heard him tell Pepper — walked in. His unflinching gaze met Rowdy's. He didn't exactly gloat, as Rowdy had expected. In fact, the detective looked resigned, dogged and frustrated.

Logan eyed the cuffs on his wrists. They'd left behind ugly bruises, proof of his efforts to escape.

The cops hadn't given him an opportunity. So far, they hadn't made a single mistake.

Pulling out a chair, Logan sat opposite him. "You're not an easy man to find."

Staring at him with red-hot hatred, Rowdy said nothing.

Logan sat back, looked down at the table-top. "Pepper didn't give you up. I —"

"I don't need you to make excuses for my sister." He fucking well knew Pepper would never do anything to endanger him, not on purpose anyway. The blame belonged to the detective.

And to himself.

Rowdy had to admit that he'd done a piss-poor job protecting her, and now, because of his incompetence, she might be hurt after all. He should have killed Morton instead of dodging him. He should have razed Checkers so that nothing remained of the club.

He should have done so damned many things. . . .

"She doesn't deserve your rage."

Rowdy laughed. "You don't know shit about what she deserves." If Logan did, he never would have used her.

Logan sat forward. "I know she deserves better than a life on the run."

Narrowing his eyes, Rowdy considered him. Anger on Pepper's behalf? That wasn't what he'd expected from the detective, but then, what better way for the cop to try to get around him than using his sister?

Again.

"I'll kill you."

The whispered words took Logan back in his seat. "Is that what you do now? Murder?" He tossed out a file. "I looked through your history, but I didn't see that one. Is there a confession you want to make?"

"Go screw yourself." It'd be better than screwing with his sister. *No, he couldn't let himself think about that.* If he did, he'd break his own arms trying to get free so he could take Logan Riske apart.

"I need information."

Rowdy said nothing. Trying to share information had started this whole fucking catastrophe. Trusting a cop, any cop, could get him killed. Not really a good trade-off.

"You worked at Checkers a few years ago, at the same time that a city commissioner was murdered. Jack Carmin."

Saying nothing, Rowdy looked away.

Logan pressed on. "I know you remember. You went to the reporter —"

No, he hadn't, but he said only, "The reporter who got his throat cut open? Yeah, I remember it well." It was something he'd never forget. Now he prayed Pepper wouldn't forget, either. "Where the fuck were the boys in blue back then? You ever wonder about that?"

"Often, actually."

That surprised Rowdy enough that he started to reassess. "No shit?"

After a second of indecision, Logan leaned forward with purpose. Rowdy didn't know if Logan planned to slug him, murder him or make a confession of his own.

Before Logan could say a word, the other detective opened the door. "You have a call, Logan."

Logan scowled at his buddy. "The lieutenant?"

"No."

Irate over the interruption, he said, "So take a message."

The big man's gaze crawled over Rowdy, then returned to Logan. Voice lower, he said, "It's about his sister."

The chair crashed backward as Rowdy launched out of his seat. With his hands shackled to the table, he could do nothing more than cause a disruption. "Where is she?" Helplessness strangled him. "What's happened?"

Logan reacted almost as badly. "Watch him," he ordered the detective, and in two long strides he left the room.

Breathing hard, Rowdy stared at the other man. "If she's hurt —"

"Emotionally, I'm sure she's devastated." In a show of insouciance, the cop put his hands in his pockets and took a relaxed stance at the edge of the table. "The two of you seem hell-bent on ensuring that."

Taking him to task? And including Logan in the censure?

"I'm Detective Bareden, by the way. Reese Bareden."

"Fuck off." This was the weirdest situation he'd ever experienced. An arrest that maybe wasn't. Questioning that didn't cover the expected. Casual introductions. And now concern for his sister? Not just from Riske, but from Bareden, too?

None of it made sense — yet.

"You don't know anything about her." But the detective was right. Pepper needed him now, more than ever.

Still with disregard for the extreme circumstances, Bareden rolled one shoulder. "I know she's a young woman who's been put in an untenable position, with few choices left to her."

Unfortunately, Rowdy had even fewer choices than his sister. "Damn you, tell me that she's all right."

"I have no idea," Bareden said. "But I do know she slipped away from my officers."

It took a few seconds for that to sink in past the fear, for the gnawing panic to recede. Pepper had eluded the hawks.

Thank God.

Rowdy needed to sit, but he'd toppled his chair. He folded his arms on the table and put down his head instead, intent on regaining his calm.

Helplessness was not a comfortable happenstance.

He felt Bareden approach, tensed for an attack, but then heard the chair legs scrape as the detective righted it.

"My officers are diligent."

Not diligent enough, obviously. Not for Pepper. Rowdy sent more thanks heavenward before lifting his head. He smiled at Bareden. "The evidence would prove otherwise, yeah?"

Bareden ignored that to say, "That was some extreme reaction you had."

"Fuck you again."

"I'm curious." He studied Rowdy's face. "Are you worried about her giving up info on you, or for her safety?"

Gratefully, Rowdy dropped into the chair. "She'll never talk." Not that she had anything incriminating against him anyway. He rubbed tired eyes and prayed that Pepper would disappear, then stay gone. Arrangements had been made to enable her.

But would she leave him?

Logan stormed back in. He hit the door so hard that it bounced off the wall with resounding force. Reese tried to stop him, but he shoved past with uncensored aggression to grab Rowdy by the shirtfront. *"Where the fuck is she?"*

Unfazed by the anger, Rowdy eyed Logan's taut features, the bunched muscles, the clenched jaw. Huh. If he didn't know better, he'd think Detective Riske was actually worried for her.

Interesting.

He glanced at Bareden. "And you thought my reaction was extreme?"

Logan shook him. "Tell me, damn you."

"Sure thing." Knowing it'd get to the cop even more, Rowdy let his satisfaction show.

"She's where you'll never find her." And now, finally, he could relax a little — at least on that score.

Pepper stood at the sink, scissors in hand. Bold streaks of lighter blond now enhanced her natural blond color. Because she'd often cut her and Rowdy's hair, she wasn't totally inept. A salon would have been better, but it was too late for that.

It was too late for hesitation. Too late for a lot of things.

She got started, and within half an hour she'd finished. Though her hair was still long, she now had layers, more fullness and a little style.

It didn't take her long to go all out on the makeup. Shadow, liner, mascara, blush, gloss . . . She now looked nothing like the mousy, plain, timid spinster.

As awful as everything else might be at the moment, it felt good to be herself again.

Rowdy had stocked up on everything she'd need, including some of her old clothes. But the only bra she had was the awful, restrictive sports bra — and she tossed it toward a rusted barrel. With luck, she'd never have to wear that uncomfortable thing again.

She pulled on a dark tank top and skinny

jeans with ankle boots. After strapping a leather belt through the loops of the low-slung jeans, she secured her folding tactical knife in her left boot and drew her cross-body purse over her head and shoulder.

No one who knew her two years back would miss her now.

Finally, after hiding so long, she wanted to be seen. After all, if Morton's cretins didn't see her, they'd go after Rowdy instead. In jail, he was a sitting duck.

So she had to be a visible target instead. She owed her brother that much.

She'd start the night by visiting the station.

If Morton had heard of the arrest, his henchmen would be watching. Logan had known of her, so it stood to reason that Morton did, as well. She'd draw attention.

She'd draw Morton Andrews.

With any luck, his people would come after her instead of her brother.

She couldn't imagine what Logan might think when he saw the real Pepper Yates instead of the fabricated Sue Meeks.

And she didn't care!

Damn him, none of this was about him. It was about her brother, about keeping them both alive.

And if she said it enough, maybe her heart would finally start to believe it.

CHAPTER TWELVE

Lieutenant Margaret Peterson, having just arrived back at the station, stared at Logan with ill humor. Even in her off hours, Peterson didn't dress casually. She wore her suits and starched white shirts like a suit of armor.

Logan knew her to be a ballbuster of the first order. But then, at thirty-two years old, she'd seen a lot of ugly things while serving the city. Law enforcement was in her blood; she came from a long line of cops, with an even longer line of commendations.

She wanted to make a difference. She wanted to clean out the corruption.

A woman would have to be tough to do that.

They didn't come tougher than Peterson. "You have him . . . where?"

"Here." Logan handed her a cup of fresh coffee and refilled his own. "Reese is keeping him in the interrogation room."

"Detective Bareden." Her displeasure couldn't have been plainer. "I thought we agreed to keep this sting between the two of us."

"I trust Reese."

"Obviously." Big blue eyes, short but silky brown hair and a slender body were in contrast to a will of iron. "I'm not convinced that's wise."

So she didn't trust Reese, and Reese didn't trust her. In other circumstances, Logan might find that more amusing. But not now.

Not with Pepper off on her own, scared, hurt, unprotected.

"How did this happen, Detective?" Peterson perched her hip on the edge of a table in the empty conference room — a room she'd chosen for privacy. "How is it Bareden knows about this before me? I was to be kept informed first and foremost. Did you forget that little detail?"

"I needed Reese for backup." And Reese had chosen not to tell her. Logan drank more coffee, impatient with the delay.

"I could have supplied the appropriate backup."

"Unexpected things happened. When I realized I could grab Yates, I had to act fast."

"So you somehow stumbled on Rowdy

Yates? Is that what you're telling me?"

"Sort of." Logan rubbed the back of his neck. It was going to take more than a dose of caffeine to set him right tonight. "I was working on my contact — Rowdy's sister —" *who even now could be in danger, damn it* "— and he broke into my apartment."

The lieutenant's eyebrows lifted. "The apartment you're using for cover?"

"Yes." Had some of Andrews's cohorts grabbed Pepper as insurance, to keep Rowdy from talking? Fear for her safety kept his thoughts churning, all but obliterating his tactical reasoning. "I think he was somehow on to me, or he was just being extra cautious. Whatever his reason, he was probably hoping to find proof of my identity."

Speculation narrowed the lieutenant's gaze. "And Reese just happened to be hanging around to assist in the arrest?"

Here's where the lie got iffy. "I overheard Pepper on the phone, and from her side of the conversation, I made some assumptions." Logan held up a hand. "I wasn't positive of what I heard or I would have contacted you immediately. Hard to believe Rowdy would be that ballsy, you know? I asked Reese to be there mostly as a precaution."

Setting down the coffee, she pushed away from the table to pace. "A precaution that paid off."

"We have him." How valuable that'd be, Logan didn't yet know. "I'd like to get back to questioning him."

"You do that." She turned to admonish him. "But this time, you will keep me informed of every single detail. Is that understood?"

"Of course." They left the room together, the lieutenant headed for her office, Logan headed back to Rowdy. He'd get the information he needed, even if it took all night.

And then he'd find a way to get Pepper.

Reese had just finished his hushed phone call in a dark corridor when an officer intruded. Never a real moment of privacy, he lamented, not in a police station.

He dropped his cell back into his pocket and faced the younger man with an expression of curiosity.

"Sorry to interrupt, Detective Bareden, but there's someone at the front desk who wants to see you."

"Who is it?"

"No idea, sir. She asked to see her brother first, and when the sergeant told her that wasn't possible, she insisted she wanted to talk to you."

The tiredness he'd felt a moment ago evaporated. "Fascinating." He started down the long hall with anticipation. "Go fetch Detective Riske, too, will you? I'm guessing he'll want to be in on this."

"Sir?"

He wasn't about to waste time explaining. "He's in an interrogation room. Tell him you'll stay behind and keep an eye on his quarry, okay? Make it fast."

Reese left the confused officer and lengthened his stride to the front of the station. Just as he rounded the corner, he drew up short in disbelief.

No way.

Before being noticed, he studied her nose, the shape of that stubborn chin, and he almost laughed. Incredible, but it was her.

And yet, it wasn't.

In that body-hugging getup she looked . . . fuck-tastic. Great ass, even better rack. Long legs, tiny waist. A face that'd make a guy fantasize.

He couldn't wait for Logan to join him. Hands in his pockets, Reese strode forward. "Miss Yates?"

She jerked around to face him, and he soaked up the tsunami-force sex appeal. Light brown eyes sparkled with vitality. Not the reserve Logan expected. Not gentleness or timidity.

This gal was bold and ready to take on the world.

Reese whistled.

She firmed her shiny lips and tossed her hair — hair that looked freshly tumbled, as if she'd just crawled out of a lover's bed. Reese nodded. "I'm impressed."

She drew a breast-expanding breath that pulled his gaze back to her chest. "I need to see my brother."

"No can do. Not yet anyway." Reese didn't bother hiding his interest in her new look. He perused her from head to toe and back again. "Logan is still questioning him."

Hands on shapely hips, she let him look. "You don't understand what you've done."

"I did it under Logan's direction." He shrugged. "He has questions that need to be answered. That's all."

She closed the space between them to poke him hard in the chest. "You're both fools."

"Ah, ah," Reese rebuked. "No striking the detective." He removed her hand and then held on to it for good measure. No way did he want her walking off before Logan got a look at her.

As to that . . . he maneuvered them

around so her back was to the hallway. Better to let Logan get close before she spotted his approach.

"Stop that." All but vibrating with frustration, she planted her feet and then tried to free her hand.

Smiling at her, Reese held on.

She relented with an indifferent shrug. "I need you to give Rowdy a message for me."

And from behind them, Logan said, "Pepper?"

She stiffened — and didn't turn to face him. Reese watched her color rise, saw her eyes narrow and her jaw clench.

"You sent for him?" she asked as if it didn't really matter, as if she didn't really care.

"Of course."

Her gaze glued to Reese's, she asked, "Well?"

He lifted a brow.

"My brother. Will you give him a message from me?"

Reese let out a long, aggrieved sigh. "You're stealing my fun." Bodily, he turned her to Logan.

And yes, the look on Logan's face was worth it.

Logan opened his mouth but then closed it again to move nearer to her. Eyes flared, body tensed, he said again, "Pepper?"

"I'm not talking to you."

"Typical female response," Reese said.

"Is that really you?"

She held silent.

"Damn. What did you do with yourself?" Logan reached for her, and she popped him hard in the shoulder.

More in surprise than pain, Logan drew back.

"Or," Reese said, almost laughing, "maybe not so typical."

After glaring at him, Pepper gave her attention back to Logan. "No touching, *neighbor.*"

"She sneers well," Reese said, and they both ignored him.

"I don't understand." Logan visually devoured her. "What are you doing?"

"Being *me.*" She thrust up her chin. "What? You thought you were the only one undercover?"

"Jesus."

Logan couldn't seem to stop looking at her long enough to speak coherently, so Reese said, "She's plotting something, obviously."

"I'm only here for my brother."

Confused and now annoyed, Logan shoved close despite the threat of her hostility. "I've been worried about you."

She didn't back up an inch. "That's a joke, right?"

Molars sawing together, Logan all but heaved. "It's true, damn it. You were supposed to be safe and sound at your apartment. I left men to watch over you. I *told* you I'd be back to talk."

She snorted. "You also told me you were a neighbor. You told me . . . a lot of things. All of them lies."

Logan softened. "Not all."

"Screw that! I won't believe anything you have to say." Almost desperate, she zeroed in on Reese. "Will you tell Rowdy something for me or not?"

Reese opened his mouth — and Logan rudely elbowed him aside. "I already told you, if you have something to say to your brother, you can damn well go through *me.*"

Nose to nose with him, Pepper said. "Fine." It was Logan who got poked in the chest this time. "Tell him I've got it covered. Tell him not to worry." And then, more tentatively, she added, "Tell him . . . it's my turn."

Reese didn't understand that cryptic message at all, and he doubted Logan did, either. Whatever she meant, it couldn't bode well for anyone.

The sounds of the station escalated as five men came in together to file complaints. Drunk and disorderly, somewhat battered from an apparent brawl, they shouted and caused quite a disturbance while sharing accusations, the occasional shove and threats both physical and verbal.

As if oblivious, Logan and Pepper continued to watch each other.

Finally Logan nodded. "I'll tell him."

She turned to go.

"Stay." Logan reached out for her, but at her killing glare, he let his hand drop without making contact. "After I talk to Rowdy, I'll let you know what he has to say."

She shook her head. "I already know what he'll say."

"Pepper."

She stopped again.

"I don't want you to worry."

"No, you just want me to be a pawn, to play my part without getting in your way."

"No —"

"There's a lot between us, all of it bad."

"No," Logan said with more force.

"But I'll tell you what, Detective." She gave him a hard stare. "Give Rowdy my message, and we can call it even."

"Not that easily." Logan flexed his fists. "I know you're pissed, Pepper. I get that."

She laughed, shook her head and began backing up.

Reese almost felt sorry for Logan as he struggled with impotent frustration. Before it got better, it was going to get a whole lot worse for him.

He had tried to tell Logan that. He'd tried to head off the inevitable. But Logan wouldn't be derailed from his hunt for justice.

And now they'd all have to improvise.

"You and I are going to talk." Careful not to spook her, Logan closed the distance between them. Even while trying to think ahead, to plan ways to keep her close, he marveled at her makeover.

He'd known that on the inside, she was as hot as a woman could be. But standing there now in skinny jeans and a tank top, no bra, her hair loose and mouth shiny, she all but took his breath away.

Now he knew what she'd hidden from him, and he could even guess why.

"Whether you want to hear it or not," Logan said while sidling nearer, "I need to explain a few things to you." Like how he'd gotten caught in his own trap, and how much she'd come to mean to him.

Pepper kept him in her sights, always

maneuvering so that he couldn't move alongside her. "Believe me, it's clear enough. I might be disgustingly gullible, but I'm not totally dense."

"You're not gullible." But she had been eager for affection — and he'd abused that need.

"Not anymore, no."

She looked ready to bolt, so he said, "I have no plans to hurt your brother."

"Another joke, right?" Her laugh held no humor. "You've already hurt him, probably more than you've hurt me — not that you're keeping track, are you?"

Her sarcasm wore on him. She looked so different, *acted* so different. Did he actually know her at all? "As soon as I get my answers, Rowdy can get on with his life. You have my word."

She glanced at Reese, then back at Logan. "If you actually believe that, then you're in over your head and just don't realize it. But do me another favor, okay?"

She seemed to have softened her stance; she looked less wary, maybe even exhausted. Right now, he'd promise anything to ensure her safety. "Name it."

"Don't trust anyone. If you truly mean for my brother to get out of this whole-hide, then *you* watch over him. You, and only you."

Reese pretended affront. "Miss Yates, are you accusing me of something?"

Her attention stayed on Logan — and she backed farther away. "Keep your cell on you, Logan, okay? I'll be checking back off and on."

"Give me your number and I'll call you after I talk with Rowdy —"

"Not happening."

Logan gave up with a sigh. Gently, hoping she wouldn't cause a scene, he said, "I'm sorry, honey, but you're not leaving."

This time her laugh almost scared him.

Still smiling, she said, "The thing is, Logan, I'm already gone."

Before either of them could move, Pepper bolted. Being slender and fast, she easily ducked through the chaos of the drunks who'd come in and the additional officers who'd shown up to help straighten out the confusion. They were close enough to the front door that she'd exited the station in seconds, her long legs covering a lot of ground.

Both Logan and Reese gave chase, but they hit the front walk and . . . true enough, she was nowhere in sight.

Logan turned a circle, looking up and down the street, searching over the parking lot, toward the garage. He saw pedestrians, he saw traffic, parked cars and a bus.

But he didn't see Pepper.

Humid night air enveloped him, adding to his heat of annoyance and rage.

She could have gone in any direction: behind a parked car, up and over the retaining wall to the lots beyond, down the street, up the street. Hell, she could be in a car right now, watching him as he floundered.

"To have disappeared so fast," Reese mused aloud, "she had a plan. She came here with it all laid out. How long to stay inside, when to leave and exactly where to hide when the time came."

Logan locked his hands behind his neck and turned again, searching, trying to decide —

"You can't start looking for her," Reese said before Logan headed off to do just that. "You made the lady a promise about her brother. But the longer Rowdy Yates is here unattended, the less likely it is that you can keep that promise."

Irritation boiled over. From the get-go, this whole sting had gone upside down on him. Logan headed back in with a purposeful stride. The worry on Pepper's face had

258

been something he couldn't ignore. "She thinks someone here will hurt Rowdy."

"That's what I got from it, yeah." Keeping pace beside him, Reese said, "We both know there are dirty cops. Who, that's the question."

Logan cut his gaze over Reese. "She doesn't trust you." And neither did Lieutenant Peterson.

"She doesn't know me," Reese reasoned. "But you do, and that's what matters. Besides, I get the feeling the only person she does trust is her brother."

"She trusts me." No, she didn't want to. Logan got that. But she did. Otherwise she wouldn't have asked him to ensure Rowdy's safety. "She's furious, but she's smart enough to understand why I —"

Reese clapped him on the back. "Yeah, keep telling yourself that if it makes you feel better."

Without slowing his pace, Logan thought of how Pepper had looked. Not shy. Not withdrawn. Definitely not plain.

Bold. Sexy. Living, breathing temptation.

Yes, he knew what she'd been hiding: *herself.*

"Now what?" Reese asked.

Logan rumbled low, "Did you see her?"

"No man would miss her — including the

cutthroat bastards who murdered Jack."

Jesus. Was that her intent? To draw attention? He just didn't know. "This whole thing is fucked three different ways."

"It occurs to me that we have those few years where Pepper was entirely off the radar."

Logan had assumed her timid personality explained that. He had so easily pictured her staying behind while Rowdy took the lead.

Now? He didn't know what to think. "Your point?"

"I don't really have one," Reese said. "It's just that maybe you don't know her at all. Maybe you should scrap any and all assumptions and start over at ground zero."

Though he'd already had that thought, Logan dismissed the possibility. He had to believe that some part of her was real.

The vulnerable woman who talked of her painful past.

The messy housekeeper who liked late-night movies and pizza.

The runner. The cook.

The incredibly inventive lover . . .

"Why did she risk coming here when she obviously didn't want to stay?" Reese asked. "She could have called you with that message for her brother."

Logan saw the officer standing outside the interrogation room where he'd left Rowdy. "Part of her motive was to make me suffer." He'd felt it, witnessed it in her light brown eyes. "She wants to hurt me like I hurt her."

"By showing you that she's smoking hot?" Reese snorted. "That was a gift and you know it."

Actually, her appearance had shocked him, but it didn't make him want her any more than he already had. Such a thing wasn't even possible.

He shook his head at Reese. "After I talk to Rowdy, I'll know more." He stopped in front of the officer. "Did he give you any trouble?"

"Hasn't made a sound."

"Anyone else come by?"

"No."

Logan thanked him, then asked Reese to take up the guard duty. "I don't want to be interrupted again."

"Sure thing. But let's not take this too late, okay? I'm now a responsible pet owner. I can't be out all night."

Seriously? Reese was worried about his dog when they finally had Rowdy Yates in custody, and when Pepper was out doing God-knew-what?

Or maybe there was more to Reese's impatience.

Reese shook his head in resignation. "I'm here as long as you need me. You know that. But let's not drag it out, okay?"

Logan accepted that and went into the room.

Calmer now, he pulled out his chair opposite Rowdy.

The man's enigmatic gaze bored into him. "How long are we going to do this?"

"Why?" Logan asked. "You have somewhere to be?"

Rowdy shrugged. "I'm getting hungry, I need to take a piss, and I left a warm woman waiting in my bed."

"Did you tell her you were leaving to break into my apartment?"

"Actually, I wasn't really breaking in since I own the building."

At Logan's pause, Rowdy laughed.

"Yeah, you gotta wonder who the bigger fraud is, right? You undercover as a tenant, or me as an absentee property owner."

"You own the building?"

"That's right."

"Why?"

"I needed a safe place for Pepper. A place where I could touch base with her, where she could be easily overlooked." Rowdy leaned forward. "But you can get that look out of your eyes. She's long gone from there now, and she won't be back."

If Rowdy spoke the truth, he'd gone above and beyond to keep Pepper off the grid. "She'll have to go back there eventually."

"No."

"She left with nothing. All of her belongings are still there."

For a short beat of silence, Rowdy considered things, then he shrugged. "There's nothing there that she needs, believe me. I didn't count on someone like you tracking her down, but I didn't leave it to chance, either."

"Meaning?" In order to figure out where she might be now, Logan needed to learn more about how she and Rowdy had operated.

"I had contingency plans in place. Pepper has already covered her tracks."

That sounded far too final, so Logan pressed him. "Your tracks, too?"

"Yeah, mine, too." Slowly, Rowdy grinned. "I just thought of something."

Hopefully a clue he could use. "Let's hear it."

Rowdy actually laughed. "I was staying at a dump motel for a few days, and I really did leave a naked woman in my bed."

"Who?"

"I don't remember her name, but she had a world-class rack."

Logan's temper ratcheted up another notch. This was the man closest to Pepper, and it made him sick. "I don't give a shit about —"

"Odds are, Pepper went there first."

It took all Logan's concentration not to show his rage. "To cover your tracks?"

"That's right." He shook his head, still amused. "Pepper would have found her there, and knowing my sister, she probably tossed her out."

An image Logan couldn't quite fathom. "When the hell did she have time for a makeover?"

The humor fled Rowdy in a heartbeat. "What are you talking about?"

"She's only had a few hours, and if she spent part of that time cleaning up your messes —" The ringing of Logan's cell phone kept him from finishing that question.

"What do you mean, a makeover?"

It was curious how Rowdy's tone dropped, how his entire demeanor darkened.

After giving him a long look, Logan glanced at the phone. A private call, without a number or name listed. The entire night had been filled with disturbances. He flipped open the phone. "Hello?"

"Did you tell him yet?"

Pepper. Hearing her voice reassured him. For this instant, at least, she was still safe. "Where are you?"

"None of your business. So did you tell him or not?"

"He's been so talkative, I haven't had a chance to say anything yet."

Rowdy went perfectly still, listening in with interest.

"Yeah, right," Pepper said. "So tell him now."

"Soon." She'd said she would check in. How often? If she called every half hour, he might be able to track her cell. "If you'd stop running off, I could tell you a few things that you might find interesting." Like how he hadn't been pretending to care about her, and he definitely hadn't pretended to want her.

What he felt for her was as real as it could get, and it ate him up to think of her out on her own, playing hide-and-seek with a ruthless murderer like Morton Andrews.

"You want to talk about interesting tidbits, Logan? Here's one for you — you arrested the wrong person."

His heartbeat slowed. "That's as confusing as your transformation. After all, he did break in."

Rowdy sat forward. "Let me talk to her."

Logan ignored him.

"My brother is a *saint,*" Pepper said. "Everything he's done, he's done for me. He's protected me when no one else could. He's cared for me when no one else did."

That truth hurt. "Pepper . . ."

"I have to talk to her," Rowdy insisted. He reached for the cell, but the restraints held him back. "Damn you!"

Logan stood to move out of range. "Come back to the station, honey. You can help me to figure this out." *And this time I won't let you get away.*

"She was *here?*" Rowdy came to his feet so fast, he half lifted the heavy table.

Reese stepped in, but Logan waved him back out. Reluctantly, Reese withdrew.

"In an hour I'll call again. One hour, Logan, you got that?"

"Why an hour?" he asked her, hoping to keep her on the phone.

"Everything should be done by then. If you haven't yet told Rowdy, I won't call you again. And you'll never get the answers you want."

"Don't let her hang up," Rowdy shouted. He thrashed against the cuffs. "Pepper! Goddammit, Pepper, don't you dare —"

266

"She's gone."

"Gone?"

"Hung up." Closing the phone, Logan leaned on the table toward him. "You will stop shouting at her, do you understand me?"

"Do you know where she is?" Fear colored Rowdy's face, filled his tone. "You have to stop her!"

"I'd love to." His urgency became Logan's. "Why don't you tell me what it is she intends to do? Something else in your contingency plans?"

"You have no clue." Rowdy leaned across the table to speak to Logan in a harsh whisper. "You want answers about that city commissioner that was killed? You want to rein in the fucks who shot him in cold blood? You want to know why he was shot?"

Ice filled Logan's veins. "Yes." Yes to everything.

"Well, I'm not the one who saw it all go down."

"Bullshit. The reporter said —"

"It was Pepper."

The ramifications of that couldn't sink in. Logan shook his head. "No."

Watching the door, still pulled taut against his restraints, Rowdy said softly, "Understand this, you bastard. If I had any other

267

choice, I wouldn't tell you shit. But if Pepper was here, then she's not following the procedure we laid out. And that means her life is on the line."

No, and no again.

"Make up your mind and fast, Detective. Shit's about to get ugly. Whose side are you on here?"

CHAPTER THIRTEEN

For an answer, Logan stepped to the door and locked it. He doubled-checked that the intercom was off, too.

Reese heard the lock click, tried the knob, then looked in the window with a dark scowl. He pounded on the door, demanding entrance.

Of course Reese didn't like being cut out, and the lieutenant would be livid, but he'd deal with them both later.

Close to Rowdy again, he said, "Tell me."

"It's . . . complicated. Convoluted."

"So give me the short version. Fast." If Pepper was in direct jeopardy, the sooner he knew the details, the better he could help her.

Rowdy waffled only a second. "Pepper and I both worked at Checkers. I was a bouncer, guard, doorman, you name it. Pepper was an evening maid."

"A maid?"

"Cleaning the offices, the bathrooms, that sort of thing. It was a great-paying job for me, and Pepper made a decent wage. Working nights, downplaying her looks, and keeping a low profile left her mostly off the radar of the boss. She was . . . insignificant to the operation. That's how she and I both wanted it. If she'd been a waitress or something . . ." Rowdy shook his head.

Hatred burned like acid in his stomach. "Andrews would have hit on her."

"Hit on her?" Rowdy snorted. "He thought women were his for the asking. No one dared say no to Morton."

"Not even a city commissioner?"

Rowdy rubbed a hand over his face. "You knew him?"

"Jack Carmin was my best friend."

Rowdy looked down at his hands. "Morton had cops in and out all the time, helping him with his business. I saw more bad cops than I ever saw good."

"Jack wasn't a cop, but he was definitely one of the good guys."

Rowdy accepted that without question. "The cops . . . they were well paid to look the other way when Morton did deals around town."

"What type of deals?"

"Drugs, guns, muscle . . . whatever was

needed. You name it, he did it."

"You know this how?"

"Not the way you're thinking. Morton trusted me only so far as the door. As the bouncer, I let in the guys on the payroll and stalled the cops who came to snoop. When I couldn't stall them, I hit an alarm that sounded only on the third floor to let Morton know they were around. That gave him time to clear out the upstairs rooms. By the time the cops got through all the locked doors, there was nothing to see."

"You interfered with justice."

He made a rude sound. "Hard to know when justice came calling. You guys all look the same."

"Meaning you couldn't tell the good from the bad?"

"I knew who to let in and who to block. But I didn't have details on what, when or where. I wasn't kept in the loop on arrangements. Far as I knew, creeps fed off creeps. If one died, another just as bad took his place. I didn't have firsthand knowledge of any of the corruption, but I didn't see any angels in the mix."

"You said you were muscle?"

"Not to beat down Morton's adversaries. The muscle I supplied was in restraint and booting out the guys who got too unruly, or too drunk. I never killed anyone, although I sent a few home with blood and bruises."

That didn't make Rowdy a saint, as Pepper claimed, but it didn't really taint him with the same corruption as Andrews, either.

"I was already making plans to get us both out of there. But it all went to hell before I could."

"Jack?"

"I don't really know that much about him. From what I could figure, Morton wanted more influence, so he went to your friend. Being the city commissioner, he could have reassigned Morton's cops to certain areas so they could be more effective."

Areas they had since occupied, maybe because Jack was out of the way. Without a single doubt, Logan said, "Jack refused."

"I assume so. There'd have been no reason to make an example of him otherwise."

"Jack was the type of man who would have done what he could to expose it all." There was one thing that didn't make sense to Logan. "He went there to meet with Morton? Without backup?"

"I'm guessing they grabbed him off the street," Rowdy said, his expression dark, his hands fisted. "I was down on the main floor, and we had a crowd that night, so I didn't see any of it. Pepper had cleaned that area earlier and was supposed to be working on the main floor with me. But she realized she'd left the keys to the storage room upstairs."

Shit. Thinking of what she'd blundered into, what she'd seen, how close she'd been to danger, Logan went rigid.

Rowdy spoke in a quiet whisper that showed he felt the same as Logan. "She stayed hidden in the boardroom and kept quiet. But she could hear everything."

"Jesus."

Almost tortured, Rowdy looked away. "She said they dragged in your buddy. He'd already been worked over and was in a bad way, not really fighting back. Pepper heard Morton say that he'd use him as an example to others."

Knowing what his friend had gone through, how he'd been beaten, Logan breathed deeper.

"The thing is . . ." Rowdy stared hard at Logan. "There were two other cops there. One of them fired the gun."

Though Logan already knew how it had ended — with a bullet — knowing that Jack had died at the hand of a cop twisted him with rage.

"You know the cops?"

He shook his head. "You all look the same to me — self-righteous with a hard-on for exerting authority."

Logan let that fly. "Male or female, black or white —"

"Men, white." He shrugged. "At least, that's what Pepper assumed from what she heard."

"She came to you?"

"Not right away. She sat in that room for over an hour, afraid to move." His mouth quirked in a sad smile. "She said she was afraid if they found her, they'd kill me, too."

"They knew you were related?"

"No, but Pepper's always been like that. A real mother hen. Protective." Rowdy closed his eyes. "I try to keep her safe, but I'm all she has, and —"

"She loves you."

Rowdy looked him in the eyes and said again, "I'm all she has."

Sick, more scared for her than ever, Logan dropped back in his seat. "When did you find out?"

"We were swamped that night. I had six hours overtime. I could tell something was wrong, but I didn't want to risk talking to her overlong, and whenever I did catch her to ask, she said she was fine."

"If they'd caught her that night . . ."

"She didn't know who to trust," Rowdy explained. "She knew the cops were involved, so how could she go to them? She didn't want them to just get away with it, so she tried talking to a reporter, but that idiot talked to the wrong person about his scoop —"

"A scoop he got from . . . Yates." Not necessarily Rowdy Yates. Just a last name.

All this time, it was Pepper. And here he'd thought in the long run, he'd be helping her, freeing her from an inconsiderate brother.

Instead, he'd made her a target. Thanks to him, she was now in more danger than ever.

Reese paced outside the door. What the fuck? Logan had to be slipping to get in cahoots with Rowdy. Even now they sat together at the table in hushed conversation.

Sharing details.

Coming to conclusions.

Plotting . . . something.

Logan had actually locked him out!

Perturbed, Reese again looked in the small door window. The surveillance cameras were off. Neither man paid him any mind. What did it mean?

"Detective Bareden?"

Reese wanted to groan even as he turned to face Lieutenant Peterson. "Ma'am?"

Her gaze was sharp enough to slice through his usual disregard. She gestured at his stance outside the door. "Playing guard dog?"

Which would be better — to let her think that or to tell her the truth, that Logan had excluded him? Choosing to be noncommittal, he shrugged.

"I want to talk to Detective Riske."

Reese smiled down at her — something he knew she disliked. She had the attitude of an Amazon but the stature of a runt, and it bothered her that he was so much bigger in every way. "I'm sure he'll be right out."

Her chin tucked in. "I'd like to talk to him *now.*"

Shit. Reese wanted to stall for Logan, to give him time to . . . what? Come to his senses and include him again?

Well, yeah.

"The thing is, Logan hasn't really had a chance to talk to Yates uninterrupted."

"Why not?"

"Because there have been . . . interruptions." He gave her a "duh" look.

Exasperated, Peterson folded her arms and glared at him. "Your attitude is bordering on insubordination, Detective." She gave him *the* look, the one that made most in the police force stop and reevaluate. "Maybe you need a little beach time to collect yourself."

Reese rubbed the back of his neck. He got that Peterson had to be a strong woman. But did she also have to be such a pain in the ass?

He had no choice but to spit out a fact. "Rowdy's sister came to visit."

After a blank stare, she dropped her arms. "His sister?"

"Yeah. I take it they're close. She's the one Logan was schmoozing to get to Rowdy."

"I know who she is, damn it!" She narrowed her eyes in thought. "Why did she come here?"

"To see her brother?"

Her slim brows came down. "If you don't know, just say so."

"To see her brother."

A long sigh of impatience left Peterson looking deflated. "And did she?"

"What?"

Suddenly her temper snapped. "You're doing it on purpose!"

Reese held back a smile. "Doing what?"

Jerking around, she paced a few steps away, then stormed back. A cold facade now hid her irritation. "I'm a nanosecond away from disciplinary action. In fact, few things would please me more."

"That's a pity." To his way of thinking, women should have many other pleasurable options. "I'm only trying to answer your questions."

Her smile was mean. "Detective Bareden, you will either open the door or get out of my way. *Now.*"

Gallant when it suited him, Reese moved to the side and gestured for her to do as she pleased.

She reached for the knob, turned it and realized the door was locked.

Once again on the edge of exploding, she said, "What, *exactly,* is going on here?"

"Since I'm on the same side of the door as you, I can't really say." He lounged back against the wall. "But I assume Logan will fill us in the moment he wraps it up." God willing, that'd be soon.

Squeezing his eyes shut, Rowdy said, "The same people who murdered that commissioner when he wouldn't play ball also cut the reporter's throat to keep the story from going public. They're the same people who would kill *anyone* who knew the truth."

Including Pepper.

The puzzle pieces fit together to create a complete picture for Logan. "When the reporter got murdered, you stepped in as the snitch? You encouraged everyone to think it was you."

"It was more believable that I'd have been the witness, so it wasn't hard to get that idea circulating. All I had to do was take off and my guilt was assumed. Pepper objected, of course, but I figured . . . better me than her."

Logan agreed. "All this time . . ."

"I've done what I could to keep her safe. As soon as she told me, we booked. I used what cash we had to get alternate identities. With the cops involved, I didn't dare try catching a plane or even a train. I won the apartment building in a card game from an old guy who's since passed away. I got Pepper set up there, and then I kept my distance so no one else would stumble on the truth or try to use her to get me."

"As I did." Logan ran a rough hand through his hair. "You were good at covering your tracks. I spent a lot of time looking for you, doggedly chasing down every possibility."

"I figured most would look for a brother and a sister together. So I hid, and Pepper changed everything, her entire life."

"Her appearance." While Logan understood Rowdy's intent and the protectiveness that drove him, Pepper's life had not been ideal. She deserved so much more.

"I hate what this has done to her. I didn't know which cops were dirty or how high up the corruption might be. All I knew for sure was that those involved were coldblooded enough to murder one of their own without a blink. Disappearing seemed to be the only option."

"It probably was — then."

"And now?"

It was actually smart for Rowdy to lay low while hiding Pepper out in plain sight, not close to Morton, but not so far away, either. Even with all his resources, it had still taken considerable time for Logan to catch up with them.

"I can help."

"You've blown her cover."

Unable to deny it, Logan accepted that — and more. "She wanted me to tell you that you've done enough. That now it's her turn."

Pained, Rowdy looked away. "She was back to her old self?"

"I have to assume." Urgency drove Logan to his feet to pace. "I tried to keep her here, but —"

"Unless you find her and stop her, she'll move heaven and earth to try to end this."

"End it how?"

He rolled a tired shoulder, his expression ravaged. "She'll probably head to the night-club to go after Morton. It's the only way she knows to protect me." Rowdy narrowed his eyes. "The big question now is whether or not she'll actually trust you enough to let you help her."

Logan could say with certainty that she wouldn't. She was hurt, angry and adamant that he needed to be kept at a distance. He deserved that — especially after taking her brother, the most important person in the world to her.

The only person she could rely on.

Making up his mind, Logan pulled the keys from his pocket. "Together, we'll convince her." It was the only way he could think of to locate her and to keep her safe.

Whether he liked it or not, his priorities had all changed.

Number one on the agenda was protecting Pepper.

After that, he'd get Morton Andrews, and the dirty cops, and anyone else involved in the corruption.

Once Logan freed him, Rowdy flexed his hands and nodded at the door. "Want to tell me how you're going to get past that one? Because I don't think he's going to willingly look the other way."

Logan turned, saw Reese eyeing them through the door window, and said, "It'll be fine. Just follow my lead."

"Not like I have a choice." Rowdy followed him to the door. "But if you're wrong, if he hurts her, I'll kill him."

Logan didn't correct Rowdy. But if Reese hurt Pepper, Rowdy wouldn't get a chance to touch him.

Logan would take care of it himself.

It made Rowdy edgy enough to be in a packed police station, but to have to trust Logan to guard his sister, too? That was asking a lot.

Never mind that Logan Riske maybe had valid, very personal reasons for tracking him down. And the detective did seem to genuinely care about Pepper, and vice versa.

In Rowdy's experience, cops were not his friends, period. They protected the ordinary people, the middle class, the privileged few — and each other.

Those forced to take drastic measures to survive? They were a nuisance at best, disposable at worst. In his lifetime, he'd been referred to as a troublemaker, a bottom feeder. To ensure he and Pepper stayed together, he'd spent years skirting legit jobs. Once she was of age, he'd still felt compelled to keep her as close as possible.

Didn't take a genius to figure out what drove him; at an early age, he'd lost everyone and everything important in his life — except for Pepper. She was it for him. *Numero uno.* His entire world. He'd die for her.

And he'd kill for her.

But God Almighty, he'd never wanted her to feel the same.

He and Pepper had spent their lives trying to steer clear of the criminal element and cops alike. Neither fit into their lives.

Survival. That's all they'd really wanted. Enough shelter, enough food, comfortable clothes, occasional entertainment.

Safety. Security.

And for him, a warm, willing woman when the past weighed too heavily on his brain. He needed nothing else.

He definitely didn't need the steel-eyed official-looking gal now showing her disdain.

"Detective Riske?"

They stood clustered outside the interrogation room. It was clear that Logan hadn't counted on running into the woman.

Angry tension all but vibrated off her

petite frame. She was more than a little pissed and not succeeding much at hiding it.

With worry for Pepper prodding him, Rowdy considered making a run for it. But more than a few cops stood between him and freedom. If he ran, they would assume him guilty of something — and he was. Hell, he was guilty of all kinds of shit. Not all of it was illegal, but that probably wouldn't matter much in the big scheme of things.

Not in a police station filled with guys who got a stiffie over carrying a piece. To him, it seemed that most cops were trigger-happy and waiting for an excuse to exert their limited clout.

If he got himself locked away again, who would save Pepper from herself?

Reese spoke up. "Lieutenant Peterson had hoped to join the interrogation, but, ah, Logan, you'd locked the door, so . . ."

Lieutenant? Huh. Rowdy surveyed her and had to be impressed.

Fury brought her forward so that she faced them all, one small woman challenging a trio of big men.

Yeah, he was sexist. Not the worst of his faults.

In a clipped but icily polite tone, she

ordered, "Gentlemen, back inside if you please."

For someone so diminutive, Rowdy noted, she carried herself with enough brass to back up the attitude. She strode into the room he and Logan had just vacated, and then stood there with the door open, waiting for them to join her as ordered.

Damn it, they did not have time for this.

Reese went in first, and Logan, the mistrustful bastard, stayed at Rowdy's back until he entered.

"So." She shut the door, crossed her arms and leaned back on it. "What is this?"

Reese looked at Logan. So did Rowdy.

"I don't have enough to hold him."

Her mouth firmed. "Did he tell you who killed the commissioner?"

"Apparently that story was blown all out of proportion by the reporter," Logan lied. "He didn't see much and remembers even less."

"But the reporter —"

"Must've jumped the gun," Rowdy interjected. "He offered to pay me for info, and I agreed. But he never came back, so I forgot about it."

Unconvinced, the lieutenant narrowed her eyes. "The breaking and entering? The apartment you were using?"

"He just wanted to see his sister," Logan said. "And since he wants to be helpful now, I'm letting that go."

"I really do," Rowdy told her, trying to sound sincere when every beat of his heart made him more anxious to get on the move. If he didn't find Pepper soon, she'd get in over her head — or worse.

But first, he had to win over the lieutenant — so he'd turn on the charm and see where that got him. Not a hardship. She was sort of cute in a buttoned-up, too-rigid way.

When next the lieutenant glanced at him, Rowdy gave her his wickedest, most intimate smile.

Her attention snagged on him for a longer look. After a lengthy silence, she frowned. "And just how do you think to help?"

Since he had no clue what Logan wanted him to say, he shrugged. "However I can." The way he said it, sort of low and suggestive, brought color to her face.

Reese coughed.

Logan stepped in front of Rowdy. "We're going back to the apartment to go over the time line, dig out what paperwork I have on my computer, see if there's any trail at all. We'll try to match up dates, share some photos with him, and see if he recognizes anyone who was with Jack right before he was murdered."

The lieutenant considered all that. Her big blue eyes met Rowdy's again. "You worked at the club?"

"Bouncer." Rowdy shifted to the side of Logan. "I saw a ton of people come and go. I remember many of the regulars. Maybe with some pics . . ." He looked at her mouth, then back up to her eyes, and he smiled again. "Who knows? Something might click."

Her compressed lips softened, but she said nothing. After a start, she turned to Logan with renewed purpose. "His sister was here?"

Both Logan and Rowdy went still; neither of them looked at Reese.

"She was," Logan finally said. "Briefly. When I told her I wanted to interrogate him before she could see him, she bounced."

"Where did she go?"

"No idea," he said with feigned disinterest. "Probably back to her apartment. Why?" Logan stared at her. "Did you want me to pick her up?"

The lieutenant waved that off. "No, no need for that. I'm sure she's been through enough tonight." She emphasized that with a frown at Rowdy. "Actually, I prefer you treat her with utmost respect and care. The last thing we need is for her to lawyer up."

"She wouldn't," Rowdy stated. "Too costly, and there's no reason, right, since I'm not under arrest?"

"And since he's cooperating," Reese added.

"Make sure." The lieutenant encompassed them all in that order. "I do not want the press to get hold of this, not unless we get something concrete to go on."

Rowdy let out a breath.

"I'm sure you understand the importance of keeping those under investigation in the dark as long as possible."

"Absolutely." Logan waited.

Still not satisfied, the lieutenant asked, "Does anyone else know he was here?"

"The three of us," Logan told her. "That's it."

She scowled at Reese.

"Hey," Reese said. "I can keep a secret."

There were obvious bad feelings between the lieutenant and Detective Bareden. Later, Rowdy thought, he'd ask Logan about it. But for now —

"The night isn't getting any younger," Logan said abruptly. "Hell, morning will be rolling around soon. I'd like to get going. So if there's nothing else . . . ?"

The lieutenant opened the door and gestured for them to go. Reese headed out, then Rowdy. Before Logan could clear the doorway, she caught his arm.

"If Andrews has even a clue that we're onto something, it could mean another death. Yours," she said. And then with a look at Rowdy, "Or his."

Or his sister's, Rowdy thought, but he tried to keep his expression impassive.

"Keep him, and his sister, under wraps," the lieutenant ordered. "Understand?"

Logan nodded. "Will do."

She sent another frown toward Reese. "You better know what you're doing, Logan. All this coming and going, dead ends and loose ends. You've had enough time. Wrap it up, and let's move on." And with that, she walked past them all.

Alone in relative privacy, Reese turned to Logan. "So what's it to be? Leave me in the dark, or let me help?"

Rowdy knew how he'd prefer to leave it: trust as few people as possible.

When Logan's phone rang, they all froze. Rowdy held his breath, but as soon as Logan answered the call, he knew it was Pepper.

CHAPTER FOURTEEN

After ending the call, Morton placed the phone on his desk and turned to pace the small confines of his office space. Even at this ungodly hour, the club remained in full swing, both the first and second floor crowded with men anxious to spend their money.

He expected his guest to show up any minute now. New ventures would have been cemented. More money made. More power acquired.

He did not need this new problem. And that's what it was: a grade A, supernova problem. *"Motherfucker."* Snatching the phone back up, he hurled it into a wall, narrowly missing one of his bodyguards.

The outburst did little to vent his rage but caused quite a reaction as others jumped, yelped and flinched. He paid no attention to them. They were disposable grunts, there to serve him, to protect him.

The idiots had failed.

But they weren't the only ones.

Rowdy Yates was alive and in police custody. That meant the cop had failed him, too.

Glancing around at the bodyguards who, through orders, had a certain look — a look that mirrored his own — Morton knew what he had to do now. It was inconvenient but not as much so as prison. He'd handle this as he handled everything else.

He would destroy the problem, bury it and move on.

Logan started everyone walking again while saying, "Pepper. Where are you?"

She ignored the question to say, "I'm really burning up the phone lines tonight, right?" She laughed, but he heard the strain and what sounded like fear. "I'm going to keep this really short and sweet, so pay attention. I'm going to the club."

"No, don't do that."

"Too late. If you want Andrews, get your behind over here and you can catch him in the act. Rowdy can tell you how to get in. But no fanfare, Logan. Do not send in your police buddies, or you could get me killed."

His heart lodged in his throat. While he walked fast toward the lot where he'd parked, he infused as much calm into his tone as he could drum up. "Listen to me, honey. Your brother —"

"If they hear you coming, I'm screwed. So seriously, Logan. If you don't want me dead —"

"You know I don't, damn it!" He swallowed the ferocity and tried for another dose of calm reason. "I want to protect you, I want —"

"Great," she said, cutting him off. "So don't screw this up."

And she disconnected the call.

His discipline shattered, Logan broke into a jog. "She's going to the club."

Both Rowdy and Reese kept pace alongside him as they maneuvered through the sally port and out to the lot. Rowdy grabbed his own cell but muttered, "Damn it, she's not answering."

"For the love of . . ." Reese grabbed Logan's arm, pulling him to a halt. "This is insane. You go in through the park. I'll circle around from the other side. Whoever finds her first can head her off from doing anything stupid."

Rowdy started to protest, but Reese said, "Not a word from you! We don't have time to argue about it."

Logan agreed. "It'll take twenty minutes

to get there, but don't use your siren."

"Noted." And with that, Reese jogged to his car.

Forcing aside all uncertainty, every ounce of hesitation, Pepper studied the setting before her. She knew that guards protected Checkers not only from within but also from the exterior, every minute of every hour of every day. Morton Andrews spent a small fortune on security. Getting to him wouldn't be easy.

After shutting Logan down midsentence, she'd set her phone on vibrate. The last thing she needed was a call in the middle of her setup. She'd already felt her phone buzzing, so that had to mean he was concerned, right?

Fortified by that thought, she started forward.

She prayed that she hadn't entirely misjudged Logan, that deep down he was just a good cop trying to find justice.

She had to believe that, because anything else was unthinkable.

Anything else meant her brother might already be gone.

Several yards away from the club, she saw two goons, each wearing an earphone, no doubt armed, chatting to each other while keeping watch on all coming and going down the walk. In the business area, well-lit establishments lined the street, everything from liquor stores to tattoo parlors to restaurants and gas stations.

Neon signs flashed. Night owls laughed and talked, some outside their cars, others hailing cabs, a few just loitering. No one should have paid undue attention to a woman alone.

But with her gaze zeroed in on the men, they *felt* her approach — as she'd intended.

Without glancing away, Pepper walked right up to them. The one closest to her looked her over with appreciation. The other faded back a little, probably to keep the advantage.

Like a woman without a care, Pepper stopped before the biggest goon. "I need to see Morton."

A mean smile curled his mouth. "Yeah, you and a dozen other women."

Now, that was funny. Pepper copped a stance that she hoped hid her jitters. "I seriously doubt any of them see him by choice."

The condescending arrogance darkened to irritation. "Get lost, honey."

"Here's what you'll do, *honey.* Inform Morton that Pepper Yates is here, and if you behave, I won't tell him that you tried to send me packing. Because you know, if he found out, he'd probably kill you for being so incompetent."

Skepticism showed, but it couldn't win out over the guy's healthy respect for Morton's ruthlessness. He gave a slight nod, and his buddy made the call. He spoke so softly that Pepper couldn't hear him over the human congestion spilling out of the club, but she knew he spoke to Morton's number one guy.

And judging by the look on his face, Morton had agreed to see her.

Few at the club had ever noticed her while she worked there, and the only photos available were the same that Logan had. Morton might not recognize her, but he knew the name.

Because she was Rowdy's sister.

And Rowdy had set himself up to be the snitch.

Too many people wanted her brother, all because he'd tried to protect her. She *had* to do this.

"Let's go," the big goon said. He reached for her arm, but Pepper stepped back.

"Morton is inside?" She assumed he was, but she needed it verified. If she'd miscalculated, if they tried to stuff her into a car to transport her somewhere else, she'd scream bloody murder.

It might not save her, but at the very least, others would notice.

"He's in his offices."

"Above the club?"

Impatience shortened the goon's temper. "Are you coming along or not?"

Pepper got her stiff lips to form a smile. "I am." She stepped ahead of the guy and marched toward the club. Her heart beat in time to her every footfall. The closer she got to the hubbub around the club, the sicker she felt. Nausea churned in her stomach and her temples throbbed, making her almost light-headed.

In an iron grip meant to hurt, the goon took her arm to steer her around to a back entrance. Breathing too hard and too fast, Pepper willed her feet to keep moving, one in front of the other. She didn't want to be dragged. She wanted, *needed,* to do this on her own terms.

Morton Andrews had plagued them long enough. If Logan didn't get there in time, well then, she'd find a way to end the miserable cretin one way or another.

At the back of the building, beneath bright security lights, he stopped. One of the additional guards, stationed to keep anyone from intruding, scowled. "What are you doing? You can't bring her back here."

"Andrews's orders."

"Ah." There was a pause as the men looked at her with carnal assumptions. They chuckled in shared appreciation of the situation.

The bastards.

Pepper didn't look at any of them. She didn't look at anyone until the goon turned to her.

She saw his slack-jawed expression, the intent in his gaze; he would frisk her, and she knew he would make it as unpleasant as possible.

Raising her chin, she feigned indifference — and suddenly a deafening boom sounded above the clamor of patrons, music and conversation. *Gunshot?* Where? Who?

Glass exploded from third-story windows, raining down around them. Acrid smoke clogged the air, burning her nostrils. No, not a gunshot. Then . . . ?

Before that thought could fully form, a shrill alarm cut through the night.

Covering her ears, confused by the commotion, Pepper cowered. At that first loud blast, her nerves had shattered. A mingling of fear and confusion kept her heart racing double-time.

What had happened?

Weapons drawn, two other guards ran past them while talking into headpieces. Screams sounded out front, followed by a stampede of bodies fleeing the building.

Shoved to the side, Pepper fell to her rump, then scampered back farther. She crouched there until in the midst of shouted orders she heard the word *bomb.*

Oh. Dear. God.

Everything suddenly made sense. She looked up to see smoke pouring from the windows. Someone had exploded a bomb on the third floor of the club.

The floor Morton Andrews used for his office.

The office . . . where he'd been waiting to talk to her.

"We might not be able to find her." Rowdy, who rode with him, got more uneasy by the moment. "She knows how to hide."

Logan had firsthand knowledge of just how adept Pepper could be at hiding. Hell, he'd had sex with her and hadn't gotten a good look at her. "I hope you're right." Going a little too fast, he turned the corner. They were now only minutes from the club. "She can't very well launch an attack on anyone while hiding away."

A distant siren sounded, growing louder

by the moment.

Rowdy sat forward. "Smoke."

"What?" More sirens, joined by flashing lights.

"In the sky." Rowdy's shoulders bunched. He tunneled his fingers into his hair, and his jaw loosened. "Son of a bitch . . ."

A fire truck pulled up to the club just ahead of them. Another was already there. Firefighters launched into action. A small crowd milled outside, some sitting on the curb, others bent double coughing. An ambulance blazed onto the scene, but they didn't see anyone injured.

"She wouldn't," Rowdy said. He grabbed Logan's arm. *"She wouldn't."*

Acid burned in Logan's gut. His jaw clenched so tight that his temples throbbed.

Smoke poured from the shattered windows of the upper floor of the club. Most of the damage appeared to be in the back of the building. From the look of it . . . "A bomb."

Furious, Rowdy jerked Logan around. "Pepper would never do anything like that, so get that idea out of your head right now." Then, breathing fast and hard, his expression bleak, he sank back. "Jesus, what if she was inside?"

"No." Logan couldn't bear that thought.

At the moment, his brain felt almost numb. Possibilities chewed on his conscience, each one worse than the one before.

He had to think. He had to figure out what to —

Rowdy lurched against his door, trying to get it open, but Logan hit the locks.

Turning on him, Rowdy shouted, "She could be *in there*! She could —"

Logan's cell rang.

Both men stalled. Logan jerked out the phone and opened it on the first ring. "Pepper?"

"Logan." Her voice was high and shrill. "Oh, my God, Logan."

"Where are you?" He scanned the area, looking for her, praying he'd find her.

"There was an explosion."

He heard the trembling of her voice. He heard the shock. She needed him to take over, and that's exactly what he'd do. "It's okay now. Tell me where you are."

"There were people inside," she continued, as if she hadn't even heard him. "Music and noise and I was . . . a guard was ready to frisk me, and then he was going to take me in to see Morton."

"So you're still outside?" Was she even now being watched by Morton's men? "Is anyone with you?"

300

"The guards all ran off. At first, I wasn't sure what had happened, but then someone mentioned . . . a bomb." She choked. "I don't know if anyone was hurt. I don't know if Morton is still alive."

"It'll be okay, I swear." He could hear her breathing, but she said nothing. Going with sudden inspiration, Logan said, "Pepper, Rowdy wants to talk to you. Don't you dare hang up on me, honey. Do you understand? I'm giving the phone to your brother."

Rowdy grabbed the cell from Logan, saying in a rush, "Are you okay?"

Rowdy hesitated, nodded, and as he slumped back in the seat he closed his eyes. "Thank God."

"Tell her to come to us." Logan continued scanning the outskirts of the area. Reese approached from the other side of the devastation, walking, staring in amazement. He looked as stunned as Logan felt. "This is dangerous, Rowdy. Too damn dangerous."

Reese faded back into the shadows, out of the main flow of the milling throng.

Rowdy hesitated, maybe thinking of a way to keep Pepper safe from one and all.

The sense of menace amplified, the pressure built inside Logan. "We can't linger here, damn it. She's a sitting duck. If anyone sees her —"

Making up his mind, Rowdy sat forward. "I'm with Logan, in his truck. You need to come with us."

Rowdy shushed whatever argument she gave — if indeed, she argued. Logan couldn't be sure.

"We'll be safe, both of us, but not if you don't get your ass over here, right now."

Logan kept watch while Rowdy told her where to find them.

"No, stay on the line," Rowdy said, "until I see —"

And just like that, she appeared across the street, hovering behind a bus stop shelter, her gaze watchful.

Again Rowdy tried to get out of the truck. Logan cursed as he held him back. Considering Rowdy's size and the added strength of his emotion, it wasn't an easy feat. "People will recognize you! Stay put, and tell her I'm coming to get her."

Rowdy relented. "Logan is coming for you, hon. I'm in the truck waiting. Don't you dare budge an inch."

"Get behind the wheel," Logan told Rowdy before leaving the truck and jogging over to Pepper.

She stood there, her hair tossed by the evening breeze, her expression wounded but her stance defiant.

In his lifetime, Logan had faced injustice of every kind. He'd dealt gently with rape victims, survivors from random shootings, the bereaved, the insane, evil and immorality.

Nothing and no one had ever leveled him like this.

As he got closer to Pepper, she took a step back, then planted her feet again. "If you hurt my brother, I swear I'll —"

Logan grabbed her up against his chest, crushing her close, his face in her hair, his hands opened against her back.

She didn't exactly return his embrace, but she didn't shove him away, either. "Logan?"

He had her, and he'd be damned before he let her go again. To reassure himself that she wasn't injured, he held her back, smoothed her hair, searched over her.

She released a broken breath. "Don't you dare think that I —"

"We have to move. You can explain everything later." He turned with her tucked close to his side.

"Nothing to explain."

"Fine." With so much confusion surrounding the area, no one appeared to pay any attention to them. But that didn't mean they were safe. Hell, no.

He feared a sniper, another bomb, even

an ambush.

Reese didn't approach the truck, but then, he'd have enough sense not to once he saw everything unfolding. Rowdy had the truck idling as he waited for them. Logan tucked Pepper into the middle of the bench seat, then got in beside her.

"Drive."

With the truck already in gear, Rowdy asked, "Where?"

"Out of here for now." He fastened Pepper's seat belt, then his own. She didn't fight him when he took her hand.

Rowdy glanced at them both before carefully turning the truck and driving away.

Pepper took an audible breath. "I need the stuff out of the car."

"Forget it." Logan wanted only to get her as far away from the area as possible.

She didn't appreciate his consideration. "No, *you* forget it! It's important."

"I see you're recovering from your shock." Now that he saw her unharmed, all his worry coalesced into rage. She could have been killed. She *would* have been killed. "What you did, coming here like this, it was incredibly reckless."

"Yeah, well, if you hadn't —"

"You cleared out my motel room?" Rowdy asked with an abrupt interruption.

That redirected her anger. "Yes, including the bimbo you left in the bed!"

Watching the road, Rowdy turned a corner and said, "She was a very nice girl." And then, "Everything is in the trunk of my car?"

Deflating, Pepper crossed her arms and glared at Logan. "Yes."

If the situation weren't so dire, Logan could have appreciated the irony. He'd wanted Pepper to get Rowdy. Now he had Rowdy, but all he could think about was keeping Pepper out of harm's way. He rubbed the bridge of his nose. "Where is the car?"

"I parked it two blocks north of the club, in the lot of a pawn shop. The keys are under the passenger seat."

"Anything . . . incriminating inside?"

She turned dagger-eyes on him. "You mean, since we're such heinous criminals and all that?"

In the face of her hostility, being reasonable wasn't easy. "I didn't say that."

"Not in those exact words, maybe. But you thought it all the same."

He gave her a quelling look that she tried to ignore. "We'll clear all that up very soon. But for now, I meant is there anything that could be used to trace you?"

"No, I just felt like visiting Rowdy's most

recent conquest for some small talk. I mean, what better way to get my jollies, right?"

Rowdy whistled.

"Your sarcasm isn't helping anything."

"You're lucky all you're getting is sarcasm!"

Counting to ten didn't help. "What kind of car is it, Rowdy? I'll send Reese to take care of it."

After Rowdy gave him the make and model, Logan withdrew his cell. "You any good at losing a tail?"

He checked the rearview mirror. "Are we expecting that?"

"No. But be prepared just in case." He called Reese.

Reese answered with a blunt, "I saw. What do want me to do?"

He couldn't believe he'd doubted Reese, even for a second. "For now, get out of there without being seen."

"I left when you did. Want me to meet you somewhere?"

Knowing his friend wouldn't like it, and aware of both Rowdy and Pepper listening in, Logan said, "Not just yet, but soon."

Rowdy's shoulders eased a little. Did he really distrust Reese that much? Or had he still been worried that Logan would betray them?

Not likely. He wanted to do many things to and with Pepper Yates, but betrayal was permanently off the list. "I have to sort this out, and it'll be easier to slip away unnoticed if I do it alone."

"That's the problem, Logan. You're not alone — you're with people that, until only recently, you considered dangerous. Since you cut me out, I have no idea why you've changed your mind, but I do know that I should be there with you. I should —"

"Can you trust me on this?" He didn't have time for explanations.

Without hesitation, Reese said, "One hundred percent."

"Thanks." At the moment, trust was a high-priced commodity — and in short supply with the siblings sharing his truck. "I've got a laundry list of things to be done, but for now, can you move Pepper's car without being seen?"

Clearly puzzled by the request, Reese said, "I can do that, yeah."

Logan gave him the details on the car and where to find it. "Put it someplace secure, all right?"

"No problem."

"I have to switch phones, so it'll probably be a few hours until I can touch base with you again. Find out what you can about the club before then, but be subtle. I'd as soon no one knew we were there."

"Consider it done."

"Appreciate it." Logan disconnected the call and then turned off his cell. To Pepper, he said, "Where's your phone?"

Subdued, she handed it over to him, and he turned it off. No reason to make it easy for others to track them through GPS.

"Rowdy?"

"Already done." Vigilant, he glanced in the rearview mirror again. "But I'll hang on to mine."

Yeah, Logan didn't blame him. "Take another left and then hit the highway. Go south for now." He twisted to look out the back window, but he didn't see anything suspicious. He gave his attention to Pepper.

So many sentiments flashed over her face, distrust and hurt at the forefront. She tried to conceal it with bravado, but her hands were shaking, her face pale.

"I'm sorry," he told her, and he meant it.

"Jam your apology, Logan." She leaned farther away from him, crowding close to Rowdy. "I don't want to hear it."

Rowdy briefly gripped her knee. "You'll be okay now," he told her.

Putting her head to his shoulder, she gave him a brief, hard hug.

God, she was beautiful.

And she wanted nothing to do with him. Knowing she'd need time, Logan said, "What the hell were you doing at the club?"

Rather than answer, she said, "I didn't cause the explosion."

"I told him that," Rowdy said.

"Thank you." She hugged him again while giving Logan a quick, disgruntled frown. "God, Rowdy, I've missed seeing you."

For a second there, Rowdy looked overcome with emotion. "Same here."

Logan touched her back. "Let him drive, honey. It's doubtful, but if he suddenly spots a tail, he'll need both hands on the wheel."

Nodding, she straightened again. She settled her purse in her lap and, without further prompting, said, "I was counting on you to get there in time, but if you didn't, I would have killed them."

"Them?" Logan asked.

"Morton Andrews. His bully boys." She rubbed her palms over the denim covering her thighs. "Anyone in his circle who got in my way."

CHAPTER FIFTEEN

Pepper seemed so fragile, Logan couldn't keep from smoothing back her hair. She'd put a lot of faith in him getting to her on time, and in him *not* being involved with the corruption. "Morton was in the club?"

"I assume so." All but oblivious to his touch, she chewed her bottom lip. "After I told the guard who I was and that I wanted to see Morton —"

Rowdy cursed low.

"— he made a call, and then agreed to take me into the club. We had just reached the back entrance, and the guard was ready to frisk me when . . ." She clenched all over.

Logan wanted so bad to hold her, but in the short time he'd known her, he hadn't taken her preferences into consideration.

From here on out, he would.

She shook her head, swallowed hard. "When I heard that noise, I had no idea what had happened. At first I thought someone was shooting at me. But then the windows above us blew out, and an alarm sounded."

Rowdy turned down the road that'd take them to the highway ramp. "While you were scoping it out, did you see anyone suspicious go in? Anyone who stood out in any way?"

"No." And then to Logan, "It's a busy place. Even on a weekday, people are coming and going at all hours, usually in big groups." Seconds ticked by. "Used to be," she whispered, "I'd have recognized Morton's car and known if he was inside. But now, it's just been too long. There were some fancy wheels in the parking garage, but who knows if any of them belonged to Morton."

Logan opened his glove box and took out a pen and notebook. "Write down the models and colors — anything you can remember. I'll try to find out what Morton drives now."

"He gets chauffeured by his own driver," Rowdy cut in. "And he always has an entourage with him. Bodyguards and the like. It'd have to be something big to hold them all, but probably not anything as showy as a limo."

Her hands now steadier, Pepper wrote

down what she could remember.

"What will you do?" Rowdy asked Logan.

"Ensure you two are safe, first."

"We were safe before I met you," Pepper said in an aside while still writing. "Thanks a lot."

Rowdy held silent.

Considering what she'd been through and how he'd deceived her, Logan let her slide on the continued animosity. "I know a place we can go."

"And then?"

Thinking out loud, he said, "I'll get a prepaid cell, call Reese to see what he's found out about Andrews and the bomb, any suspects." Logan shrugged. "I'll go from there."

Eyes dark with concern, Pepper said, "I don't know if anyone was hurt. I took off as soon as I realized what had happened."

"I'll find out." He took the pad of paper from her but held on to her hand. "Okay?"

After a long searching look, she nodded. "Okay." She squeezed his hand before letting him go.

Logan took heart at the sign of her softening. Or was it simply desperation over a critical situation that had tempered her animosity?

"I'm in the dark here, boys. You two have

obviously come to some understanding, so does anyone want to fill me in?"

"I told him everything," Rowdy said. "You can trust him."

Her eyes narrowed, and then she nodded. "All right. I'll trust him." She gave Logan a look. "With this."

It was going to be a cluster-fuck of the first order. No doubt about that. "I'll need a pay phone. If you see one, pull over."

"Food would be good, too," Pepper said. "Not to downplay the drama, but I'm starving."

Rowdy smiled over that. "She eats when she's upset or nervous."

"Do not."

Watching them interact, Logan couldn't deny their closeness. So many of his assumptions were disproved with the natural, loving way they treated each other. He and his brother were often the same — irreverent, but there when needed.

"Fast food?" Rowdy asked.

"Let's get over the bridge into Kentucky first. Another ten minutes, tops." Still awed by how different Pepper looked, Logan studied her profile. "Is that okay with you?"

She rested her head back and closed her eyes. "I won't starve."

But it was nearing dawn. She'd missed

dinner and had been running for hours, probably on adrenaline and fear alone.

Pepper wrapped her arms around herself. "At least I don't have to wear those ugly clothes anymore."

"You're crossing the line, aren't you?" Rowdy switched lanes. "This could cost you your job."

"Maybe. I don't know." It all depended on how things rolled out. So far Peterson had been accommodating when he needed extra time, when he wanted to follow vague leads. She'd even given him the go-ahead to be undercover at Pepper's apartment building — something most detectives wouldn't be involved with. But this? The lieutenant could only be so forgiving and understanding. "I'll figure it out somehow."

Rowdy flexed his hands on the steering wheel. "I can make a suggestion."

"I don't know if I want to hear it."

On a groan, Pepper said, "I know I don't."

At a rest stop, Rowdy pulled in and put the truck in Park. He turned to face them both. "Sorry, Logan, but you need to cut me loose."

Pepper said, "No!"

Unsure where he was going with the suggestion, Logan studied Rowdy. "Why would I do that?"

"It's the best way to get info. I have contacts. In a single day I can probably find out more about Morton and anyone who wanted him dead than your whole damn police department can in a week."

"*No,* Rowdy."

He hugged his sister up close, kissed the top of her head. "Sorry, hon, but you don't get a vote in this." He looked at Logan. "I'm not hampered by the law. I don't need search warrants or even a key to go snooping. Because Morton has remained a threat to us, I've kept track of him. I know the people working with Morton. I know where they'll hide, and who they'll turn to."

"So you can find out who might have wanted him dead?" Assuming Morton Andrews was the target — instead of Pepper.

Rowdy gave him a hard stare. "I have ten times the motivation of anyone on the force."

Because he wanted to protect his sister.

Much as Logan hated to accept it, especially knowing how Pepper would react, Rowdy had a point. "I'm listening."

"Your buddy Reese can bring the car to me. Everything I need is in the trunk."

"Like?"

"A half dozen prepaid phones for one thing."

No need to pick up more. Smart. Logan nodded at him. "What else?"

Rowdy didn't sugarcoat the truth. "Gun. Knife. Computer." He shrugged. "Contacts."

Shit. "You can't expect me to give you carte blanche on murder."

"The Glock is for protection!" Pepper snarled not an inch from his face.

Rowdy pulled her away from Logan. "You want to clear up this mystery once and for all? Get my car to me, and I'll take it from there."

Notably silent, Pepper curled in on herself, her legs pulled up on the seat, her head on her knees.

Had she learned not to argue when Rowdy had a plan? Or did she simply trust him that much to make it all right?

One day, Logan thought, she'd trust him in the same way.

"I can do this," Rowdy said. "But I have to know that she's safe."

"I'm not going to let anything happen to her."

It surprised Logan when Pepper didn't object. It also helped to make up his mind.

He had to call Dash and Reese, and after he got Pepper stowed away he'd have to tell the lieutenant something. "I'll agree, on one condition."

Ready to impose his will, Rowdy said with silky menace, "Yeah, what's that?"

"If at any point you find yourself in real danger, you let me know so I can send backup your way."

Suspicious, Pepper lifted her head to stare at him. Speculative, Rowdy narrowed his eyes.

At this point, they both had reason to doubt him. Logan shook his head. "I understand your reservations, I really do. But whether you accept it or not, there are trustworthy people in the force." Through the open truck window, he snagged the receiver off the pay phone. "I know, because I'm one of them."

After a few quick phone calls, they'd gone back to driving. They decided not to stop for food; it made more sense to get settled for the night. Logan had assured her she'd be eating soon.

Pepper didn't know where he was taking them, and her thoughts were fractured enough that she didn't bother to ask. As she'd said, if Rowdy trusted him, then he was trustworthy. Period.

At least with this. With security.

But not with anything personal. Not with

her heart.

Oh, God, she hated to admit that her heart had gotten involved. She wanted to tell Logan to go to hell. She wanted to hate him.

But instead, his nearness comforted her.

And excited her.

How sick was that?

Even now, after everything that had happened, she was so incredibly aware of him. His shoulder bumped hers. His thigh pressed to hers no matter how many times she tried to scoot away.

Over and over, she took deep breaths to capture his scent.

Tonight, she could have been killed; Logan wasn't wrong about that. A bomb had exploded over her head. Morton Andrews had possibly died.

But instead of concentrating on that, her thoughts repeatedly went to Logan, to his involvement, to what he'd done to her and how he'd used her, how he'd abused her trust.

She put her head back and closed her eyes, but she couldn't avoid the truth: she'd abused his trust, too. Sure, they each had their reasons.

Were his any less valid than hers?

He spoke quietly, giving Rowdy directions,

making additional plans, discussing things that involved her.

The road got bumpier, and she opened her eyes to look around. The headlights of the truck cut through the obsidian night. Woods lined the sides of the narrow gravel road.

Just to irk Logan, she said, "Planning to dump us somewhere?"

He didn't take the bait. "We're going to my brother's cabin."

"It's secure?" Rowdy asked.

"Other than Dash and me, and now you two, no one knows about it."

"Dash?" Pepper asked.

"Dashiel. My younger brother." Uneasy, he rubbed the back of his neck. "He owns the construction company where I . . ."

"Pretended to work?" Resentment welled up again. "Great cover for you, right? Not that it took all that much to con me." Disgusted, she said, "I made it pretty damned easy."

Rowdy blew out an uncomfortable breath.

Logan went right past that gibe. "Dash enjoys the physical work, but he also enjoys getting away on occasion."

They came upon a split in the road, and Logan said, "Turn here." A minute later, the headlights landed on a large, rustic cottage.

Rowdy put the truck in Park but kept it running as he took in the house. "You say your brother owns the construction company?"

"Yes."

It hit Pepper, and she turned to him. "Your brother is well-to-do?"

For too long, Logan stared out the passenger window. "Actually, we're both pretty well set for life." Finally he faced her. "Family business and all that. We work because we want to, not because we have to."

More resentment had her puffing up, on the verge of blasting him.

Rowdy shook his head. "Are we going in, or waiting here?"

"Dash and Reese will be here soon. We might as well go in and air it out." Without comment, he reached past Pepper to remove the truck keys but left the headlights on. Latching on to her arm, he said, "Let's go."

Even the firm touch of his hand on her arm affected her. "I don't need your help."

"You do, but right now I'm more concerned with discouraging you or Rowdy from leaving me here. So you're sticking close."

"Oh, that's rich!" She didn't really fight

him as he got out, hauling her with him. To do so might instigate a brawl between him and her brother, and the night had been chaotic enough already without any bloodshed. They were each so capable that, once started, a fight could prove damaging — to them both. "You're accusing us of being dishonest?"

"Not dishonest, just misguided." He nodded for Rowdy to go ahead of them.

Contrary to her reaction, Rowdy didn't seem to find anything amiss. Using the headlights to guide him, he stepped carefully over a stone walkway and made his way around to a side door that Logan unlocked.

Logan stepped inside with Pepper held close to his side, then fumbled around at the wall until he located a flashlight.

After he turned it on, he handed it to Rowdy. "Flip the breaker box in the last bedroom."

"Right." Rowdy moved the flashlight around the interior.

They'd stepped into a kitchen and dining room, with a modest sitting area at the other end of the house. They ran together in a U-shape, bisected by four doors that Pepper assumed to be bedrooms and hopefully a bath.

Rowdy glanced at her, then said, "Be right back."

As he disappeared into the darkness, she felt her tension expand.

Alone, with Logan. Almost.

His hand on her arm contracted, his fingers sort of caressing. "Once the lights are on, I'll open the windows. Let in some fresh air."

She barely heard him. The urge to turn to him, to lean on him, kept her tightly strung. The knowledge that she no longer had to hide from him teased her senses.

"With all the shade trees," Logan continued, "it doesn't get too hot in here, even in the middle of summer."

Somehow he moved closer so that he stood partially behind her, his warm breath near her ear.

"You're still shaking." His arms slowly closed around her, and he eased her back into his chest. He wasn't that much taller, but he was so much stronger, thick with muscle and so incredibly hot.

His thighs made contact with her rump. His broad chest pressed into her shoulder blades. That indescribable scent of his cocooned her, robbing her of animus. She remembered how he'd touched her this way, taking her from behind, following her instructions, both of them wild with lust —

The sudden intrusion of light had her flinching away. He released her, but one glance at him had her ducking away from his knowing gaze. Logan didn't follow her, and he said nothing about her retreat, but she had no doubt he'd been thinking the same thing.

She went to patio doors on the longest wall to look out. Rowdy returned and put the flashlight back in its holder on the wall by the front door.

He glanced around with interest at the fishing poles in brackets in the dining area, the wood stove, the well-worn furniture. "This is nice."

"Thanks." Logan pulled aside the drapes and opened the patio doors, then two windows. "I don't get out here as often as I'd like, but whenever I do, it's peaceful."

They heard the approach of another car. Rowdy narrowed his gaze, Pepper went still.

Logan touched her arm, saying, "Stay here," and he went out the door.

Rowdy went to the door and looked out, then came back to Pepper. "You okay?"

Because she didn't know what to say, she nodded. The last thing her brother needed was more worry.

Still checking out every nook and corner

of the house, he said, "I don't know Logan's brother, but I've met Detective Bareden."

"Reese."

"Yeah." He watched her. "You know him?"

"I met him when you did." When he'd arrested Rowdy. God, she couldn't think about that right now. Never in her life had she felt more exposed, or more helpless. "He was also at the station when I tried to see you. He's . . . I don't know."

"Yeah, that's what I think, too." Glancing over his shoulder toward the front door, Rowdy kept watch for Logan's return. "There's something about him."

"He's not entirely up front." That didn't necessarily mean that Reese was bad, but he was . . . something.

"No, he's not. I can't get a fix on him, so I want you to be extra careful around him."

They heard Logan speaking quietly and the crunch of feet on leaves and gravel.

"Stick close to Logan, okay?" Now in more of a rush, Rowdy added, "Until I figure him out, avoid Reese as much as you can."

Stick close to Logan? Surely he didn't mean —

Logan came in, and right behind him was a man who had to be his brother. Logan was six foot tall, but his brother looked more on par with Rowdy, around six-four. Construction work had left him leanly muscled. Dash's hair was a little lighter, but he and Logan shared the same dark eyes. Except that Dash's gaze was more mischievous. He looked at Pepper and grinned like a scoundrel. She had no doubt that Dash would be popular with the women.

He said, "Hi there."

Before Pepper could reply, Reese pushed in behind him, all but knocking Dash over. "Stop ogling her. She's been through enough tonight, ya know?"

Not in the least insulted, Dash went to the dining table to set down three big bags of groceries and then came forward with his hand extended. "And you must be Rowdy?"

Her brother accepted the handshake. "Nice place you have."

"Yeah, it was plenty private till Logan decided he had to take it over. I've never even brought a woman here." He turned to Pepper. "I might have to make him buy me a new place now. What do you think?"

Without censoring her thoughts, she asked, "Can he afford to do that?"

"Shoot, yeah. He didn't tell you that he's loaded?"

He sort of had, but . . .

"Knock it off, Dash." Logan closed and

locked the door. "Make yourself useful and show her a room to use."

Dash grinned some more. "Any preferences?"

"Let her pick. I don't care."

"I'll give her one next to the bathroom, then." Dash opened a closet to retrieve fresh bedding, then waited for her to join him.

Rowdy pulled her close first. "I'm going to take off. The sooner I get on this, the sooner we can put it behind us." She opened her mouth, and he said, "No, don't argue, kiddo. I know what I'm doing. Just remember what I told you, okay?"

Logan scowled over that. Dash turned away to give them a modicum of privacy. Reese just crossed his arms and leaned back on the table.

"I won't forget."

"Yeah, well, this time it'd be great if you remember *and* follow along."

Pepper couldn't help but squeeze her brother tight. "I will, if you promise to come back in one piece."

"Guaranteed."

In such a small and open space, with three big men listening in, there could be no such thing as privacy.

At the moment, she didn't care. "I love you, Rowdy."

He hugged her right off her feet, stealing her breath for a double beat of time. Then he turned away and headed for the door, saying to Logan, "Walk me out."

Pepper stood there, staring at the open door, until Reese said, "I brought in the clothes you had in the trunk."

That drew her from her melancholy thoughts. "So you went through our belongings?" Jerk.

Reese just shrugged. "Looked to me like you were well prepared."

"Not for a bomb."

That gave him pause. "No, I guess not." He handed her overloaded bag to Dash.

If he wanted a "thank you" he was doomed to disappointment.

But he said only, "Go on with Dash. While you settle in your room, I'll put together some food. You have to be getting hungry."

Damn it. She could go on disliking him more easily if he'd stop trying to be nice. Grudgingly, she nodded. "Thanks."

Dash smiled at her. "If your brother is anything like mine, he's probably unstoppable. Try not to worry too much."

It'd be easier not to breathe.

Rather than follow Dash into the bedroom he opened, she looked at each door. "Where does Logan usually sleep?"

"The room here in the center. It's a security thing for him. He can't turn it off even when he's sleeping."

"What about you?"

"I'll take whatever room you don't use. Reese will use the couch."

So Reese was not only sticking around, but he'd be near the front door, ensuring she couldn't sneak away? Not that she'd planned to anyway, but it bugged her all the same.

"Fine. I'll take the room closest to Logan."

Dash bit off a smile. "There's a bathroom through here. The water heater is miniscule, so if you want a hot shower, you have to make it fast."

The bedrooms were spacious but sparsely furnished. Twin-size beds, one dresser, one nightstand, one small lamp.

Dash set a couple of plain quilts, sheets and a single pillow on the bed. "Want me to make it up for you?"

"I can do it." She took the bag from him, gave him a pointed look so that he'd leave, and then shut the door behind him. Dropping down to the bed, she wondered what to do now.

She was hungry, damn Reese. But with the windows now open, she could smell the lake — and that made up her mind for her.

Forget the shower. As soon as she got the bed together, she'd freshen herself with a late-night swim.

CHAPTER SIXTEEN

Reese stepped out to the front deck. He had to move around a bit before he finally got reception on his cell. No calls from Alice something-or-other. But she had to wonder why he hadn't returned yet.

Disgruntled, he punched her number and waited past four rings before she answered in a very sleepy voice.

"Hello?"

"I woke you?" Where the hell was his dog?

"Who is this?"

He heard the uncertainty in her voice, but he didn't understand it. "It's Reese."

Silence.

"You have my dog?"

"Oh. Yes."

He looked around, but Logan was still with Rowdy, and Dash was inside keeping watch over Pepper Yates. Hoping the fresh, cooler night air off the lake would revive him a little, Reese filled his lungs. "I hate to ask this, but do you think you could keep him overnight?"

"Okay."

He waited. And waited some more. But she didn't ask a single question. He cracked first. "I have a situation with work."

"It's all right. We'd already gone to bed anyway."

We? No, he wouldn't pry. "Is Cash behaving?"

"He snores, but he's very sweet."

"Snores? You have him in bed with you?"

A longer pause, and then, "Since he joined me there, I assumed that was where you let him sleep."

Ah, she'd allowed Cash to stick close. Nice. He did do the same, but then, it was his dog. "I really appreciate this. I should be able to get him sometime in the afternoon." Or not, depending on how things went with this whole exercise in idiocy. "But let me know if anything comes up, okay?"

"He's fine. I'm off tomorrow, so it's not a problem."

It occurred to Reese that he didn't know enough about her — like where she worked. But maybe they could set up an arrangement. She appeared to like Cash, and he was gone too damn much to be a really good pet owner. Maybe he could pay her as

331

a pet sitter or something —

"Is there anything else, Detective Bareden?"

"Yeah. Call me Reese."

More silence.

He gave up. "I'll let you get back to bed, then. Again, thank you."

"You're welcome." And she hung up.

Frustrating. Confounding. A little annoying . . .

So then, why was he smiling?

Logan waited while Rowdy went through the belongings in his trunk. Though he'd had a motel room, he obviously lived out of his car.

Always ready to bolt at a moment's notice.

Logan made note of the clothes, food, water, first aid and shaving kit, a few weapons with additional ammo . . . and a stuffed bear?

While Rowdy rearranged things, Logan lifted the tattered bear. A faded red ribbon remained around the brown bear's neck. One ear hung loose. Certain spots were worn thin.

A sick feeling twisted his heart.

Glancing at him, Rowdy said quietly, "That's Pepper's."

He'd assumed as much. "She's kept it?"

Rowdy shrugged. "She wanted me to keep it for her."

In the trunk, ready to go . . . in case they had to leave.

What if Rowdy had gotten spooked by his presence? What if he'd uprooted Pepper and taken off? Logan could have lost her before he'd even realized how much she meant to him.

With practiced ease, Rowdy dropped the clip in his Glock, checked that it was loaded, then put it in again. "That shabby little bear is the only toy she's ever had. She used to sleep with it when she was little. Every so often our folks would . . . overimbibe, and Pepper would hide the bear."

"Why?"

"She didn't want them to take it away from her."

Meaning they did things like that? Most of the stuffing had settled in the bear's legs and arms. The middle felt empty, almost flat. "You bought it for her?"

Without looking up, Rowdy gave a crooked grin. "Stole it for her, actually. The folks weren't big on gifts. Hell, if we got socks or underwear, it felt like Christmas." He paused, put his hands on the open trunk and looked off in the distance.

Logan understood his mood. "She'll be

safe with me." It was important for Rowdy to know that.

"Hurt her again," Rowdy said, "and we're going to have problems." Finally he straightened. He took the bear and placed it in a corner, behind the ammo, then covered it with the edge of a spare blanket. After handing Logan three prepaid cell phones, he slammed the trunk and went around to the driver's seat. "Just so you know, I don't trust your buddy, Reese, so I'll be boosting a new car. If you'd thought to track me, think again."

"Understood." Logan kept him from closing the door. He leaned in. "And just so you know — I'm trusting you to be as honorable as Pepper thinks you are."

That made Rowdy laugh with derision.

"Share any info you get before you act on it." Logan continued to lean into the car. "If you can find out who planted the bomb, if Morton is dead or alive, anything at all, let me know. Under no circumstances will you play vigilante."

"Sure thing." Rowdy started the car. "You have my sister, so I'll call often to check in. And when I do, I'll want to talk to Pepper, so keep her close."

That suited Logan just fine. Maybe if he told her Rowdy wanted it that way, she wouldn't protest too much. "All right."

Rowdy rested his wrists over the steering wheel and tipped his head at Logan. "You might want to get back inside now. If I know my sister, she's probably already stirring the pot."

It seemed with every minute he got a better understanding of the siblings. And with each of those minutes, he gained new respect for Rowdy and a deeper fondness for Pepper. "Drive safe." He closed the car door and stood back as Rowdy drove away.

The night sky felt like a heavy, oppressive weight on his shoulders. He hoped he was doing the right thing, but he just couldn't be sure. Since meeting Pepper Yates, the "right thing" seemed more and more like an open-ended idea.

Barefoot, wearing only an oversize T-shirt that fit like a short dress, Pepper stepped out of the bedroom. She felt both men staring at her, but so what? Since Rowdy stored only the basic necessities at the safe location, she didn't have the advantage of a big wardrobe. She didn't even have a swimsuit.

She wanted a swim, she wasn't a prisoner, so they could stuff their disapproval.

She didn't care.

Veering into the bathroom, she grabbed a

white towel off a shelf and a bar of soap from the sink. When she emerged again, Reese and Dash were both standing, a little incredulous, a lot undecided on how to "handle" her.

Ha! Let them try. "I'm going for a swim."

Dash sidestepped into her path. "It's dark." As if he couldn't help himself, he dipped his gaze down her body, then shot it right back up to her face again.

"So?" She'd grown up swimming in the river, night and day. More often than not she'd taken her baths in the cool river water. She stepped around him — and almost ran into Reese.

With a roll of her eyes, she said, "Move."

He did but then kept pace alongside her. "Why don't you wait for Logan?"

"I don't like him very much right now, that's why."

"Okay, fine. Then —"

"I don't like either of you all that much, either."

"What did I do?" Dash asked with comical affront. He had a look similar to Logan's, but his disposition couldn't have been more different.

Reese made a sound of impatience. "It's not all that safe to —"

"Sure it is. I know how to swim, and I

336

don't need anyone's supervision or help." She looked back and caught Dash staring at her butt. He gave her a rascal's grin that she dismissed. "Just so you both know, I'll be skinny-dipping, so you can keep your peepers up here and out of my business."

They both went mute, which worked for her.

As soon as she opened the patio doors, they were both with her again.

"Swimming at night is a lousy idea." Dash spoke loudly — no doubt hoping Logan would hear. "There are snakes in the water."

She laughed. "Is that your attempt to scare a girl? Get real. The only pets I ever had growing up were rodents and snakes, so try again."

"Seriously?" Dash stepped in front of her once more. "That's . . . well, really sad."

With a loud snarl, Reese took a position next to Dash. "Be reasonable, Pepper. This is a bad idea."

"Screw you." She made to shove past him, but he blocked her. Pepper leveled an evil gaze on him. "I would suggest you get out of my way."

"It's all right, Reese."

Logan. Pepper didn't look back at him. She'd have rather been in the water before he returned, but she was nothing if not adaptable. With her life, she'd had to be in order to survive.

Reese made a great fanfare of moving aside, and Pepper stepped around Dash to continue on down the hill toward the water. Beneath her feet, the grass was cool and dewy. She knew Logan was behind her. She'd felt Dash's stare, but it was nothing like this. When Logan watched her, she more than felt it.

She experienced it.

"You might want to stay on the path," he said from right behind her. "There are twigs and rocks everywhere that can cut your feet."

The "path" wasn't all that defined in the dark, but she navigated carefully, each step measured.

"The dock is sturdy, but the floodlights don't reach all the way." He didn't quite touch her, but she knew he was *right there.* "When we fish, we usually bring down a lantern."

"I've been swimming off sunken stumps, often in the middle of the night, since I was three. I think I can handle it."

"All right."

His calm tone and reasonable manner irked her. She walked out on the wooden dock, stopped and pulled her top off over her head. "You gonna skin out of your clothes and swim with me?" Refusing to show any modesty, she pushed down her panties.

Palpable expectation throbbed in the damp evening air. "If you want me to."

Most definitely, but she wouldn't admit that to him. "Suit yourself."

"Then I will."

Her heart rapped against her ribs. Stars glittered overhead, and the wash of moonlight left murky, blue-tinged shadows everywhere. "My shirt and panties are on the dock. Don't kick them in."

"I saw."

She felt him getting nearer. He could see? More than the faint outlines that she detected?

"There's a ladder off the front right side of the dock. Don't dive in until you judge the depth. It can get pretty low in dry seasons."

"You think?" She heard the quiet hiss of his zipper being lowered, and it left her far too warm. "Until Rowdy and I had to take off, I spent more of my summers in the water than out."

"You mean before your parents died?"

No, she wouldn't discuss this with him. Moving away from him, she stared through the inky darkness until she found the top of the ladder jutting above the dock. Little by little, her eyes adjusted.

She looked out at the lake. Starry diamonds sprinkled the black velvet water, disturbed only by the occasional ripple of a fish. She went down the flat rungs until the water lapped at her waist.

"Cold?" Logan stood over her.

Her face was probably even with his knees. Could he see her? She wished she could better see him.

"Not bad." She pushed back and into the water, submerging her head and coming up several feet away. If she dunked herself a foot or so, she could touch bottom. Not deep at all.

Something bumped her foot, and she knew it was Logan. He tread water near her. Sticking close. Being protective.

Being male.

A frog began croaking somewhere along the shore. She loved the sound, just as she loved the water. "You have a boat?"

"Rowboat, and a little fishing boat with a trolling motor. Nothing fancy."

"Dash said you're rich."

He went under, then came up a few feet away. It felt so intimate, being here with him like this. The moon played peekaboo with his dark, wet hair, sometimes shining down on him, sometimes concealing him. The night sky surrounded them, cozy, sort of sexy.

Other than the undulation of the water, Logan stayed still and quiet.

She wouldn't ask again. If he didn't want to talk, then fine. She'd bathe in silence.

She swam over to the dock. Water sluiced down her body as she went up the ladder to get the soap. While she lathered herself, she glanced up at the house. Someone stepped out onto the deck with the lantern Logan had mentioned earlier.

Since she preferred not to be ogled by the others, she got back in to rinse.

Halfway down the hill, Dash called out to them. "All clear?"

Logan said, "Leave the lantern on the bench."

"Sure thing." The light bobbed as he walked, dancing over the dew-wet ground and the occasional tree trunk, and casting an eerie wash of yellow over Dash's face.

He put the lantern on a big stone bench that she hadn't even noticed on the shore. A warm glowing light expanded out to the end of the dock, exaggerating shadows and showing their twin piles of clothes.

Which meant when she got out, anyone

looking would see it all.

"Reese said the hash will be done in another five minutes if you want to eat. He cooked canned green beans and rolls with it."

"Thanks," Logan said quietly.

Keeping her gaze on Dash, Pepper watched him go back up the hill. At the patio doors, he met with Reese. The two of them looked back down to the lake before going in and closing the door.

Her thoughts scuttled about; worry for her brother tried to dig in, but she fended it off. If she started down that path, she'd be bawling like an infant.

Going to her back, she floated lazily — well aware that the moonlight combined with the lantern would show her body.

The water felt amazing. Refreshing. Almost relaxing — though not much could really help her unwind tonight . . . at least, nothing as simple as a swim.

The surface of the lake whorled around her as Logan moved closer again. "Are you hungry?"

The way he said that, all husky and deep, told her a lot. Would he make a pass? Would he have assumptions based on what they'd already done and the way she showed herself now?

Why should she suffer just because of him? She shouldn't.

Mind made up, Pepper turned in the water again, dunking her head, then emerging with a splash. "Actually, I'm starved. Let's go so we can get food out of the way." Not waiting to see how he interpreted that, she swam to the ladder and climbed out.

Seconds later, Logan did the same. She heard his wet feet on the rough boards. The stillness in the air amplified her awareness of him.

Slowly, she turned to see him standing before her, naked, wet, *gorgeous* . . . and erect.

Breathing deeper, her body alive with need, she looked him over while drying. When she finished, she handed him the towel.

He didn't dry; the towel hung limp in his hand, his arms at his sides.

"I'm glad your brother brought the lantern."

His broad chest expanded on a breath; he took a step closer, his gaze on her body. "Me, too."

Knowing her willpower wouldn't last, Pepper pulled on her T-shirt and stepped into her panties.

Logan still didn't move. On impulse, she

343

reached out and clasped his penis.

His hand fisted on the towel; he shifted his stance, and then, other than the flexing of his erection, he held still.

"Bring the soap up with you." Releasing him, Pepper turned and walked away. If she stayed, they wouldn't make it off the dock, and she was still really pissed at him.

She knew what she wanted, but she also knew how she wanted it done. This would happen.

On her terms.

Dinner first, and then Logan would get to know her a little better.

Logan watched her dig into her food. Hell, he couldn't take his gaze off her. Little by little her hair dried in tangled waves, and even that was sexy. She'd pulled on jeans, but the sight of her standing naked beneath the moonlight would forever be branded on his brain.

She had a killer body.

A body that she'd successfully hidden from him even while having sex. He'd been inside her, but he hadn't gotten to touch her.

God, he wanted to. He was so coiled with lust, everything else faded.

"Great dinner, Reese."

344

"Thank you. Glad someone is appreciating it."

Both he and Pepper ignored the inane conversation between Dash and Reese. She finished off a glass of milk and sat back.

Reese waited, and when she only stared back at Logan, he asked, "I take it you like hash?"

"When I'm hungry enough, I'm not particular." Her gaze moved over to Reese. "But it was good."

Dash said, "Since Reese will be taking off in the morning —"

"Where are you going?" Pepper asked with suspicion.

"— I'll be cooking breakfast."

She glanced at Dash. "I can feed myself, but thanks anyway." Then back to Reese, "So you're not hanging around, huh?"

"I'll be back and forth. Logan didn't explain?"

Her narrowed attention came back to him.

Logan finished off his own milk, then mimicked her pose, relaxing back in his seat. "There's no reason to just wait on your brother when Reese can do his own research at the same time."

"Yeah, because that sort of thing has worked out so well for you, right?"

Reese said, "I can go through legal channels that Rowdy can't touch, and vice versa. I like to think we'll complement each other."

"You can think whatever you want. But if you trip him up and he gets hurt —"

"Yes, I know. I've heard the threats from you both already. I don't know how I'll sleep tonight with so much fury heaped my way."

Derision brought her forward, palms flat on the tabletop. "How do I know you won't lead anyone back here?"

Reese's expression went taut. "Is that an accusation of complicity or incompetence?"

"Reese," Logan warned. He saw no reason to prick Pepper's already prickly temper. "I trust him, honey, so —"

"I'm not your honey," she shot at Logan, and then with a glare at Reese, said, "and I *don't* trust him."

Dash held silent, and Logan couldn't tell if he was amused, awed or aghast at Pepper's ferocity.

"Now my feelings are hurt."

"Ha!"

Reese leaned into her anger, all kidding put aside. "Before this gets out of hand, understand that I know how to spot a tail, and I take my position as a law enforcement officer seriously."

"Well, hallelujah for you, but that doesn't

reassure me a bit." She scraped back her chair.

Assuming she'd go off angry, Logan stood, too. He'd follow her, try to appease her, hopefully put her more at ease.

But instead of storming off, she snatched up the emptied plates and headed to the kitchen.

The way Dash grinned now, there was no confusing his amusement. Reese threw up his hands.

Logan picked up the glasses and followed her to the kitchen. Since it wasn't that far from where Dash and Reese sat at the table, with no walls separating them, he knew both men looked on.

"Calm down." He kept his voice low. "Everything is going to be fine."

She scraped the plates into the garbage. "I've got a feeling that your idea of fine differs from mine." She rummaged around under the cabinets.

"What are you looking for?"

"Dish soap."

Logan took her shoulders and, mindful of their audience, set her away to get the soap himself. He put the plug in the drain and filled the sink.

Dash came over. "So. Why don't I do the dishes and you two can —"

"No." She elbowed aside both men and got to work. "I carry my own weight."

Logan already knew she wasn't a fan of domestic chores, but she looked so strained, he didn't want to do anything to set her off.

He shook his head at Dash, and then said to Pepper, "Mind if I help?"

"As a matter of fact, I do." She gave him a molten look. "Why don't you go busy yourself elsewhere?"

Dash cleared his throat. "We're going to play cards. Want to join us when you're done here?"

"No." She looked at Logan again. "And neither does he."

With no idea what that was supposed to mean, Logan held up his hands. "I still have to put sheets on my bed, anyway. It'll be morning soon and we all need to get some sleep."

She made a rude sound that he couldn't interpret, and didn't dare ask her to explain. He turned and headed to his room.

The bedrooms were all utilitarian. Whoever had first built the house hadn't meant it for luxury but for hunting and fishing and getting away. Neither he nor Dash hunted, but they did enjoy fishing, swimming and being close to nature.

Their parents had a condo on a resort lake

that they could use whenever they wanted. Golfing, horseback riding, restaurants, dancing and more. They had speedboats and a sailboat, and . . .

Pepper had one stuffed bear.

He had both parents, a brother he was close with and an entire network of relatives.

She had only Rowdy.

Logan glanced at the bed, ran a hand through his hair and accepted that he wouldn't get any sleep. He could almost understand why Pepper had taunted him with her body and with that maddening way she'd stroked him.

Before she'd turned away.

He'd added to her hurt when she'd already been hurt so much, and now she wanted payback. Clear enough. He got it. If that's what she needed to feel better, he'd man up and take it without complaint.

But he'd give a lot to hold her, to keep her tucked close through the remaining hours till dawn.

After tossing a pillow on the freshly made bed, Logan stripped off his shirt, stretched and stepped out to check on Pepper.

She finished drying a pan and put it back on the stove. She glanced up, caught his gaze, and without looking away, she dropped the dish towel over the sink and started toward him.

Both Reese and Dash paused in their card game as she went past them, her intent gaze zeroed in on Logan.

Given the way she watched him, with so much obvious determination, he had no idea what to think. She stopped before him, trailed her hot gaze over him, then snagged a finger through a belt loop at the front of his shorts. Without a smile, without a word, she led him back into the bedroom he'd just exited.

"Pepper?"

Uncaring about the others, she closed the door and leaned back on it. "Get naked," she said in a husky whisper, "and get in the bed."

CHAPTER SEVENTEEN

Feeling daring and hot and far too needy, Pepper held her breath as Logan hesitated, his expression both confused and concerned. She knew he wanted her. Already he was semierect, dark eyes glittering, cheekbones flushed.

"Go on." She stepped away from the door — and peeled off her own shirt to bare her breasts. She dropped it on the wooden floor and turned to him.

He looked at her body in minute detail, then back to her face. He'd grown so rigid, he looked ready to break. In contrast, he kept his tone gentle. "What are we doing here, honey?"

"*Not* your honey," she reminded him again — and she opened the snap on her jeans. "But I like having sex with you, so why should I do without? Now that we're both out in the open, well, no more need for restraint, right?" Teasing him, she eased down the zipper.

Logan's breathing deepened, but still, he didn't lose the shorts.

Pepper considered him, then gave a shrug. "Feeling shy?" She knew that wasn't his problem. "I can go first. Modesty isn't one of my virtues."

And with that, she pushed the jeans down her hips, stepped out, and dropped them with the shirt. She wore only tiny panties.

"Pepper . . ." His sharpened gaze moved over her body.

"What? You're sorry that you hurt me? You don't want to hurt me anymore?"

"Yes."

"Then give me what I need." She sat on the bed, scooted back until she could recline in the middle, and smiled at him. "I need to shake off some tension. That means I need you."

Seeking self-discipline, he worked his jaw, finally got his attention on her face and came to sit on the side of the bed. "I'm not sure —"

She sat up. "You want me to go to Reese or Dash, instead? Is that it? I don't know if either of them would be interested, but, hey, if you're not willing —"

"No." With anger overshadowing other emotions, he turned to her and caught her

352

shoulders. "You're not going to any other man."

She trailed her fingertips over his chest. "No, I won't." Enunciating carefully, she said, "Not if you. Get. Naked."

While he struggled to figure her out, he contracted his fingers on her shoulders, caressing her. "You want . . . sex?"

"Oh, yeah." Done waiting, she pushed him to his back — and he let her. God, he looked good. Even while *almost* hating him, she wanted him.

So damn much.

She opened the fastening to his shorts. "What we did before, Logan? That was pleasant, you know? Discreet. Naughty." She pulled his shorts down, taking his boxers off at the same time. "It satisfied me."

He lifted his hips to help her. "It was special to me."

"Baloney." Not wanting to hear his explanations, to maybe be fooled again, she wrapped her fingers around his erection, stopping him in midprotest. He made a half-hearted effort to stop her, but when his hand covered hers, it was to squeeze. "Like it firm, huh? I can do that."

Sensation closed his eyes, stiffened his shoulders. He growled her name.

"Shh. No talking, okay?" If he tried to

reason with her, to do more lame apologizing, she'd get off track. "Let me enjoy you."

He hesitated, but in the end, they both knew he would agree. "You think I used you, so using me will make you feel better?"

"You *did* use me." She stood in a rush and finished stripping off his shorts, then looked at his body while removing her panties. He had powerful thighs, hairy calves and big feet. "No reason to overanalyze it."

"No, I won't." He relaxed back on the bed, offering himself to her, for whatever she wanted.

And she wanted a lot.

He wasn't an overmuscled brute like Reese, and while tall, he didn't have the extraordinary height of Rowdy or Dash. But he was so incredibly sexy, the perfect combination of muscle, bone and body hair. She couldn't imagine a man being more masculine, or more . . . perfect.

Shaking off that thought, she crawled up over his thighs and stared down at his cock.

Logan watched her through heavy eyes, breathing deep, expression severe with expectation. Slowly, he cupped her breast.

Ah, God, that was so wonderful. His hands were big and hot and strong . . . For only a moment, Pepper tipped back her head and closed her eyes.

That must've encouraged him, because he cupped both breasts, stroked her, brought his thumbs into play over her now tight nipples.

"I don't know the rules here, honey, but I'd love to kiss you."

She didn't have any rules, not for this.

"Yeah." She got herself under control. "I'd enjoy that, too." Sprawling out over him, her legs open over his hips, she took his mouth.

In her mind, she'd wanted to stay in charge, to show him her strength.

To prove that he hadn't hurt her.

But now that she had him naked and in bed, now with his mouth on hers . . . He so easily took over, leading while she followed, and she didn't care.

It shocked her, how devastating a kiss could be. Wet and deep and somehow so right that she knew she'd been starved for him. How had she not known the potency of his kiss?

Had he been holding back before this?

Or was it that she now felt free?

Keeping her involved with the play of his tongue, he moved his hands over her back, down to her bottom, then to the backs of her thighs.

He urged her legs open more, spreading

them until she lay flat against him. His arms came around her, keeping her that close.

Right where she wanted to be.

Pepper lifted her head and breathed urgently, "Do you have a rubber?"

"Just one." More kisses, each hotter than the one before. "In my wallet."

"Tomorrow," she murmured, "get more."

As if that pushed him over the edge, he turned and pinned her under him. His mouth was at her neck, and she just knew he would mark her.

That turned her on, too, so she wrapped her legs around him.

He sucked and licked his way to the upper swells of her breasts — and then down to her left nipple. He sucked her in, his rough tongue laving, his mouth hot.

"Logan." Holding his head to her, she arched up.

He groaned. "You are so sweet."

No, *sweet* was not a word that applied to her. "I need you, Logan. Right now."

"Not yet." He kissed his way to her other breast, drew on that nipple, too.

"Logan." Voice high and thin, she said, "It's too much."

"Let me help." He insinuated his hand between their bodies, cupped over her mound with his fingers softly playing, searching. He parted her swollen lips, then paused. "You're already wet."

"I need you inside me."

He worked two fingers deep. "Better?" he asked while kissing the corner of her mouth, her jaw, her throat.

"Yes, but not good enough." She caught his face to end his teasing. "I need this, Logan. Right now. No seduction. No reservations. Definitely no apologies."

His fingers still deep inside her, his chest hair tickling her nipples, his weight a warm comfort, he said, "God, I need you, too, Pepper. But —"

"Shh." She kissed his mouth. "I've thought about this ever since you first moved in next door to me. So, please. Put on the condom and let's both take what we need."

After a searching look, he kissed her long and hard — and rolled away. In seconds, he had the condom out of his wallet and rolled on.

Throbbing with need, Pepper reached out to him. He settled back between her legs, kissed her again and kept on kissing her while opening her with his fingers, pressing in a little.

She freed her mouth to groan.

He captured it again — and thrust deep.

Ah, now this was what she wanted. His

taste, his warmth, the press of his body over hers, his breath on her face, his scent all around her.

He tangled one hand in her long hair, and with the other he held her breast, a little rough, a lot amazing.

The bed bounced against the wall, but neither of them made a move to readjust. She didn't care, and she wasn't sure Logan even noticed. In minutes, pleasure began to coil, growing tighter and tighter. Her groans turned into throaty moans. Her heels pressed into his back. Her fingers dug into his shoulders.

She strained against him, reaching for release, needing the oblivion so badly . . .

Logan put his head back, his jaw tight, his teeth locked. She knew he fought off his own release to wait for her — and that did it.

Pleasure rolled over her, a giant, pulsing tide of sensation. She arched hard, crying out, holding tight to Logan until she heard his vibrating groans fading.

Slowly, he settled his weight back down over her, then rolled to his back while keeping her close. It was dangerous, but she allowed herself a single minute of luxuriating in what they'd shared. Her heart continued to pound — and Logan continued to idly stroke her.

There were no words. What could she say? You owed me that? Well done? Thanks? Hell, no.

Not only didn't he deserve that from her, but . . . it would cheapen it all. Even hurt and angry, she couldn't do that.

But she could get herself together and protect her heart from further damage.

She stroked his damp chest, touched his whisker-rough jaw and sat up.

His hand trailed from her shoulder down to her wrist to catch her fingers. When she looked at his face, she found his gaze wary but relaxed, possessive and yet watchful.

Don't do it, don't do it, don't — she leaned down and kissed him, a complete wimp when it came to resisting him. Thankfully, she summoned the wit to keep it light. "Sleep well."

She stood and reached for her shirt.

Logan came up to one elbow. No longer so mellow, he asked sharply, "What are you doing?"

No way would she look at him again. Already the hurt in his voice knotted her stomach. She pulled on her shirt and tried to sound cavalier when she said, "Heading back to my own room."

Finally catching on, his expression hardened. He sat up on the side of the bed. "You could stay here with me."

"Thanks, but no." She pulled on her panties.

"Pepper —"

Please don't let me crack until I'm alone. " 'Night, Logan." She opened the door, slipped out and pulled it closed behind her. Both Reese and Dash remained at the table, cards spread out in front of them. They tried not to look at her, but they failed.

Chin up, feigning as much attitude as she could muster, Pepper went to the room assigned her. She closed her door with a soft click, then pushed in the lock.

Awful pain squeezed her heart, and emotion choked her until she couldn't breathe right. Slowly, she slid down the door to sit on the cold wooden floor, her knees drawn up, her eyes burning. She hugged herself and did her best to swallow back the tears.

She'd always known that a normal life wasn't in the cards for her.

But then, she'd never figured on meeting a guy like Logan Riske.

Logan was the first up the next morning. Then again, he hadn't gone to sleep. On the couch, Reese stirred, grumbled at Logan and rolled to his side.

Reese overflowed the couch by a good foot. He had to be miserably uncomfortable. Today he'd go back into town armed with a story for the lieutenant and a cover that would allow Logan to stay with Pepper.

He carried the cell with him, but so far, Rowdy hadn't called.

Standing in the kitchen, he waited for the coffee to finish. He'd made a big pot, so it was taking longer.

A door opened, and, stiff, Logan walked to the end of the kitchen to see. But it was Dash. He had on jeans but hadn't fastened them. After a quick look at Reese, Dash asked quietly, "Coffee?"

"Should be done soon."

"Thanks." Dash went on into the bathroom, then joined Logan a minute later. He leaned back on the counter, crossed his arms and waited.

Now that he wasn't caught up in the hottest lust imaginable, Logan knew that Dash and Reese had to be well aware of what had transpired last night. Hell, he could still remember how Pepper had tightened all around him, how wet she'd gotten, how hot.

Her raw, broken cries as she came.

How she'd held him as close as she could.

And then she'd left him.

The second the coffee finished brewing,

361

Dash was on it. As he poured two cups, he said, "Okay, I know I'm up with the sun because that's how it is in construction, and I'm a creature of habit. Work or not, I'm awake. What's your excuse?"

Logan took his mug and went to the table to sit. "A shitload to do today."

"Yeah, about that." Dash pulled out a chair. "I wouldn't mind a clue or two. Am I playing watchdog? Errand boy? What?"

"Probably all of the above."

Another door creaked, and Pepper stepped out of her room. She looked first at Reese on the couch, then toward Logan and Dash. With no inflection whatsoever, she asked, "Coffee?"

Logan took in her disheveled hair, her heavy, sleepy eyes and her "just tumbled" appearance. He burned for her all over again. She was back to wearing just a T-shirt, and she had beautiful legs.

Legs that she'd wrapped around him while he rode her . . .

Dash said, "Just got done. Cream and sugar?"

"Please." She yawned inelegantly and headed into the bathroom.

Dash prepared her cup of coffee, set it on the table and cleared his throat.

Logan was doing a good job of ignoring

his brother when they both heard Reese get up. In his boxers, Reese started for the bathroom, but Dash said, "Occupied."

That stymied Reese for a moment until he shrugged and stepped outside.

Pepper noticed the opened patio doors when she emerged. She looked at the couch again, found it empty and smirked.

Still without jeans, she came to the table and dropped into a chair. Head propped on a fist, she indicated the extra coffee mug. "Mine?"

Dash smiled at her. "Let me know if it's okay."

She sipped, sighed dramatically and said, "Perfection. Thanks."

Even after Dash nudged him, Logan couldn't stop staring at her. He hated it, the way she made him feel so fucking . . . lost. He was a man who liked to act, not wallow in indecision and confusion. He knew right from wrong, and he enforced it. He went after what he wanted, whether it was a woman or a criminal, physical or emotional.

With Pepper, he didn't have a clue what to do.

Reese came in, saw her at the table, and sidetracked to the couch to get his pants. "Please tell me there's coffee left."

"Logan made a whole pot. Mugs are over

the stove." Dash nodded toward the kitchen. "I can put on more after we go through it."

"Thanks." Reese folded his blankets and put those with his pillow back in the closet before heading into the kitchen.

Pepper stared at the couch he'd just vacated, then turned to Dash. "Make your bed already?"

"Uh . . ." He shrugged. "Yeah."

She rolled her eyes at Logan. "I know you already did."

"Yes. But don't worry about —"

"Be right back." She scraped back her chair and disappeared into her room.

Reese came to the table with a cup of black coffee and a package of cookies. Minutes later when Pepper returned, he silently offered them to her.

She took two.

For some reason, even that turned him on. Shit. Logan turned to look out the window. Thick fog lifted off the lake, visible through the gray dawn. In another hour, the heat and humidity would be suffocating.

The table squeaked, and he turned to see Pepper carrying her cookies and coffee out to the deck.

"If Rowdy calls," he said to Dash and Reese, "let me know." He went after her.

Watching the sun creep over the hills, she sat on a dew-wet bench and sipped her coffee. The sunrise cut through the fog with blinding force, reflecting off the lake like colored glass.

Fuck it, Logan decided. He sat close beside her. "Did you get any sleep?"

"Not really, no." She sipped her coffee and, voice thick, said, "I might take a nap on the dock today."

"It'll probably hit ninety."

"I know." As if a thousand conflicts didn't exist between them, she smiled. "I always loved being outside. Even when the heat would chase everyone into the air-conditioning, I'd stay out and swim. Rowdy would harp at me about too much sun. Every time I turned around, he was trying to drag me into the shade. But it usually ended with him joining me."

Not touching her cost Logan. It was like holding his breath or going hungry. "He loves you a lot."

Her gaze drifted off to the lake. "The sunrise on the river is something to see, too. It colored our old rusted trailer and the carcasses of abandoned cars until they almost looked pretty." She closed her eyes and put her face up to the sun. "That was the best time to fish — before anyone else got up. Near shore, you could see to the bottom. I learned to clean and cook fish when I was about seven."

"That's awfully young."

She opened her eyes. "Sometimes we even had fish for breakfast."

Because she had nothing else? He couldn't bear imagining her in that type of poverty. The people he knew who lived on the river did so in extravagant condos or ostentatious homes. "Rowdy taught you?"

"He taught me . . . everything." She nibbled on a cookie. "He hasn't called?"

"Not yet, no. But it's only seven." How the hell had she disguised that body? How had she hidden that face? Seeing her now, with the morning sun in her eyes, she was the most beautiful woman he could imagine. "Try not to worry. It really hasn't been that long."

"It's weird," she said. "But I think I'd know if he was hurt. Or maybe I just tell myself that, so I don't go nuts worrying."

Almost on cue, the cell in the house rang. Pepper and Logan both turned as Dash stepped out to hand Logan the phone. "It's Rowdy." And then to Pepper, "He says he's fine."

Pepper let out a breath and nodded. "Of course he is. Thank you."

Dash didn't intrude. He immediately went back inside but left the patio door open to let in the cooler morning air.

Logan looked at Pepper, saw the anxiety she tried so hard to veil and made up his mind. He handed the phone to her. "I'll talk to him after you."

Something shifted in her expression — surprise, maybe gratitude, although she didn't thank him. She took the phone. "Hey, Rowdy."

Rowdy smiled while keeping watch out the window. "You didn't cut Logan's throat just to get the phone first, did you?"

"He gave it to me."

"Ah, did he now?" She sounded surprised and secretly pleased. "Wising up, is he?"

"I don't know."

Yeah, he didn't really know, either, but he was glad that she stayed cautious. Logan might have good intentions, but in reality, the best intentions could prove deadly.

As he looked on, officials went in and out of Checkers, a few in plain clothes, others in uniforms. "I might have some good news."

"I could use some."

"I heard that Morton is dead."

A long beat of silence preceded her soft

exclamation of "Wow." And then: "So the bomb got him?"

"That's what I'm told." It had gotten a few other people, too, but Rowdy didn't want to go into that with Pepper just yet. "We might not have to worry about him anymore, but until I figure out who detonated the bastard, I want you to stay put, okay?"

"We can't hide forever."

"We can hide a little longer, though, so promise me."

The smile sounded in her voice when she said, "Do what you need to do, and then come get me. I'll be here, I promise."

"Thanks, hon." Better to get this over with. "Now put Logan on."

"Love you."

He knew it, but he never tired of hearing it. "Love you, too."

A few seconds later, Logan said, "Morton's gone?"

So he picked right up on that? "That's the word on the street. Just dumb luck on his part, though. I don't know who yet, but someone dropped a shitty little homemade bomb into his office. Two inch pipe, gunpowder — and plenty of sharp projectiles. And get this — I'm told it exploded in his face."

Logan gave a low whistle. "That'd make a convenient mess."

Exactly what he'd been thinking. "He died a couple hours after getting to the hospital."

"I'd rather have him rotting in jail."

Rowdy didn't care one way or the other, as long as the bastard was gone.

But . . . death by bomb would work for him. Except that, with all of Morton's minions around, why would he get anywhere near a bomb? "Will you be able to do your thing, check fingerprints, get a coroner's statement or something? I want it confirmed that it's Morton."

"The medical examiner's office will want the coroner to send the body for an autopsy. I'll check on it first thing. Anything else?"

"Morton wasn't the only one to die."

There was a beat of silence, then Logan asked, "Who else?"

"No one innocent, so don't worry about that. The short version is that Morton was trying his hand at human trafficking. A rep was there to cement the deal when shit went sideways. After the bomb, the guy fled the building, and bit a sniper bullet on his way out the door."

"So that guy dodged the bomb somehow, but died anyway?"

"The plot thickens, right?" Rowdy kept

watch on the club while making his way back to his car. "Reese still there?"

"He's heading out today."

"Will you be able to stay with Pepper?"

"I'll have to leave for a while, but Dash will watch over her."

"You don't leave until Reese is gone." Rowdy got behind the wheel and started the old sedan he'd kept hidden at the same place where he'd stowed other necessities for Pepper. "And make damn sure Dash understands —"

"That you don't trust Reese. I'll tell him. But it's not necessary."

"Gamble with your own life if you want, but not with my sister's."

"I take it you do trust Dash?"

Other than Pepper, Rowdy didn't completely trust anyone, but . . . "He's your brother."

"And that says it all?"

"No, but being a brother myself, I assume he cares for you." Dysfunctional families existed, but in his gut, he sensed that Dash and Logan were close.

"Yes."

"And you care for her." More volatile by the second, Rowdy waited for confirmation.

He didn't have to wait long.

With a gruff edge to his tone, Logan

admitted, "I care."

"Good." Now that he was away from the club, Rowdy moved on to other matters. "Speaking of my sister, how is she really?"

A long pause.

"I'm guessing she's still there with you?" Listening in, drawing conclusions and maybe mooning over Logan — though she'd never admit it.

"No. She went in for more coffee."

Ah. That made Rowdy smile. Pepper did love her coffee in the morning. "Then why the suspense?"

As if goaded, Logan groused in reply, "You already know there are personal issues between us."

Personal? Rowdy winced. He really didn't want to think about that too much. "All right, I'll let that one go." After all, they had company in the house, so he didn't have to worry about Logan using her. "Just know that she's a lot more sensitive than you might imagine."

"She hides it well," Logan said, "but, yes, she's plenty sensitive."

And if Pepper heard that, she'd annihilate them both. "I know some people who were dealing with Morton on drugs and guns. I'm going to track them down for a little chat."

"Meet someplace neutral. Don't get drawn into a trap by going to —"

"Save the advice, Logan. This isn't my first rodeo." In many ways, he and Logan were alike — both take-charge and proactive. "I'll let you know if I find out anything."

"Fine, but remember that you're to touch base with me before acting."

Yeah, right. He'd been on his own far too long to start asking permission before doing what he considered right. "If possible — maybe." Rowdy disconnected the call before Logan could get up in arms about that.

He didn't bother to tell Logan that after he talked to his sources, he intended to do a little investigation into Lieutenant Peterson *and* Detective Reese Bareden.

For the foreseeable future, they were both on his do-not-trust list. Until he felt confident that they were honorable, he'd keep digging for the truth.

Someone was running a game; eventually, he'd find out who, and then he'd handle it. It was time to put the past to rest — once and for all.

CHAPTER EIGHTEEN

The second he stepped back into the house, Logan zeroed in on Pepper in the kitchen talking with Dash. By the concentrated look on her face and the pained look on Dash's, he knew she was interrogating his brother.

It made Logan nuts that she wore only that damned revealing, sexy T-shirt — but he could just imagine how it'd go over if he tried to dictate modesty to her.

He thought of himself as a perceptive man, but she'd really pulled one over on him. He'd bought her shy maiden act hook, line and sinker. Hell, he'd fallen for the shy maiden.

But this persona, the independent and volatile hellcat . . . yeah, that was even more tempting. With her body, face and "screw you" attitude, Pepper Yates personified every male fantasy. She was a woman comfortable in her own skin, a woman unconcerned with decorum.

His brother and Reese were both honorable guys. That didn't stop them from being affected by her in-your-face sex appeal, but it did stop them from acting on it.

Speaking of affected . . .

The chillier morning air left her nipples pebble-hard, noticeable beneath the soft cotton tee. Dash went nearly cross-eyed with the effort to keep from eyeballing her body.

Reese, being less discerning, didn't bother with any effort: he openly studied her chest and her every on-display curve.

Not that Pepper seemed to care, or even notice. Her dislike and mistrust of Reese was even more pronounced than Rowdy's.

How could he dismiss that? They weren't fools; they'd survived by being sharp, by noticing things that others might not.

Logan set his coffee cup on the table. "Dash?"

Grateful for an excuse to escape, Dash pulled his attention away from Pepper. "Yeah?"

"I need you for a minute."

"Yeah, sure thing, Logan. No problem." After one last unwilling peek at Pepper, Dash skirted her and the table and came to Logan with a mixed expression of relief and guilt. "What's up?"

"In private." Logan caught Reese's eye, and Reese, the ass, said, "Never fear. I'm nothing if not vigilant. Not that I expect her to attempt an escape in that getup." He smiled. "At the very least, she'd need . . . shoes."

That set off Pepper enough that she left them all, going into the bathroom and shutting the door.

As if that had been his end goal all along, Reese smiled with satisfaction and lifted his coffee cup in a salute. "There you go."

Logan couldn't really say anything to Reese without Pepper overhearing, but he shared a look of warning. "I'll be ready to get out of here in ten minutes."

"Good." Reese ran a palm along his jaw. "I need to go to my apartment to shave and change clothes before heading into the station."

Knowing his brother would follow, Logan went into his bedroom. The walls here were sturdy, but still he kept his voice low. "I don't know how long I'll be gone today, but don't let her out of your sight."

"God Almighty, Logan, that's going to be tough." One hand in his hair, Dash dropped to sit on the bed. He pinned Logan with a desperate look. "What if she skinny-dips again? In broad daylight? I already saw too much last night, you know, even when I was trying not to, but —"

"You looked?"

Dash grinned. "It was shadowy, but you know how it is. A naked woman just sort of draws my eye."

Damn it. His Lothario brother would have to learn to avert his gaze. "I'll talk to her before I leave."

Dash gave a mocking laugh. "Yeah, right, good luck with that."

"I don't need luck. I need leverage — and I have it." He had to make sure Dash understood. "Pepper is unpredictable. Everything I thought I knew —"

"Yeah. From what Reese said, she did a major about-face on you, huh?"

"Not entirely." There were many facets to Pepper Yates. Sensitive, as Rowdy claimed. Also proud and independent. Cautious out of necessity, but also bighearted.

Deep down, he believed her to be the same person he'd connected with. And there had been a definite connection. He realized it, and sooner or later she would, too.

"Be as nice as you can be, but if that doesn't work, if she tries to leave or get out of your sight . . ." Logan hated to think it, much less say it, but he had no choice. "Do what you have to do."

That stalled Dash. "You mean . . . like *restrain* her?"

Logan pulled on his shirt. "*Without* hurting her." If only he could stay . . .

"Damn, make this a little more challenging, why don't you?"

Temper breaking, Logan barked, "Can you do it or not?"

"Yeah, I can. Somehow I'll figure it out." Dash stretched as if he didn't have a care. "You don't actually think she'll try to run off, do you? I mean, where would she go? On foot, it'd take her over an hour just to get to town."

Logan found his shoes and sat beside Dash to pull them on. He had one irrefutable fact on his side. "She's here because this is where her brother wants her to be."

"You're saying for him, she'll stay put?"

Praying he was right, Logan gave one firm nod. "But keep an eye on her just to be extra safe."

"Got it covered. Anything else?"

"Yeah." He rubbed the back of his neck but couldn't put it off any longer. "Rowdy doesn't trust Reese. I promised him that I wouldn't leave Pepper alone with him, so —"

"Fuck me sideways." Incredulous, Dash

half turned to glare at Logan. "Let me get this straight. While you're gone for this indeterminate amount of time today, I might have to wrangle with a naked woman —"

"No!"

"— while fending off a partner you've trusted for years?" Dash lifted a brow. "Am I to make sure I don't hurt Reese, either?"

Rather than let Dash continue annoying him, Logan took the question seriously. They *had* been friends for years, and it felt traitorous, but Rowdy's concern chipped away at his trust in Reese. "I can't see it happening, but if he gets out of line, then do whatever you have to."

Mimicking Logan's mood, Dash sobered. "C'mon, Logan. You don't seriously think Reese would hurt her?"

"No." He didn't want to think it. "But I can't ignore Rowdy's gut feeling, either. He says Reese is hiding something." And given Rowdy's street smarts, he had to respect his instincts.

Dash waited.

"The more I think about it, the more I . . . agree. Until I know what's going on, I'm not taking any chances."

Done dressing, he stuffed his wallet into his pocket, grabbed up his keys and left the

378

bedroom.

Pepper came out of her room at almost the same time. Tendrils of damp hair clung to her face, so she must've washed up.

She looked at him and lifted her chin. "I used your mouthwash, but I need a tooth-brush."

That stalled Logan.

Dash moved around them, opened the hall closet, and offered a new-in-the-package toothbrush. "Here you go."

She accepted it with an offhand "Thanks," then thrust a paper toward Logan. "I have a list."

"A list?" He looked at the paper.

"Of things that I need you to pick up for me." She leaned against the hallway wall, arms crossed, watching him.

Condoms were listed as number one.

So she hadn't changed her mind about that? She waited for his reaction.

He nodded and went back to the list.

Bathing suit, size six; a certain type of lo-tion, shampoo and conditioner; sunglasses; running shoes . . .

Dash started to look over his shoulder, so Logan folded the note and put it in his pocket. "If you think of anything else, call me on the cell Rowdy gave me. You have the number."

"How long will you be?"

"Let's talk about that." To Reese, who still waited in the kitchen, he said, "Give us just a minute." He took Pepper's hand and urged her out the side door toward the truck.

As soon as they were out of sight of the others, she pulled away.

"Pepper." With a hand on her shoulder, Logan stopped her from stalking ahead of him. She could and would be as pissed as she wanted, but he wouldn't let her take any risks. "It could be late before I get back."

Something close to uncertainty passed over her features. "But you will be back?"

Oh, God, what did she think? That he'd leave her? "As soon as humanly possible." With condoms on her list, could she have any doubt about that? "How long it takes will depend on what's happening at work. You know about Morton, so you can imagine all the follow-up I'll have." Like seeing the body himself, to determine if it was in fact Morton Andrews. He'd studied that scum for so long, he knew every tattoo, every scar and flaw on his body.

Andrews could maybe fool others, but he wouldn't fool Logan.

"You have other cases?"

"Usually, but not right now." It was a sore subject for her, but that didn't change the facts. "My work against Morton took precedence. As the lead on a small task force, I'll be able to dedicate my time to that."

She nodded in understanding. "I'm glad Morton's gone, but now we need to know who's responsible."

If Morton was gone. He'd have it confirmed beyond Rowdy's street sources. "I'll be looking into it, and so will your brother. We'll get it sorted out."

"Okay then." She hugged her arms around herself. "You don't need to worry about me, you know. I can entertain myself while you're gone."

A perfect opening. He tipped up her chin so he could snag her gaze. "It's how you entertain yourself that concerns me."

Immediately, she dropped her arms and copped an attitude. "Is that so?"

Even smug, she looked so beautiful to him. Logan stepped a little closer to her and said succinctly, "No skinny-dipping."

"Until you get back with a swimsuit —"

"You'll swim in shorts and a T-shirt, minimum."

Her anger flared. "You don't —"

"And," he said, interrupting her, "you won't even think about giving Dash a hard

time. Don't let his attitude fool you. He can be ruthless, and he will be if you test him."

Her eyes narrowed. "Spell it out for me, Detective. What exactly will your baby brother do if I don't toe the line?"

"You don't have to toe the line. You have to be reasonable." She started to debate the point, but Logan spoke over her. "I know you're furious with me." *And hurt,* but he wouldn't say that. "I understand."

"You do, huh?"

"You're entitled. No problem." More gently, he added, "I hope we can eventually work through that —"

She snorted.

Locking his back teeth, Logan sought long-lost patience. "You need to understand that my brother is just helping out. He's not me, Pepper. It's unfair to put him in the middle by deliberately making him uncomfortable. And if you push too much, if you deliberately provoke him, you'll find that he's more than capable."

Logan realized that he could be blowing his chance at a repeat performance in the sack. But this was important, so he'd do it anyway.

"News flash, Detective. I've been dealing with the king of difficult brothers for most of my life. Dash doesn't scare me."

A smile almost got him. "I know." Before she knew his intent, he stroked her jaw. "But you'll behave all the same."

"Or what?"

"Or I won't keep you in touch with your brother."

That took her back a step.

His hand fell. Her expression was so wounded, so accusing, that it cut him. "No, honey, I'm not saying I'd let your brother be hurt."

"Ha!"

"But he'll be checking in often." He searched her face. "To me."

Realization dawned in her expressive eyes. "And you'll withhold info from me if I'm not playing nice?"

Spelled out, it sounded even worse. "Something like that."

"Jerk."

"I know." God, what he'd give if things could be different. "Look at it this way. You need to be here —"

"Where would I go, Logan?" Arms spread wide, she turned a circle. "We're in the middle of freaking nowhere!"

"True. But it hasn't escaped my notice just how ingenious you and your brother can be."

That flash-fire temper of hers faded until

her mouth quirked. "Oh, my God, you think I'm Houdini? You think I can somehow arrange for an airlift? What am I, a damned ninja?"

"No, but you are incredibly sexy, and you're out for payback —"

"Get over yourself!"

"And that's fine," he continued. "Heap all the anger on me that you want. I deserve it."

"Something we agree on."

His own temper edged up there. "Dash does not."

Reese stuck his head out the door. "Can you two resolve the most immediate issues so that we can get on the road?"

"You're leaving now," Pepper said. "*Both* of you." And then lower, to Logan, "Don't sweat it, Detective. Baby brother will be safe from my evil clutches."

She started to storm off, but Logan stopped her again, this time with a single, soft apology. "I'm sorry."

She stopped, faltering a moment, her back still to him.

Logan moved closer. "I'm going to keep saying it until you believe it."

"Damn it," she muttered low. She breathed harder, then suddenly turned around and grabbed his face.

Her kiss was so hot and deep that he almost forgot where they were and that he was about to leave.

Slowly she eased away. "Oh, I believe it, Logan," she said against his mouth. "But it doesn't matter enough. Yet."

He watched her walk away, her ass looking very fine beneath the T-shirt, her shoulders back with stubborn pride. It took Reese snagging his arm and drawing him away to finally get him to the truck. He turned to watch as Dash held the door open for Pepper, then waved them off and followed her in.

With no reason left for lingering, he got behind the wheel and turned the truck around to leave.

They drove in silence for a good fifteen minutes before Reese chuckled.

"Fuck you." While staring out the windshield, Logan went over all that had to be done, everything he needed to address today — things that Reese would know about and some he wouldn't.

His foul mood only enhanced Reese's hilarity. "She has you on the run."

Maybe. But he wouldn't discuss that with anyone. "Where's your car?"

"I left it in a lot near where I picked up Rowdy's car. You can drop me off there. I'll head home to check on my dog, clean up and change, before coming to the station."

"The dog's been closed up all this time?"

Reese grunted. "I wouldn't have an apartment left if I'd tried that." He turned his cell back on, glanced at it, then shook his head. "A neighbor lady has him. Alice-something-or-other."

"She's watching your dog, but you don't know her name?"

"Thanks to you, I was left to quick improvisation. She was handy, she likes Cash, so . . ." Reese shrugged. "She and the dog get along great. She has the magic touch with him, and believe me, Cash needs a little gentleness. I don't know how I'd have worked it, but I wouldn't have just left him alone that long. He'd feel abandoned. So it's a good thing Alice was around."

It left Logan curious, hearing such an outpouring over a dog Reese had just gotten and a neighbor he'd never before mentioned. "Does she have a dog of her own?"

"No. But it's clear she loves animals."

"A good quality, right?" How would Pepper feel about a pet? Maybe a cat or dog — or both. He had a feeling she'd love it, and that gave him something to consider.

"She's a single woman, super tidy, so you'd think she'd be on me to come get him, right? But last night when I called to check on him, I woke her. And get this — she'd taken Cash to bed with her because that's where he wanted to sleep."

Single and over-the-top friendly to his dog — seemed clear enough to Logan. "She's on the make."

"Definitely not. Hell, most of the time she won't even acknowledge me. If it wasn't for Cash, she still wouldn't. She's a strange one, I'll give her that."

"Define *strange.*"

Reese pondered that. "I guess self-contained covers it. And alert — like a cop, but in a different way. Maybe with more worry than caution."

"But you trusted her with your dog?"

"Cash loved her on sight. What can I say?" Reese grew introspective. "It's a hell of a conundrum."

Sounded to Logan like Cash wasn't the only one taken with the woman. They drove another twenty minutes in relative silence, each lost in their own thoughts, before Logan asked, "Have you heard from Peterson?"

"Strangely enough, no. My cell was off, of course, and we were on our own time . . . but, yeah, I half expected a dozen messages when I turned my phone back on." He glanced out the window, indifferent.

"She'll probably chew both our asses when we get in."

"Because of the club snafu, you mean?" Reese shook his head. "I doubt she knows we were anywhere near there."

"The thing is . . ." Logan flexed his hands on the steering wheel. "Morton Andrews died last night."

"The hell you say!" Reese scowled in surprise. "I saw the site, Logan, and the situation could have gone either way. It's not like the floor was obliterated."

"It was a homemade bomb. He died at the hospital after getting hit with shrapnel." While gauging Reese's reaction, Logan shared the few details he'd gotten from Rowdy on the second death.

Reese shook his head. "We'll need to find the sniper, but I doubt anyone will miss either of the men." Rife with disgust, he muttered, "As far as I'm concerned, good riddance to them both."

He was good — but there was something missing in his response. "You knew about Morton's newest venture into human trafficking?"

Reese didn't deny it, but he did clarify. "I didn't know much, only that he hoped to dabble. Why?"

"You didn't think to share it with me?"

"You're not a slacker, Logan. You know the club dealt in prostitution, and you knew Morton was brutal. It only made sense that he'd cut corners where he could."

"By buying women?"

Reese took in his skepticism. "Don't tell me you're surprised?"

That Morton Andrews would peddle flesh? No. But that Reese had info he hadn't shared? Yeah, that was an unpleasant revelation. "You should have told me."

"The way you researched him, I assumed you knew, as well. And with you on your stakeout of Pepper Yates, we didn't really have a lot of time to chat."

Bullshit. They'd talked, but Reese hadn't mentioned it. "I got sidetracked a few times. What do you know about it?"

"Only had a few leads, nothing concrete." Reese rolled a shoulder. "I hadn't checked into it yet, but one of my snitches told me that suspected traffickers were contacted by Andrews's cronies." Reese gave him a quick look. "Speaking of snitches . . . have you checked this truck for GPS tracking?"

"Yeah." No way in hell would he have taken Pepper to the lake house if he hadn't known she would be safe there. "Rowdy had me tagged with a mini-device, but he'd

389

already removed it. There wasn't anything else."

"Damn. He actually told you that?"

"He says he's come clean about everything." And for the most part, Logan believed him. So far, everything he'd said had added up.

"Guess he wasn't taking any chances with his sister."

"No, Rowdy Yates is not a man to take chances." Logan could only be grateful for Rowdy's diligence. "Turns out he had reason to mistrust me, right?"

Reese directed all his attention on Logan. "He had reason to doubt your motives — that's a different thing entirely. His gut told him you weren't being up front."

"Because I wasn't." Logan slowed at an exit ramp. Thanks to the highways, the lake house wasn't far from where he lived and worked, but it was secluded. "Gut instincts are usually dead-on."

Reese conceded the point. "I've never understood why so many people ignore them."

Logan felt the same — which was why he had to take Rowdy's concerns about Reese seriously.

"But now he knows what motivated you," Reese pointed out. "And in all instances, the end goal makes a difference."

"You think so?" Logan didn't feel very righteous about any of it. If he could turn back time . . . then what?

If he'd never gone after Rowdy, he'd never have met Pepper. She'd remain in hiding, living her life as a lie.

"I know so. Rowdy might be too involved to have a clearheaded perspective, but you're not, so stop berating yourself."

Did Reese hope to justify deceptions of his own? "There's never a good reason for hurting a woman."

"There's hurt, and then there's hurt." Reese smiled. "Last night, Pepper proved she's not exactly a delicate flower."

She'd proved . . . something. Logan didn't know what. "Stow it."

"In fact, Dash was afraid you'd knock a hole in the wall, the way you two were rocking that bed."

His temples pounded. "Shut up."

Reese grinned. "In all seriousness, seeing her on her way to and from your room, she appeared far from wounded. In fact, I'd say you're all but in the clear already. So how about we appease the lieutenant, I'll research that bomb, we'll track down a sniper, and then we can both get back to our lives."

Logan nodded, but he knew it wouldn't

be that simple. Nothing ever was — especially when dealing with Pepper Yates.

The closer he got to his apartment, the more anxious Reese became. He'd spent a near sleepless night on a too-small, narrow couch. He'd put up with an irascible and accusing female. He'd dodged Logan's subtle inquisition and condemning silences. And then he'd had more driving to do to get his car back home. He was exhausted, concerned, feeling a little cornered, and yet . . .

The majority of his thoughts centered around his neighbor.

A quick glance at his watch showed it to still be early. He had a little time before he should put in an appearance at the station.

Was Alice up? Should he call her?

Or surprise her by knocking?

Knocking, he decided.

Fighting off an absurd smile, Reese parked. Morning sunshine already baked the parking area. It'd be another scorcher.

Despite the exhaustion, he went up the steps with a sense of keen expectation. Was Alice still in her pajamas? What did she wear? Probably not anything sexy. Maybe something staid and shapeless. His grin widened at that image.

At her door, he raised his hand to knock — and heard Cash's berserk barking. The door opened without him knocking, and Alice stood there, well-wrapped in a peach-colored cotton housecoat.

He barely had time to register her soft expression, mussed hair and small bare feet before Cash leaped up against him.

Giving up his perusal of warm, sleepy woman, Reese knelt down and showered the dog with the attention he wanted.

Cash almost knocked him over in his effort to lick his face. Laughing, Reese stood again.

Alice handed him the leash. "He hasn't been out yet. I wouldn't delay on that."

"Hang on." Flattening a hand on the door, Reese kept her from shutting him out.

She looked down, let out a sigh and said, "Too late."

Damn it. Reese looked down, too, and saw Cash now cowering in what looked remarkably like embarrassment. "No worries, buddy. It'll mop up."

Cash thumped his tail in relief — and went back to excitedly yapping.

Reese laughed.

Alice tipped her head to study him.

Given the manners of his dog, he should have been embarrassed, too, but what the hell? It was funny. "Leave it," he told her. "I'll take care of it as soon as I come back in."

"Okay."

"Alice?"

She paused.

"Answer when I knock." And then, rather than let her dismiss him, he dismissed her by walking away.

In an absurd voice reserved only for the dog, he said, "Come on, Cash. Let's go, my man. That's a good boy."

He was all the way to the bottom of the stairs when he heard Alice's door click shut.

So she'd watched him go? Great.

Cash continued to bound around him, so Reese walked the dog out to the grass and let him do as he pleased. After sprinkling a half dozen areas to claim them, Cash chased a bee, barked at a squirrel and ran after the stick Reese threw for him.

After a good five minutes of playing, Reese dropped down next to a tree so Cash could get in his lap.

It was odd, but he accepted the truth — he'd missed the dog, too. Smiling at that silly idea, he hugged Cash and even kissed the top of his furry head.

The dog went bananas again, making him laugh.

"You really did miss me, didn't you? Was she cruel, is that it? Did she feed you birdseed or smack you off the couch?"

"Of course I didn't."

Reese looked up — and there Alice stood. She'd quickly dressed in casual slacks and now wore slip-on shoes, but she hadn't yet combed her hair.

"I was teasing." Reese patted the ground beside him. "Care to sit with us?"

"I'm fine, thank you."

So why had she joined them? Just to keep him from getting near her apartment again? Interesting. "Did he behave for you?"

"That depends on your idea of behaving." But she smiled at the dog. "He ate a throw pillow while I was . . . that is . . ." The words fell away, and she ducked her head.

Interest spiked, Reese said, "While you were what?"

She cleared her throat. "Away from the couch."

Away from the couch doing *what?* "Cooking?" Thinking of the occasions when Cash had done the most damage to his place, Reese offered, "Changing? On the phone? The computer?"

"Showering, actually."

He'd have paid good money to see that. "So . . . you were in there long?"

"Ten minutes, tops." She turned brisk. "But after scratching at my bathroom door, he quieted. I assumed all was well. Until I found the stuffing everywhere."

Great. "Sorry about that. I'll pay for the damage."

"No need. I made the pillow, and I have fabric left, so I'll just make another."

Somehow it fit that she could sew. But what else? "You're sure?"

"Don't give it another thought."

Cash finally plopped down, his chin on Reese's thigh. His tail thumped hard on the ground as Reese stroked him.

"He obviously adores you."

Was that surprise in Alice's tone? "I'm an adorable guy."

The slightest of smiles quirked her mouth. "Did you need me to watch him today?"

"I wanted to talk to you about that." He checked his watch again. "Come on. Sit for a minute."

Unsettled, she searched the ground and again shook her head. "I'm fine."

"Actually you're skittish. Why is that?"

"I'm not!"

Whoa. Slowly, keeping his gaze on her, Reese got to his feet. Cash went on the alert, unsure what they were doing. Hell, Reese was unsure, too. "Could we sit on the steps then?"

She looked back at the apartment, drew a breath and nodded as if she'd just agreed to enter a burning building.

With grave seriousness, he said, "Thank you."

One way or another, Reese knew he'd figure out the problem. But not now, not with such a limited time frame, not in the lot of his apartment building with his dog craving attention.

But soon. Probably a whole lot sooner than Alice whatever-her-last-name-might-be would like.

CHAPTER NINETEEN

By silent agreement, they headed back toward the steps. "Where do you work?" Reese asked.

"Here." She waited for him to sit on a step, then put herself as far from him as she could get without actually sitting on the blacktop. "I'm self-employed."

"Really?" Interesting. "Doing what?"

"I'm a virtual assistant."

Never heard of it. When he continued to stare at her in confusion, she launched into a rehearsed explanation.

"Other people who work from home often need help with databases, phone calls, filing and other general forms of organization. That sort of thing."

Enjoying how she'd opened up — in a miniscule way — Reese kept her talking. "How's that work?"

"It's easy enough with the internet and email. Different clients send their information to me and I keep their business lives running smoothly."

"So you're here . . . pretty much all the time?" That was so convenient, it almost felt like fate. Not that he believed in fate. If he did, he knew he was screwed big time, given that fate so far seemed to have a sick sense of humor.

"I . . . Yes." She frowned. "I'm not sure I understand why you're asking."

Reese put his hands on his thighs in sudden decision. "Here we go. I found Cash in a box in the middle of a street. The box was taped shut, so I know someone put him there on purpose."

"Dear God!"

He liked that reaction because it mirrored his own. "It was sheer luck that he hadn't already been hit by the traffic. I saw the box move, got suspicious and stopped. The second I lifted it, I knew there was a dog inside, so I put him in my car, cut the tape — and out popped Cash."

Hand covering her mouth, Alice looked at Cash with a wealth of emotion. She moved in closer to hug Cash tight.

Sensing her deep sympathy, the dog looked at Reese with worry. Expressive dog.

"I didn't really think it through," Reese explained. "I just took him to the vet, then

399

spent a small fortune getting him a flea dip, his ears cleaned, his blood checked . . . the whole shebang. Thus his name, Cash."

"That was so kind of you."

Great. Melodrama. Just what he didn't need. "That was *human* of me. Whoever put him in that box is lacking humanity." And should be beaten, at the very least. "But the point is, now I have a dog, and I'm fond of him and he of me, but unfortunately I sometimes have to work weird times of the day so —"

"You'd like me to be the dog sitter?"

In case she thought to refuse, Reese went about convincing her. "He's smart, so I know he can learn about tearing up stuff and waiting to go outside. Of course I'll supply all his food and anything else you'd need. And —"

"I'd love to."

"I'll pay you," he said at almost the same time.

They stared at each other.

Reese moved down a step to be closer to the dog — and to Alice. "I'm sure we could come up with an agreeable wage, and I could even pay overtime whenever my hours get too screwy." Like they were bound to be again today.

"I like Cash." She held the dog protectively to her chest. Cash's eyebrows went up and down as he looked at Reese with uncertainty. "I don't mind watching him."

"But I'll still insist on paying you." He patted his thigh. "Come here, Cash."

The dog bolted over to him, crawled into his lap but then stretched out to lick at Alice's hand.

A diplomat or an affection hog — Reese wasn't sure which.

Alice looked ready to melt. "Okay."

On to the next hurdle. "You can't watch Cash and ban me from your apartment."

Her gaze shot up to his. "I wasn't banning, exactly . . ."

Before she could get too worked up, he said fast, "It's okay. I'm not going to pry." Yet. "But I'm a cop, you know. I'm trustworthy. And I need to know Cash is safe."

Umbrage put her shoulders back and stiffened her neck. "If you're suggesting —"

"Not suggesting a thing." More like setting up the rules. "I'm only saying that ours will be a friendly business arrangement, and there's no reason for you to worry about me overstepping, in any way." Just because he suddenly wanted to kiss her silly . . . no reason at all. "I want everything clear up front."

"Everything?"

"The details of our arrangement."

She continued to regard him in stiff wariness.

Better to save that discussion for later. He checked his watch to drive home his lack of free time. "But right now, I have to go shower and shave and get to work. Are you okay for now?"

"Yes."

Still stiff. Great. So far he batted a big fat zero. "Today will probably be another lousy day. But I might —" as in definitely would "— come by during my lunch so that Cash doesn't think I've handed him over."

"Fine."

He rubbed his bristly jaw, but time did run thin. "We'll talk more as soon as I get a chance." He cupped Cash's furry face. "You be good, my man."

Almost as if he understood, Cash did an army crawl over to Alice. He rolled to his back on her lap and gave her a big doggie grin.

Alice cuddled him like an upset child.

"You big mooch." Reese had to laugh. Well-laid plans went to shit all around him, but at least he had a handle on this. "Thank you, Alice. It means a lot to know Cash is well cared for."

She didn't look up at him. She kept her

face tucked close to Cash's. "My pleasure."

And that was something else he'd like to see.

Alice's pleasure.

There were a lot of reasons why he should curb those thoughts. She was a neighbor. She had some issues going on that he didn't yet understand. And she was his dog sitter.

But . . . He looked down at a crooked part in her hair. No, he really didn't care about any of that. He wanted her. Eventually he'd have her.

"I'll see you, Alice."

She didn't say goodbye. But then, she'd never said hello, either.

Logan and Reese stood together while the lieutenant briefed everyone on the bombing.

Without looking at Logan, she said to Reese, "I want you to take the lead on this."

Given her apparent mistrust, that surprised both men. Logan was heading up the task force; it didn't make sense to switch things up right now, but what could he say? He needed as much free time as he could get. The fact that Peterson was working an angle of some sort could be used to his benefit.

Reese stared at her, then nodded. "Of

course."

She went on to name the officers covering the scene at the club and the hospital. "We have two of Andrews's men under watch. They're injured, but should survive."

That was news to Logan. Rowdy hadn't mentioned it, but it made sense. "They haven't said anything yet?"

"They were being treated, then went to sleep with painkillers."

"And no one pushed for info?" If their injuries weren't life-threatening, someone should have picked their brains at the first opportunity.

"There's enough bad press on us at this point. They aren't going anywhere, and no one has been allowed in to see them."

"I'll head there now —"

She shook her head. "I want you to interview the witnesses."

"We have witnesses?" Other than Pepper, whom he had under wraps. "Who?"

"Clubgoers, passersby, employees . . . typical lineup of possible observers. So far no one seems to know anything, but keep picking. You never know when a clue might present itself."

So she wanted him grounded at the station? Reese sent him a curious look, but Logan could only shrug.

Peterson went on to detail the officers working behind the scenes in supporting roles. There'd be computer checks to do, video cam footage to watch, warrants to obtain.

All in all, Logan wasn't displeased with his assigned duty. When the lieutenant finished, he followed her to her office and tapped on the door frame. "Got a second?"

As if expecting him, she seated herself and opened a file before saying, "What's on your mind, Detective?"

"Are you having Andrews's death confirmed?"

That brought her head up. For several seconds she scrutinized him. "It's going to be difficult. He must have been holding the bomb when it detonated." She held up her hands and wiggled her fingers. "No fingerprints."

"Shit." That was too damned convenient for comfort.

"The blast did considerable damage to his teeth as well, and his face . . . it's gone."

More than ever, Logan needed to see the body.

"I'm expecting an official report later this morning, but who knows? DNA sampling would be the last option."

Too expensive. "Relatives?"

"None that we're aware of." She closed the file folder. "You have reason to believe it's not him?"

"I wouldn't leave it to chance."

"Of course not." She swung her chair from side to side. "So Morton Andrews is presumed dead, a human trafficker is murdered, and you let Rowdy Yates go."

The accusation stiffened his spine. That's why she wanted to keep him at the station? "I had no reason to keep him."

"Hmm."

The noncommittal sound grated. Logan held her gaze and waited.

"Was Rowdy able to give you any useful information at all?"

Disliking the line of questioning but determined to hide it, Logan took a seat across from her. "He confirmed that some from the police department were on Andrews's payroll around the time Jack was murdered."

"Old news." She flagged her hand in indifference. "You know where he is?"

"Rowdy?" *He's off doing my job for me* — but of course Logan wouldn't inform her of that. "Not specifically, no."

She frowned.

Logan offered, "I could probably find him."

"Good. You do that." Almost like a dismissal, she checked her watch.

Logan didn't budge. Because they still didn't have reason to arrest Rowdy, he said, "You want me to ask him to come back in?"

"He and his sister, yes." She lifted her brows at him. "I have a meeting with the press in five minutes."

Trying to show no reaction to her order, Logan stood. "Is there something I don't know?"

"Given that you were running the task force, I shouldn't think so." She put her fingers together and studied him. Finally she said, "But then, you and Detective Bareden were out of touch last night."

Irritation sparked. "For a little while. Did you try to reach me? I didn't see any missed calls on my cell."

"So you didn't know about Morton's death until this morning?"

Straight-faced, without a single sign of deception, he said, "No."

"You didn't watch any television, listen to a radio . . . ?"

"My personal time is my own," he said, and he told a half lie. "But I was with a woman, and, no, we weren't watching television or listening to the radio."

"Ah. Well, that would explain it, I guess."

She stood. "I take it Detective Bareden was similarly preoccupied?"

Logan shrugged. "You'd have to ask him."

Taking a big verbal leap away from her inquisition, she said, "The club is of course shut down, the scene secured, but it won't do us much good. The place was mobbed — all three floors. Everything had already been trampled and tossed by the time we got there."

"Morton's office?"

"The scene is safeguarded, but even without the damage of the bomb, do you really think he's dumb enough to keep anything incriminating where others might get to it?"

Not really, no. "How was he identified?"

"You mean, given that his face was blown off?" She smirked at him. "Clothes, hair and ID in the wallet in his pocket." She strode past him. "The build matches and the hair color — what wasn't bloodied — matched up. Now if there's nothing else?"

"No."

"Then I suggest you get to work on those witnesses."

Logan followed her from the office and then kept going to his desk to get the report on the witnesses he'd be interviewing. He wanted to call Rowdy, but not yet. He needed complete privacy for that, and that meant getting through part of the day first. He had questions to answer, plans to make, reports to fill out.

He locked gazes with Reese.

Where to start, he wondered . . . and with whom?

Moseying barefoot around the property, Pepper saw that it was more weeds than grass, without a speck of landscaping in sight. The sun was so incredibly bright that it hurt her eyes — and she loved it.

The old house could use a new coat of paint. The windows needed a good cleaning. A few flowers would really be nice.

Like a vigilant shadow, Dash trailed silently behind her. He wasn't intrusive, but he wasn't an irritant, either.

Knowing he'd hear her, she said, "If I had a place like this, I'd plant wildflowers everywhere."

"The point of wildflowers," he replied, "is that you don't have to plant them."

"But I would." She stopped at the corner of the house to pull up a sturdy weed. "There are some really pretty ones, and they don't need much care."

"Meaning my house looks bare?" He smiled at her.

He was so incredibly handsome that if Logan didn't already have her so twisted up inside, she might have been more admiring. "You're supposedly rolling in dough, right? So why don't you pretty up the place a little?"

He bent to pull a weed, too. "I'm not *rolling in dough,*" he told her. "But I am comfortable."

She snorted. Comfort could mean a variety of things to a variety of people. Only the well-to-do used it to describe a lifestyle filled with security and extravagance.

"If I lived here," Dash said, "maybe I would decorate more. But the draw for me is that I don't have to do anything when I'm here. I cut the grass —"

"You mean the weeds," she quipped, and pulled another.

"— when it's necessary. But mostly I just laze around in the sun, go swimming, row out the boat, that sort of thing."

"Do you come here often?" If it was her place, she'd never want to leave.

"A day here, a day there, and a couple of times a year I find a week or more." He bent, turned over a rock and watched a fat spider scurry away. "I don't want this to become a big responsibility, and that's what it'd be if I felt like I had to get here to water

410

bushes or flowers, or trim the lawn."

"I guess. But you could hire someone." Since he *was* so well-off.

"Then others would know about it."

And Logan wouldn't have felt comfortable leaving her there. Dash hadn't complained, but she still felt she owed him an apology. "I'm sorry that we intruded on your privacy."

Standing in the shade of a shed, he looked around at the fallen branches and twigs from tall trees, and at the rusted lock on the shed door. "Don't be. Logan knows he can count on me for . . . anything." He checked the lock. "Damn, I guess I do need to do a little maintenance work."

"You have a lawnmower?"

"Push, yeah." Using his wrist, he cleaned sweat off his forehead. "The hill is too steep for a rider."

"I'll cut the grass."

He paused. "You don't need to do that —"

"I want to. I love the sun and the heat and the fresh air." Grudgingly, she confessed, "I'm a little bored, and I'm feeling sluggish. Since I don't have a suit for swimming, and Logan got his boxers in a bunch over the idea of me skinny-dipping —"

"Would you have?" he interrupted her to

411

ask. "I mean, without Logan here to know you're doing it?"

The grin came slow and easy. "You think I only did that to irk him?"

"Yes."

And he'd be right. "You've got me there. But if you tell him, I'll make you sorry."

He joined her in grinning. "Why would I do that?"

"Logan is your brother."

"That he is, and even though I love him, last night was mighty entertaining."

Entertaining? That hadn't been her intent at all. But it was so nice hearing Dash openly admit to loving Logan that she let it slide. "Most men aren't so honest with their feelings."

"Men who aren't wusses are."

She laughed at that. "I'm not overly modest, you know, but I'm not really someone who runs around in the buff, either."

"You impressed me. It was a diabolical payback, the type only a woman could connive."

"I'm not sure I like the way you say that." He made her sound really vindictive and wicked. Was she? Okay, she *could* be. But Logan had it coming . . . didn't he?

"I just meant that Logan's too serious. I like it that you're keeping him on his toes."

"Yeah, well, I'm still mad at him." She went to the shed and tugged at the flimsy lock. "You have a key?"

"Tucked out of sight on a hook inside the lazy-Susan cabinet." He crossed his arms. "Are you really that angry with him, even knowing why he had to dupe you?" Understanding softened his tone. "Or is it that you're still hurt because you care about him, and you trusted him?"

Pepper took in his sincere gaze, the dark brown eyes so much like Logan's, the breadth of his shoulders and the way his biceps bunched with his crossed arms. Beard shadow darkened his jaw and gave him an appealing, rakish look, and that smile . . . He probably broke hearts on a regular basis.

"Did I grow horns or something?"

She shook her head with amusement. "I bet you have an easy time of it with the ladies, don't you?"

"Dodging the answer?"

"Just making an observation. And the answer is . . . both."

He considered that before nodding and giving an answer of his own. "Women aren't too difficult once you understand them."

"What's there to understand?"

"Number one is that they're different from

men — more tenderhearted, gentler and far more emotional."

"That's awfully sexist." Was she being too emotional about Logan's ruse?

"But true all the same." Dash winked. "Later, when it cools down, we can work on cutting the grass if you really want to. For now, why don't we swim? There's heavy-duty sunscreen inside, and you can borrow my drawstring shorts and a T-shirt to use. I promise, no matter how awesome you look in the getup, I'll do my best not to notice."

Such a charmer. "Okay, sure." Maybe she could use the time with him to dig into Logan's psyche. No way did she want to be the overly emotional one. "You'll tell me more about Logan?"

He started them both back toward the house. "What did you want to know?"

"Everything." And to ensure he didn't disagree, she said, "It's the least you can do to entertain me while I'm stranded here."

"All right. But be prepared to dislike us both even more. Overall we've led pampered lives filled with love and indulgence." He smiled while saying that. "Our mom is a natural-born coddler and our dad is a real stand-up guy. Life has been good."

Oddly enough, she was glad to hear it. "I don't dislike either of you."

"No?" He looked pleased with her confession.

"No." She wouldn't wish her childhood on anyone. "I'll treat your story like a fairy tale." And maybe it'd make it easier for her to sleep at night.

That is, after she got a little more retribution with Logan.

Logan found her in the rowboat, stretched out on her back across one of the hard wooden seats, a floatation cushion under her head, her feet hanging over the side. Dappled sunlight came through the tall trees shading the lake. Rippling waves kept the boat rocking lazily, occasionally bumping the dock.

She slept on.

The heat of the day had dried her hair after her swim, leaving it in twisted hanks with a crooked part. A little too much sun kissed her nose and the tops of her cheekbones. Wearing a pair of Dash's shorts, cinched tight around her hips, and one of his large T-shirts, she should have looked silly.

Instead, she looked . . . relaxed. Happy. More at ease than he'd ever seen her.

Finding her like this worked as a buffer against the futile efforts of the day. He wouldn't mind ending every shift this way — coming home to find Pepper there, knowing she'd be his for the night — and longer.

Interviewing witnesses had proved a waste of time. He'd tried to check out Andrews's body, but the lieutenant had that locked up pretty tight. He'd have drawn suspicion if he'd started poking around too much.

Hopefully Reese found out something more.

Sitting on the dock, Logan took off his shoes and socks, then unbuttoned his shirt and rolled up his pant legs. A humid breeze licked over the bared skin of his chest, ramping up his edgy need.

His gaze tracked over her body, from her breasts to her long legs to her narrow feet.

"Thinking of joining me?"

His attention shot to her face. He found her watching him through heavy eyes, a slight smile on her mouth.

"I didn't mean to wake you."

"That's okay." She stretched, and even in the absurd clothes, she made his blood boil. "I've been napping too much today."

Enjoying this mellow mood of hers, Logan smiled. "You needed to catch up on your sleep." God knew, they hadn't gotten much rest yesterday.

"So do you." She sat up yoga style and, shielding her face with one hand, squinted up at him. "You get the rubbers?"

So bold, and so damned tempting. She left him savage with lust, but it was the overwhelming emotion he found difficult to contain. "I got everything on your list."

"Good." She looked around at the lake, at the sun now dropped in the sky. "What time is it anyway?"

"A little after seven. I meant to be back here sooner, but —"

"You have a job to do." She reached out a hand to him, and when he took it, she stepped from the boat and stood beside him. "Anything new to share on Morton?"

Eye-level with her knees, he stirred more. It'd be so easy to lean forward, to put his face against her warm thighs, breath in her scent, made muskier by the hot sunshine. "Not a whole lot."

"That's too bad." She touched his hair. "What about the rest of your day?"

Did she actually want to talk about that with him? It'd be unique for him to share his work with a woman, but then, Pepper was a unique woman, and this situation involved her as much as — maybe more than — him. "I went through a string of witnesses today."

She tugged him to his feet. "Bet that was a waste of time, huh? Hear no evil, see no evil, speak no evil."

"That's about it." When she started on the buckle to his belt, his abdomen tightened. "Reese went to the hospital to talk to a few of Morton's guys who were injured, but they're pretty dopey on pain meds."

"They'll live?" she asked without much concern. With his pants now open, she abandoned them to strip his shirt off his shoulders.

"Yeah." He helped her with the shirt, freeing his arms and dropping it to the side. When she went back to his pants, he caught her wrists. Not wanting to dissuade her but unsure how to continue, he asked, "What are we doing here?"

"I thought maybe you'd like a quick swim to cool down." She pulled a hand free and smoothed it over his chest. "You're a little sweaty."

Only a swim? That was probably better than getting busy in the water with his brother in the house, but still . . . "How could you sleep in this heat?"

"I told you I like it." She went back to his slacks, pushing them down so that he could step out. Eyeing him in his boxers, she said, "I like swimming even more, though. So what do you say?"

"Dash will have dinner ready in a few minutes."

"Then we better get to it." She held out the big T-shirt. "As you see, I was a good girl and stayed covered up today."

As sincere as he could be, given he was already half hard, Logan said, "Thank you."

That made her grin. "I like your brother."

Absurd jealousy stirred. "Meaning what?"

The grin turned into a laugh. "Meaning that, all in all, I had a nice day."

"I'm glad." He'd have to talk more with Dash. He'd taken only a cursory report before heading down to the lake to see her.

"You might want to take a nap yourself after dinner." She went on tiptoe to kiss him. "Now that we have the rubbers, I'm expecting to have an even better night."

She turned away and made a clean but shallow dive into the water, proving that she'd already gauged the depth.

Logan stood there, sporting full wood and wishing he could bypass everything else and go straight to bed with her.

Dash yelled down the hill, "Burgers in five minutes."

Damn. Hoping the water would be cold enough, Logan dove in behind her.

CHAPTER TWENTY

"Everything tastes better off a grill," Pepper said as she finished off her hamburger.

Dash agreed. "Doesn't hurt to have that view, either."

"Or the fresh air," Logan said.

The setting sun sent a splash of crimson across the cloudless sky, reflecting the rich colors on the surface of the placid lake.

Dash propped his feet on the railing, a Coke dripping condensation onto his abs.

Pepper sprawled out in a lounge chair, still in the same clothes she'd worn to swim. She looked so carefree that Logan wished he could keep her there forever.

With him.

She swatted away a mosquito, took another drink of her cola, and swiveled her head toward him. "So Reese isn't joining us?"

"Not tonight, no."

"I trust him more when I can see him."

Dash gave a short laugh. "I'm guessing you and your brother feel that way about everyone."

"With good reason."

Almost on cue, Logan's cell phone buzzed.

"Speak of the devil?" Pepper asked.

Since the call came in on the cell phone Rowdy had given him, Logan shrugged. "Reese or your brother. No one else has this number."

As soon as he answered, Reese said, "What was all that with you and Peterson today?"

They hadn't had a chance to talk earlier, not at the station with ears all around. And with Reese gone most of the day, they hadn't even passed each other that often.

"Hang on." He covered the phone and said to Pepper, "I'll just be a minute." He started to stand so he could seek some privacy.

Pepper waved him back. "I'm going to take a shower and wash the lake water out of my hair."

Dash stood, too. "You'll have to make it fast if you hope to have hot water." He gave Logan a look and said, "Think I'll put away the dishes."

Which was code, meaning he'd keep an eye on Pepper. Logan appreciated his help

— and resented it at the same time.

"Thanks. I'll lend a hand in just a minute."

"No rush."

Standing so he could watch Pepper through the patio doors, Logan said to Reese, "No idea what's going on with her, but I have to admit, I didn't expect her to make you lead." He'd been given carte blanche on the specialized task force duties, and he *had* made headway — though, of course, Peterson wasn't entirely up to speed on everything.

"Maybe she recognizes my superior sleuthing abilities."

That obvious joke fell flat. "Or maybe she knows I'm in a little deeper than I'm letting on." He visually tracked Pepper's every move as she rummaged through the items he'd brought back. She went through the bags, carried the shampoo, conditioner and lotion into the bathroom, and took the rest to the bedroom.

"Or she hopes to pit us against each other. Who the hell knows?"

Pepper came from the bedroom with clean clothes. She spoke to Dash for a moment, then went into the bathroom and shut the door.

The small shower barely accommodated one person, so no way could he join her —

even if she'd invited him. But he could picture her naked, wet . . . and he did.

"Don't let her get to you," Reese said, interrupting his thoughts.

"Who?"

He made a sound of exasperation. "Peterson." He muffled the phone for a moment, then came back. "Sorry. Cash is underfoot."

Without the view of Pepper to hold his attention, Logan walked to the railing and stared out at the lake. "How's the crazy lady who's been keeping him for you?"

"Never said she was crazy. And, in fact, she's been incredible. Cash is happy, I'm happy, and she's available 24/7. So . . . if you need me, I'm there. But if not, I figured I'd spend the night with Cash, then show up at work early tomorrow, maybe throw Peterson off the scent a little."

"We're fine here. Don't worry about that." The lawn, though more weeds than grass, was now evenly cut. He hadn't even noticed before, not when he'd been so intent on Pepper sleeping in the rowboat. "What now?"

"I saw the body." Reese didn't bother to disguise his disgust. "The face was a mangled mess, jaw destroyed, one ear blown off, teeth missing. There was too much blood in his hair for me to tell if the color was exact, but definitely blond. The size, weight and bone structure seemed right."

"You're not convinced it's him?" Did anyone really believe that Andrews had died so easily?

"The thing is, the two bodyguards at the hospital? They'd been drugged."

Logan straightened. "Come again?"

"The bomb did some damage to them, but mostly they were out because someone dosed them. I'm thinking they were props, like the wallet in the pocket of the corpse."

A corpse that could also be a prop.

Reese continued, "Didn't you tell me once that Morton had a scar on his shoulder?"

"Yes." As a younger man, Andrews had done his own dirty work — and hadn't always gotten away intact.

"Well, the upper body is pretty singed and mangled." Before Logan made any mental leaps, Reese said, "And I never saw the scar firsthand, but . . . I didn't find anything like that on the body."

So it was a stand-in. "He's still out there."

"*Maybe.* If it's not Morton, well, what will we do about it? That's the riddle, yes?"

"Yeah." Logan's eyes burned from a combination of tiredness and lake water. "Jesus, I want this over with."

"Now more than ever, I suppose."

"Meaning?"

"You have Pepper to consider, not just a need for vengeance."

"The way I see it, I have more reason for vengeance than ever before." Andrews had killed his friend Jack — but he'd also made Pepper's life miserable and continued to be a threat against her. "One way or another, I wanted Andrews to pay. If he's dead, okay. But even if he's not, he'll never get near Pepper."

"Speaking of finding Andrews . . ." Reese paused, and then asked, "What's Rowdy up to?"

Logan didn't have to lie. "No idea, really. He's following some leads or something. That's all I know."

"What leads?"

"He said he has reliable contacts on the street — same as most cops do."

"Make no mistake, Logan — he is not a cop."

"No." But that made him no less reliable.

"It's a little dangerous, isn't it, letting him off the leash?"

Logan snorted. Never had Rowdy Yates been leashed, definitely not by him. "I have no choice but to trust him." Same as he did Reese — with limits on both of them.

Reese hesitated again. "If he turns up

anything, you'll let me know?"

"First thing." Logan was ready to disconnect the call when Reese spoke once more.

"I almost hate to miss the show tonight. Hope Pepper takes it easy on you — or not, depending on your preference for that sort of thing."

The call disconnected in the middle of Logan's heated reply. He stalked into the house in time to hear Pepper squawk when the hot water ran out.

Dash grinned. "I did tell her."

Joining him in the kitchen, Logan said, "You two seem to be getting along." He picked up a dish towel and began drying the few plates and utensils they'd used.

"She won me over," Dash told him.

"So she didn't give you a hard time?"

"A little maybe." A crooked smile came and went. "She's genuine, you know? And funny, and not at all unreasonable."

"To you." With him . . . well, she had grounds to be difficult, so he'd just accept it. For now.

"True." Dash finished with the dishes. He dried his hands and leaned back on the counter. "She's also as sexy as a woman can be."

"I know."

"Killer legs."

Logan tensed. "I know."

"And the rest of her —"

Throwing the dish towel onto the rack, Logan considered throttling his brother. "Do you have a point, Dash?"

"Yeah, I do." Sincerity chased away the humor. "Pepper Yates is a keeper."

At that moment, the "keeper" shut off the shower. Logan knew she'd emerge any minute. Freshly washed, soft and damp . . . maybe ready to torment him some more.

In bed.

God, he hoped.

Dash gave his shoulder a shove. "Damn, Logan. You are so far gone, it's almost not funny." But he laughed anyway. "On top of her other qualities, she has the constitution of a bulldozer."

Glad to give Dash a new focus, Logan asked, "How so?"

"She cut the grass. All of it," he stressed. "And damn, but she seemed to enjoy herself. I got her to put on sunscreen first, but she didn't have the right shoes."

Logan scowled. "The hill . . ." Without care, someone could slip and lose a foot.

"Yeah. Makes it treacherous. It was hot as hell this afternoon, so I thought I'd have to insist. But she's smart enough that before I could even mention it, she put on her jeans and boots, and she got to it."

It didn't surprise Logan that Pepper enjoyed working outside. Soon he'd be able to jog with her, and maybe that'd help her to burn off excess energy.

Unless they could burn it off tonight in bed, instead.

"It wasn't easy, but halfway through, I talked her into taking a break. We drank iced tea, took another dip in the lake, and then . . ." He shrugged. "She wanted to finish cutting. I felt like a damned slug, sitting around watching her. And I did promise you I'd keep an eye on her, so I ended up pulling weeds."

It was Logan's turn to grin. "I thought you wanted to leave the place untouched so it wouldn't become a chore."

"Yeah, I did. But she outmaneuvered me on that. I swear, I was ready to call it quits long before she was. If I'm not careful, she'll have me relocating wildflowers with her tomorrow."

Logan pictured that, grinned again — and Pepper emerged. She paid the brothers no mind as she went out to the deck to comb her still wet hair.

Definitely sexy, as Dash had claimed. With her ruse as a wallflower no longer necessary, she had a way of walking, of infusing just the right amount of swagger and sway to her hips. Thanks to the chill water of the shower, her stiffened nipples showed beneath the soft cotton of a clean T-shirt.

Logan drew in a breath — and realized that Dash was staring after her, too.

He gave him a shove.

Unfazed, Dash saluted him. "I think I'll kick back in front of the boob tube."

They got crap reception and didn't have cable, but Dash kept a store of DVD movies in a cabinet under the television.

Seeing his brother settle in on the couch, Logan said, "Keep an eye out while I get my own shower." A cold shower, which he needed. He stuck his head out the door to speak with Pepper. "I'm going to wash up, too. I shouldn't be long."

"Good." She kept her back to him while dragging a wide-toothed comb through her long blond hair. It was still so hot that it wouldn't take long for it to dry. "Make it quick, though. I feel like turning in early tonight."

With him? She was so unpredictable, he couldn't be sure. He hated to give his lust free rein on assumptions, when this could be more of her torment. "Pepper . . ."

Looking over her shoulder, she gave him a

sultry stare. "Keep the condoms someplace handy."

And just that easily, she got him semi-hard. Maybe tonight he could convince her to spend the night in his room. He wanted to take as much time with her as he could, while he could.

And with any luck, it'd be enough.

Rowdy sat toward the back of the bar. While waiting for his contact to join him, he watched for trouble, and he watched for the petite waitress. He saw stacked women, lush women, blondes and brunettes, but he didn't see the hot little redhead.

Had she quit? Changed her hours?

No, he wouldn't accept that. Eventually, he'd see her again.

His attention shifted to five men who'd just entered, their gazes searching the crowd. They wore jackets — likely to conceal their guns.

Without a shadow of a doubt, Rowdy knew they were looking for him. It was a hazard of asking questions.

Snitches weren't loyal. Most were just plain desperate.

When he'd asked specific questions, he'd known that others would come after him, curious as to who had been curious, and why. It was almost funny — but not quite.

Slipping out of his chair, Rowdy stuck to the darkest shadows and moved along the wall to the hallway that led to back rooms — the kitchen, bathrooms, perhaps an office.

It pissed him off that he had to go without new info. The men's arrival here meant he'd gotten too close with his questions today, and someone had noticed.

One guy, even two or three, he'd have taken his chances in the hopes of uncovering something important. But going up against five trained thugs would be suicide.

He started for the bathrooms but changed his mind at the last minute. Instead, he veered off to swinging metal doors that opened into the bustling kitchen. He pushed through — and almost ran into his little redhead.

Juggling a tray of drinks, she pulled back, and he stepped forward, taking them both out of view of the customer seating.

An automatic apology tripped from her soft mouth.

Until she saw him — and went mute.

One emotion after another shadowed her beautiful blue eyes — surprise, delight, suspicion and then reproach. "You can't be back here."

Rowdy couldn't believe his bad luck at finally seeing her again at such an ill-fated time. Knowing what he wanted to do, and what he had to do, he weighed his options.

"This tray isn't getting any lighter."

As spirited as ever. He chewed his upper lip in indecision but didn't really put up much of a fight. "I was hoping to see you again."

"I can't imagine why."

Cutthroat thugs searched the premises for him, and if they found him, it wouldn't be polite conversation on their minds. But he grinned all the same. "We have unfinished business, you and I."

Her pale blue eyes stayed direct. "And here I thought we were quite finished."

"Not by a long shot. But much as it pains me, now isn't the time. So —" He took the tray from her hands and plunked it down on the counter.

"What do you think you're doing?"

Seriously. What *was* he doing? "Going on the assumption you'd as soon not see me murdered."

"Murdered!"

"Shh." He looked over his shoulder. The men drew nearer. "I need to find a back way out."

Her mouth dropped open but almost immediately snapped shut. "Are you in trouble?"

"Pretty much always."

"I am *soooo* surprised," she said with crisp sarcasm.

Their chitchat would have to be cut short. "It isn't the cops coming after me, honey. And just so you don't think I'm a wimp, there are five of them. I'll get in a few hits of my own, but it's not going to be pretty. I have about thirty seconds left before —"

"Of all the . . ." Already turning with his hand held in hers, she led him toward the back exit but stopped suddenly and instead pushed him through another door and into a pantry, closing the door behind them.

Reaching up, she pulled a cord and the small room went dark.

Rowdy crowded closer to her back. "Maybe you didn't understand —"

"Shh." She reached back, accidentally patted his junk, and jerked her hand away. He heard her audible swallow, then her whispered, "Sorry."

Near her ear, he breathed, "Quite all right."

She turned her face a little to explain softly, "Men were at the back door."

Ah. So the detour was to protect him? Nice.

Almost as nice as her breath on his mouth, her scent wrapping around him, and the innate trust she'd just exhibited.

Unfortunately, he couldn't enjoy it as much as he'd like because if they found her with him in a pantry, she'd be in as much trouble as he was.

Rowdy put his hands on her shoulders, started to ease her back behind him — and voices sounded outside the door. He and the waitress both held their breath.

"You see him?"

"Not yet."

"He's probably cowering in the johns."

Rowdy scowled. He did not cower. Okay, so he hunkered down in a pantry. But that was just good common sense. Not cowering. Hell no.

She reached back and patted him again, this time on the thigh.

"We'll check it out, but in case we missed him, I want you outside the back door, Hicks. Smith, you stay at the front. If either of you see him, remember, we need him alive, but not necessarily kicking."

The men laughed.

Rowdy could feel her trembling, and he wrapped his arms around her. They both waited another thirty seconds. Finally she turned toward him, and, both hands flat on his chest, she backed him up. "Carefully," she whispered. "There are bags on the floor, cans everywhere."

Rowdy dug out his cell phone, opened it and used it like a flashlight. He saw a narrow opening behind a shelf.

"Stay there," she said. "I'll turn on the light and step out. If no one is watching, I'll call the police."

Rowdy caught her wrist with his free hand. The blue light of the phone shone on her face, exaggerating her lashes, the shape of that tempting mouth.

"No police," he told her.

She paused. "Do I want to know why?"

" 'Course you do, but I can't go into it right now." Damn, it was insane, but he wanted to kiss her. And he would. But not yet. "Check the back door. If there's only one man there, no problem. I can handle that."

"Don't be an idiot."

"Shh," he told her with a smile, even though she'd whispered. She had her head way back to glare up at him, and the differences in their sizes — her petite and so feminine, him taller and much stronger — turned him on. He felt like a caveman, but so what? "I swear to you, I'm not a threat." Not to her. Not to anyone innocent. "But I do need to go, or others might be hurt."

She searched his face, gave him a light punch to the shoulder, and said, "I'll be right back. Don't move."

Praying she wouldn't betray him, that she wouldn't go ahead and call the cops, or worse, give him away to the goons, Rowdy stood beside the shelving and . . . waited.

Seconds later she came back. "There are four men now at the front of the bar. They're starting to question customers. If anyone saw you duck back this way —"

"Doubtful." So only one man remained at the back. Perfect. Rowdy pulled her farther into the room. "Give me your name."

That threw her. "I don't —"

Pulling her to her tiptoes, he pressed a firm kiss to her mouth. Her lips were soft, warm, and he wanted more than the three seconds he took. A whole lot more. But that'd have to come later.

When he released her, she stared up at him, softened by the same things he felt, looking a little dazed.

"I'll be back to explain everything, you have my word. But I'm not leaving without your name."

She shoved a hand into her hair, ruining her bangs, and said, "Avery Mullins."

Yeah, that suited her. She looked like an

436

Avery. Rowdy kissed her one more time. "You're a lifesaver, Avery. Thank you."

He started to head out, but she grabbed him by the waistband. "Hold on."

Stepping out ahead of him, she gave a casual glance around, gave him a subtle nod, and retrieved the tray of drinks.

He saw her push through the metal doors and disappear from sight. Wasting no more time, Rowdy went through the rest of the kitchen to the back door. Along the way he snagged a hand towel, an apron and a knife.

Making no noise at all, he peeked out and found a guy staring back at him.

Grinning at the guy's surprise, Rowdy slugged him hard. He was a big man with big fists, and when he hit a guy point-blank, the dude felt it.

Content with the way the goon crumpled, Rowdy bent to gag him with the hand towel while checking the area, but saw no one watching him. He used the apron to tie the guy's hands behind his back. Salvaging what he could of the night, he dragged his victim to his car and shoved him into the trunk. Satisfaction filled him; it looked as if he'd get his information after all.

Seconds later, he got behind the wheel and drove away unscathed.

Well, unscathed except for that kiss.

Avery Mullins. He had a feeling he wouldn't be content until he got a better taste of her, and more. Much, much more.

CHAPTER TWENTY-ONE

Wearing unsnapped jeans and nothing else, Logan left his door ajar when he went into his room to turn down the bed. The icy shower had revived him a little, but it wasn't enough to temper the sharp, edgy lust.

He needed Pepper to appease that particular ache.

He was just about to go after her when he heard her come in. Voice mellow, she asked Dash, "Where is he?" He didn't hear his brother reply, so presumably he'd only given a nod of his head.

Taut with anticipation, Logan stood at the foot of the bed; she didn't keep him waiting.

She stepped in, closed the door and devoured him with her gaze. Nothing more. She didn't say anything, didn't do anything other than provoke him with her obvious interest in his body.

Her silent, mysterious gaze was so tactile,

he felt stroked.

Did it give her satisfaction to leave him unsure of her intent?

Screw it. He knew what he wanted, so he'd make the first move and she could deal with it — or not.

Watching her, he took the box of condoms and set them on the nightstand at his side of the bed.

Her mouth curled into a sensual smile.

"Take off the T-shirt," he told her.

Without hesitation, she pushed away from the door and did just that. She grasped the hem and tugged it — slowly — up and over her head to drop it on the floor. Wearing only miniscule panties, she went to the bed, crawled on her knees across it, and stopped in front of him.

"Your turn." She gave a brief caress to his chest. "Lose the jeans."

With her so close, he picked up the light scents of her shampoo and lotion, along with the scents of sunshine and fresh air. Together, on her, they were enough to take out his knees.

He shed the jeans without reserve and, once naked, reached for her hips. When she didn't protest, he slowly moved his hands over her ass, her hips and thighs, relishing the feel of her. He had big hands, and they covered so much of her silky skin. That turned him on, too, seeing his darker, rougher hands on her sweet, pale flesh.

It amazed him, how incredibly sexy she was, but what he felt was so much more than physical attraction.

Keeping iron control, he smoothed his hands to her narrow waist, up to her breasts. Lush, full, firm . . . her nipples drew tight.

Damn. It took all his concentration not to lower her to the mattress right now.

Pepper tipped her head back, arching her spine and pressing her breasts toward him — an invitation he couldn't ignore.

He teased her nipples, first kissing lightly, licking and then drawing on her.

While she remained so accepting, he slid his hands into her panties and dragged them down her thighs.

Gaze warmed with lust, she put her arms around him and whispered, "I've been thinking of fucking you all day."

Her phrasing hit him like a cold slap, but he tamped down any reaction. Keeping one hand curved on her derriere to hold her still, he pressed his other hand between her legs.

As he searched over her, a vibrating sound of appreciation removed the taunt from her expression.

"Already wet?"

"I . . ." She swallowed, drew in deeper breaths. "I told you I'd been thinking of this."

"Of me." He wanted her clear on that. What they had was special, whether she'd admit it yet or not. Keeping her gaze captured in his, he opened her and slowly pressed a finger deep.

Breath catching, she said, "Logan . . . that feels so good." Her eyes sank shut and, as he worked his fingers in and out of her, she bit her bottom lip. "God, I missed sex so much. Maybe more than anything else —"

To silence her, to keep her from reducing their time together to nothing more than physical release, Logan kissed her hard. She accepted that with enthusiasm, kissing him back, sucking at his tongue, and clamping her internal muscles around his now slick fingers.

When he knew she was close, he pulled free and eased her to her back on the bed.

He skimmed her panties off the rest of the way, stroked his hands over her body, down to her knees — and parted her legs.

Body flushed, lips parted, she lay there, waiting to see what he'd do.

Giving herself to him.

It wasn't everything he wanted, but for

right now, it was enough. He bent and kissed the inside of her knee, up her tender inner thigh, over her taut belly. Her hands tightened in the bedcovers — but she didn't resist him.

"You smell so fucking good." He brushed his nose over her curls.

She made a sound of excitement.

Settling on the bed between her legs, Logan used his thumbs to part her swollen lips, drew his tongue over her, up to her clitoris. She went still, held on a precipice of sharp pleasure.

And he covered her with his mouth.

They groaned together.

She tasted even better than she smelled, and the small, rough sounds she made, the way she moved under him, all worked against his restraint.

He wanted it to last, so when he felt her tightening, he changed tactics, licking into her instead. She groaned a complaint, then lifted her hips up to him when he returned to teasing her in just the right spot.

Again when she neared a climax, he eased off.

One small fist clenched in the sheets. "Damn you."

He smiled and bit her gently. "Trust me."

"Stop teasing."

He hoped to tease her for the rest of his life, but he said only, "It'll be better if you wait."

"I don't want to — *Ah.*"

This time she clamped her hands into his hair to keep him close as he worked her with his tongue. Her hold was tight enough to sting, but he didn't mind; he liked knowing he'd gotten her to that point of desperate need.

Wanting to feel her release, he pressed three fingers into her, nice and deep, and the orgasm rolled over her. She squeezed his fingers tight, bathing them in silky wetness. She let him go to snatch a pillow over her face, trying to muffle her harsh cries. Her strong thighs tensed even more, her heels digging into the mattress at either side of his shoulders. It went on and on until she sank boneless onto the bed.

So overwhelmed he could barely draw breath, Logan sat up and grabbed for a condom. When he turned back to her, she had her eyes closed, her legs still sprawled.

He touched her knee. "Pepper."

She drew one more big breath, let it out slowly, and opened her eyes. Three seconds ticked by and then . . . "That was worth the wait."

He trailed his fingers up and down her

thigh. "I'm glad."

"If you're waiting for an invite, you got it the minute I stepped into the room."

A half smile hid his deeper thoughts. Truthfully, he didn't want to rush it, because he knew she'd want to leave him again afterward. But telling her that would be too emasculating, so he lowered himself over her without comment.

"Mmm," she said. "So you *were* waiting for another invitation."

He kissed the side of the neck, her jaw. "I like how you taste, Pepper." He drew on the soft skin of her throat, put a damp love bite to her shoulder. "And I love seeing you like this." In his bed, soft and accepting.

The mention of love threw her for a second, then she teased, "Well-sated, you mean?"

He kissed her jaw again, the top of her cheekbone, the bridge of her nose and her forehead. "Not yet, honey." Guiding his cock to her, he sank deep, to be held in snug, slippery warmth. Emotion caught in his chest, stilling him, forcing him to take a moment to regroup.

A little breathless, she agreed, "Not yet."

And that did it for him. He held her head and took her mouth in a deep, tongue-thrusting kiss. Locking her tight to him, he started the rhythm they both needed. Never in his life had he felt so connected to a woman. Less than two minutes later, she hugged him hard and cried out as another climax rippled through her.

His heart thundering, he put his face in her neck and gave in to his own release.

Minutes later, when his heartbeat finally slowed and his breath evened out, it struck Logan that she still held him. Every so often he felt the soft brush of her mouth on his shoulder.

The gentle touch leveled him as nothing else could. Hell, a sucker punch to the chin couldn't have left him reeling the same way. He lifted up to his elbows to see her face, but the second her gaze met his, he knew.

She would leave him again.

He saw the regret in her eyes, felt the way she emotionally withdrew. Was it pride that pulled her away, even when she wanted to stay? Or did she not feel the same things?

Persuasive arguments formed alongside his hurt — a hurt he buried under irritation. "Damn it, Pepper, this is ridiculous. You know you want —"

His cell phone rang. Given her dark frown, the interruption had probably stopped him from saying too much.

Logan eased away from her and stretched

out a hand to snag it off the dresser. In case she had thoughts of leaving before they talked, he held her ankle with his free hand.

She came up to her elbows. "My brother?"

"I assume so." He flipped open the phone. "What's up?"

"I'm sitting here with one of the traffickers."

Logan straightened. "You're okay?"

"He's an ugly fucker — more so now that we've finished our chat — but yeah, no problem."

He relaxed and gave Pepper a nod, smoothed his hand over her calf. "Your sister is here with me."

Rowdy's voice dropped to a whisper. "That's your way of saying I shouldn't scare her?"

"Pretty much."

Rowdy snorted. "Feel free to edit things however you want, but don't make the mistake of keeping anything from her."

No, he wouldn't do that. Pepper had proven more resourceful than any woman he knew. She could handle the truth — and she deserved nothing less. "I wouldn't."

"No names, and nothing incriminating, got that?"

So the guy was listening to him? "Understood. Tell me what happened."

"I was set to meet with a *friend* at a local bar, but instead, five bozos came in looking for me. I managed to get one of them —"

"How exactly did you do that?" Visions of Rowdy maiming someone, totally screwing the case, got his temples throbbing.

"He was stationed by the back exit, waiting for me. But I'm a faster, harder puncher than him."

"He was alone?"

"Yeah. The other guys were going through the rest of the bar, asking questions, looking under tables, doing God knows what."

A muffled protest ensued, followed by a thump. It got quiet again.

Logan choked back his annoyance. "So you punched him, and he decided to spill his guts to you, huh? He didn't call out to the other four guys?"

Pepper jerked upright. "*Other four guys? What are you talking about? Rowdy's okay?*"

"He's bragging," Logan told her, making sure Rowdy heard. "I'd say he's still in one piece."

Rowdy laughed. "Before he came to enough to start squawking, I stuffed him in my trunk and drove to a secure location to . . . question him."

The muffled complaints escalated again.

Logan blew out a breath. "Care to tell me

where this secure location is?"

"No."

Pepper leaned against his back and twined her arms around his throat. He felt the cushion of her breasts, and her warm breath on his ear.

It maddened him.

Cutting to the chase, Logan said, "How bad is he hurt, and what does he know?"

"He's alive, but not real happy. He says he's a top guy for the trafficker — and the guy who took a bullet to the noggin was a negotiator. Seems old Morton had planned to buy several young girls."

His guts cramped. "How young?"

"Seventeen, eighteen. Thereabouts."

Bastard. "He'd have used them at the club?"

"The idiot is unsure about that. All he knows is that Morton wanted a shipment, made a deal, but then tried to renege when it came time for final arrangements."

"He didn't want the girls after all?"

"Oh, he wanted them. He just didn't want to pay the asking price." As if coming to grips with the reality of human trafficking, Rowdy took several slow breaths.

Logan heard a thump, a groan and another thump. He didn't need to be a psychic to know what happened. "Rowdy, listen to me." He infused authority into his tone. "You need to get a handle on that temper. He's scum, and he deserves it, but if you kill him I can't help you."

On alert, Pepper leaned back. She left her hands on his shoulders, idly caressing him.

"Help me what?"

"Stay clear of this." Logan stood to put some space between himself and Pepper's luscious naked body. She didn't know the ugliness of the conversation or the fine line her brother walked right now. He needed his wits to talk Rowdy off the ledge before he did irreparable harm. "I know you'd like to kill him."

"With my bare hands," Rowdy said in a gravelly rasp. He breathed too fast, too low. "Do you know that he talks about women, about *girls,* like they're fucking property?"

"I know." He hadn't dealt much in human trafficking, but there were other things just as revolting. The ones responsible seldom put any value on human life, and they almost never felt any real remorse. "I don't blame you for roughing him up —"

"Good." A few more solid punches and a few more groans. "I'm only giving him a little of what he deserves."

"I'd have done the same." Logan locked his jaw. "But you have to stop."

450

Silence.

It wasn't concern for the trafficker that kept Logan pacing, but Rowdy didn't seem to be in the mood to listen, so he redirected his attention. "Tell me what you've found out so far."

He practically heard Rowdy gathering himself before he finally said, "Morton tried blackmail."

"Against who?"

"The traffickers. He said he had cops on his payroll, and on a whim, he could bring the force of the law against anyone on his shit list."

"Why would he do that?"

"He wanted his supply dirt cheap, but that was a no-go. He got threatened in return, and he found out the trafficker has his own considerable means of retribution. For a lot of people, that sheds suspicion on his timely death."

"It'd be good motivation to fake it." If Andrews was believed dead, the traffickers would forget about revenge — and then Andrews could strike against them first.

"The theory is that Morton would get his shipment free, and maybe even try to take over the business. The two were battling for the rights to buy and sell women . . ." Rowdy sucked in several tight breaths.

"Honest to God, I might have to slug him a few more times."

Recognizing that as less volatile bluster, Logan asked, "He'll live?"

"Unfortunately."

It was easy enough to understand Rowdy's rage. Any good man would feel the same. Any man who'd ever loved a woman would be especially outraged at the idea of trafficking.

Glancing over at Pepper, Logan found her on her knees, her hands resting on her thighs, her blond hair curled down and around her breasts. Jesus, she twisted him up inside.

He turned his back on her and dropped his voice. "You know I'm not going to let anything happen to her, right?"

"So you've said."

"You have my word." He'd die before he let anyone, especially anyone as corrupt as Morton Andrews or a flesh peddler, get anywhere near Pepper.

"Some things are out of your control."

"No, not this. Not ever."

Rowdy took that in, then murmured, "I appreciate that."

"The same goes for you, Rowdy."

"Whoa. What the fuck does that mean?"

Turning back to Pepper, staring into her

beautiful light brown eyes, he said, "I don't want there to be any fallback on you, either."

"Forget that shit." He snorted. "I don't need a damned babysitter. Just concentrate on keeping my sister in the clear."

No, Rowdy didn't need a babysitter — but he needed a friend. And he needed a real life. "Everything your sister deserves, you deserve, as well." Before Rowdy could get insulted over a perceived slight on his ability, Logan added, "Think how happy it'd make your sister to know you were safely settled somewhere, with no reason to look over your shoulder."

It amazed Logan, but big tears filled her eyes. They didn't fall. She didn't sniff or make a big deal of the emotional vulnerability.

The tiniest, most endearing smile lifted the corners of her mouth.

Logan knew he was in it for the long haul, and he knew how important Rowdy was to her. But even if he'd never met Pepper, he'd feel the same. Rowdy was a good man who'd never been given a break.

In another whisper, Rowdy said, "I hate it that she worries about me."

"Let's stop giving her reason to, okay?" Logan walked over and stroked Pepper's hair. Before it all ended, he'd make it right for them both.

"First things first. You're getting ahead of yourself."

Right. He had to determine if Andrews was dead or alive, and now he had traffickers to deal with, as well. He needed to take Rowdy out of the equation — which wouldn't be easy while Rowdy kept a bludgeoned perp on hand.

Logan gave it quick thought and came up with a viable solution. "Here's what we'll do."

Pepper listened as Logan made note of the information against Morton. Not once did he question the facts Rowdy gave him.

He trusted her brother.

That made him smart and intuitive — on top of being hot in the sack.

"Does he know who you are? Good. You haven't used any names, either, so he can't connect any of us to this. Do you think you can leave him tied up somewhere secure so no one else will find him? Not for good, but until we give the cops an anonymous tip about where he's at. No, not just any cop. Reese." Wonderfully naked, Logan continued to pace the limited space in the bedroom. "I know how you feel about him, but he's the only cop I trust to do this. Once

Reese takes the guy in, it shouldn't be difficult to link him to the dead trafficker, especially with the info we'll share in the tip. That'll give us reason enough to hold him."

A little awed, Pepper realized that Logan wanted to protect Rowdy. Other than her, who had ever done that?

No one.

Her brother would be the first to say he didn't need protection. In fact, he'd deny it with his dying breath.

But for so long now, he'd stood alone against the world, a barrier between her and every bad thing that could ever have happened. He slept around a lot, and even though she harassed him about it, she understood.

It was the only comfort he ever got.

More tears burned her eyes; her heartfelt sigh drew Logan's attention. Frowning in concentration, he listened to Rowdy while studying her.

Her body, but also her face. Especially her eyes. She had the feeling Logan wanted to decipher her, her moods and her vendetta against him and . . . everything that concerned her. She hadn't made it easy on him. But maybe that should change.

By championing her brother, he'd just

stolen a small piece of her heart.

"Yeah," Logan said while watching her. "Reese will have to take him in, but Peterson will oversee things. No, she won't have him killed." He rolled his eyes. "No, she won't. Even if she was inclined to do that, and I'm not convinced she would be, there are still too many loose ends for her to try it." He listened a moment, then shook his head. "*No,* you can't just kill him yourself."

That outrageous statement made her grin. So Rowdy blustered, and Logan bought into it? Or was that just men being men, letting each other save face?

Not that she cared much what happened to the snitch. He'd been in on selling women, working with Morton, and he'd tried to gang up with others to hurt her brother. Far as she was concerned, he had three major strikes against him.

But as she'd told Logan, Rowdy wasn't a murderer.

"Look at it this way. The guy will probably try to bargain, and he'll give up his boss."

And women would be saved. Pepper softened more.

Rowdy must have agreed, because Logan nodded. "Fine. Leave him hobbled until the morning. It's no skin off my nose. I don't give a damn if he suffers a little. But, Rowdy, don't do any serious damage to him. I mean it."

Again drawing Logan's attention, Pepper moved to the top of the bed and leaned against the headboard, getting comfortable. He evaluated her new position with interest.

"Sure, you can call Reese yourself if that's how you want to handle it. Just know that I'll be calling him, too." He listened, shook his head. "It's not up for negotiation, so just deal with it."

Two such controlling men, Pepper thought. Knowing they respected each other left an unfamiliar tightness in her chest.

"Rowdy, before you go . . ." Logan hesitated, then said, "You did good with this. Thank you."

And there went the last of her reservations. Damn it. How could she hold on to her hurt feelings still?

Logan closed the phone but didn't join her on the bed.

Without righteousness to fuel her brazenness, she felt a little shy. "You need to call Reese?"

"In a minute." He folded his arms and regarded her. "Your brother wants to talk to him first."

More than a little aware of her own naked-
ness, she struggled against the urge to get
under the covers. "You're okay with that?"

He shrugged. "If that makes Rowdy feel
better about things, then I don't see the
harm. They can figure out a good place to
leave the snitch before Reese picks him up."

"You trust Reese, don't you?" Just as he
couldn't discount her brother's misgivings,
she couldn't discount Logan's judgment.

"Ultimately, I do, yes."

"But you're not willing to ignore Rowdy's
concern?"

"How could I? He knows what he's doing."

The space between them got to her, and
she patted the mattress beside her.

Gaze contemplative, Logan unfolded his
arms and approached. He stopped at the
side of the bed. "I'd like for you to stay here
with me. In the bed." He reached out and
fingered a lock of her hair. "Sleep with me."

Being truthful, she said, "I'm pretty
zoned. I'm not sure I'll be up for anything
other than sleeping."

"I don't need anything else." He sat on
the side of the bed and cupped his hand
around her skull. "I want to hold you,
Pepper. All night. Not to get too poetic, but
I want to feel your heart beating, breathe in

your scent and . . . just touch you."

Her heart melted.

Brushing his thumb over the corner of her mouth, he said, "Stay here with me tonight."

Something new and different and wonderful blossomed inside her. She needed to lighten the mood or she'd soon be an emotional mess. "If I snore, no complaining in the morning."

Recognizing her acquiescence, his grin came slow and easy. "Give me ten more minutes to make sure Rowdy and Reese have worked out the details, and then we can make it an early night."

Yeah, that worked for her. No reason to go face-to-face with Dash after what he'd probably just heard. Besides, Logan looked as exhausted as she felt. "Same here," she said around a yawn. "Until then, why don't you fill me in on what Rowdy had to say."

He did, and soon after that, they both fell asleep.

Logan forgot all about calling Reese.

CHAPTER TWENTY-TWO

Reese sat on his couch, his feet propped on the coffee table, a can of beer at his elbow and his dog sprawled over his lap. A sports program played on the TV, but he wasn't really paying attention.

Cash's fur was sleek and soft — because Alice had given him a bath and brushed him. For some absurd reason, that really got to him.

He could almost picture it, her gentleness, that soft way she spoke . . .

Great. Instead of putting his brain power to the mystery surrounding Morton Andrews, he was daydreaming about a woman's voice.

Pathetic.

He looked down at the dog and found Cash looking back. That made him grin. "You're thinking of her, too, aren't you?"

The dog's tail started thumping in excitement. He lifted his head in expectation.

"No, we can't go bother her right now. But I know she likes you a lot, too." He tipped up his beer for a deep drink and muttered, "Me, she's keeping at a distance. I'm going to have to do something about that, but I don't want to screw up our arrangement with you."

Cash's eyebrows raised and lowered; he tipped his head.

Reese laughed. When his cell rang, the laugh almost changed to a groan. Sitting forward, he snagged it off the end table. "I just got comfortable, damn it."

Assuming it must be Logan with another glitch, he answered.

But it wasn't Logan, and it was a hell of a lot worse than he'd expected.

He could only juggle the issues and players for so long before everything crashed down around him.

And with every day, the crash seemed more imminent.

As soon as Logan got to work the next day, Reese pulled him aside in the hallway. He looked haggard, tired and itching for a fight.

"What the fuck were you thinking?"

Logan studied Reese. "I take it you got the anonymous tip?"

"Not funny, damn it!" A uniformed cop

glanced their way, and Reese, with a strangled breath, tried to rein in his temper. "He's here, but Jesus, man, how do you expect me to fix this?"

Fix it? Is that what Reese thought? That he expected him to find some magical solution to the mess? Not likely.

In fact, he'd already realized that he owed Reese an apology. "I shouldn't have pulled you into the middle of this."

Reese drew back. "What?"

"I was trying to figure out how to keep Rowdy out of it and still use the information we got. But I shouldn't have put you in that position. It's not you —"

"Fuck that!" Reese crowded in close, nose to nose, eyes burning. "I'm not talking about involving me, damn it. I'm your partner. I've got your back, no matter what."

Narrowing his eyes, Logan said softly, but with ultimate command, "Step back."

Reese heaved, searched his face, and then with another rank curse, he turned away. Logan watched him rub his neck, saw his spiraling frustration.

Something was going on with Reese, and he'd had enough of subterfuge. "Now might be a good time to come clean."

Reese laughed, turned to look at him, and laughed again. "You know the guy was roughed up pretty bad. Broken nose, black eyes, even a damned broken finger."

Logan just waited.

"I had to turn him over to Peterson. She's in there now, jawing at him, stepping in where she doesn't belong."

Doesn't belong? "She's the lieutenant."

"And it's your case. But from the get-go, she's been in it up to her stubborn chin. Micro-managing, snooping —"

Snooping? "What the hell is wrong with you? Peterson wants to clean up the corruption, that's all. You know she's always been a hands-on lieutenant." Her determination to stay involved and on the street hadn't won her any favors in the force, but she didn't seem to care.

"No, Logan, it's more than that."

"You know that . . . how?"

"Detectives," said a new, more feminine but no less strident voice.

They both turned to see Lieutenant Peterson bearing down on them. Logan nodded at her.

"How propitious to have you both here together."

Logan checked his watch. "Only ten minutes early."

Reese crossed his arms over his chest and dropped back negligently against the wall.

All signs of his agitation were now under wraps, the cagey bastard.

Peterson looked between the two of them. "I got a description of the man who worked over our prisoner. He sounds remarkably like Rowdy Yates."

"Really?" Reese smirked. "Tall, blond and muscular could describe a lot of men."

Since that also included Reese, Logan had nothing to add.

The lieutenant waited, then said flatly, "Morton isn't dead."

"No?" Logan didn't even bother trying to look surprised. "Did that come from the perp or through the coroner's report?"

"Both, actually."

Shit. Reese didn't change expressions or posture, so Logan asked, "Do we know the deets on the corpse?"

"One of his lackeys." She waved that off. "No doubt Morton hired him because he had the same body type and hair color."

"Bleached blond?" Reese asked.

She shrugged. "It's possible Morton had him bleach his hair. At this point, we don't know, and it doesn't matter anyway."

To carry on his part, Logan asked, "Did you get any good info from the guy Reese brought in?" The sooner he could get out of the office, the better. He needed Andrews removed as a threat. He needed —

"Actually, yes." She rubbed her face tiredly, then dropped her hands. "The apartment building burned to the ground."

Plots and plans stalled as Logan assimilated what she'd said. It wasn't at all what he'd been expecting. "What apartment building? When?"

The lieutenant slanted a guarded look at Reese, but since he didn't budge and continued to look neutral, she turned back to Logan. "The apartment building where you stayed while cozying up to Pepper Yates."

The slow burn of red-hot rage coursed through him. If he hadn't gotten Pepper out of there . . .

"The apartment building," Peterson stressed, "where we assumed we'd find a lead. The apartment building that, according to you, gave us nothing viable to work with."

"When?" Reese demanded.

At the same time, Logan said, "Was anyone hurt?"

"I got the call while I was in interrogation. Likely arson. The place was torched pretty good. Gutted. A total loss."

It was difficult for Logan to get around the idea that Pepper had lived there, and whoever set the place ablaze apparently wanted her dead. He tried to think of who else might have been in the four-unit building.

"We didn't find any bodies inside." Before his relief could sink in, Peterson said, "Have you located Rowdy and Pepper?"

Logan shook his head, but to help cover that lie, he said, "Given the fire, I'll make it a priority."

"You do that. Both of you."

Reese went very still beside him, his expression enigmatic.

"You think one of them set the fire?" Logan hadn't even considered that. He knew Pepper hadn't left the cabin, but Rowdy . . . damn, he just didn't know. "Why would they?"

"Perhaps to destroy evidence." She gave him a sideways look. "You hadn't yet cleared out your belongings?"

"No." He'd been too busy hustling Pepper's sweet behind out of the line of fire. "I didn't have that much there. A few clothes, bedding . . . enough stuff to make it look like I lived there."

"Were you still seeing Ms. Yates?"

She sounded merely curious, so Logan replied with equal nonchalance. "I haven't been back to the apartment at all." His thoughts jumped ahead. He needed to get hold of Rowdy first thing, then check with Dash to ensure nothing had happened at the lake.

"So you didn't lose anything valuable?" the lieutenant asked.

"Not really, no." What had Pepper left behind? She was too smart to get tripped up by loose ends — but not everyone would know that. Had the fire been an attempt to hurt her, or to remove a trail?

"First a bomb at the club, a dead body double, now a fire and a task force that's turned up nothing at all." The lieutenant shook her head. "Explaining this and the department's involvement is getting more and more complicated by the minute. The very least we can do is get the Yates siblings back in here."

"I'll get right on it," Logan promised.

"Understand, Logan, I want them in here before the end of the day. No more delays. Even if they know nothing about the fire, they could be in danger. We'll offer them protection. Keep them safe." She glanced at Reese. "From everyone."

Reese took an aggressive stance — but Logan put up a hand, stalling any arguments from him.

Complacent, the lieutenant said, "I don't care how you accomplish it, but I want them here, where I can talk to them. Understood?"

"Loud and clear," Reese said.

The second Peterson walked away, Reese dropped back against the wall. "What now?"

Logan struggled with himself, undecided.

"I don't entirely trust her, you know that," Reese said. "But Peterson is right. The cabin would be secure unless anyone digs into your family history — but that's something another cop can do. Then it's easy enough to find out about your brother, and a property search will —"

"Disclose the cabin." Logan tensed even more. "The fact that her building burned down means someone knows she was living there."

"Could be a fluke, a coincidence," Reese said, "but neither of us is going to buy that. They're onto you, or Rowdy and Pepper . . ." He shrugged. "Possibly both. I know you weren't followed —"

"Even the best cop can trip up, so, no, we don't know that for a fact." Awful possibilities chewed on Logan's already churning discontent. "Andrews is sick enough on his own, but this just jumped to a whole new level. With organized traffickers involved now, too, I think we're better to trust our luck here, at the station, than someplace remote."

Reese gave a nod of agreement. "Sucks, but there it is. What can I do to help?"

"I'm going to get Pepper myself." No way in hell would he trust that to anyone else.

Reese caught his arm. "Understand something, Logan. I'm here, I have your back."

But Logan knew that Reese was still hiding something. "Meaning what?"

Reese narrowed his eyes. "You can trust me, damn it."

Logan gave a tight smile. "I know."

"Then no more surprises. If you have Rowdy digging around, tell me."

"Rowdy is his own man, checking things his own way."

"That's not smart."

Logan disagreed. With so many unknowns, he liked having Rowdy on the outside. But for Reese's benefit, he conceded the point. "Maybe not, though I'm not sure it matters much at this point. I'm bringing Pepper in, and if I can, I'll round up Rowdy, as well. In the meantime, see if you can get anything useful out of our prisoner."

Relenting, Reese nodded. "I'll let you know."

Pepper remained silent on the drive in. Logan didn't like it, but he knew she was worried with the sudden change of plans. Until she reached her brother, he didn't expect her to relax much. Rowdy had promised to meet him at Dash's home so they could all go to the station together, but Pepper didn't know about his detour.

Dash followed behind as a precaution. No, he wasn't a cop, but he was a cop's brother and loyal enough to do whatever had to be done.

It made Logan edgy, having Dash and Pepper in potential danger.

And Rowdy . . . he'd agreed to come in, but Logan knew him well enough now to pick up on his suspicion. He had a distinct feeling that Rowdy would make his own detours before meeting with them at Dash's.

"Pepper?"

Keeping her gaze out the window, she said, "Hmm?"

He tightened his hands on the steering wheel. "I wanted to give you more time, but unfortunately, time's a commodity I just don't have now."

She turned to look at him. "What do you mean?"

"You're going to have to trust me."

Silence fell. The only sounds inside the truck were of the passing traffic and the air conditioner blowing. Logan didn't break the quiet; at this point, what could he say?

He felt the scrutiny of her light brown eyes as she studied him. Tension escalated until he thought he might snap.

"It's not easy," she finally said.

Not easy — but not impossible. Logan saw promise in her words. "I know."

She half turned in the seat toward him. "You made me feel like a stupid fool."

His guts clenched in remorse. "That was never my intent."

"No, your intent was to use me however you wanted so that you could get your hands on my brother."

There'd be no point in denying it; never again would he lie to her. "Yes." With one clarification. "That was before I really knew you, though."

"You knew me when you had Rowdy arrested."

He wouldn't let her get away with that accusation. "I knew Sue Meeks, an uptight, mousy neighbor who liked sex."

"You knew that wasn't my real name!"

"Names have nothing to do with it. Sure, I realized you were Pepper Yates using an alias, but I didn't know *you.* Parts of you, yes. Important parts." She wouldn't like it, but he spoke the truth anyway. "Like your vulnerability."

"You're deluded," she said with a lack of steam.

"At first I was determined to get closer just so I could find Rowdy. You're right about that. But after we talked a few times, I felt equally drawn to you, and . . . sympathetic."

"You —"

"It was tricky," he interrupted, "how you handled it, how you handled *me.* But you're a natural-born sensualist —"

"And you used that to your advantage!"

He accepted that accusation. "Just as you've used it to your advantage since then."

"Complaining?" she asked with a sneer.

Logan understood her. Whenever she worried, she got more sarcastic, almost as a cover to her real thoughts. "The sex is amazing, so, no, you won't hear any complaints from me."

She narrowed her eyes.

"But if I wanted only sex, I could have that without you."

She drew in a sharp breath.

Rushing so that she wouldn't misunderstand, he said, "I wanted shy, withdrawn Sue Meeks. I sure as hell want Pepper Yates. You're stronger than I ever realized. More independent. Loyal and funny."

"I haven't denied you, Logan. You don't

need to pour on the compliments."

"Only speaking the truth." He desperately wanted her to understand. "The thing is, last night, holding you while you slept, waking with you tucked close this morning . . . that is and always will be special to me. I'll never take it for granted."

Anger deflating, she eyed him. "Never?"

Emotion left his voice gravelly. "Even before I saw the real you, I had regrets and reservations. I'd wanted Morton Andrews for so damned long. I wanted to avenge my friend Jack. That need drove me. Hell, it almost consumed me." He glanced at her. "But then there was you, and I hated that you were involved . . ."

"You involved me," she whispered.

"No, Andrews did that. But I brought it all back out in the open, and I'm sorry for that, too." He pawed the steering wheel. "For a while there, I wished that I'd done things differently. The thing is . . ." He felt the beating of his own heart, and he sensed her suspended breathing. "Now I know you, Pepper, the real you, and I wouldn't want to give that up, no matter what."

After a small eternity, she reached out a hand to him.

Acceptance — of his explanation, or . . . of him? Praying for the latter, Logan squeezed her fingers. "I need you to trust me, honey," he stated again.

She gave one small nod. "Okay."

He was glad to have that settled, but he couldn't relax yet. "We're going to Reese's apartment first."

Confused, she looked out the window. "I heard you tell my brother to meet us at Dash's house."

"Yes, and we'll get there eventually. But I want to double-check on things first, and if I'm not satisfied, I want a safe place to stash you until I can work it out. My house is probably being watched, so we're going to Reese's apartment."

"And my brother?"

It wouldn't be easy, because they both knew that, regardless of the danger involved, Rowdy would put his life on the line for her. Logan knew what Rowdy meant to her, and because he now accepted that he loved her, too, he wanted her happy.

"You have my word, honey. I'll do whatever I can to keep him safe."

More than a little displeased with his promise, she gave him a disgruntled frown, murmured an insincere "Thanks," and looked away.

Morton ran a hand over his new, darker

hair, cut in a ridiculously shabby way. He didn't like it; it made him look average, when he was anything but. The beard shadow, sunglasses and bulkier clothes helped conceal his identity.

He missed his fine wardrobe, as he missed his caravan of cars and toadies. But it wouldn't be for much longer. The cops thought him dead. Business associates discounted him as a continued threat.

As always, he had the upper hand.

He only had a few loose ends to tie up, and thanks to his plebian pretense, he'd have that handled very shortly.

Sitting alone in a compact car under a shade tree, the irony struck him: so many masquerades at work. Rowdy Yates had dodged him by disguising his sister, and now he'd use that knowledge to kill them both.

Rowdy had cost him a great deal, but today he would pay up — with nothing less than his life.

CHAPTER TWENTY-THREE

Rowdy checked his watch. Very shortly, Logan and Pepper would be at Dash's home. He didn't have much time, but before he allowed his sister to be taken into police custody — even for her own protection — he wanted to check out Reese Bareden. The easiest, most expedient way to do that was to go through his apartment.

On his way into the building he passed a woman heading out with a dog. Giving away nothing of his purpose, he nodded at her, but she avoided his gaze, edging away with a tight hold on the dog's leash. Rowdy glanced back and saw her heading for the sidewalk.

Dismissing her from his mind, he went up to Reese's apartment. There were two doors on that floor, but he saw no one, so he got out his tools to pick the lock.

"You'd think a cop would know better," Rowdy whispered as the lock easily gave way. After checking one more time for curious spectators, he slipped into the apartment and closed the door behind him.

Detective Bareden was an orderly guy. That made it easier. He went to the desk and laptop first. He wasn't a computer expert, and Bareden had a lot of his online files password protected. But he still found plenty.

On him. On Pepper.

And on Lieutenant Peterson.

"Huh." Strange. Why all the curiosity about his lieutenant?

Every cop he'd ever known kept a hard copy of his records. Since he couldn't quickly access the computer files, he'd look for the paper trail and hope for the best. Rowdy checked the desk drawers but found only the usual inside. It appeared Bareden had a healthy savings account, plenty in his checking, organized receipts.

Nothing that Rowdy could use.

He left the desk and went into the bedroom. He checked both nightstands without much success and then, on sudden inspiration, removed the drawers to look behind and under them.

That's where he found the file — taped inside the nightstand behind the drawer. He flipped it open, skimmed it quickly, and then not so quickly.

Sitting on the side of the bed, the file open on his lap, he read over the lieutenant's history on the force, her rise in the ranks and her efforts to clean up corruption.

He also read other, more interesting accounts. Four in total. It looked pretty damning.

It was not what he'd expected.

The front door opened and closed. On alert, Rowdy considered the window, or maybe the closet —

As if he'd expected to find Rowdy there, Detective Reese Bareden strode in. He was armed but had left his gun in his shoulder holster.

He came right into the bedroom, right up to Rowdy. "Is there a good reason why I shouldn't beat you into the ground?"

Whoa. That calm was a surprise. Rowdy took his measure, felt no real sense of menace and shrugged. "Might not be as easy as you expect."

"The way I feel right now, I wouldn't want it to be easy." But he rubbed his face as if merely disgusted. "What are you doing here, Rowdy?"

"You know the answer to that already."

"Right. When it comes to your sister, you don't take chances."

Despite Reese's lack of real aggression, it seemed prudent to get to his feet. "I thought you were at the station."

"And so you felt free to let yourself into my apartment?"

"Something like that."

He shook his head and propped his shoulder on the wall in his typical stance. "Alice called me."

Alice? Who the hell was . . . the lady with the dog. Damn it. She hadn't looked concerned. In fact, Rowdy wasn't at all sure she'd even noticed him. "She's a neighbor?"

He nodded. "She was taking my dog out for a walk, saw you, and became apprehensive."

Reese had a dog? He hadn't counted on that, either. "She must be a suspicious sort then, because I gave her no reason."

As if that bothered Reese, he murmured, "Yes, she is. Very much so." To clear away that thought, he shook his head. "Luckily for you, she gave me a detailed description of the *intruder* — otherwise you might have found yourself staring down the barrel of my weapon."

So Reese had known it was him? "And . . . what? You don't mind me visiting?"

"You have reason to be extra cautious." Reese loosened his tie and opened the top button of his shirt. "And unlike you, I'm not nearly so mistrustful."

Rowdy held up the file. "I'd say that's debatable."

"You read it?"

"The gist of it, yeah." Puzzle pieces came together. "Logan doesn't know?"

Reese worked his jaw. "I won't demolish a reputation lightly. I wanted solid proof before saying anything. A few secretive visits are nothing more than circumstantial evidence."

Suddenly Lieutenant Peterson stepped into the room, her gun already drawn. "Would one of you care to tell me what's going on here?"

Shit. "Dude, you need an alarm system."

"Apparently so." Reese glanced at the lieutenant's gun.

Rowdy considered his options, but the idea of being caught by anyone other than Reese hadn't crossed his mind. He'd known Reese was at the station, so he thought he'd have time.

He hadn't counted on his neighbor making that call.

And now the lieutenant had joined them. When the two of them only shared an accusatory stare, Rowdy asked her, "Why are you here?"

"So I need to go first? Fine." She motioned for Reese to step back. "He's been cagey, secretive. Before bringing you and your sister in, I thought I'd find out why." Her gaze went back and forth between the two men. "I didn't expect to find you here. Are you working with him, then?"

Rowdy didn't understand her. "Him who?"

"Reese." She nodded at the file in his hand. "The two of you have joined Morton's ranks?"

Slowly, Rowdy grinned. "That's what you think? Seriously?"

Reese didn't see the humor. "I would have loved to be wrong."

"You *are* wrong, Detective." Her gaze skittered over to him, and her eyes narrowed. "You really believed I'd let you get away with this? Not likely. I've known for weeks that you were up to something."

"He's been following you." Rowdy fanned the folder in the air. Because he believed it to be a misunderstanding, he gave her a verbal nudge. "Detective Bareden thinks you're the one who's been cozying up with Morton."

Her delicate jaw clenched. *"Never."*

"Bullshit." Reese took a forceful step toward her, drawing her aim. "You've kept

481

your more personal association with Morton under the radar."

"What personal association?"

To free up his hands, Rowdy dropped the folder onto the nightstand. If anyone started shooting, he had to be ready. "It's all in there," he said, hoping to give them a chance to sort out the confusion. "Dates and times documented."

Slowly, after an impressive visual standoff, the lieutenant lowered her gun. "Seriously, Reese? That's what you've been doing?" She curled her lip in disgust. "All this time you were watching *me*? My God, are you an idiot?"

Reese frowned at her vehemence. "No."

"The proof says otherwise." She holstered her gun. "I detest Morton and his ilk. Yes, I've had conversations with the man. But that's all."

"Why would you do that?" Rowdy asked.

"He tried to buy my involvement, and we both know what happens to those who deny him. So I met with him. He made veiled offers, and I strung him along. But I gave him *nothing*."

"Yes, but you were quite charming," came another voice, "so I allowed you the ruse." Morton Andrews stepped into the room. He held a Sig Sauer 9 mm with a silencer attached. Beside him stood another thug, a big, bald, sweating menace, and equally armed.

"Fuck me sideways," Rowdy said. "Is there a damned turnstile on the door now?" Incredible that so many would come trooping in when he'd thought to be the only one.

"Give it time," Morton all but purred, "and I can guarantee you will be fucked in every way imaginable."

"Is that a come-on or a threat?"

Morton laughed.

He'd done what he could to change his appearance, but Rowdy would know those cold, dark eyes anywhere. "Gotta tell you, Morton, you look like shit."

"It's temporary." At his leisure, utterly relaxed, he stood blocking the bedroom door. He smiled at his cohort — who pointed the gun at Rowdy — then addressed the lieutenant. "If my business dealings hadn't gotten so complicated, I'd have tended to you next."

At that open threat, Reese tried to step in front of the lieutenant, but Morton wasn't having it. "Ah-ah, now. None of that." He aimed his gun at Peterson. "Hand over the weapons, slowly. Place them on the floor and then walk to the other side of the bed. Make one wrong move, and I'll put a bullet through her brain."

Reluctantly, both Peterson and Bareden were forced to hand over their weapons. Morton used his foot to kick them across the hardwood floor, out of the bedroom and into the hall. He produced chain-lock handcuffs and tossed them onto the bed. "How convenient that you have a slatted headboard. Put one cuff on your wrist, thread the other through the headboard, and then she can cuff herself to you."

"On a bed?" Peterson said. "No way."

Reese gave her a quelling frown. "You wish."

Morton sighed. "Do it now," he said as if reciting a boring litany, "or I shoot her in the head. Your choice."

"Great. Fucking great." Reese attached the cuff to his left wrist, threaded it through, and raised a brow at Peterson.

"I knew you weren't dead," Peterson grumbled while attaching the cuff to her right wrist. They were both forced to sit in the middle of bed, close together. "It couldn't be that easy to get rid of you."

"No, not easy at all. I'm here and I'll be here long after the rest of you are gone."

Both Morton and his man were watching Reese and Peterson. This might be his only opportunity. Sure, he'd probably get shot, but what did it matter when that's exactly what Morton intended anyway?

Masking his hatred, Rowdy started to move, and Morton said, "Try it, and after I've shot you, I'll rape her. Detective Bareden can watch."

Impotent fury brought him to a standstill. Yes, Pepper was his number one priority, but he couldn't sacrifice another woman so easily.

Morton smiled again. "So the infamous Rowdy Yates is also a gentleman? Who knew?"

"Anyone who'd met him," Peterson said. "That is, anyone not too dense to see the obvious."

Reese spoke quickly, probably to keep Morton from reacting. "How do you expect to get out of here?"

The rage in Morton's gaze subsided. "Don't look so hopeful, Detective. It's true, I'm not currently in contact with most of my staff, but hiring a man to guard the entrance of the apartment building was easy enough. Money talks — you should know that by now, given the cops I've bought."

"Not always," Peterson told him. "You couldn't buy me."

"Ah, but you see, those I can't buy, I destroy."

"You still have the traffickers to deal with," Reese pointed out. "After the way you tried to cheat them, they're not feeling real understanding."

Peterson rounded on Reese. "You knew about that?"

"Of course."

Her exaggerated gasp nearly choked her. "But you didn't see fit to report it to *me*?"

"I didn't trust you, if you'll recall."

Rowdy could see that Morton disliked losing their attention. He spoke over them to regain center stage. "I'll be dealing with the traffickers next. They believe I'm dead, so they won't be expecting me when I show up."

"Show up?" Rowdy asked.

"After I take over, I'll reestablish myself under an alias and be more powerful than ever."

"The traffickers are close enough for you to just drop in, huh?" If they found the resources to get out of here alive, Rowdy would take great pleasure in destroying that operation.

Discounting any interference with his plans, Morton said, "They have absurd accommodations at a ramshackle house down on Third Ave. Filthy, really. Not at all up to my standards." He shivered as if repulsed.

486

"I'll enjoy killing them all, but not as much as I'll enjoy killing you."

Reese said, "He's not the one who saw you kill Jack Carmin. All this time, you've been chasing the wrong person."

"Shut up, Reese." Whatever plan he might be forming, no way in hell did Rowdy want his sister's name bandied around in front of Morton.

"Had the incompetent fools questioned the reporter before cutting his throat," Morton muttered, "they'd have known it was his sister, not him, who'd snitched. But no matter. I'm told that Rowdy and Pepper are inseparable. Find one, you find the other."

Every muscle in Rowdy's body went taut. "You won't get anywhere near my sister."

"Actually, men are seeking her right now."

"You don't know where she is," Peterson said. "Even I don't know."

"And you would have told me if you did?" he inquired.

"I would have killed you — when the time was right."

Rowdy knew he'd find a way to destroy Morton with his bare hands before he let him get anywhere near Pepper. If he died in the process, so be it.

Logan pulled up to Reese's apartment and the first thing he saw was the woman with the midsize black dog held on a leash. She looked toward him, and misgivings kicked him in the gut.

"Something's not right."

Pepper looked around. "What is it?"

Just inside the front doors, a burly thug loitered. "They're here." He called Dash. Keeping his attention on the area, he said, "Pull up beside me. When I get out, switch over to my truck and get Pepper away from here."

Without question, Dash said, "You've got it." He pulled up alongside Logan as directed, but Pepper wasn't so obliging.

She locked both hands on Logan's arm. "Who's here? What's going on?" She looked around the area.

Logan cupped a hand around the back of her neck. "Don't do that, honey. Just act normal so you don't draw attention." He pulled her in for a quick hard kiss. While staring into her eyes, he reminded her, "You trust me. Don't forget that."

She nodded, forced her shoulders to relax so that she appeared casual — and didn't budge. "What's going on?" she asked calmly. "Tell me who's here."

The dog barked, and Logan looked up to see that the woman watched him more closely. "Morton's goons, or the traffickers, hell I don't know. But Reese is here, too. That's his car."

"You think —"

"No." Logan shook his head. "Hell, no. Reese might be up to something, but not that. Not ever."

She searched his face. "You're sure?"

"Positive." Reese would never deliberately put a woman in harm's way, or assist anyone else with that agenda.

"Okay then. If you trust him, I do, too. So I should probably tell you . . . I see Rowdy's car."

Flummoxed, Logan stared at her. "I thought he was going to steal something."

"He's not a car thief," she complained with ire, then she drew a breath. "He kept old beat-up cars, weapons, changes of clothes . . . everything he or I might need, at the warehouse. That old sedan parked about six or seven cars down? It looks like his."

So Reese wasn't alone. Hopefully that meant he had backup — instead of two victims. "If I can get inside, I can work it out."

Suddenly the woman and dog started toward him. She smiled, waved as if she'd just seen him, and Logan didn't know what to think.

"Who is that?" Pepper asked with accusation.

"I think she might be Reese's dog sitter." When the woman strode over to his side of the car, Logan rolled down the window.

Still smiling, she leaned down to speak to him. "You're a friend of Detective Bareden's?"

More than a little confused, Logan said, "I am."

"You're a police officer, like him?"

"Yes."

"I thought so. You have the look."

Logan had no idea what the look might be.

"Something is going on, so play along, please." Faking a friendly chat, she leaned on the frame of the window. "There's been a parade of people going into his apartment. One is a particularly sinister character who has a bodyguard of sorts with him. I don't think we have a lot of time, so if you want to come with me, I can get you inside. We'll act like old friends. Does that work?"

Jesus. He didn't know what to think. "You're Alice?"

"Yes. I'm a neighbor. Now do you want in or should I try to think of something else?"

Like what? "I do." Logan turned to Pepper. "You're going to leave with Dash."

She licked her lips. "There are probably men around back, as well."

"I don't think so," Alice said. "I took the dog for a walk around the perimeter and didn't see anything else amiss."

With effort, Pepper pulled her gaze away from Alice and back to Logan. "I can stay and help —"

"No."

She spoke in a rush, both urgent and offended. "You promised my brother that you'd stay with me. You promised *me.* And, Logan, you know you can't do this alone."

"I can and I will." But he hated to let her out of his sight, she was right about that.

Alice said, "If I could offer a suggestion? Bring her in, and she can stay in my apartment with me. It's secure."

Secure? An odd word choice for a run-of-the-mill neighbor lady.

She looked over her shoulder at Dash, who pretended to adjust his radio. "He's with you?"

Unbelievable. "Yeah."

"He can handle himself?"

"He can," Logan said.

"Good. He can keep an eye on the bully at the entrance." She opened his door as if greeting a longtime friend. "Let's go then."

Giving her a stern frown, Logan hesitated before getting a gun out of the glove box. He put it in the waistband of his slacks, under his shirt.

"Walk over and greet Pepper," he told Alice. "Both of you wait by the side of the car for me."

The dog barked excitedly, and Alice said, "I do believe he's enjoying himself." With no apparent cares, she went around the car to carry on an animated faux conversation with Pepper.

Few things really threw Logan for a loop anymore, but he had to admit, Alice had him reeling. He walked to Dash and slipped the gun in to him through the open window. "It's loaded, so be careful." He'd be left without a weapon, but he could improvise.

Dash rested the gun over his thigh and lifted a brow. "Who am I supposed to shoot? The gorilla up front there?"

"If necessary, yes." Briefly, he explained Alice and her dubious plan. "I'm going in. Pepper will wait in Alice's apartment with her while I check on Reese."

"And kick ass — if necessary?"

Yeah, if it came to it, with or without a gun, he'd demolish all threats, because that's what it'd take to keep Pepper safe. "If this setup goes south . . ." *shit, shit, shit* ". . . get Pepper away from here. Preferably across state lines. Then you can go to the police. But not here." There were too many unanswered questions, and he didn't know who to trust.

Dash clasped his arm. "Much as I'm enjoying the adrenaline rush, I'll enjoy it more if you come out of this whole-hide."

"Count on it." He looked over at Alice, who alternately played with the dog and treated Pepper like a long-lost friend.

Other than appearing a little shell-shocked, Pepper played along well enough.

Best to just get it over with.

Pasting on a huge smile, he joined the ladies, and together they strode back into the building. He kept the women on his right, away from the jackass guarding the door. Except for an appreciative look at Pepper, the man barely gave them any attention until the dog started snarling at him.

Like a cool, seasoned pro, Alice said, "Cash, behave." After stroking the dog's head, she smiled at the guard. "Sorry. He's usually well mannered."

The guard gave her a dismissive nod.

A minute later, Logan saw the ladies safely ensconced in Alice's apartment. Pepper wore an empty look, twisting his guts in a sick knot of dread.

"None of that," he told her.

She looked at him, nodded, but he could see what it cost her to find her grit.

Alice said, "One moment, please." She offered the leash to Pepper.

Absently, Pepper stroked the dog with a gentle hand, but her expression turned feral. "I don't like this. If anyone has hurt my brother —"

"The guard wouldn't be there if that was the case," Logan told her. "I still have time."

"You aren't armed," Pepper argued.

"He will be." At the hall closet Alice went on tiptoe to retrieve a box. She took out a revolver and handed it over to Logan. "Don't worry. I have another in my bedroom. We'll be safe enough."

Reese had said she was strange. Well, he couldn't have been more correct. "Get the gun now." He wanted to see it in her hands before he left.

While Alice left to do that, Pepper watched him take off his hard-soled shoes and set them on the floor. Next he stripped off his dress shirt and pulled his T-shirt free from his slacks.

Carrying a Glock, Alice reentered but faltered when she saw him removing his shirt. "What are you doing?"

"Preparing," Pepper said, grim-faced. "He needs to be unhindered, and he has to be able to get in there unannounced."

Logan put the gun in his waistband.

"Do you need a knife, too?" Pepper asked.

"I don't want to cut his throat, honey." He pulled his T-shirt over the gun.

After giving the leash back to Alice, she went about checking the locks on the windows and closing the drapes.

"I already got the windows in the bedroom and bathroom," Alice told her.

"We'll dead bolt the door behind you." Pepper checked the lock and nodded in approval. "As Alice said, it looks sturdy. And don't worry, I'm not opening the door to anyone I don't know."

Seeing she had more to say, Logan waited.

"We won't interfere, but, Logan . . ."

She braced her shoulders and her courage, as he knew she'd had to do too many times in her life.

Touching her soft, warm cheek, he said, "Try not to worry, honey. You have my word, I'll do everything in my power to see that Rowdy isn't hurt."

Lips trembling, she knotted a hand in his T-shirt. "Damn you, Logan."

It amazed him that one woman had become so precious to him. On the off chance he failed, he wouldn't walk away without her knowing. "I love you."

Her eyes flared and her hand fell away from him. "What . . . ?"

"I *love* you." Smiling, he said, "Think about that while I'm gone, okay?"

And with that parting shot, he left.

Chapter Twenty-Four

One of the many precautions they'd taken as partners was that Logan had a key to Reese's apartment, and Reese had one for his home. As it turned out, he didn't need the key to get in.

Someone — probably Andrews — had left it slightly ajar, no doubt so he could sneak in on Reese without risk of being heard when the door closed. Logan followed suit and left it slightly open.

After scanning the entryway and finding it empty, he followed the drone of conversation in a back room. On silent feet, the gun now in his hand, he inched forward.

"You won't get away with this," Peterson said. *What was she doing here?*

Andrews laughed. "Of course I will. I didn't become a powerful man by being ineffectual. But I'm not in a rush, so we'll just bide our time until I have word that Pepper is under wraps."

Logan didn't let the sick threat affect him. Pepper was safe; Andrews couldn't threaten her now.

Reese gave a huff of scorn. "With the club shut down and you playing a zombie, you don't have the resources needed to go after Pepper."

"You have no idea how my operation has grown. But as it turns out . . . you're right. It's tough to build a large entourage of truly trustworthy, capable gunmen. That's why I'm utilizing new contacts."

"The traffickers?" Peterson asked.

"Exactly. After the untimely assassination of their boss —"

Reese interrupted to ask, "Were you the sniper, by chance?"

Peterson curled her lip with disdain. "I wish I could take the credit. But I'm guessing that was Morton."

Apparently they'd worked out their differences. Logan was careful not to cast a shadow, not to bump anything.

Was Andrews here alone?

And where was Rowdy? *Please, God, don't let him be hurt.* It would devastate Pepper.

Andrews laughed. "He brought me the bomb to use but I couldn't very well fake my own death and leave behind a witness, now could I? That's not smart business. He knew too much, and I decided his dealings would be more profitable for me without him taking a cut."

Finally he heard Rowdy say, "You are such a cowardly fraud."

It relieved Logan that no one sounded hurt or even too fearful. Rowdy and Reese were both cool and analytical. Peterson sounded outright pissed.

He took a small step forward.

"By now," Andrews said, "the traffickers will be closing in on your sister."

Glacial with defiance, Rowdy said, "Fuck you. She's safe."

"Logan Riske has a brother. The brother owns property," Andrews stated. "These things are easy enough to know when you have police contacts."

Logan peeked around the door and saw Andrews and another, bigger man, both armed. Rowdy stood at the foot of the bed, Reese and Peterson on it.

In that split second of time, he saw Reese staring at Peterson with accusation.

Judging by her tone, it infuriated her. "Say it and I'll beg him to shoot you first!"

"Then how?" Reese asked.

"I thought it was you," she told him.

"You're the one who's been suspicious. You're the one who met with the bastard."

"Oh, please," Andrews said. "The conniving bitch only wanted to know the other cops who are on my payroll. Isn't that right, Lieutenant?"

"Yes. And they have been uncovered. I have a full report ready to go. Whether you kill me or not, I've accomplished that much."

So neither Peterson nor Reese was dirty? They'd only been suspicious of each other? Later, after he had Andrews locked away, he'd allow himself to feel relief.

But right now, with menace throbbing in the air, he didn't lessen his focus.

Reese said, "Why didn't you tell me?"

"I don't . . . *didn't* . . . trust you," Peterson snapped.

"But you do now?"

"Well . . . yes."

"Great." Irony dripped from Reese's tone. "At least I can die knowing I eventually won you over."

"And you think I feel any differently, you impudent ass?"

Logan understood their ploy. Stall, distract, redirect the attention. He appreciated their efforts because it gave him a chance to peek in again, to better formulate a plan.

Andrews kept his gun loose at his side,

but his goon maintained a dead aim on Rowdy.

Proving he had a streak of cruelty a mile wide, Morton spoke with sick anticipation. "Your sister will go missing, you know. No one will ever see her again, but believe me, she'll be put to good use."

Instead of going into a fury, Rowdy grew calmer. "No, I don't think so. She's safe — and you're pathetic."

Did Rowdy want to enrage Andrews? If they started shooting, Reese and Peterson were sitting ducks. Or . . . had Rowdy noticed him? Was he drawing their fire to save the others?

Logan couldn't let that happen.

He only needed to distract the men for a single second. He knew, given any opportunity, Rowdy would react. Between the two of them, they'd make it work.

If he shot Andrews, the goon might kill Rowdy.

If he shot the goon, Andrews could take aim on Peterson or Reese.

The room was small enough that, if *anyone* started shooting, they'd all be eating bullets. Best to avoid that if at all possible.

With that decision made, he put the gun back in his waistband and slowly inched into the door frame.

Proving a keen awareness, Rowdy's gaze went right on past Logan so that he wouldn't give away his position.

Reese flattened his expression and leaned a little in front of Peterson.

To assist him, Rowdy frowned and looked at the closet. He widened his eyes.

Taking the bait, Andrews jerked around to face the new threat, and Logan was on him. He caught Andrews's wrist and pressed his gun hand down, squeezing hard until the weapon fell from his hand.

Rowdy and the other man crashed into them, and Logan heard a whispered *pop, pop, pop.*

The silencers made the shots barely detectable, but a searing burn cut through his right upper arm. Damn it.

Refusing to let any injury slow him down, Logan brought his left elbow up and into Andrews's face and smashed his nose. The bastard howled in fury and grabbed for him. Logan drove him forward until they fell into the dresser, then landed hard on the floor in a tangle.

As he reared back to demolish Andrews, he saw the odd twist of his neck, the wide sightless eyes and slack mouth.

Morton Andrews had broken his neck and faded away with little fanfare.

Disbelief obliterated the pain in his shoulder.

Reese shouted, "Damn it, Rowdy, stop it!" He rattled the entire bed with his objections. "You're going to kill him!"

Logan saw the gunman sprawled under Rowdy, unmoving, his face bloodied and battered. "Rowdy." He got to his feet and clasped Rowdy's shoulder. "That's enough."

Breathing hard, fist cocked, Rowdy pulled back, paused and then shoved to his feet. He stood heaving for only a moment before bending to go through the man's pockets.

After finding the key to the cuffs, he turned to Logan and flattened his mouth. "Sit down, why don't you?"

Logan ignored that to collect the guns now strewn every fucking place. He tossed them on the bed near the lieutenant's feet, and in the process, managed to get blood everywhere. Shit.

Rowdy stepped in front of him. "Seriously, Logan. *Sit.*"

He glanced at his arm, at the slow oozing of blood and blackened flesh, the swelling. Disgusted, he said, "I'll ruin the bedding."

"Damn you, Logan," Reese snarled as he struggled with the key. "I can buy new bedding!"

"You're sounding hysterical," Logan told him.

Reese drew a deep, strained breath. "No." He drew another. "I'm perfectly fine. Please sit down before I get free and *kick your ass!*"

Now that the others kept pointing it out, his arm went from numb to screaming pain. "Yeah, all right." But rather than join Reese and Peterson on the crowded mattress, he went to the wall and slid down to the floor.

Rowdy crouched down in front of him to check the wound. "Damn, man. I'm sorry. I tried to control his gun hand, but he —"

"You're not hurt?"

Rowdy gave him a comical look and laughed. "Bruised head to toe, but otherwise fine — thanks to you." Gingerly, he lifted Logan's arm. "It looks like the bullet passed through. Do you think it hit bone? Does anything feel broken?"

"No. It'll be fine." It had to be; with Andrews out of the way, he wanted time with Pepper. He did not want to be incapacitated.

"Sucks that it's your right arm."

Done discussing it, Logan said, "Dash is outside keeping an eye on one of Andrews's men."

While continuing to poke and prod like a damned doctor, Rowdy asked, "My sister?"

It astounded Logan that Rowdy didn't

seem more concerned for her. "In the apartment with Alice."

"Ah. Good. I was counting on you keeping her safe, and you did. I owe you for that."

"You don't owe me a damned thing." Majorly pissed off at himself, Logan put his back to the wall and stretched out one leg. "I don't fucking believe this."

Peterson said, "I'm calling it in."

Reese flipped over the fallen thug, now coherent and groaning in pain. He pulled his arms behind his back and fastened the cuffs to his wrists. Taking his gun from the bed, he said, "I'll let the ladies know we're in the clear, then take our third man off Dash's hands."

Rowdy walked out — but surprised Logan again by coming right back with two towels from Reese's bathroom. They'd really done a number on the apartment. Blood, bodies and bullet holes . . . Reese would need a damn cleaning and repair crew.

"Maybe you should lie down," Rowdy said as he pressed one towel to his arm.

Logan eyed him, snorted and shook his head. "Not happening."

That made him grin. "Yeah, I'd probably fight it, too." He held the towel against Logan and spoke quietly. "Morton had bad plans for Pepper. He was going to —"

Logan cut him off. "I heard. But he's dead now. And she's safe."

"She's . . . free," Rowdy agreed. He held silent a moment. "He told us where the traffickers are set up."

Peterson covered the phone and scowled at him. "You will *not* get involved, Rowdy Yates, do you understand me?"

He readjusted the towel. "Yes, ma'am."

"I mean it. I'm already preparing a team to go there. We'll handle it —"

"Yeah, sure. No problem."

Peterson stalked away while barking orders into her phone.

Logan couldn't help but chuckle. "You're a miserable liar, Rowdy Yates, and a worse nurse." He took the towel from him. "Go fetch your sister. You know you're dying to."

"She's going to kick my ass when she sees you got shot."

"I don't know about that. But if *you* got shot, she'd probably kill me herself."

Rowdy gave him a funny look, then laughed. "Boy, are you in for a surprise." He left to find Pepper.

So Rowdy thought she cared about him? That'd be nice, Logan decided. Better than nice, and worth a bullet.

Less than a minute later, the dog barked,

and Pepper hurried in with her long-legged gait — until she saw him sitting on the floor.

Logan got caught in her mesmerizing gaze. He smiled to put her at ease. "Hey."

Fury straightened her backbone and squared her shoulders. "You're *shot.*"

"I'm fine." And he was. Yeah, he hated it that Andrews had gotten off so easily, especially after the verbal threats toward Pepper. But . . . it was over.

He'd now be free to put all his considerable concentration into winning her heart. Anticipation started a slow burn that all but blocked the pain of his injury.

When she just stood there, staring at him in horror, Rowdy gave her a nudge. "It's just his arm, sis. He won't expire on you."

"Don't be a jerk!" She shoved away from him to step over and around Andrews, then came down beside Logan. She took the towel from him and lifted it. "Ohmigod."

She didn't mention his declaration of love, but she must care for him, given her reaction. Logan pressed the towel back to his arm. "Kiss me. It'll make me feel better."

Rowdy snorted.

"You're both insane," she complained, but she did kiss him.

Peterson finished her call, took in their cozy position, and rolled her eyes. "Ambulance should be here any minute."

That got his attention off Pepper. "I don't need a damned ambulance."

"Tough. You're getting it anyway."

Alice stood there, stoic and silent, holding the dog's leash. He whined and lurched this way and that, unsure what to do, still uncertain of the situation.

Probably smelling the blood.

Sitting on the side of the bed, Rowdy held out a hand, and the dog came to him like a long-lost friend.

Reese strode back in with Dash but froze when he saw Alice. It was only then that Logan realized she still held the gun loosely in her hand.

Without taking his gaze off her, Reese said to Logan, "A couple of units showed up. They have a handle on things."

"Good."

"Paramedics will swarm in soon, probably along with a half dozen uniformed cops." They both spoke quietly.

He nodded toward Alice. "You want to deal with that before they do?"

"Yeah." Reese moved closer to her. "Alice?"

Eerily mute, she freed her finger from the trigger, turned the gun around, and offered it to him.

He took it with alacrity. "You were going to shoot someone?"

"If it came to that, of course I would." She couldn't seem to pull her gaze off Andrews. "Dead?"

"Unfortunately, yes."

"Why is it unfortunate?"

The men all shared a look. Logan said, "I wanted to take him in."

Hands locked in fists, Peterson agreed. "I wanted him to stand trial. I wanted —"

"Sometimes," Alice interrupted, "it's better when they're dead."

"Whoa." Pepper leaned into Logan's good side.

Sharing that sentiment, he hugged her with his uninjured arm. *Better when they're dead.* So who else had Alice tangled with? And who were *they*?

"Alice?" Reese touched her chin and brought her face around toward him. "Any second now I'm going to have my hands full. Are you okay?"

"Yes."

Pepper glanced at Logan with sharp worry. He understood her concern, but he didn't know what he could do about it.

"You'll watch my dog?" Reese asked her.

Alice stood there, lost in thought for too many heartbeats until she finally pulled herself together. "Yes, Cash will be safe and waiting for you when you return."

"I want you to be waiting, as well."

She lifted her chin. "I'm not running off."

"Good to know."

Logan figured there was a whole lot going on there, but now wasn't the time to ask about it.

"Let's go." Reese hauled the other man off the floor and, ignoring his complaints, half dragged him from the room. Alice took the dog's leash and followed Reese.

"Dash?"

Being a cop's brother, Dash knew enough to stand just outside the perimeter of destruction. Smart. Logan drew his attention. "Would you mind making sure that no neighbors wander in?"

He scrutinized Logan, glanced at Pepper, and rubbed the back of his neck. "Yeah, sure. No problem."

Amused, Logan said to Pepper, "My brother is concerned for me, but he's manning up so he won't upset you."

"He's considerate." She narrowed her eyes at Rowdy. "Unlike my brother."

Rowdy tossed a sheet over Andrews. "How's that for consideration?"

She shuddered. "It's morbid but . . . thank you."

Logan would have worried about him taking off, except that he knew Rowdy wouldn't leave his sister.

Pepper was damn good insurance toward a new life for Rowdy. And that pleased Logan, because they both deserved so much.

Pepper gazed in the direction Alice had gone. "I think something very tragic must have happened to that poor woman."

"Probably." Logan drew her closer to kiss her brow. "But she'll be okay." Reese would see to it . . . somehow. "What about you?"

She stroked back his hair, touched a bruise on his jaw. "What about me?"

He'd already told her that he loved her; no reason to belabor the point right now. "You're doing all right?"

"Andrews is gone, thanks to you." She exchanged the bloody towel for a fresh one and winced. "Where are those damned paramedics, anyway?"

Peterson said, "I'll check on them."

Logan struggled to his feet.

"What are you doing?" In a near panic, Pepper scrambled up beside him.

He didn't want her to be in the same room with a dead body, and beyond that, he had no intention of sitting on his ass while others around him handled things.

Unfortunately, he barely made it out of the room before the paramedics were on him. He clasped Pepper's hand. "I want you with me tonight."

"Ha!" She kissed him again, quick and hard. "Just try getting rid of me."

In the predawn hours of the following day, after a lengthy stint at the hospital, too many questions and far too much time away from Pepper, Logan finally got into his own bed, in his own home. Peterson had called just a few minutes ago to update him on the progress with the human trafficking ring.

They'd busted a lot of people and were now en route to intercept a transfer . . . of women.

Over and over, Logan had to remind himself that Morton Andrews was dead, and Pepper was no longer in any danger.

He sank into the mattress with a great sigh of relief.

"Okay?" she asked while touching his jaw.

"Yeah."

"Do you want something to drink?" She smoothed back his hair. "To eat?"

This was a quirky mood for her, being so touchy-feely while pampering him. "No, I'm fine."

"Thank God Reese brought you a clean

shirt." She opened the buttons while saying that. "Tell me if I hurt you."

As long as she didn't leave him, she wouldn't hurt him.

She eased the shirt away and went to work on his shoes and then his pants.

"I'm not an invalid, you know."

"No, but you are right-handed and the doctor said your deltoid is going to hurt like crazy for a while, so I'm helping, end of story. Now, can you lift your hips?"

Charmed by the mix of bossy and nurturing, Logan did as directed. "Okay if I keep my boxers?" he teased.

"If you insist." Her hair fell around her face as she dragged the pants down his legs. She plumped a pillow behind him so he could rest back on the headboard, then drew a sheet up and over him.

Trying to ignore the constant throbbing in his arm, Logan watched her move around the room, putting his clothes on a chair, tossing his shoes in a closet.

He had her in his house, in his bedroom, and whatever it took, he'd keep her there.

Strain showed in her drooping shoulders, the shadows under her eyes. Her hair hadn't seen a comb since early the previous morning.

"You are so beautiful."

A secret little smile peeked through the fatigue as she dug in a drawer and found a clean T-shirt. She shook it out. "Pain must be affecting your vision. Are you sure you don't want a pill?"

"Not yet." He'd already gotten a shot for pain along with a load dose of antibiotics in his backside. He'd be taking more antibiotics for a week and wearing the damned sling for longer than that. He had pain pills to take, but he wanted to be clearheaded for his conversation with Pepper.

He waited for her to remove her clothes.

Eyeing him, she held the shirt to her chest and chastised him with another indulgent smile. "You realize that hot stare is wasted. You're in no shape to do anything."

"I can hold you." He patted the left side of the bed. "Right here." He wanted to feel her heart beating with his. He wanted to breathe in her scent and listen to her sleeping. He wanted to tell her that no one and nothing could ever hurt her again — but in many ways, he was the one who'd hurt her the most.

Worry etched her brow. "What if I bump you in the night?"

Bumping he could take. Sleeping alone — no way. "I *need* to hold you."

She said nothing, just stood there, his shirt

in her hands, several feet from the bed.

He tried for patience, but it wasn't easy when he so desperately wanted her beside him. "Are you hungry?"

"No. Dash got me a sandwich at the hospital."

Thank God both his brother and hers had stuck around to keep her company until he'd finally been released. After dropping off clean clothes, Reese had joined Peterson in a sting against the traffickers.

"The master bath is through that door. There's another in the hall if you want privacy."

"It's a nice house."

A house she hadn't even noticed as she'd hustled him through it and into bed. "Thank you." He started to tell her that she could change anything she wanted, but maybe that'd be moving too fast for her. She needed time to acclimate to an entire transformation in her life.

"Rowdy will come by tomorrow."

"He told me." As soon as the hospital released him, Rowdy had taken off. Logan didn't know where he'd go, and Pepper seemed to take it for granted that he'd do his own thing, in his own way.

Dash had driven them to Logan's home, and Logan knew he'd wanted to hang around, but like Rowdy, he understood that Logan wanted time alone with Pepper. "If you're worried about him —"

"Rowdy?" She shook her head. "No, that's not what I'm worried about."

He'd already shared Peterson's report about the trafficking ring, so she knew that was over. And while they were both concerned for Alice, they had no influence there.

"Tell me what's wrong."

She licked her lips. "I don't have . . . anything." As if they were a longtime couple, she stripped off her clothes without fanfare or modesty and pulled on the T-shirt.

Logan would never tire of looking at her. "What do you need?"

"Everything." Warming to that subject, she explained, "What little I owned was in the apartment that burned down or at the warehouse, and now that the police know about it, they've taken it over, at least for now."

So much had happened in the past twenty-four hours, he hadn't thought that far ahead. "We can go shopping tomorrow."

Absently, she said, "No, tomorrow you have to rest. The doctor said so." She put her clothes on the chair with his. "I was trying to think about it, but . . . now that I don't have to hide anymore, the list just keeps growing in my mind."

Rowdy said he and Pepper had enough money to endure, but what did that mean? Logan wanted her to do more than endure — he wanted her to thrive.

With him.

She sat on the bed near his hip. "Everything is so different now."

Logan couldn't deny that. "I want it to be better." He'd wanted that almost from the day he met her.

"We have money, you know. Rowdy's always seen to that. And he probably has a car for me." The corner of her mouth lifted. "He usually thinks of everything for me. But there's no job, no home, no clothes or food or dishes or furniture."

How unsettled must she feel? Logan needed to reassure her. He'd be happy if she moved in with him, if she let him take her shopping.

But how could he suggest that without insulting her independent nature or stepping on Rowdy's toes?

She licked her lips. "The thing is, there's no fear, either. No threat, no worry." She inhaled. "And I hope no more . . . loneliness."

A hint? God, he hoped so. "Do you think

you can forgive me?"

As if he hadn't spoken, she said, "I want to jog. God, I miss jogging."

"As soon as I can, I'll jog with you."

With the softest expression he'd ever seen on a woman, she touched his wounded arm in a butterfly caress. "I want to go to movies and restaurants. Maybe the park. And the lake. I'd love to go swimming, boating, too."

"I won't be up for all that today, but tomorrow . . ." He shifted, felt the burn of his wound, and retreated. "Maybe day after tomorrow?"

She paused, a little self-conscious, and said in a barely-there whisper, "What if that bullet had struck a little higher?"

"It didn't. It's just my arm, and that will be fine soon enough."

Her eyes went glassy; her lips trembled. "You could have been killed, Logan, and I . . ."

He took her hand and lowered it from his arm. If she cried, it *would* kill him.

To distract her, he said, "Give me a few days, and I'll do everything with you."

"Everything, huh?" Her hand smoothed over his abdomen, making him twitchy. "There's no more risk for me, you know."

Meaning she'd rather do those things

alone? She kept him so bemused, his head started to pound. "I never want you at risk again."

Looking impish, she whispered, "Well, maybe a little risk . . ."

"No." He sat forward — and she immediately protested the stress on his injury. Logan didn't care. He caught her upper arms and held her still. "The only risk I want you to have is my last name."

Slowly, she stopped fussing at him and gifted him with a smile so scorching, his arm could have fallen off and he wouldn't notice. "Seriously, Detective Riske? I don't know. I was thinking more about risking my heart."

His blood rushed. "With me."

She outright laughed. "Yes, with you." She leaned forward and kissed him. "Though I have to say, the last name works for me, too."

His heart skipped a beat. "You'll marry me?"

"You need to understand, Logan. When you left me in Alice's apartment and went off to tangle with Andrews . . ." She closed her eyes a moment. "God, I was so scared."

"I know, and I'm sorry."

"No, you don't know. Because I haven't told you." She touched his chest where the white sling wrapped over his shoulder, and shuddered. "But I'm not a coward."

"No, definitely not."

She met his gaze. "I let you think I was only worried for Rowdy. I even told myself that's all it was, because I was still mad, and hurt, and . . . a little afraid."

"With reason." He folded her hand in his. "I never should have used you like that."

"But I'm so glad you did." She smiled at his surprise. "You're the best thing that's ever happened to me. If you hadn't come into my life, what would my life be right now? You not only freed me, you freed my brother, too."

He wanted no misunderstandings. "I love you."

She breathed a little faster. "You're a part of my life now — a better life — and I don't ever want to lose you."

He'd damn well hold her to that — right now. "Tell me you'll marry me, Pepper."

Laughing a little, she said, "I will. And I'll love you. And spend my life with you."

Contentment moderated his aches and amplified his exhaustion.

"But for right now," she said, easing him back in the bed, "I'd really like to just sleep."

"With me." He pulled her down with him, locking her in close.

"Yes." She hugged him carefully, kissed his chest. Sleepily, she asked, "Big wedding or small?"

"Whatever you want."

She yawned. "Tomorrow we can tell Rowdy and Dash about our plans to marry." She snuggled closer. "And of course we'll tell Reese."

It pleased him that Rowdy and Pepper now trusted Reese.

"Maybe, if Reese wants, we could even invite Alice to the wedding. I don't really have any female friends, but I liked her. And I think she's more than earned the chance to celebrate with us."

"A terrific idea." Alice could probably use a few friends. He started to ask Pepper more about her, but he heard her breathing even into sleep.

Logan smiled. His arm was badly swollen and hurt like a son of a bitch, there was chaos at the station as the disloyal cops were exposed, and he'd soon gain a headstrong, overprotective brother-in-law used to living on the edge.

And still, he felt like the luckiest man alive. For the sake of justice, he'd run the risk, and despite the odds, he'd ended up with love.

He ended up with Pepper.

As long as he had her, he had it all.

Hindered by indecision, Reese stood outside Alice's apartment door, his hand raised to knock while he warred with himself.

Damn it, his apartment was off-limits. They had the body out, but the blood, general destruction and bullet holes remained. Until the department finished their reports, he didn't want to disturb anything. Exhaustion left him weaving on his feet. He was starting to see double, but he wasn't sure —

The door opened and there stood Alice, Cash beside her.

The dog leaped forward to greet him with his usual enthusiasm and maybe something more, something like worry and relief. Reese stroked his back. "Too much confusion, buddy? For me, too."

Wearing a vintage-looking nightgown under a loosely fastened robe, her feet bare and her hair rumpled, Alice watched him.

Best to just spit it out and take it from there. He opened his mouth.

Alice said, "You can't go to your apartment."

His mouth closed. He scrutinized her and puzzled over her uncanny ability to see things a timid woman should never notice. "No."

"You need to get some sleep."

"Yes."

Her mouth screwed up, her gaze dropped down his body, then shot back to his face. She cleared her throat. "Why do you have an erection?"

A direct attack? Huh. Interesting . . . and somehow exciting. "Hell if I know." God, this was awkward. "But you don't have to worry about that." Stupid. How could she not worry? She had all kinds of secretive shit going on, and here he was, dead on his feet while his Johnson wanted to stand at attention.

He'd been fighting a boner ever since pulling up to the apartment with the realization that he'd *probably* have to impose on Alice for a place to crash, at least for a couple of days.

She rubbed at one eye but came to a quick decision. Handing Cash's leash to him, she said, "Let him out while I make up the couch for you."

"I won't be in your way?"

"I made the guest room into my office, so for the most part, you'll be undisturbed."

"I was worried about *you* being disturbed." He was so tired, he could sleep through a train wreck.

Her face colored a pretty pink, intriguing him further.

The blush lifted his exhaustion, encouraged his libido, and made it near impossible to get his physical reactions under control.

She glanced at his lap again, then quickly away. "Take Cash out, then you can sleep. And afterward . . . I suppose we have to talk."

Reese smiled at her. "I can hardly wait." He started to go but thought better of it and caught the door before she could shut it. "You aren't just waiting for me to walk off so you can lock me out?"

For the longest time she stared at his feet. Finally, she lifted her chin. "Truthfully, Detective, I'd as soon not spend the day alone anyway."

Was it memories that wrought that confession? "Then I'm glad I'm here."

She pulled her robe tighter around her, nodded and whispered, "Odd as it seems . . . so am I." Gently, she closed the door in his face. He listened for the sound of a lock clicking into place but heard nothing.

"Great," Reese said to the dog as he led him down the steps and out the front door. "Isn't it just like a woman to get in a parting shot guaranteed to keep a guy stirred up?" Cash made a noise that, to Reese and his tired brain, sounded like agreement. "We're going to have our hands full dealing with that one."

But damn if he wasn't already looking forward to it.

The employees of Thorndike Press hope you have enjoyed this Large Print book. All our Thorndike, Wheeler, and Kennebec Large Print titles are designed for easy reading, and all our books are made to last. Other Thorndike Press Large Print books are available at your library, through selected bookstores, or directly from us.

For information about titles, please call:
(800) 223-1244

or visit our Web site at:
http://gale.cengage.com/thorndike

To share your comments, please write:
Publisher
Thorndike Press
10 Water St., Suite 310
Waterville, ME 04901